*Jitterbuggin' with the Renaissance: A Jazz Age Thriller* "…is a triumph on every level. Don Swaim leads us through some of the most vivid events of the 1920s—from Al Capone's stranglehold on Chicago to murders in Hollywood to the stock market crash—in a narrative that is as vibrant and rollicking as the decade he is portraying. And throughout, we are regaled by H. L. Mencken's nose-thumbing of politics, religion, and American culture in general. If you can only read one novel about the Roaring Twenties, this should be it." —S. T. Joshi, leading authority on H. P. Lovecraft, Ambrose Bierce, and H. L. Mencken, and winner of the World Fantasy, Bram Stoker, British Fantasy awards

Great wit, clever prose, and an exhilarating story that, sadly, also displays the outrage of racism. Easy to lose oneself in the language, the humor, and the lore, and the real people who lived it. The wild, audacious events that populate this love letter to a courageous time and place in history are priceless. —Chris Bauer, author of the Maximum Risk series, the Blessid Trauma Crime Scene Cleaners series, and the Counsel Fungo series

*Jitterbuggin' with the Renaissance* has all the hallmarks of a Don Swaim masterpiece: perfectly drawn characters who insert themselves in absurd situations at their own peril, explorations of mostly forgotten historical events and figures well worth revisiting, and gorgeous writing that compels the reader to turn the page as quickly as he can. —William J. Donahue, author of *Only Monsters Remain*

# by
# DON SWAIM

## FICTION

*Jitterbuggin' with the Renaissance: A Jazz Age Epic*

*Man With Two Faces*

*The Assassination of Ambrose Bierce: A Love Story*

*Bright Sun Extinguished: Ode to Norman Mailer & Dank Tarn of Auber*

*Steampunk Electroblaster Romance*

*The H.L. Mencken Murder Case*

## ESSAYS

*Deliverance of Sinners: Essays & Sundry on Ambrose Bierce*

## ANTHOLOGIES

*Shocking Verbs, Lawless Nouns* (executive editor)

*Covid-19: The Pandemic Project* (editor)

## JOURNALS

*Neshaminy: The Bucks County Historical and Literary Journal*
(executive editor)

# JITTERBUGGIN'
## — WITH THE —
# RENAISSANCE

## A Jazz Age Epic by
## DON SWAIM

A Montag Press Book
www.montagpress.com
Montag Press
777 Morton Street, Unit B
San Francisco CA 94129 USA

Montag Press, the burning book with the hatchet cover, the skewed word mark and the portrayal of the long-suffering fireman mascot are trademarks of Montag Press.

Printed & Digitally Originated in the United States of America
10 9 8 7 6 5 4 3 2 1

*It was an age of miracles, it was an age of art,*
*it was an age of excess, and it was an age of satire.*

—F. Scott Fitzgerald

# CONTENTS

(One) Sahara of the Bozart . . . . . . . . . . . . . . . . . . 1

(Two) Tommy the Choirboy. . . . . . . . . . . . . . . . . .30

(Three) Homicide in Hollywood . . . . . . . . . . . . . . .71

(Four) ~~Hell~~ Heck in Havana. . . . . . . . . . . . . . . . 128

(Five) Jitterbuggin' with the Renaissance . . . . . . . . . . 177

(Six) The Crash . . . . . . . . . . . . . . . . . . . . . . . 221

Acknowledgments. . . . . . . . . . . . . . . . . . . . . . 259

About Don Swaim . . . . . . . . . . . . . . . . . . . . . 260

# ONE

# SAHARA OF THE BOZART

*They took me out*
*To some lonesome place.*
*They said, "Do you believe*
*In the great white race?"*
*I said, "Mister,*
*To tell you the truth,*
*I'd believe in anything*
*If you'd just turn me loose."*

—Langston Hughes

I, Gart Booker Asquith III, descendant of slaves, joined the Ku Klux Klan during the hot and humid summer of the Year of Our Lord nineteen twenty four; I being a negro.

At the time I took the oath, I naively thought the Klan issued you your sheets, but, no, you either had to bring your own or buy them from Calhoun's Dry Goods on Main Street in Royal Prong, North Carolina. Earl Calhoun was a Klan brother and gave us a five percent discount. But you had to cut your own peepholes, which I managed to botch. Cut 'em too high or too low or too far apart, and then I'd be stumbling around blind at the cross burnings, missing out on the best parts. Also, you had to wash and iron the sheets yourself unless you had an obliging spouse or a doting mother, and I roomed alone at Ma Gable's boarding house so it would have been impolite to borrow her sheets.

One might think it odd, my joining the Klan, being colored. But I had a white father and a mixed-race, light-skinned mother so I could pass as white or black whenever it suited my purposes. Like Jean Toomer, the Harlem Renaissance author who published his highfalutin *Cane* one year earlier and who married white.

To me, there seemed to be a certain nobility to being a descendant of slaves and acknowledging it.

But I was always black—or tried to be even though I didn't look it—when I partook at Aunt Ethel's Rib and Okra joint on the far side of the tracks where the Royal Prong's negroes lived. Aunt Ethel's was the unrivaled eating emporium in all of North Carolina's Mundrickus County, where I was on undercover assignment for the Baltimore *Sun*. I rarely worried about being caught at Aunt Ethel's by my Klan brethren because they only crossed the tracks late at night when they intended to burn a cross outside of someone's house or at an African church or school or maybe just wanted to scare the bejesus out of some poor widow and her kids.

---

Henry Mencken was a regular at the Hotel Rennert in Baltimore, feasting on oysters and beer while entertaining a gaggle of admirers, chief of whom was myself. We were all wary of the Prohibition cops, against whom Henry railed as co-conspirators in the uncivilized war on the right to quench one's thirst. Officially, the Rennert sold nothing stronger than birch beer and apricot juice.

Henry's height was middling, slicked-back hair parted in the middle, and clinched between his teeth an unfired Uncle Willie, which he described as the cleanest, mildest, and best-made five-cent cigar in the world. Inevitably, he gripped a stein of pilsner. He had once been the managing editor of the *Evening Sun*, but didn't like being boss and gave it up for his first love: punditry in which he exercised more clout than most mere mortals.

I was a bespectacled cub reporter at the *Sun* when Henry, still the paper's mainstay, took me under his wing. He also co-edited *The American Mercury* with George Jean Nathan, and it was my hope he'd accept one of my oft-rejected submissions. But I was still a long way from being an actual writer. That would change, I figured, the longer I consorted with Henry, who was unaware I was once a theology student who failed in every particular, not the least of which was a lack of faith.

The KKK had just staged a monumental march in Washington, DC, some forty-thousand Klansmen and their frauen strutting on Pennsylvania Avenue in their whites, fists raised. They were hoodless because a local ordinance prohibited the wearing of masks—and the Invisible Empire claimed to be law abiding. The marchers were escorted by Klan guards in snazzy uniforms, white caps, Sam Browne belts, and black puttees. It was an astonishing turnout, marking the moribund Klan's resurgence.

Henry was in fine fettle at the Rennert bar following the KKK's gaudy display. He said to me, "The marchers were clothed in robes decorated with scarlet trim, and carried miters of the sort affected by the patriarchs of a Greek rite. They had their wives with them; fat, amiable gals with make-up dripping from their noses. The Pennsylvanians were the first troupes in line, the chivalry of Kutztown, Kunkletown, Kratzerville, Kleinfeltersville, and Schwenksville."

"I hear some of them were three sheets to the wind, Mr. Mencken," I said, clinking my mug against his. "That's a joke."

"As is the Klan. Their gown was only the beginning of their attire. Some wore the cloaks of Spanish grandees of the sixteenth century and others the robes of Shinto high priests. One platoon was in green baldrics emblazoned with vermilion crosses. Another sported huge special shakers bespattered with gilt stars."

Henry was hard to peg. He often mixed sweeping and liberal social commentary with his petty prejudices. At times, he appeared contemptuous of those with dark complexions and spoke pejoratively of what he called Hebrews of the wrong stripe. In fact, Henry didn't care much for anybody. He christened the Church the Ku Klux Klergy, referred to God as a third-rater, and labeled President Coolidge a farce. But he was the most celebrated intellectual in America, author of *The American Language*, and he'd just published another in his essay sequence, *Prejudices: Fourth Series*. Educated America listened to him, and I didn't want to miss out on that.

I hoped desperately to impress Henry, as well as rising to the level of crime reporter—a status well above my current role as a cub. So I came up with the brilliant scheme of infiltrating a Klan chapter and landing a scoop that would make my name in the *Sunpapers*. I was hungry for a byline. I could visualize it now: *Inside the KKK: An exclusive by Gart Booker Asquith III.*

"I like your proposal," he said. "I admire reporters who actually go out and cover a story instead of waiting for the story to come to them."

"The *Sun*'s slogan on its masthead is *Light for All*. To reach that light, Mr. Mencken, I would travel all the way to the Deep South or to Hell. You name it."

"And I'd be fine with either." He chuckled, although I'd never seen him laugh outright as it would displace the cheap cigar in his mouth. "I've almost become fond of you, m'boy. Call me Henry."

"Henry, sir, there are fears for the fate of the black race in the South, as evidenced by the comeback of the KKK."

He peered into his beer contemplating the bubbles.

"There is no immediate path for the African to evolve gracefully in our society. However, I read an article by an intelligent black writer claiming that light-skinned negroes can pass as Caucasian in the South because many Southern whites have distinctly negroid features."

"Which is why I think I can pull it off, my infiltrating the Klan."

"And why shouldn't you, Mr. Asquith…"

"…Gart, sir."

"What sort of name is Gart?"

"Short for Taggart."

"Then why not call yourself Taggart? It's more distinguished, You *are* a Caucasian, are you not?"

"Uh, isn't it apparent?"

Knowing Henry's disposition, I wasn't going to tell him otherwise.

He said, "The African in the South may be oppressed, yet he has made strides and is realizing faster cultural progress than the hillbillies and lintheads. It's no accident that the only visible esthetic activity in the South is in black hands."

"That's a hopeful sign for the negro."

"No Southern melodist has written music so fine as that by a half dozen black composers. Even in politics, the negro reveals a curious superiority—and yet he knows his place."

"Henry, sir, I'm going to pack my grip and abscond on assignment to Dixie posthaste, although I'm unsure as to where to start."

He drained his mug, then waved to the waiter for a surreptitious fourth refill. For a moment, he remained thoughtful.

"I happen to know a small-town editor in the debased state of North Carolina who holds an honored position among the local booboisie. A man named Custis. He's the proprietor of the Royal Prong *Democrat*, which is barely more than a rag in a town that's primarily a collection of pie eaters, pig stickers, and privies. But he owes me a favor, which I shall now collect, insisting that he take you on, no questions asked. The perfect camouflage for an ambitious, youthful reporter such as yourself. I'll write—nay, telegraph—him tomorrow."

"Then my path is clear, Henry, sir."

"But, Taggart, m'boy, as you marvel at the absurdity you'll observe down there, keep it to yourself. An indiscreet word and the whole of Dixie will be upon you, bitterly denouncing you as a scoundrelly damned Yankee or a Bolshevik Jew—or worse. You should fully understand what you'll be getting into."

I was giddy as I stumbled from the Rennert to my modest room on West Biddle Street. How many people received actual advice from H.L. Mencken?

I bought a battered old Dixie Flier, a two-seater, barely a step up from a horse and buggy, but it would move me around, more or less. Henry Ford had just lowered the price of the vintage Model T with a crank to two hundred-ninety bucks, more if you insisted on the convenience of a self-starter, but I was still saving my pennies, planning to become a Wall Street investor one day. I was fortunate to be a go-getter in the nineteen twenties when the economy was tenacious and optimism so great. All the financial prognosticators agreed that the nation's future was limitless.

Maryland was below the Mason-Dixon Line, although few considered it the Deep South, the geographic area that Henry's invective specially targeted. Back at the Rennert, he had told me, "The South is as sterile, artistically, intellectually, and culturally as the Sahara Desert. If the whole of the late Confederacy were to be engulfed by a tidal wave, the effect upon the world's enlightened few would be no greater than a piddling flood on the Yangtze River. The entire South is a vast plain of mediocrity, lethargy, and almost a dead silence."

"Strong words, sir."

"The North is also gross, crass, and vulgar, not to mention obnoxious; however, nowhere but in the South is there such complete sterility and an absence of any civilized gesture or aspiration."

"Is there any hope for it?"

"Not in our lifetimes. The South has not only lost the capacity for producing ideas, it's taken on the worst of ignorance and stupidity. Even if only a few of its Saharan anthropoids were aware of the graceful French term for the study of the arts, *les beaux arts*, they'd still murder the pronunciation. Which is why I titled one of my most read essays 'Sahara of the Bozart.'"

Thus, my expectations weren't positive.

My main route south to Mundrickus County was the Atlantic Highway, which was about to be rechristened as Highway 1. It was mostly paved, occasionally merely improved, and took me deep into North Carolina where I encountered an A&W Root Beer stand at Raleigh. There, I chugged two mugs before veering west through Greensboro, sustaining only two flats, which I patched and reinflated with a bicycle pump. I admired the image of the flying red horse Pegasus, so I gassed up mostly at Mobil filling stations.

There were few roadside amenities on the road, so I slept in the car one night, and another in a rooming house. I sang to myself all the way down. Somehow, I couldn't get Vernon Dalhart's Victor recording of "The Prisoner's Song" out of my mind, and by the time I got to my destination I loathed the ditty.

Royal Prong was hardly a surprise, a collection of weather-beaten shops clustered around a town square with the requisite bronze of a Confederate general on horseback, all dominated by a brick courthouse marked with a clock tower. The general's name was Royal Prong, for whom the town was christened. He was neither the best nor the best-known rebel leader, but he was celebrated for fighting the conflict's shortest battle: three and a half minutes. Prong's battalion saw what they thought was an enormous force of Yanks emerging from the mist, but the specter turned out to be a herd of cows on which the Rebs fearlessly opened fire. Before sounding retreat, General Prong declared victory. For that, in nineteen twelve, the Loyal Daughters of Dixie raised the funds to erect an effigy in his honor.

Mr. Custis, owner of the weekly *Democrat*, put me to work typing obituaries, running senseless errands, checking out twaddle for its two bumpkin reporters, and then on Fridays binding the press run and dropping off copies at pick-up points. A Baltimore *Sun* it wasn't. As I was unknown and never had a byline, I didn't bother to use a pseudonym, as I would on later clandestine assignments. Custis had little to say to me, and I to him. We both knew I was there because of his grudging obligation to Mencken, which went unspoken. I performed my tedious labors while scouting for the right opportunity to hook up with the Klan. It had no recruiting office so I was on my own.

Like the nation as a whole, the county was dry, but despite the apostolic supremacy, I found no lack of hush-hush ginmills trading in moonshine and Canadian bootleg—while Sheriff Ownbe and Deputy

Upchuck wisely turned a blind eye. That proved to be a benediction for a sham Christian like me.

Thanks, God, old chum. Now, all I need is for you to let me worm my way into the Klan.

----

It was at a juice joint called Jethro's—where the password was "Lem sent me"—that I met a lantern-jawed local named Ezra Potts, who split rock at the town quarry, and after his shift habitually boozed himself into a stupor. The bartender had hinted to me that Ezra was involved with the Klan, not surprising since most whites in town were connected in some way.

That night, Ezra and I became nigh on inseparable after I sprang for the first round, then the second, and the third. The flavor of the astringent sheepdip we swallowed was undiluted, but I manfully managed to down it while we exchanged what turned out to be Klan humor.

"Y'know, Gart," he said, draping a brotherly arm around my shoulders, "there's only two types of folks worse than racists."

"What's that, Ezra?"

"The blacks and the Jews."

He almost split a gut laughing. I roared too, hoping it didn't sound forced. Ezra could help me make the right connections.

He said, "Hell, my wife actually accused *me* of bein' a racist."

"How's that?"

"On account of I got into a lather when I found out her boyfriend's black."

Gales of laughter.

"I got one for *you*, Ezra," I slurred, the hootch catching up with me. "This guy's in the city who wants to join the bowling league, which is whites only. But the man who runs the league tells him the only way he can join is if he takes a revolver and goes out and shoots four blacks, two Jews, a Mexican, and a rabbit. The guy says, 'But I'd feel awful bad about shootin' the rabbit.' So the bowling league proprietor waives his initiation fee."

Ezra doubled up in laughter.

"Butt me," he said, wiping the tears from his eyes. "I'm out of smokes."

I tossed him an almost empty pack of Luckies.

"You're a good egg," he said, lighting up. "Racism's just plain stupid. You shouldn't ever treat no one no different just on account of them being from an inferior race. Those is the immortal words of Nathan Bedford Forrest, one of the South's greatest heroes."

Forrest had been the founder and first Grand Wizard of the KKK. I played along, keeping Ezra on the string without making it obvious I wanted to join. I didn't want to appear to be an anxious, would-be infiltrator.

"Say, Ezra, stop me if you've heard this one. A murderer, a wife beater, and a racist walks into a bar, and the bartender says, 'What can I get you, Sheriff?'"

"Hell, I can do better'n that. Whad'ya call a group of racist white chickens?"

"The Coo Clucks Clan?"

"Damn, ya heard that one already." Then he turned contemplative, as much as possible for such a bitty brain. "Y'know, in all seriousness, flyin' our beloved Confederate flag don't make no one a racist. It's the other way around. Say, Gart, you ain't so bad for a Yankee."

He punched my arm in a sort of locker-room affection.

"Hell, I ain't no Yankee, Ezra. I'm from Maryland."

"Which don't count 'cause you folks never resigned from the Union. Anyway, lemme ask you. How much do you know about the KKK?"

At that instant, the door was unlocked. Which is how I got my invite to join the Klan.

Damn, I was trying like hell not to hate this stubbly-chinned soak with bad teeth, who hadn't the faintest idea that the guy he was getting free drinks from was actually his worst enemy.

---

I was sworn in at a Klonklave in the damp basement candlelight of Clyde Scroggins's farmhouse in the tobacco fields six miles west of town, Ezra

Potts being my sponsor. Ezra's title was Grand Kighthawk, whose sole official duty was to tote messages between the Exalted Cyclops and the other KKK potentates, although some of the muckety-mucks now had telephone party lines, which made communication simpler. Everyone in the Klavern seemed to have a title: Klaliff, Klabee, Kladd, Kligrapp, Klokard, Klonsel, Kludd, Klokan, but I never did get them all straight.

Ezra attested to my decent character as a native-born gentile Christian citizen of the US of A, of sound mind, over eighteen, and with a full commitment to the furtherance of the white race. Dozens of hooded shapes surrounded me in ceremony, their paunchy shadows reflecting on the walls, as I took the vow.

"I, Gart Booker Asquith III, in the presence of God and man most solemnly pledge, promise, and swear, unconditionally, that I will faithfully obey the constitution and laws and willingly conform to all regulations, usages, and requirements of the Knights of the Ku Klux Klan, which do now exist or which may be hereafter enacted, and will render at all times loyal respect and steadfast support to the Imperial Authority of same, and will heartily heed all official mandates, decrees, edicts, rulings, and instructions of the Imperial Wizard thereof, I having knowledge of same, Providence alone preventing." Blah, blah, blah.

There was more drivel, of course, lunacy about secret signs, signals, words, and handgrips, and my promise never to yield to bribe, flattery, threats, passion, punishment, persuasion, nor any enticements whatever coming from or offered by any person or persons, male or female, for the purpose of obtaining secrets or secret information of the Knights of the Ku Klux Klan, and to die rather than divulge the same.

"All to which I have sworn by this oath that I will seal with my blood. Be thou as my witness, Almighty God. Amen."

I figured any oath to the Klan under God didn't account for anything, so I felt no guilt. After which the pointy white hats flew off and there were huzzahs, hoorays, handshakes, and slaps on the back from the cream of Royal Prong, practically anyone who was anyone. For a negro, I almost felt like I belonged.

Finally, they brought out the white lightning.

The Exalted Cyclops, who proved to be Pastor Buckalew of the Royal Prong Southern Methodist Evangelical Episcopal Church, said to the assembled, "Brothers, as you know, the KKK officially endorses Prohibition, the total abstinence of all alcohol, and the outlawin' of the saloon. I, as a man of the Lord, know that consumin' fermented and distilled beverages is an affront to God as well as family and home. Alcohol leads to degradation and pauperism and sometimes death. However, individual Klaverns, such as ours, have wide discretion on the matter—so let's drink the hell up, boys."

All the good Klavern jobs were taken so they appointed me a temporary Klexter, an outer guard, the person standing watch outside our secret meeting place to ward off spies, eavesdroppers, and women. Unless it rained. Then I became acting assistant to the Imperial Klarogo, the inside guard, imbecilic Bert Cubbedge, who ran the feedlot and poultry farm where he was the reigning king of chicken excreta.

Cubbedge was a foul-mouthed cracker who, as I was to learn, personally inspected your sheets to make sure they were cleaned and pressed, and if they weren't, he'd publicly humiliate you, fine you a quarter, and send you home for the night. He somehow thought that I was less than masculine, and started calling me Daisy. Maybe it was my eyeglasses.

After the ceremony, the talk turned to plotting a motorcade and rally in the town square to show off the vast power of the local Klan, which boasted of a few dozen paid members, plus a ladies' auxiliary.

Pastor Buckalew gave me some fine-tuned words of advice.

"Stop calling 'em sheets, son. It's white robes we wears, lightweight cotton, or, preferably satin. Only our horses wear sheets. Also, make sure there's a white strap around your waist so the robes don't go flappin' the hell everywhere. Our insignia is a red cross inside a black circle, and it's gotta be on the left breast. Plus the tassel attached to the peak of your cowl has to be red. The Klan likes things neat."

I was ordered to report to Biff Upchuck, the deputy sheriff, for a class on cross burnings, floggings, and tar and featherings, which was required of all new members. Upchuck told me that occasionally there would be some Republican to run out of town, so such knowledge was mandatory. Even an inadvertent praise of a Republican might get you shot.

Finally, before I could flee Clyde Scroggins's cellar, I had to fork over my fifteen-dollar initiation fee and promise to pay my monthly dues of two bucks. I kept my fingers crossed that the *Sun* would reimburse me for my expenses. I was pretty sure Henry would put in a good word for me.

***

Royal Prong was roughly divided in half by the Carolina, Clinchfield & Kentucky Railroad tracks, the white neighborhood, town square, and shopping street in the east, all the blacks to the west, wherein was Aunt Ethel's Rib and Okra joint. Her's was something slightly better than a shack with a noticeable lean, yet inside was an almost indefinable tumble-down warmth. A neon sign on the wall flashed OKRA.

The first time I walked in, a dead hush fell. It wasn't often someone appearing to be white intruded, other than Sheriff Ownbe or Deputy Upchuck who occasionally invaded to serve a warrant, make an arrest, or simply throw their weight around.

But I broke the ice.

"I've heard about your ribs," I told the lady at the counter who turned out to be Aunt Ethel. "But how's about what *really* matters?"

"What's that, chile?"

"The sauce."

The buxom chef broke into a bellyful of laughter. She was so flattered, I never had to stand at the counter like the hoi polloi waiting for my ribs. Aunt Ethel seated me at a rickety table and served me herself, and even gave me seconds on the house.

She said, "My secret ingredients is—and don't you go spillin' the beans—a touch of maple syrup, two pinches of cayenne, and a whole bottle of Dr Pepper."

White-appearing outsiders didn't come around much, so the other customers peppered me with questions. Was I a real, authentic Yankee?

How comes I talked so good? Had I ever seen Bert Williams on stage? How's about Bojangles Robinson? Was all Yankees like me? My exotic first appearance at Aunt Ethel's was tempered a bit when I revealed that I worked at the *Democrat*, but that I was only an errand boy.

Aunt Ethel said, "Still, chile, it ain't often I gets a white customer."

"What makes you think I'm white?" I said, winking

Before long, next to the barbecue sauce, I was treated to the worst kept secret this side of the tracks: Aunt Ethel's back room where the band kicked up its heels on weekends, which made Farmer Scroggins' moist basement seem like a Homo erectus hallucination. Ragtime piano, trumpet, slide trombone, clarinet, rhythm banjo, and the beauteous Ruby Glam singing vocals.

I was smitten by Ruby, a statuesque Nubian with delicate facial features and stygian flesh that cried out to be licked by a tongue. It was either love at first sight on my part or I was a monumental idiot. Probably both.

Lordy, how the musicians, with their own touch, performed the hits: "Tin Roof Blues," "The Sheik of Araby," "Dinah," "Sweet Georgia Brown" I jumped in to play a mean washboard solo on "The Dixieland Jazz Band One-Step." Pump a little hooch into me and, with thimbles on my fingertips, I was terror on the washboard. My quick feet once won a trophy at a dance contest in Baltimore, tripping the Charleston with a young lady who nearly kept up with me.

Aunt Ethel said, "Ain't you gonna get youself in trouble comin' over here, chile? 'Specially you workin' at the newspaper and all."

"Why should I?"

"On account of the Klan keeps watch on this place."

---

The KKK's motorcade got underway a week later, but first, Pastor Buckalew, our Exalted Cyclops, summoned us to prayer.

"Dear God, bless our brotherhood who are akin in race, belief, spirit, character, interest, and purpose. So that we may relieve the oppressed. To succor the unfortunate, especially our white widows and orphans, and to affirm the commitment of the Knights of the Ku Klux Klan to the sacred duty of shieldin' the chastity and good name of womanhood. To preserve blood purity and the integrity of the traditions, ideals, and heritage of our superior race. Amen. Gentlemen, crank your engines."

It looked like something out of the annual auto show at the Fifth Regiment Armory in Baltimore. The motorcade included one of the new Ajax models made by Nash Touring, Dodge Roadster, Olds 43A, Napier, Marmon Speedster, Willys Overland Speedster, Durant Model A, the usual Model Ts, and even a Leach-Bitwell Sedan. It almost included a cart pulled by a billy goat, but the driver was a seven-year-old kid who was disqualified. I had offered my Dixie Flier to the motorcade, but it was deemed a classic, far too fragile, and more deserving of preservation behind an outhouse on the negro side of the tracks. Most of the autos were open-air to accommodate our stylish, pointy Klan hoods.

The scheme was to drive around the town square several times honking and shouting, park the vehicles, and then parade on foot in full Klan regalia to the bandstand for a spirited rally to demand that hotel and restaurant owners preserve their hallowed right to refuse service to anyone, especially the colored; to curb the mongrelizers who'd use our schools and government agencies to destroy the white race; to imprison or execute all bomb-happy anarchists, agitators, and assassins; and to promote patriotism to God, country, and flag—the Confederate flag in particular.

But it never got that far.

The Willys Overland driven by Carl Depriest, who ran the hardware store, rear-ended the new Leach-Bitwell Sedan owned by Rufas Stembridge, president of Royal Prong Savings and Loan. Naturally, this infuriated Rufas, who had imported the Leach-Bitwell from the city just a fortnight earlier. Rufas exited his sedan, surveyed the damage, and, throwing his hood aside, began angrily remonstrating with Carl. This produced a furious response, with Carl accusing Rufas of stopping short and therefore was himself responsible for the collision. Rufas demanded that Carl spill for the damages and to cough up now, by God, while Carl told Rufas to take a flying leap. The upshot was that the two peckerwoods began throwing punches before rasslin' each other to the ground, mucking up their clean, white robes with dirt, sweat, and blood. It wasn't long before all the brothers, choosing sides, joined the brawl—everyone had been drinking, don't you know—which got Sheriff Ownbe and Deputy Upchuck into the farce. It took twenty minutes before everything calmed down and Doc Peavy could reset Carl's broken nose and patch up Rufas's black eye.

Furious, Exalted Cyclops Buckalew threw in the towel as far as the rally was concerned and ordered everyone to get the goddamed hell home.

"You'll be hearin' about this at our next Klonklave!" he yelled while using various phrases not usually associated with a man of the cloth. "There's fines to be had."

The Klan had hoped their rally in the town square would produce a sizeable crowd of onlookers, which it did, but not in the way they expected. Although I was a mere Boy Friday at the Royal Prong *Democrat*, I took copious notes on the melee in the square and typed up a decent little dispatch, which Mr. Custis ran on the front page of that week's edition.

It was my first byline, which I cut out to insert into my scrapbook, maybe someday to show my grandkids. And I wanted Henry to be impressed—assuming that was even possible.

---

I was carrying the torch, although not in the way the Klan did, for the stunning Ruby Glam, who seemed to be taken by my Northern-style erudition and sophistication—although the name Mencken was as unknown to her as that of Wladyslaw Stanislaw Reymont, a former railroad crossing gateman who'd won this year's Nobel Prize in Literature.

Late one night at Aunt Ethel's, after the funambulists did themselves wicked and bringing down the rafters, I invited Ruby to drive with me to the shore of Lake Occaneechi for a romantic, moonlight rendezvous. She was shocked at first at what appeared to be a crude overture from a white man to a negress in clear violation of custom and propriety, not to mention the statutes prohibiting the delightful practice of fornication, a custom of which I was personally in favor. I was surprised yet pleased that she, however hesitant, accepted my less-than innocent invitation.

She was spellbound by my tales of life in the metropolis of Baltimore, about the great ships that berthed in the Inner Harbor right downtown, its horse tradition at Pimlico, and the story of "The Star Spangled Banner" and Fort McHenry. Not to mention my dexterity on the washboard.

But therein was a problem. She was black while I appeared to be white, and I dared not reveal the truth for fear of exposing my subterfuge in infiltrating the KKK, the sort of thing that could get you stuffed and mounted over a Klansman's mantel. Under the law, to be a Caucasian one had to be more than seven-eighths white, and if the Tar Heel State deemed a person with as little as one-eighth negro blood, he or she was considered black. Period. Technically, Ruby and I were of the same race, yet, still undercover, I couldn't speak to her about it.

On my lunch hour, I'd gone to the Mundrickus County Court House to research some of the state's laws regulating behavior among consenting adults, and came upon a statute dating to eighteen-five reading to the effect that "...if any man and woman not being married to each other shall lewdly and lasciviously associate, bed, or cohabit together, they shall be guilty of a Class 2 misdemeanor, resulting in one-thousand dollar fines and six days in jail." Little doubt, the offending couples would fare dramatically worse were they of different races.

Nevertheless, a tender moon nestled in a blue-black sky reflected from Lake Occaneechi's clear waters, and as we sat side by side on the shore, soothed by a comforting breeze, I put my arm around her and she didn't shy away.

"I'd like to take you to Baltimore," I said. "We could get lost in the city where no one knows us or cares what we do. Maybe buy a quaint little rowhouse in Fells Point."

She didn't say no, nor did she object when, the stars sparkling like jewels overhead, we willfully violated North Carolina's fornication law.

My next interaction with the Klan was a cross burning outside the house of an uppity negro by the name of Willie Jefferson, by trade an auto mechanic.

"Here's what happened," my Klan guarantor Ezra Potts explained over tiger milk and reefer at Jethro's. "It seems Willie walked through the front door of Huckabee's Luncheonette to buy a po'boy instead of goin' round to the back. Old Huckabee sold him the samwich, but he had a fit because Willie was so damned brazen, and right in front of the luncheon crowd. Huckabee don't serve no negroes at the counter, but he makes allowances if they come to the back door, so he's sometimes suspected of being a progressive, even a Republican, which he denies. He didn't want to make no scene inside the luncheonette, although he let Willie know what he thought by givin' him the evil eye.

"But, wait, that ain't all. Missy Calhoun, wife of Earl Calhoun, who runs the dry goods place, was walkin' down the street when she passed Willie and he winked at her. Winked. Hell, that's negro eyeballin' of the worst sort. Can you believe it? Why, she was fit to be tied.

"And listen, Gart, it gets even worse. Willie works over at Ulrich Motors. He repairs cars real good by all accounts, which is why Ulrich keeps him on in spite of his snippy attitude. He's the best mechanic in town. So one morning when Ulrich is in the city at the dentist's, Carl Depriest walks in to see how Willie's comin' along fixing the slipping clutch on Carl's Willys Overland. Carl's in a hurry but Willie's takin' his sweet time, and Carl gets impatient and starts snappin' at him, like, boy, get along on this. You know how Carl is. You saw when he had that ruckus with Rufas Stembridge on the square.

"Willie gets all high and mighty and tells Carl—actually calling him by his first name—to hold his water and it would be damned ready when it was damned ready. Of course, Carl goes—what's it called?—apoplectic and later bitches to Ulrich, who puts him off, 'cause he don't want to lose Willie. That's why us boys is gonna pay a little visit to that smart-alecky porch monkey's house tomorrow night. Gotta put him in his place. We already got the cross built and it's ready to be lit."

The reporter in me wanted to go, but the thought of it was repellant.

"What happens if I can't make it?" I said. "I might be busy washing my sheets."

"You gotta go, Gart. Cross burnin' attendance is mandatory for greenhorns like you."

"And if I don't?"

"If you rack up enough infractions they'll bring you up before the whole Klonklave."

"What can they do to me?"

"Reprimand, suspension, banishment, or the extreme penalty, which is unwritten. You don't wanna truck with the Invisible Empire. And, Gart, wear your best robes. At cross burnins', the Klan likes to look high class. I'm the guy who got you in so don't disappoint me."

"Anything for you, Ezra."

Only Sigmund Freud could explain how someone like me could become fond of a lummox like Ezra, a member of the most grotesque, loathsome, and repugnant cadre since the days of the witch hangings in Salem.

Sometime after midnight, my Klan brothers and I arrived at Willie's little frame house out near the negro cemetery in a parade of four cars, one of which had a big wooden cross strapped to the roof. We were ordered to walk on tippy toes and keep our lips zipped until the cross was set ablaze, so as to enjoy the full advantage of Willie's shock and fear. His house was dark as we expected, presumably he and his family having gone to bed. We struggled mightily lifting the heavy cross, then dug a hole in the front yard in which to plant it. We poured gasoline all the hell over it, although my aim was bad because I had trouble seeing out of the hood's cockeyed peepholes. Plus my eyeglasses kept slipping under the hood.

Earl Calhoun, who was especially aggrieved because his wife claimed that Willie had winked at her, said in a sotto voice, "That's enough gasoline, boys. Now hand me the match."

There was a pause, some fumbling, and a few mutterings.

"I said gimme a damned match so I can light up this bastard."

More whispering and dawdling.

Then one of the brothers said, "Earl, we ain't got no match. We forgot to bring 'em."

"What?"

"I said—"

"I heard what the hell you said. You tellin' me you didn't bring matches to a damned cross burnin'?"

All of a sudden, the lights went on inside Willie's house, then the porch light, where Willie opened the door and stepped out toting a shotgun and a lantern.

"Can I help you gentlemens?" he called.

A stupefying silence belted us as hard as Jack Dempsey's knuckles. We were like deer caught in the headlights of a Model T, and it was clear none of the caulkies, including myself, had any notion of what to do in case things backfired—so to speak. We had no alternate plan, and no one ever thought Willie would actually confront us, armed no less. We weren't prepared for it.

Earl finally assembled what amounted to a few wits, shouting, "Let's skedaddle, boys!"

Abandoning our flammable but unfired cross, we clumsily loped from several directions to our parked vehicles and clawed our way inside. Three of the cars roared off spewing billows of dust, but the auto driven by Dr. Peavy, the one I leaped into, damned wouldn't start. The doc tried again and again to get it going but it refused to kick over.

Willie, dressed in slippers and a nightshirt and still holding the shotgun and lantern, casually walked over to us.

"Doc Peavy, sir, that you? Thought I recognized your car. I worked on it plenty of times. Say, what y'all wearing? Looks like bedclothes to me. A bit chilly tonight. You folks wants me to bring you out a blanket or two?"

Peavy desperately geared the clutch and pumped the gas pedal, but the car was as dead as a twice-flattened possum out on Poon Pie Road.

Willie said, "Doc Peavy, sir, sounds like you got carburetor trouble. Why don't I open the hood and take a look? Bet I can get it fixed in no time."

We sat, cringing, squeezed inside Peavy's Dodge Roadster, mortified in our farcical robes and hoods, as Willie tinkered with the car's guts under lantern light. It was one thing to commit some travesty when your face was covered, but another when your intended victim, unflinching, knew exactly who and what you were.

"Now try it, Doc Peavy, sir," Willie said.

Which he did and the Roadster rumbled back to life.

Willie said, "Think it was mostly flooded, but I seen a couple of loose cables which I fixed, so you should be in good shape now. No charge."

Peavy said sheepishly, "Well, uh, thanks Willie. Uh, give my best to your wife and kids. And about that cross in your yard..."

"Yes sir, Doc Peavy. It'll make some mighty fine firewood, and I'm real appreciative. I'm figurin' to put it on my woodpile in the morning. And you know what they says about woodpiles and folks who look like me."

So went my first cross burning, and I marveled at the Klan's incapacity to make the grade, come up to snuff, or cut the mustard—call it what you will. As soon as I got back to Ma Gable's, I added to my growing pages of Klan notes, one section of which I labeled, "Idiocy."

---

Clog dancing wasn't fashionable in what passed as the urbane precincts of Baltimore, although I once found a smoky Turkish joint on the waterfront, hidden among the warehouses and patronized by merchant seamen. There, belly dancers did their shimmies accompanied by oboe, clarinet, oud, ney, kanoon, and finger cymbals. Although I'd never witnessed a clog dance, I was familiar with the sound, particularly late at night hearing "The National Barn Dance" on WLS out of Chicago, courtesy of a robust transcontinental radio signal. So when I read a flier about a barn dance featuring a clog dancing competition in Royal Prong, I invited Ruby to go with me—as insane as the idea now seems. I don't know what I was thinking.

She looked at me in astonishment.

"Don't you know, Gart, in the Carolinas, barn dances aren't for my kind."

"And what sort of dances are for your kind?"

"The Black Bottom, the Fox Trot, and the One-Step. I also do a nasty tango. But they'd never let me into one of their barn dances."

My own Baltimore, like all the East's big cities, was segregated in many ugly ways, yet one might understand why, in my infatuation, I increasingly wanted to safely spirit Ruby away to anywhere the Klan wasn't.

So I wound up in the company of Ezra Potts. The barn dance was at Homer Riddick's pig farm on a dirt road five miles south of town. Riddick once farmed melons and squash, but decided there was more gravy in swine. Fortunately, his farmhouse and its original barn were upwind of the pig operation.

We heard the twang of the banjos and screech of the fiddles even as we drove up to the overflowing red barn, where Riddick's homely daughters charged a quarter for each admission, which included free non-alcoholic liquid of some sort, cookies, and something that resembled cake but was hard as a rock.

The clogging competition was already underway, with teams of men in overhauls and women in ruffled skirts, arms loosely at their sides, wearing heavy work shoes, and stomping in precision on a huge plywood platform to a familiar two-quarter time hoedown rhythm.

"They don't always call it cloggin' in these parts," Ezra told me. "Sometimes it's known as flatfootin.'"

I loved the rhythmic stomp and the boisterous, unstudied, unaffected country string music, a far piece from the syrupy dance bands of Nathaniel Shilkret, Jean Goldkette, and Jacques Renard and his Cocoanut Grove Orchestra, which performed at Baltimore's Alcatraz Ballroom.

Ezra said, "I see lots of our brothers is here tonight, Gart. There's Bert Cubbedge over by the punch bowl."

Cubbedge, my nemesis, was one philistine I had no desire to connect with. But as I was dragged over to join him by the refreshments stand, he said to me, "Say, Daisy, I been meanin' to talk to you."

"Why, Bert? I've kept my robes clean and pressed just like you said. Even put a little starch in 'em."

"Ain't that." He spat out a mouthful of whatever was in the punch bowl. "Say, there ain't no firewater in this here watered-down cow piss. Let's go out behind the barn so's we can talk private-like. I got a bottle of canned heat that'll grow hair on your chest, especially yours, Daisy, on account of guys like you can use a few hairs."

"I love you, Bert."

"And keep your fuckin' paws to yourself."

Outside, with the crickets chattering in the weeds and the fainter ringing from the banjos inside, we passed around Cubbedge's bottle, a Mason jar. The libation scorched my esophagus like fire as it went down, but I took some comfort in knowing that the heat was intended and that it may even have rendered me somewhat manly.

"What the hell's with you, Daisy?" Cubbedge snarled at me. "You turnin' into a swamp donkey or somethin'? We seen you walk into that colored rib joint the other night, on account of we got it staked out, and you was in there for hours with all them blacks. White folks don't go in there—unless maybe you *ain't* white."

"Don't I look white?"

"Which ain't the point. Africans got their place and we got ours."

"I was hungry, Bert, so I ate a few ribs, and then I heard the music in back and got curious. They call it jazz, you know."

"Jazz?"

"Yeah, kind of like your—our—white Baptist hymns only with rhythm. But, really, I wanted to figure out exactly what went on inside so's I could report it to the Exalted Cyclops. You should thank me, Bert. I put my life on the line."

"I think you *crossed* the line."

"You don't understand. I found a dangerous agitator inside Aunt Ethel's. The Klan needs to know about him, Bert."

Cubbedge's eyes narrowed. "Yeah, who?"

"Some old, dark-complected fella up from Gulfport, Mississippi. A tent revivalist by the name of, uh, Reverend Lemuel Seymour Boothe. Better known as Brother Boothe. You should of heard him in there, stirring up folks, so un-American. He was actually talking about judging people by their character, not their complexions."

"Say what?"

"And that it was time to spring from the dim and desolate valley of exclusion to the sunlit path of racial equality."

"Bolshevik talk."

"That he was taking his tent revival all the way to the coast of California. Then he said something about now being the time to alter racial injustice into the sturdy rock of brotherhood."

"Fuckin' sedition is what it is."

"It doesn't get any better, Bert. Brother Boothe said the whirlwind of revolt will one day shake the nation's foundations until justice happens. But that the negro must face violence by reaching the majestic heights of the soul."

"Even worse that sedition. Treason. He needs to be the hell deported or worse. What's his name again?"

"Brother Boothe."

"Whereabouts he stayin' at? We're gonna pay him a little visit."

"That's the thing, Bert. He was about to leave for, I think he said Tennessee. He travels all around, stirring up trouble in the colored communities everywhere he goes."

"Hell, he's tryin' to start a race war is what he's doin'. Your report ain't complete but it's tolerable. Listen, Daisy, you better damned well stay out of that black bitch's rib shop from now on because we got somethin' big planned for her."

"What are you saying?"

"I'm sayin' for you to keep your yap shut about it 'cause it's a matter of Klan security."

Brother Boothe was imaginary, but I had little doubt that someone, someday, would come along to lead the way, speaking words much like his.

———————————

It was now too dangerous for me to further patronize Aunt Ethel's. If I was spotted by the Klan again it might prove to be godawful for all of us—but that didn't rule out my courting Ruby secretly. Late one night, after parking as far away as I could and hiding my jalopy in the bushes, I sneaked in through the back, trailed by a curious yellow and white alley cat, to spoon with Ruby, preserving enough breath to later warn Aunt Ethel about the Klan's threat.

Even though I didn't know when or how they would strike, the old gal seemed to be resigned to what I told her. Still, she was a bearcat.

"We's aware of what's goin' on with them damned fools," Aunt Ethel said. "The only question is when. But we'll be ready, chile. We hopin' this place won't turn into another Greenwood."

"You mean Greensboro. I drove through it on the way to Royal Prong."

"You ain't never heard of Greenwood? Out in Oklahoma. Place called Tulsa, where lynch mongers looted, then burned the entire neighborhood while murderin' hundreds of black men, women, and babies with their machine guns and turpentine bombs dropped from airplanes. They called it a race riot, but it weren't. It was a race massacre. The Klan, which saw a great opportunity, was partly behind it and the police was in on it too. And their National Guard. The folks in Greenwood tried to defend theirselves, maybe shot a few crackers, but not enough of 'em, so they didn't stand no chance."

"Were there arrests?"

"Hell, no. None of them goobers out there was ever charged. But plenty of black folks was put in jail, those who survived it. The whole community was burned down. I can't believe it never got out, and it may never get out. It oughta have been in all the papers, instead of bein' mostly spread by word of mouth."

"I should have known about it."

"You ain't alone, chile, sorry to say."

I pussyfooted away as stealthily as I came in. The alley cat followed me back to my bucket of bolts, but didn't get in. I was almost disappointed.

At our next Klonklave, Exalted Cyclops Buckalew announced that negro church leaders were launching a registration drive to enroll black voters, which was anathema to the Klan, and vowed to put an end to it.

Buckalew said, "We'll assemble outside of their Zion African Methodist Baptist Church right after what passes as their services. I expect y'all to be there. That's in two weeks. Two. Write it down. Attendance is required, and any Klansman who don't show up faces a gelding. We ain't gonna let 'em register one damn name. The last thing we needs is more nappy-headed voters—or Republicans, who're almost as bad. Never forget, the Republicans declared war on the South contrary to the principles of liberty and freedom. So I say, hell no to voting rights for jackasses, leftists, Zionists, and woolly-headed nincompoops."

This brought a round of applause from the brothers, and I was the most ecstatic.

I got mighty antsy in the period that followed, writing my KKK notes and performing my usual menial tasks at the *Democrat*. Twice, I managed to spirit Ruby to Lake Occaneechi. But it was clear that a morass of fear abetted by social tensions and my Klan undercover work were making a relationship like ours insurmountable—despite the complications of our mutually shared race. Our goodbye was a tearful one.

At the same time, I was pining to return to the cosmopolitan atmosphere of a big city and anxious to again listen as Henry peerlessly skewered pretense, sham, buffoonery, and baloney.

---

Finally, the big day arrived for the KKK to bust up the negro voter registration drive.

In full Klan attire, we motored in a caravan to the Zion African Methodist Baptist Church, where we gathered outside the white, steepled building, each of us assuming what we considered were menacing postures.

Exalted Cyclops Buckalew kept the brothers enthused by whipping them up with race rubbish.

"The Knights of the Ku Klux Klan is on a mission to remind Americans of its duty to preserve the nation's precious racial heritage. Our country was founded by the finest elements of the white race, which established our very government. They passed it on to posterity to be maintained by white men as a white man's country for whites only. They bequeathed to their descendants the responsibility of preservin' the integrity of our kind by keepin' pure the white man's blood. The race must and shall be secured from all tainted blood and kept supreme in all the affairs of this here white man's country."

I couldn't have said it better—had I been an ignorant, white bigot, which I was trying like hell to appear.

Then Buckalew led us in awkwardly singing "Bringing in the Sheaves." Despite my abortive theological studies, I had only a passing acquaintance with Jesus and the gospels, and didn't know the lyrics. I just mouthed the words, which prompted Bert Cubbedge to eye me suspiciously and mutter some sort of recriminations under his breath, one word of which appeared to be "Daisy."

We heard the sound of a competitive choir. Joyful gospel singing and clapping from inside the church, a far cry from our own clumsily disingenuous groaning.

As Sheriff Ownbe and Deputy Upchuck leaned indolently against their prowl cars, butts dangling from the corners of their mouths, the church doors opened, and the black parishioners in their Sunday best swarmed out en masse, not seeming startled to encounter a bunch of preposterously-garbed men all puffed up and trying to look apocalyptic.

One of the parishioners, who turned out to be their pastor, Reverend Lysander Jackson, was still holding his Bible as he approached the white line. He was a plucky sort, all smiles and teeth and cheer.

"Gentlemens, this is truly a pleasure. What brings y'all here on such a beautiful Sunday so full of God's grace? And I see you is dressed in your finest threads for the occasion."

Buckalew, speaking from within the protection of his hood, said, "We're here to show the power of the KKK and to make sure you people don't register one single, new voter today. If the great state of North Carolina won't keep y'all in your place the Knights of the Ku Klux Klan will. Even if it takes force."

"Why, there must be some mistake," Jackson said.

"Ain't no mistake, boy. The worst thing our state done was to eliminate the poll tax, which only encouraged you people to vote."

"I ain't talkin' 'bout that. Our voter registration drive was *last* week. Yessir, we signed up over two hundred folks, who are now going to vote in November. Y'all came here too late."

"What?"

"But listen, why don't y'all go around to the rear of the church? Our ladies got picnic tables laid out with fried chicken, yams, sweet and spicy collard greens, and watermelons. They's plenty of food for all, and I 'spect you folks must be hungry."

The Klan's incursion again broke up in agitation, confusion, and chagrin, with angry reproofs among themselves as to who screwed up the goddamned date. Somebody was going to take the fall for that and fall hard. If we'd worn white tails as well as our white hoods, the tails would have been dragging in the dust.

As we slunk back to our cars, I overheard Bert Cubbedge say that he and some of the boys, armed to their molars, intended to spring an unheralded visit to Aunt Ethel's Rib and Okra joint the next night, and it would be a lollapalooza. Cubbedge had just imported a secondhand, barely-used tommy gun from Chicago, and they planned to shoot up the shack and everyone inside until they ran out of bullets.

———

After alerting Aunt Ethel as to when the KKK's planned attack would take place, I decided it was time to put the lid on my intelligence gathering in Royal Prong, pack my bag and Klan notes, and crank up my little flivver for the long haul north. Mentally, I previewed my planned tell-all about the Klan's inner workings, nearly swooning in my fatuous visions of scoring a Pulitzer. Two reporters for the *Chicago Daily News* had just won the prize for their work on the thrill killing of young Bobby Franks by Nathan Leopold and Richard Loeb, and none other than an impassioned defense by the lawyer-god Clarence Darrow saved the duo from collecting the celebrated electric cure. I didn't know then that I would not only meet Darrow one day, I would sleep in his house. Would my exposé of the Invisible Empire's imbecility be any less of a story than the prizewinner about two Chicago scions murdering a child merely for the buzz? No, I thought, even if in Royal Prong, the Klan couldn't be straight, act straight, or shoot straight.

Which is just about what happened outside of Aunt Ethel's.

I watched as the brave Klan raiders descended only to find that the entire black population of Mundrickus County, hundreds of men, women, and children, armed with Bibles, not bullets, had surrounded the place to protect it with their bodies, folks doing more for good than the Klan could ever muster doing bad. The sight of all those people, their only defense being their common humanity, cowed the Klan into another humiliating retreat.

Not that the KKK cared about humanity, but there were simply too many people to gun down. It didn't have enough bullets.

As I steered my Dixie Flier north on Highway 1, I imagined Henry ranting to me about the Klan, in particular about the colossal KKK debouch under the nose of the Capitol's dome, that massive march in Washington.

"Taggart, m'boy, they were common folk, and their commonness radiated from them like heat from a stove. The Klan's not a club for snobs, it's a device for organizing inferiorities into a mystical superiority."

---

I figured that even if I didn't win a Pulitzer this time, I might be able to talk Henry and the *Sun* into sending me undercover to the Windy City to infiltrate Al Capone and the mob, a reporter from the East doing what the big-time newspaper boys in Illinois couldn't. Capone had just survived a hit by rival gangsters and the beer war was out of control, so there was a damned good story there.

But I could hear Henry, a journalist to his garters, excoriate the profession that clothed and fed him, accusing newspapermen of being dispirited drudges toting the mimeographed pronunciamentos of press agents, while the Washington correspondents in particular were too stupid to penetrate the fraudulencies surrounding them. I vowed that one day I'd head to the capital myself and prove Henry wrong.

Little doubt that if a man burned a cross, something he supposedly prayed to, he'd burn about anything, including a rib and okra joint run by a feisty old lady whose sauce was as savory, sweet, and hot as her jazz. Outnumbered in more ways than one, and fully in character, the Klansmen and their new tommy gun had taken a powder from Aunt Ethel's, but, no doubt, would continue to secretly plot vulgar deeds of chaos and tumult.

I suspected they'd be around at least until their sheets became too expensive. I heard rumors that *Vanity Fair* was planning a big fashion photo spread on the KKK. Yoicks! That alone could drive up the cost of sheets.

And that's -30- for this reporter.

*The night was dark and drizzly*
*The air was full of sleet,*
*Pa he joined the Ku Klux Klan*
*And Ma she lost her sheets.*

—Anonymous

# ──TWO──

# TOMMY THE CHOIRBOY

*I walked with God and Al Capone*
*beneath an alabaster sky*
*while Satan played his saxophone*
*I walked with God and Al Capone.*

—Barry Dennis Hopkins (1948-2018)

Henry Mencken never wasted a moment of that fiendishly hot summer in nineteen twenty-five. He went to Dayton, Tennessee, where, along with Clarence Darrow, he did to religious fundamentalists in print what a dog does to a bone. On the other hand, I, Gart Booker Asquith III, remained behind, performing middling labors at the Baltimore *Sun*, but basking in my first success as an investigative reporter for my inside scoop on the Ku Klux Klan. I won no Pulitzer. However, the *Sun*'s management was convinced that with Henry's continued tutelage I was ready for another challenging assignment.

Now, I was about to leave my two-seat Dixie Flier behind and take the B&O's Capitol Limited to Chicago. The purpose: to infiltrate the mob headed by the conspicuous racketeer Al Capone, an assignment Henry and I weighed over umpteen surreptitious beers at his favorite watering hole at Liberty and Saratoga streets, the Hotel Rennert. That there seemed to be no end in sight to the affliction of Prohibition only whetted Henry's thirst for hops. Prohibition was a bitch to eradicate, harder even than smallpox, and its greatest beneficiaries were, in Henry's words, knaves, mountebanks, and rogues. Namely, Capone.

He said, "I have a request to make when you arrive in the Windy City, Taggart, m'boy, assuming you're still alive after throwing in with gangsters. Kindly extend my compliments to Clarence Darrow for his fearless undertaking in feudal Tennessee. It shall be long remembered."

Henry had arranged for me to board with Chicago's legal-lord while I worked my way into the mob, although it would be folly to let it be known to the criminal element of my temporary residence in the home of such a virtuous defender of justice.

In Tennessee, Darrow had led the team defending John Thomas Scopes, a mousy high school teacher found guilty of the crime of teaching science. The prosecution included William Jennings Bryan, thrice-denied presidential hopeful and a paladin to the Bible thumpers. Humiliated by Darrow on the witness stand, he dropped dead five days after the spectacle.

Beckoning the Rennert waiter for a refill—while ever vigilant for the specter of Prohibition agents or Judases—Henry said to me, "Fitting that Bryan's final days were spent in the backwater that is Tennessee. He enjoyed waking to the tune of cocks crowing on the dunghill and gorging on the heavy, greasy victuals of the farmhouse stove.

"Bryan was widely admired as a man of the people, Henry," I said.

"Quite true. He preferred those who sweated freely and weren't debauched by the refinements of the toilet. The simian gabble of that retrograde crossroads in Tennessee wasn't gibberish to him but wisdom of an occult and superior sort. Unlike us city folk, the yokels never laughed at him."

I said, "I suspect few opinions on God and religion were changed down there, despite the unrelenting publicity and the radio and newspaper coverage."

He fired up a virgin Uncle Willie.

"The most curious convention of our age is that religious opinions should be respected. Taggart, m'boy, what exactly do you expect to accomplish from your planned foray into the archipelago of crime called Chicago? Certainly, you'll be risking your life if not your limbs."

"The same as my exposé of the KKK, Henry. Fame. Glory. Celebrity. Maybe even a big prize."

"But how do you, lacking a single mob connection, expect to infiltrate the Windy City's underworld?"

"In the guise of one Tommaso Adosti, first-generation American, born to parents from Calabria not long off the boat in the Port of Baltimore. The boss of our local crime syndicate, Vito Corbi, also from Calabria, befriended my folks. Corbi's kid, Patsy, got busted for murdering a hood called Frankie Naples. So after Patsy was sent to the Big House, I became like a son to Vito who made me his runner with special attention to the numbers. I was also an altar boy and sang in the choir at Our Lady of Pompeii Church, where I walked to Mass from my family's home on Stiles Street in Little Italy. I borrowed the name Tommy the Choirboy from a Tommy who really exists. And the reason I'm in Chi is that I'm lookin' for better opportunities on account of Baltimore's too limited."

I could see that Henry, eyebrows raised, cigar askew between his teeth, was impressed by my bogus pedigree.

"Taggart, m'boy, how the devil did you amass that unending balderdash? I salute you."

"From the *Sun*'s morgue. They've got loads of clips in the crime files."

"If a resolute reporter such as yourself can bamboozle the Klan, then assimilating with the Capone mob should be child's play. I, for one, have had my fill of coddling wrongdoers like those new criminologists who see lawlessness as a sort of disease, either inherited or acquired by contagion, and as devoid of moral content or significance as typhoid fever. Having argued against the death penalty for all of my career, I'm now tempted to take the other side."

"That's like saying Calvin Coolidge is now your Godly inspiration."

"Cal was recently found by a secretary slumped over his desk in the Oval Office. They thought he was dead and sent for the undertaker. But he was only snoozing. Had 'em all bamboozled."

"No doubt I'll have conclusive opinions about the nature of crime when I return from Chicago."

"*If* you return. Take a typewriter with you."

"I'm not sure lugging my L.C. Smith all the way to—"

"I'm talking about a *Chicago* typewriter. All you have to do is to pull the trigger."

---

Armed with a *Sun* expense account, I boarded the Capitol Limited at the Mt. Royal Station. Each car was a Pullman, so I'd get a solid night's sleep for the nearly eighteen-hour haul via DC. Best of all was the opulent dining car with an ornate chandelier, brass fittings, mahogany paneling, and leaded-glass windows.

As Tommaso Tommy the Choirboy Adosti, my hair slicked back, I dressed the part, wearing a vested, butterfly-lapeled, double-breasted charcoal pinstripe with a flashy red tie and spiffy, patent-leather oxfords, my head topped with a beige homburg. My glad rags all but declared that bootlegging never paid better, and, best of all, the suit was roomy enough to secret a gat on one side and a flask on the other with barely a bulge. My Capone-like garb was no coincidence. Also, the bulls couldn't arrest you just for your duds.

As for the rod, I bought it only slightly used on the waterfront. I figured, being new to Chicago, I ought to look like I could use it.

The porter introduced himself as William, silver-headed and immaculately dressed in a blue uniform with buttons down the front. As the train gathered steam, William brought from the club car a Hires root beer on ice, which I surreptitiously spiked from the flask in my inside breast pocket. By the time the teeming city and its bustling harbor were replaced by the streaking rural countryside, I, already feeling no pain, was engrossed in the pulp I'd brought: *Weird Tales*. For a dollop of culture, I'd also taken along the latest issue of Henry's *American Mercury*, which I was saving to read at full sobriety.

I looked up when I heard a bruhaha at the far end of the car. William was being berated by a man about my age using vulgar racial epithets, which I intended to ignore until he gave the porter a shove. That was a bit much for me, mild-mannered and bespectacled as I was; however, emboldened by the hootch, not to mention the confidence of the heat in my jacket, I went to intercede.

I told the punk, "Say, pal, keep your mitts to yourself."

He was about my size, and lo, wore a double-breasted not dissimilar to my own. Hair slicked back too. But I figured I could take him if I acted first.

He said, "Stay outta this, wise guy. This here coon stole my suitcase."

William said, "Sir, maybe you left it on the station's platform before boarding."

"Who'd take the word of a jungle bunny over mine, boy?"

"Sir, I've been a Pullman porter for seventeen years, and never once had I—"

The goon raised a fist, about to let fly, but I grabbed his wrist before he could make chin music and twisted his arm downward, forcing him into a crouching position. With his other hand, he snatched blindly into his suitcoat, obviously groping for a piece. But I was faster. Still gripping his wrist, I partially withdrew my own gat, just enough for him to see my finger on the trigger. Momentarily, I had both the upper hand and the weapon advantage, so the message was clear.

"Okay, pal, truce," he said, wincing at the pain in his wrist. "You're obviously a pro."

I let him go, but kept my hand on the persuader.

"Perhaps you oughta apologize to the nice porter," I said in my usual helpful way.

"Yeah, maybe I got carried away."

William said, "That's perfectly understandable, sir. If your bag turns up, I'll bring it to you immediately."

The goon, scowling and rubbing his wrist, returned to his seat as I did to mine, although I had a feeling the incident wasn't over. I was shaking, I hoped not visibly, by my brief flirtation with bravado. As a reporter, I invariably stayed behind the scene.

I picked up reading *Weird Tales* from where I had left off. In it, a gorgeous, underdressed maiden whose spaceship had just crashed on an enormous asteroid circling Mars was being threatened by an odious alien with four arms and fangs approximating the height of the Woolworth Building. But the handsome, square-jawed Travis Gale, armed with a powerful space obliterator, was poised to save her.

Seeing my reflection in the Pullman window with dusk falling and the distant terrain blurring, I began to ruminate on the contradiction of an America with its unlimited promise and burgeoning wealth while its frequent intolerance condemned substantial numbers to oppression and poverty. But there were positives: Hollywood flicks, Dolores Del Rio, the Charleston, chorus lines, radio, Ben Bernie's band, short skirts, hot rods and rumble seats, and, despite the Eighteenth Amendment, plenty of hooch if you knew where to find it.

I never revealed to Henry, nor to any of my fellow cosmopolitanites, that I had attended a seminary far out in the provinces but became disillusioned and dropped out. I assimilated easily with rural folks. They taught me what they knew about shooting and fighting, but never how they justified their faith. For me, Henry was my reigning authority on such matters.

As I nearly nodded off, I imagined the goon in the gangster attire sneaking up behind me and firing a bullet into the base of my skull. One lousy shot was all it would take, my visions of Pulitzer preeminence lost in a fraction of a second. I jolted myself awake, perspiring.

---

In the swanky but crowded dining car, I was sitting at a table nursing another clandestinely-spiked root beer and studying the menu when the waiter asked if I wouldn't mind sharing my table. Okay with me, I told him.

Who should the waiter produce but the goon I'd gotten the drop on.

He glared at me and I returned the favor.

The waiter said to him, "Is this table satisfactory, sir? I'm afraid it's all that's available, and the kitchen will be closing soon."

He hesitated, then said, "What the hell, I'll take it."

He sat as the waiter handed him a menu. Our mutual silence almost sprained my ears until he growled, "Don't expect me to bump gums with you, chum."

"Like I'm gonna chew the fat with you."

A lull, then…

"You and me is dressed sort of alike and you carry a piece," he said. "We may be in the same racket."

I shrugged.

He said, "Do you know the last words of an Italian gangster?"

"I'll bite."

"Who the hell put a fiddle in my violin case?"

I stifled my inclination to laugh.

"You seem to think I'm Italian," I said. "I'll bet you're Irish. Y'know why Jesus wasn't born in Ireland?"

"Spill it."

"He couldn't find three wise men or a virgin."

"I kinda like that one," he said with what qualified as a half grin. "By the way, they found my bag. I'd left it on the open platform between the cars. I think when I was out there taking a leak off the train. There ain't nothin' like it, watching your piss fly in the wind. Neat the arcs and circles you can make."

"I'll try it tonight."

"But it has a tendency to blow back on your pants."

He introduced himself as McTeer, revealing he'd been in the Big Apple on a special assignment from his boss that required a certain expertise, and was headed back to the Windy City via DC. He was Irish and damned proud of it. I introduced myself. Adosti. Italian and also damned proud of it, known locally as Tommy the Choirboy. He asked if I was on the way to Chicago too and, if so, why. I told him I didn't have to explain nothin', but I allowed that I needed more action than Baghdad on the Crab Flats had to offer, which was why I was goin' to the City by the Lake.

He said, "I made it up to that porter. Slipped him the biggest damned tip he ever got in his life."

"Whoopee, asshole. Guess all the slurs you threw at him come easy for mugs like you."

"They ain't slurs where I come from. It's just talk. Anyway, I might have been a wee bit stewed. Finished up a flask out on that open platform."

"You like to beat up on black folks when you're stewed?"

"Hey, ya know how many of us Irish have been beat up and pissed on over the years? But now, on Chicago's North Side, we got respect. Not even you Italians fuck with us."

I said, "Respect is one thing. Niccolò Machiavelli is another."

"I know that guy. Boss out of Philly, right?"

"Check out your local library one of these days, McTeer. Go to the philosophy section. Bet you don't know the difference between the mob and an acting troupe."

"Lay it on me."

"When the mob says break a leg they mean it."

"I'll have to remember that one. The leg part's true. So who are you with?"

"I'm traveling alone," I said.

"No, wiseguy, I can tell by your rags and your mane, and the fact that you're packin', that you're with a family. New York? Philly? Where?"

"Baltimore. The Corbis. Ever hear of 'em?"

"Yeah. By reputation. Small timers."

"What about you?"

"Kenneallys. North Side."

"Small timers."

"How would you know?"

"I get around," I lied.

"Hear me out, Choirboy, if you ever lay a paw on me again I'll shoot you between the eyes and bury you in a concrete overcoat. We got a big lake that keeps its secrets."

"Hey, bigmouth, bein' shot between the eyes goes with the territory. I can accept that. But I ain't going for no concrete. It would break the heart of my sainted mother, and probably be bad for the lake."

"Okay, no concrete. How's about an acid bath?"

"Speaking of acid, McTeer, I gotta flask here that needs to be drained so's I can fill it up again. Have a few belts on me."

"Alcohol possession's a Federal offense, so I don't mind if I do. Say, just lookin' at the menu here. What's this crab imperial shit? I mean, do people where you come from actually eat fuckin' crabs?"

We did, and I never missed the annual Crab and Seafood Festival in Mount Vernon Place.

While waiting for our dinner orders, I pronounced with more assertiveness than I felt, "I'm gonna hook up with Capone once I land in Chi."

He snorted. "No one just hooks up with Al, not without no connections. Why should Al trust you?"

"Back home I got a pedigree, and I'm good at what I do."

"Al come up the hard way. Nearly rubbed out by his rivals I don't know how many times. Hounded by the cops. He don't count on no one except his bodyguards. You won't get near him."

"So how's come you know so much about it?"

"Capone respects my crew on the North Side because we don't chisel in on his territory."

I swallowed a slug of root beer-flavored hooch.

"All the Micks I know are dumb as hell," I said, "so you must have some Italian blood in you. I think maybe I just found the guy I'm lookin' for."

"Who?"

"You."

"For what?"

"Introducin' me to Al Capone."

The universe outside the Pullman window raced by as a blackish whorl of auras, perceptions, impressions, countenances, and occasional lights suggesting a distant human presence. The panorama went well with the hooch. By the time McTeer and I repaired to our respective berths after emptying my flask, we were like long-lost buddies from the Great War. Fueled by the spirits we'd shared, McTeer consented to make a Capone connection for me. But while his drunken manifestations of fraternity seemed reassuring, I had no doubt that, if need be, he'd put a slug into my skull without losing a wink of shuteye.

Before I turned in, I made a final pilgrimage to the open platform between the cars to take a leak off the train. McTeer was right. It was exhilarating as I pissed arcs and circles into the windy rush of the night.

He was also right that it would come back on you.

---

The Capitol Limited steamed into Grand Central Station along the Chicago River's south branch promptly at eight in the morning. McTeer and I said our farewells after arranging to meet at The Green Door, a North Side mob hangout.

"Al gonna be there?" I asked.

"Only Al knows where Al's gonna be at any moment."

I hailed a hack to Clarence Darrow's residence, an apartment-hotel on East 60th Street across from Jackson Park. Darrow, greeting me at his front door, was taken aback at the sight of my gangster threads.

He said, "When Henry wired me that you were coming to Chicago on an assignment, I never expected you to look, so, so…"

"Dashing?"

"One might say, uh, distinctively dressed."

"Maybe Henry didn't tell you I'm investigating your local racketeers."

He said, "I'm surprised the *Sun* sent a reporter all the way from the East Coast. Chicago has more than its share of aggressive dailies and eager reporters. Ever hear about our circulation wars?"

"Yeah, some two-dozen people were rubbed out."

"We've got six daily papers, and they all used goons to burn each other's editions and shoot their deliverymen. The blood ran thicker than printers' ink."

"But how many of your local reporters have actually joined the mob to dig for dirt? Which I plan to do. I'm from out of town. Nobody knows me here. It's a natural."

"God help you, if you'll excuse the trite expression."

The craggy-faced Darrow looked exactly as he appeared in the plethora of newspaper photos of him: tall, rumpled, tie aslant, red suspenders hitching up his droopy trousers, a forelock of his tousled hair flopping over his brow.

He ushered me in, introduced me to his wife Ruth, then led me into his book-lined study where we sat in comfortable leather chairs. Darrow was no stranger to writing. He'd published any number of books including *Farmington*, an autobiographical novel about his growing up in Ohio.

I said, "Henry sends you his respects for taking on the evolution case in Tennessee. He got a kick out of the papers calling it the Monkey Trial."

"Are you aware that Henry coined the phrase 'Bible Belt'?"

"Which shows he knows his geography. What do you take from the trial?"

Darrow settled in, as if eager to share the story.

"I was astonished that William Jennings Bryan, cooling his sudoriferous face with a palm-leaf fan, took the cause of such an outrageous law: the teaching of any doctrine in conflict with the Genesis myth. It was thick-headed and senseless."

"I read that the judge opened the trial with a prayer each day."

"Any pretense at impartiality by the court was a sham. And there in that packed, sweaty courtroom, Bryan sat, a man in decay, his admirers ringing him like a human halo."

"I hear it was pretty lively outside the courtroom as well."

"Hotdog stands, popcorn merchants, sandwich sellers, cola purveyors, and sleight-of-hand artists on every corner. They sprang up like poisoned mushrooms. At night, in flocked the holy rollers, who sang, howled, twitched, and twirled, many of them obvious halfwits. The number of people in this nation who are on the borderline of insanity is appalling."

"But you lost the case."

"Which is now being considered on appeal, for what little that's worth. We're talking about Tennessee."

"I would have been there but I was busy helping the Ku Klux Klan burn crosses."

"Henry sent me your KKK piece in the *Sun*, which must have taken a degree of courage."

"I'm now focusing on bullets, booze, and bootleggers. I understand crime's more abysmal in Chicago than anywhere in the nation."

"Blame it on Prohibition, which is splendid for Al Capone, but not the virtuous. As long as it persists, lawlessness won't disappear. Enforcement in Chicago is so lax that most saloons simply ignore the law, but when it *is* enforced it's accomplished with guns and violence in a way never before. More lives have been wantonly taken by this mad effort to make America subservient to the dries than by the rest of our criminal code combined."

"Aren't the bootleggers and racketeers at war among themselves?"

"Prohibition guaranteed it. Soda shops, pharmacies, and cigar stores are now nothing more than fronts for selling illegal booze. Doctors are writing prescriptions for industrial-grade alcohol as medicine. And the racketeers are in the middle of it."

I said, "I understand a case of decent whiskey is now worth its weight in gold."

"Prohibition can never be fully enforced because most Americans refuse to be coerced by this fanatical decree. The criminals' response was perfectly predictable."

"I think fermented beverages have existed for thousands of years. Didn't Noah plant a vineyard and get drunk? Jesus supposedly turned water into wine at a wedding."

He said, "Biblical myths aside, the Volstead Act effectively brands all who take a drink, even our greatest minds, as felons. It's the first constitutional amendment that limits instead of protecting individual freedom. There would be no literature, no art, no music, no statesmanship if we relied on the Prohibitionists for our works of genius."

"Obviously, you feel strongly about this."

"Life isn't long enough, and the embargo on alcohol simply gets in the way. We're all under a death sentence. We just don't know the day or method of execution. It's only the adventure of it all that makes us realize that consciousness is life. That's why we need to make the most of what we have and how we choose to live."

"I knew I was going to like you, Mr. Darrow."

"Call me Clarence."

"And my moniker's Tommy the Choirboy."

---

The Green Door Tavern on the corner of Huron and Orleans boasted, yes, a green door. Green doors were ubiquitous throughout the Windy City, signaling that, inside, warming spirits were only inches away—for a price.

A squinty-eyed palooka, ciggy dangling from his lips, stood in my way as I tried to enter.

He said, "Password."

McTeer never gave me one, so I blurted the first thing that came to mind.

"Open Sesame."

"Close enough. McTeer's expectin' you. I gotta pat you down first."

"I'm heeled."

"No problem. Just check your hardware with me."

After surrendering my heater to the palooka, he directed me upstairs, empty except for McTeer alone at a table. He was swilling a beer and puffing a fat cigar still wrapped with the band.

"Right on time, asshole," he said.

"I'm always on time, shitface. I never know how much of it I got left. Say, I thought I was gettin' an introduction to a certain someone, but I don't see no one here but you."

"He'll be around once he's convinced you ain't no dick. He needed time to check you out. Chi-town's got all the modern conveniences like telephones and telegraphs and short-wave radio."

Which made me uneasy. For obvious reasons, I didn't need anyone to know I wasn't who I claimed to be.

He said, "If he don't arrive, Choirboy, he's either croaked or you're about to be."

"That happens often in these parts?"

"You kiddin'? A month ago, us North Side Irish couldn't put our wingtips inside this joint without gettin' popped. Now we got a truce."

He described how the North Side's overall boss Dion O'Banion was in his flower shop innocently pruning his chrysanthemums when three mugs sauntered in to pick up a floral arrangement for a mob funeral.

"Instead, they unloaded a pile of Chicago lightning. O'Banion took two slugs in the chest, one in the back of his head, and two in his throat, which was a pity because he had this beautiful tenor singing voice. You shoulda heard him sing 'Danny Boy.' Would bring tears to your eyes. The good thing was that they was able to save the floral arrangement for O'Banion's own funeral, where they sang 'Danny Boy.'"

"I'd drink to that if I had a drink."

"Lemme get the skirt." He called, "Hey, Dolly, where the hell you at?"

A waitress appeared and I was struck dumb by her good looks.

McTeer said, "Grab my pal here a tall one. And another for me."

"You got it, Randall," she said and stepped off to fetch the drinks. Her blond hair was bobbed in the latest style with finger curls, her lips in a fashionable Cupid's bow. To say I was smitten would have been an understatement.

"What's with the babe?" I asked, trying not to appear too carnivorous.

"Dolly Darling? Forget about her. I already made a go at it, and if Randall McTeer can't do it, nobody can. She's set on Hollywood and expects to plaster her mug on the cover of all the fan magazines. Got a twin sister named Dalilah who's also a looker and has the same ambitions. Dolly waits tables here and sings at the Four Deuces, Capone's joint. But for her, waitressin' is just a detour. She's got a decent voice and can belt it out when the band plays, and she's a pretty good hoofer. But put her out of your mind."

I had no intention of putting her out of my mind.

McTeer told me that Hymie the Pole was O'Banion's successor, but Hymie made the mistake of shooting up Al's sedan. Capone wasn't in it at the time but the car was wrecked all to hell.

"Al's fussy about his cars, so that really pissed him off. Hymie also made the boo-boo of keeping the gang's headquarters at the late O'Banion's flower shop, which was targeted by a chopper squad squirtin' metal with tommies. That's where Hymie got his. So many damned bullets was flyin' they accidentally shot up Holy Name Cathedral across the street."

"I'm relieved. I was afraid this burg was gonna be boring."

"Now, the closest thing we got to a top boss on the North Side is the guy who runs my own crew, Cormac Kenneally."

The beauteous Dolly appeared with two foaming mugs, and I could barely keep my eyes off of her. McTeer and I clinked glasses as I watched her graceful exit. To my mind, she was potentially more than mere movie star material, and I was already mulling over how to get to know her.

McTeer described how Chicago was carved into mob territories, Capone's the biggest.

"Al inherited the gang from Johnny Torrio, who was almost knocked off in an ambush. Torrio's a vegetarian who stays home at night and listens to the Chicago Opera on KYW. He ain't cut out for the business so he passed it on to Al. Capone's got the Loop, the South Side by the lake, and the western suburbs."

"Where do the cops figure in all this?"

"Al controls eight police districts, which means the cops do pretty much what he says. Half of 'em is on the payroll. The guy who let you in downstairs? Ten years on the force. The mayor's a do-gooder named Dever. He's vowed to drive the bootleggers out of town and to make Chicago the driest city in the nation. Lotsa luck. We got our own places to cook alky all over town, and plenty of rumrunners, so folks is drinkin' more than ever."

"But it's more than just booze," I said.

"Damn right. Chicago's got five-hundred brothels staffed by nearly three-thousand hookers. When it comes to pleasure The Windy City's got you covered. Too bad pleasure's a sin. Ours ain't a bad livin', Choirboy, although you might say there's a relatively short life expectancy."

We heard steps on the stairs and two men entered the room, one short and pear-shaped and wearing an ill-fitting suit, the other burly, the collar of his jacket pulled up, fedora pitched down to his eyes.

McTeer whispered to me, "There he is, the little, pudgy one. Jake Guzik. He's a Jew, but Capone loves him like family."

"Who's the fedora?"

"Gotta be the bodyguard because Jake's a pussy, don't carry no roscoe. Always travels with protection. They call him Greasy Thumb on account of all the palms he has to grease."

The bodyguard took a table at the far end of the room, his back turned to us, while Guzik shook hands with McTeer.

"Choirboy, Mr. Guzik here runs Al's business side," McTeer explained. "It's like he's got a comptometer in his brain. Al says he can't do nothin' without him. Mr. Guzik, this here's the guy I was telling you about, Tommy the Choirboy. He has lots of potential. Even got the drop on me. But only once. You're here, so I guess he's who he says he is."

The jowly Guzik, whose manner was prissy and who wore round tortoiseshell eyeglasses, said, "Tommaso Adosti checks out. I put in a couple of calls to Baltimore. Spoke to one of Corbi's crew who knows him. Even talked to Father Tuccillo at Our Lady of Pompeii Church who confirmed Tommaso had been an altar boy and sang in the choir, thus the moniker. You weren't in the choir for very long, kid. Why's that?"

I said, "You can't stay forever in the choir or as an altar boy, Mr. Guzik. You gotta go out and make a living. Also, Father Tuccillo had his hands all over my ass. So I began runnin' numbers for Mr. Corbi, cleaning his piece, and taking his suits to the laundry. And that's the problem. There ain't enough action in B-town. We ain't even had a mob hit in over three months."

"Impatient, huh?"

"Mr. Guzik, I may be young and all, but I'm old enough to know I wanna go places, be part of the big time."

My fingers were crossed that the real Tommy the Choirboy wouldn't be visiting Chi-town anytime soon.

Guzik said, "Al's looking for fresh talent. Our ranks are somewhat thin right now on account of a malady caused by lots of little holes where they shouldn't be." Guzik turned to McTeer. "Choirboy here's not the only reason I came here today. Al wants to talk to you about consolidating all the North Side gangs into one. There isn't room enough for all the crews to be operating separately in your part of town."

McTeer said, "Then you gotta talk to Kenneally, my boss, Mr. Guzik."

"Here's the thing. Kenneally's not going to be your boss after today."

"Huh?"

"Kenneally will die of a sudden heart attack at promptly four this afternoon because Al only wants to deal with you."

McTeer said, "I, I don't know what to say, Mr. Guzik. Kenneally's been like an uncle to me."

"Should I wait while you shed a tear?"

"When you put it like that... Will you be settin' up a meeting between me and Mr. Capone?"

"Not necessary, McTeer. Mr. Capone's sitting over there with his back to us."

Flabbergasted, McTeer almost dropped his beer.

"Didn't recognize him with the collar up and hat pulled down. Thought he was your bodyguard. That ain't like Al. Why didn't he just come over?"

"He's playing it cool. Keeping his profile low on account of the delicacy of the situation, and wanted me to feel you out first. Anyway, with Al around, I don't need a bodyguard. When some petty hood knocked me on my ass and called me a dirty kike, Al found out about it and cornered him in a saloon on Wabash. Al didn't take it kindly after the hood called him a Dago pimp and told him to get lost, so the sap wound up with four slugs in him. Al's motto is Public Service."

Al, smiling, lumbered to our table. And that's how I became a junior member of the Capone Outfit.

---

*And they tell me you are brutal and my reply is: On the faces of*
*women and children I have seen the marks of wanton hunger.*
*And having answered so I turn once more to those who sneer at*
*this my city, and I give them back the sneer and say to them:*
*Come and show me another city with lifted head singing so proud*
*to be alive and coarse and strong and cunning.*

—"Chicago," Carl Sandburg

Capone and I hit it off. I offer no excuses. He got to be almost like an older brother, although he had eight siblings, including Ralph, who was assigned to operations in Cicero, where Al owned the town government from the handpicked mayor on down. The Capones were so brazen they stored their bootleg booze in the basement of Cicero's town hall, where Al once kicked the mayor down the steps. Another Capone brother, Cincenzo, was a Prohibition agent in Nebraska, but for everyone's benefit he wisely stayed out of town.

Al wasn't an attractive man: stout, about two-hundred-fifty pounds, of average height, receding hairline, swarthy with thick red lips, and scars across his left cheek and under his ear down to his neck, the result of a Brooklyn bar brawl. He was called "Scarface," but only behind his back. Beyond the scars, I couldn't take my eyes off his behemothic, diamond pinky ring. In his wallet, he carried a deputy sheriff's badge.

Maybe Al took a liking to me because of my sweet looks and sunny disposition. Or perhaps our relationship jelled because of the soup kitchen he set up on South State Street. He wasn't a mere bootlegger, but a philanthropist. He did good works like a Robin Hood, and he was always up for a quote in the papers. Whenever he arrived at Wrigley Field to see the Cubs or Comiskey Park for the White Sox or the prizefights he got standing ovations.

Modestly, he would say, "I'm just a businessman, givin' the people what they want."

Al never signed checks or made bank deposits, so nobody could pin anything on him.

I was assigned as a flunky to the fussy Guzik at Capone headquarters, the fancy, fortified Metropole Hotel on South Michigan Avenue, where armed guards patrolled every floor and a series of tunnels in the basement led to escape routes. I helped Guzik keep the ledgers with the names of the bought cops and Prohibition agents, itemized income from the brothels, a list of the breweries, addresses of the speakeasies buying Al's booze, and the bootleg routes by truck and boat from Canada and the Caribbean. Lots of fodder to secret in my reporter's spiral notebook.

I was in the middle of totaling a line of numbers when, in a surprise raid, the cops burst in and, making no arrests, seized the ledgers—although a compliant judge ruled the evidence was illegally seized and ordered the books returned forthwith.

But I needed more action, not bookkeeping, to land my story. When I learned about Al's soup kitchen, which he visited every day, sometimes serving the hungry himself, I jumped at the chance to ingratiate myself. I slaved in the kitchen, dished out food, washed plates, mopped the floors, cleaned the crapper—and after a couple of weeks, Al finally noticed me.

He took me aside and said, "Say, sonny, I see you in here every day bustin' your ass off. What's your name again?"

"They call me Tommy the Choirboy, sir."

"Ain't you the kid from the East Coast I got workin' for Guzik?"

"Yessir, Mr. Capone, but numbers ain't for me. I mean, I love lookin' at inventory figures and processing receipts and running the comptometer and all, but I need more than office work, which is why I'm volunteering here. Mr. Guzik don't think I'm ready for the big jobs."

"Whad'ya wanna do?"

"I've heard you say your motto's Public Service. Like you, I intend to help people get what they want. The Prohibitionists care nothin' about the nature of man, the theories of government, or the lessons of history. If a man can't choose his own beverage to suit himself, what can he do?"

Al seemed impressed by my youthful savvy, although I stole the lines from Clarence Darrow.

"Look, Sonny, I opened this soup kitchen for a reason. The economy may be on a roll, but we still got plenty of poor people. What happens if Wall Street lays an egg? Just imagine breadlines formin' all over the country. We gotta be prepared for that 'cause the government ain't gonna spread a lot of free cash around, capisce? That don't mean I'm a Bolshevik or nothin'. Capitalism's a legit racket. It's got big opportunities so we gotta hang on to it. That's why we need to keep the workin' classes away from Red propaganda and make sure their minds stay healthy."

"That makes a lot of sense, Mr. Capone."

"Know how to use a piece?"

"You bet, sir."

"Tell ya what. I got a small job for you this weekend. Try you out. There's this ivory tickler I like, goes by the name of Fats. He's performin' at the Sherman Hotel. I begged him to play at this shindig I'm throwin' at the Hawthorne Inn, place I own in Cicero, but the fucker don't wanna come. Apparently, he don't like my reputation. Tough shit. Nobody turns down Al Capone. I want you to grab a couple of my brunos, head over to the Sherman, and take care of it."

"How exactly, sir?"

"What do you mean how? You said you could use a piece, didn't ya? You do this job right and we'll see where it goes from there."

"I'm grateful for the opportunity, Mr. Capone."

M'god, I thought, there I was, barely qualified as a mobster and already Capone wanted me to administer lead poisoning to some piano pounder I never heard of. Apparently, this Fats wasn't even connected to the rackets. Just some poor sucker Al felt insulted by. And he called it a small job.

---

Before my pending felony in the name of the mob, I scrambled to find out more about Dolly Darling and where she'd be working. Mr. Guzik knew where all the bodies were, in a manner of speaking, and gave me the lowdown. She performed regularly at Al's Four Deuces, and, as luck would have it, she'd be there that night.

The building on South Wabash had two entrances, one into a second-hand furniture store owned by Capone who used it as a front, the other into a speakeasy where the real action was: spotlights, stage, band, singers, dancers, waiters, cigarette girls, artificial palms, and booze flowing like a mountain stream. The joint was famous for the plethora of aldermen, judges, and police brass who indulged there. In this very room, a card shark named Martin Guilfoyle shot dead a loser called Pete Gentleman over a gambling debt. Upstairs, thirty hookers plied their trade in private rooms supervised by a portly woman who collected the cash. Rumor had it that when certain chumps were lured to the cellar, their bodies exited via a tunnel to a back alley.

But I was there for Dolly.

Chicago was America's jazz capital. Ardent spirits went with jazz the way a smoke went with bourbon and a hooker with copulation. Prohibition be damned, the city's music venues grew like a promiscuous Topsy: theaters such as the Congress, Grand, and Vendome; ballrooms like the Trianon, Dreamland, and Savoy; clubs like Friar's Inn, Royal Gardens, Panama, Elite, the Sunset Café, and, of course, the Four Deuces.

That night, down from a gig in Detroit, was Jean Goldkette's Orchestra featuring a couple of rising young performers, Frankie Trumbauer on sax and cornet by Bix Beiderbecke. The band played its hits: "Sunday," "Sunny Disposish," "Look at the World and Smile," "Dinah," "Just One More Kiss." The music was a touch syrupy, but Bix's clarion cornet cut through the mush. And when Dolly, wearing a red dress hemmed at the knees to show her sylphlike legs, got up to sing "Hoosier Sweetheart," I was a goner.

> How the lovelight in your eyes
> Lightened up the darkened skies.

*I first held you in my arms along the Wabash*

*And you promised to be true*

*As I made my vows to you.*

I sat at a small table by myself, nursing a drink, my eyes never off the lustrous Dolly, while couples swirled and swayed to the rhythm. The clouds of cigarette smoke over the parquet might have been a romantic fog. When she wasn't singing in her high-pitched, cutie-style voice, she was surrounded by male admirers, and it was obvious I'd never be able to get near to her, much less unload a word.

Until to my good fortune, an altercation broke out near the stage.

When I stood to gawk, I saw it was Dolly struggling with some guy, an obvious hood, who was pulling her by the arm. As the ruckus got louder, the dancers made a clearing around the noisy pair while the musicians in the band lowered their instruments.

"No, Guido, I told you not tonight," I heard her say.

He yelled, "No fuckin' way, dollface, you're comin' with me like you promised."

"I changed my mind."

"You don't get to do that. I'm collectin' on that raincheck, so we're goin' upstairs."

As she tried to push him away, he tightened his grip and yanked her arm. Nobody intervened.

What did I have to lose? Or so I thought at the time. I walked through the stilled dancers to the struggling couple from behind, tapped the hood on the shoulder, and when he partially turned I cold-cocked him. Due to his inebriation, it only took one blow to the jaw and he was down for longer than the count. I'd probably have been a dead duck had it been a fair fight.

Silence pervaded the packed, smoky room. Dolly looked at me in shock.

Finally, Bix Beiderbecke raised his sweet cornet and blew a note, which I recognized as the opening to "Jazz Me Blues." Then the rest of the band picked up their instruments and the music began anew while the couples resumed their rhythmic shuffling, avoiding the unconscious goon on the floor. A couple of waiters finally dragged him off.

Dolly said to me, "I know you. You were at the Green Door with Randall McTeer a while back. What's your name?"

"Tommy."

"Lemme buy you a drink, Tommy."

We went back to my table.

She sipped gin as she said, "That was a brave thing to do. But you shouldn't have done it."

"The guy was abusing you. And nobody else was helping."

"You don't know who he is, do you?"

"I'm new in town."

"He's Guido DeGrazia who runs a gang in Wabash Heights with his brothers. They operate out of a wholesale candy business."

"Figured he was a hood. So what? Chicago's filled with 'em."

"Tommy, he's likely to come back and off you, which is why you oughta blow this dump real soon. The DeGrazias get sore easy. And Guido has the worst temper of all."

"You know him well?"

"It was a one-time thing. I'm never gonna to see him again. Not if I have any choice."

"Then my smacking him in the kisser was worth it to get close to you."

"But you're also one of the trouble boys."

"Uh, not exactly."

"You were with Randall, and he's involved with the North Side gangs."

"Actually, our mothers are old friends and Randall was simply showing me around. I'm volunteering at Al Capone's soup kitchen, just trying to do some good. However, that's only while I'm attending classes at the University of Chicago."

"You're a student?"

"Uh, I'm earning an advanced degree in sociology."

Okay, it was a lie upon a lie upon a lie, something I was used to doing. But I figured I could parlay my dishonest initial acquaintance into something enduring when I explained it later. She'd understand, recognize my passion, return my love, and all would be hearts and flowers and delicious little sweets.

"Dolly, I loved the way you sang 'Hoosier Sweetheart.'"

"It came from the heart. I'm a twin, born in Indiana. Vincennes. I plan to record it for the Brunswick recording label, which is right here in Chicago. They told me I'd only have to pay half the cost for the initial pressing and I'd receive ten percent of every platter sold. When I make it big it'll be the theme song for my radio show."

"You're on the air?"

"Not yet, but I've been talking with someone at WMAQ, and I should hear back from him any day. I'm not only a singer, I'm also an actress, and I'm gonna go to Hollywood to star in films. I wrote a letter to Douglas Fairbanks and he sent me his signed photograph. I'm waiting to hear back from Menachem Stoneman, head of Rinestone Studios. And I've been in touch by mail with Metro-Goldwyn-Mayer's biggest producer, King Vidor, who told me to look him up once I get into town."

"But not *that* soon, I hope."

"When I get up enough money. I'm sharing a room with my twin, whose also a singer and actress. We'll be traveling to Hollywood together."

"Dolly, Hollywood's a long way from Indiana. It may not be safe for single young women alone out there."

"And you think Chicago is? Nothing's going to happen to me here."

"When will I see you again?"

I wanted to linger with her, but the hood I bopped might already be awake and on the prowl for me.

To my mind, I was Dolly's savior. I got between her and a thug. The gal had big dreams. Too big, probably, and she might have been a bit rougher around the edges than she looked. But she agreed to see me again, which made it jake in my concocted world. All seemed to be going right—except for the complication of that hit Capone expected me to make.

Al's crew knew I rented a room across from Jackson Park, but they had no idea it was in Darrow's flat, so I prudently waited outside for the car they sent for my rendezvous with Fats, the poor sap Al wanted deep-sixed. At the wheel was Two-Fingers McCord. His pals Baby Shanks and Ice Pick sat in the back. Two-Fingers was communicative, but the other two were silent and surly. I didn't have to ask why he was called Two-Fingers. Since he was still kicking, I figured whoever he had a run-in with was now called No Hands.

I sat up front as Two-Fingers drove. He told me Al had lent us one of his two armored cars for tonight's mission.

"You're riding in Cadillac's top-of-the-line Imperial V-Eight, a fuckin' fortress, new guy. Al had it modified to his personal specs. The windows got inch-thick bulletproof glass. When they're rolled up they leave a two-inch gap, which lets the barrel of a submachine gun move back and forth without no obstruction. It has quarter-inch steel armor plates on all sides. In the back there's a slot on the floor so tacks can be dropped through to puncture the tires of any cars in pursuit. Up front, it has police lights inside the grill that you can flash and a police siren under the hood. In the glove box is a regulation police radio."

"Looks like Al's thought of everything."

"He's even got it registered in his wife's name in case anybody tries to foreclose on it. He says you're in charge tonight. So where're we off to?"

"Hotel Sherman. Know where it is?"

"Natch. Across from City Hall. Say, you ain't plannin' a hit on President Coolidge, are you?"

"What does Coolidge have to do with anything?"

"He and his wife are visiting Chicago, stayin' in the hotel's presidential suite. I read it in the *Tribune*."

"Coolidge leaves us alone and we'll leave him alone."

Two-Fingers laughed. "Hey, that's funny." To his accomplices he said, "Hear that, guys? We got a comedian up here."

Sullen silence in the back.

I said, "What's with your cohorts, Two-Fingers? They ain't said a word to me since I climbed in the caddie."

"They're pissed is all. Al's holding this big blowout in Cicero tonight, which they're missin' 'cause we got to babysit you on this run."

"But you're not pissed, right?"

"Hell yeah, I am, but it don't pay to get too sulky. Al notices shit like that. He likes a happy shop. Say, traffic's a bitch. Let's turn on the siren and watch the cars scatter."

"I don't think—"

Two-Fingers flipped the switch and not even the caddie's heavy armor shielded us from the siren's piercing shriek. But he was right. Pedestrians ducked and gawked while competing vehicles pulled over to surrender the right of way.

"Holy shit, Two-Fingers," I shouted through the din. "It's the cat's meow, but let's not announce our job before we get there."

He shut it off, saying, "I hear they call you Choirboy."

"So?"

"With a handle like that, don't go gettin' holy on us. You oughta have a name we can relate to. Like Knuckles or Slasher or Triggerman."

"You got a point, Two-Fingers."

The elegant Sherman on Randolph Street was said to be the largest hotel west of Manhattan. A poster advertised Fletcher Henderson's Orchestra in the hotel's College Inn, famous for its chicken broth. Henderson was the band's pianist, but he wasn't our target. We were looking for a guy called Fats. Finally, I spotted another placard advertising *Okeh Recording Star Thomas Fats Waller in the Panther Room*, where the four of us made a beeline, brazen in our conspicuous mob raiment.

A pompous host with a pencil mustache met us at the door and coolly informed us the room was completely filled and told us to make a reservation for some other evening. Somehow, maybe because of our dark good looks, we politely managed to convince him that he was mistaken and there was most certainly an available table for us next to the stage.

"Of course, of course, gentlemen," he said, impressed by our persuasive powers. "You're quite correct. How did I not notice? Right this way."

Being in the rackets had their perks.

Although Prohibition was barely tolerated in Chicago, it existed not at all in the Panther Room, with its decorative motif of big, black cats and tropical forests. The bar was extravagantly stocked, the waiters bowed and scraped, and sexy cigarette girls made their rounds. One would think there would have been more decorum what with the President of the United States snoozing somewhere upstairs, but this was the Windy City—although it was doubtful Coolidge could ever be kept from his sack time.

Three-hundred pounds by my estimate and nearly six feet tall, Fats dominated the room as much as the baby grand. With a derby cocked jauntily on his head, he made a grandiose entrance, announcing, "Here comes little Fatsy Watsy Waller. You're gettin' me in the large economy size."

He took no prisoners as his fleshy fingers hit the notes with slide-style precision, effortlessly chasing trills and bass configurations. Fats relentlessly mugged before the audience while he thumped the keys and made melody, his bushy eyebrows rising and falling with every facial maneuver, eyes popping, a thin mustache over his upper lip, and a cigarette dangling from his mouth. He told funny stories, dirty jokes, sometimes adopting a faux British accent, and quipped about his alimony payments. It mattered not that he cribbed, rehashed, or outright purloined. His patter all got laughs.

*What do you call a successful piano player? A guy whose wife has two jobs. Did you hear about the cannibal who committed suicide? He got himself in a stew. How do you make a pool table laugh? Just tickle its balls. Marriage is like playing the piano. It looks easy until you try it. A vagina is like the weather. Once it's wet it's time to go inside. What does a songwriter do in his grave? He decomposes.*

There was nothing he couldn't sing or wouldn't play. A waiter kept the glass on the piano brimmed and regularly replaced the overflowing ashtray. WLS, which had its studios in the hotel, was broadcasting live a portion of Fats's show, which he cleaned up for the radio audience.

When he finished knocking out "St. Louis Blues," he said, "Ain't that a killer? And here's a ditty I'm still working on."

> Yes, your feet's too big
>
> Don't want you, 'cause your feet's too big
>
> Can't use you, 'cause your feet's too big
>
> I really hate you, 'cause your feet's too big.

When he finished, he looked directly at a young woman at a table near the stage and said, "Take me to heaven, darlin'." She swooned. He did "Honeysuckle Rose," "The Joint is Jumpin'," "Alligator Crawl," and "Doll House Boogie." To ecstatic applause he said, "This is so nice it's gotta be illegal, which just happens to be the title of my next song."

He finally made an exit after five encores. I swear, he could have gone on all night. As the room emptied, I nudged Two-Fingers's shoulder.

"No wonder Al was wild about this guy. Everyone loves him. How the hell are we gonna do this?"

Two-Fingers said, "What do you mean *we*? It's you what's got the marchin' orders. We're here to make sure you don't fuck up. We oughta be at Al's blast tonight instead of nursin' your ass."

It was my first test as a low-level mobster and I was about to mess up the job. And if you screwed up with Al… I'd actually have to go through with it, right? Whack the poor sucker. How else could I call myself an investigative reporter?

I said, "OK, we're goin' backstage to get this done."

When we barged into the dressing room, Fats, feet up, was sprawled in an overstuffed chair, smoking a cigarette and quenching his thirst, as he'd been doing all evening—the man could hold his sauce. We looked intimidating, I hoped.

I said, "Great show tonight, Mr. Waller."

"Thanks, gents. Anything I can do for you? Autograph? Photograph? But make it quick because I'm about to hook up with a sweet little charmer from Des Plaines before I hit the hay."

"Yes, there is, Mr. Waller." I drew my rod from my inside pocket and leveled it at him. "You're comin' with us."

He dropped his drink, which shattered on the floor. "Wait a minute…"

"We ain't waitin' for nothin', Mr. Waller. Gotta take you outside. Stand up. Get your coat. March. Don't make me use my piece here. It's fuckin' loaded. We don't want to disturb the guests, particularly the President of the United States, who may be asleep upstairs. And when we get to the fancy lobby, don't bloody it up."

"But, but…"

Outside, we marched Fats, noticeably panicked, to Capone's caddie, where we plopped him in the back with Baby Shanks and Ice Pick crowded uncomfortably on either side of him.

As Two-Fingers put the Caddie in gear, he said to me, "Where to, Choirboy?"

"Hawthorne Inn in Cicero. Know how to get there?"

"You must be kiddin?"

From the back seat, Fats, agitated and perspiring, said, "What you all gonna do to this harmful little armful? You gonna kill me? I gotta young son. I gotta ex-wife."

"Don't worry about it," I said out of the corner of my mouth, like a real gangster.

"But what did I do? Somethin' I sang? One of my jokes? That woman I slept with last night? Just because I forgot her name?"

"Keep your yap shut, Mr. Waller, or I'll have to shut it for you. I ain't dickin' around here."

In the dismally ugly working suburb of Cicero, we prodded him at gunpoint into Al's command post, the Hawthorne on West Twenty-second Street, where his raucous party was in full tilt. Fats was steered through the long entranceway into a ballroom overflowing with a blusterous, besotted crowd, and where a Story & Clark upright awaited.

"Sit," I ordered. "Play. Do that 'Feet's Too Big' song you just wrote."

Fats was amazed. Confused. And then he understood.

Capone, surrounded by the usual hangers on, the pols, pimps, and pros, reacted in glee when he heard the song's first notes and saw Fats at the piano.

Rushing over, he said, "Mr. Waller, so glad you could make it. I'm puttin' a C-note in your pocket for every song you play—even the repeats. Say, I actually bought the first platter you recorded, 'Muscle Shoals Blues.' About wore it out on my phonograph. In fact, I play it more than my Caruso recordings."

Play Fats did.

Virtually non-stop for the next three …days.

The clambake, to celebrate Capone's birthday, kept on without letup and Al, who loved to party, stayed right in the middle of it. Fats abandoned the piano only for bathroom breaks or short naps. He'd be returning home to Harlem thousands of dollars richer, with plenty to pay off his alimony debt.

I caught up with him between songs.

"No hard feelings, Mr. Waller?"

"Hell, I never had a chauffeured ride in a white man's car before."

"Guess you thought the worst was about to happen."

"One never knows does one?"

Everyone who was anyone in Chicago was at the party, including the nitwit mayor, the governor, both US senators, and the entire congressional delegation. I was told that President Coolidge and his wife dropped in anonymously, although my informant, Two-Fingers, was unreliable, especially when he claimed that the president had joked that he married his wife in order to have someone darn his socks. Coolidge never joked.

The soiree was a bitter-sweet celebration for Al, whose older brother Frank had been gunned down on a Cicero street the year before by a contingent of Chicago cops moonlighting out of their jurisdiction as election-day vigilantes.

At one point during the birthday revelry, Al put his beefy arm around my shoulder.

"You did good," he told me. "Exactly what I wanted. My other guys would have just plugged the guy and left it at that, but you got a lot in your upper story and figured it out. On the other hand, there ain't nothin' like a good mob liquidation when it's necessary. It's why tigers eat their young. It clears the air. But I'm also thinkin' about my poor, lamented brother who was chilled just a year ago. Choirboy, you're workin' directly for me from now on. Second-hand furniture's my official line of work, ya know."

"I don't know nothin' about furniture, Mr. Capone."

"Neither do I."

I'd passed my test.

---

As time went on, Capone gave me more duties and responsibilities, all ostensibly involving my apparent powers of persuasion. He believed I'd convinced Fats to perform at his bash through skillful inveigling—although, for the benefit of Two-Fingers, Baby Shanks, and Ice Pick, I had to seem tougher than I was. For real enforcement and strong-arm tactics he still relied on his more experienced goons. I helped Al to settle deals, reach accommodations, and make arrangements without bloodshed, but if those efforts failed, as they occasionally did, he was quick to finalize a simpler resolution on the streets.

I engineered a new pact between a gang in Wabash Heights and my pal Randall McTeer, who now bossed the North Side. We had a sitdown upstairs at the 226 Club in the Loop, which included Wabash brothers Guido and Benito DeGrazia who sold booze to two North Side delis, which were outside of their own territory. That pissed off McTeer.

I recognized one of the brothers, Guido, as the hood I'd cold-cocked at the Four Deuces, but since he never saw it coming he couldn't identify me. Because I was fresh in town nobody knew who I was, where I came from, or even my name—and even if they had, no one saw nothin' or heard nothin', and Dolly, who'd given the creep the air, wasn't going to squeal. Word went around that once Guido found out who his assailant was, the results wouldn't be pretty.

We all sat at the 226 Club's big round table, while Al tried to put both McTeer and the DeGrazias at ease by pumping everyone's gut with cheap Chianti.

Guido said, "Ya see, Mr. Capone, we know the delis ain't in our territory, but they're, like, in the family. The delis is owned by a second cousin, a Sicilian who comes from Marsala, where our family also comes from—plus we had a delivery contract from the very beginning so it ain't fair to take the outlets away from us. We're like fathered in."

McTeer banged a fist on the table. "What's fair is for everyone stickin' to their own territories like we agreed. The North Side don't go into Wabash Heights, the Heights don't go into the North Side. Them two delis belong to us."

Al said, "You both got points, boys, which is why I turned the matter over to Choirboy here. He's one of the few mugs around this place whose got a brain."

My turn, and I made the most out of it.

"The DeGrazias are also servicing a pool hall and a tobacco shop, both in their own territory. So take a look at this map, which I redrew with a black Crayola. You'll see I drew the lines so the pool hall and the tobacco shop are now within McTeer's boundaries and the delis are in the DeGrazias'. It's what you might call redistricting."

Guido said, "I don't like it. Don't know why us DeGrazias gotta lose two venues we already had."

"But you're keeping the delis, which you wanted because, you say, they're family. You shouldn't have had all four to begin with."

"But—"

Al interrupted, "There you are, boys, the matter's closed. Now let's order. I'm starved. The Tagliatelle alla Bolognese here is the best outside of Umbria."

The compromise wasn't completely satisfactory to the DeGrazias, but Al, as always, had the last word. Gregarious as he was, he could be touchy when he didn't get his way—and he himself was said to be handy with a tommy gun. Plus there was never a time when he didn't think he wasn't right.

After the unhappy DeGrazias left, he told me, "Those boys are greedy. You watch, they're gonna try to muscle McTeer, so this ain't over. I've always been opposed to violence, shootins' and throwin' pineapples. Yeah, I've had to mix it up, but it's always been for peace. I try to treat everyone with kindness, which ain't the same thing as weakness. A smile can get you only so far, but a smile and a gun…"

---

As he got to know me better, he started fussing over me.

"Hey, Choirboy, I gotta put some weight on your bones. You ain't eatin' enough macaroni. I'm gonna fix that."

Al was famous on his block in Park Manor, not just for being a gangster, but for his spaghetti sauce. And no one had to worry that it might be spiked with prussic acid. Often, he fed me dinner at the two-story brick house he owned on South Prairie Avenue, where he lived with his mom Theresa, his wife Mae, and Sonny, his boy. It was where the bullet-riddled body of Al's brother, Frank, had been laid out in a silver-lined coffin festooned with blossoms and rose pedals, and where hundreds of mourners passed through to pay their respects. After our dinners we'd play gin or dice, and he'd spin his operatic recordings, particularly *Pagliacci*, and pretend he was conducting the orchestra with a baton.

He also had a hideaway on Austin Boulevard in Cicero, an ordinary brick building that was heavily fortified with an outside wall and a steel-plated front door. A tunnel connected the building to the garage, and bodyguards were stationed outside day and night. Al retreated regularly to the lair with his cronies and gal pals to party in privacy. He had a mirrored ceiling in his sumptuous bedroom. That I was invited there many times to drink and snort cocaine showed the confidence he had developed in me—and where he liked to philosophize.

"All I got in life is my word and my balls, and I ain't breakin' 'em for nobody," he told me. "They call me a racketeer. The real racketeers is the banks. Sure I violate the Prohibition law. Who don't? The only difference is I take more chances than the guy that drinks cocktails before dinner and a bunch of highballs after it. But I ain't ever gonna knock the American system. Look what it's done for me."

He believed that capitalism was actually made stronger by Prohibition, which opened up many more doors and made everyone richer. But he wasn't sure that I should be in the rackets at all.

"Whad'ya wanna do, Choirboy? Get yourself killed before you're thirty? I been in the business long enough to know that once you're in it too long you can't ever get out. You'd better listen to some common sense while a few of us like me is still alive. Put a nest egg together and go legit."

I said, "Al, I read a story in the *Trib* quoting a preacher who told his congregation that you're not only a public enemy but you're headed to hell."

"Then hell must be a pretty swell spot on account of the guys what invented religion are bustin' their asses tryin' to keep everybody else out. Anyhow, I'd rather be rich and greedy and go to hell when I die than to live in poverty here in Illinois. The country wants booze and I supply it. So why should I be called a public enemy?"

Al truly saw himself as a victim.

"I'm spendin' the best years of my life as a public benefactor. I give the folks pleasure and show 'em a good time. And all I get is abuse. I got a mother who never misses Mass unless she's too sick to get out of bed. I got a wife who loves me. They got feelins'. They're hurt by what they read about me. I can't tell you what it does to my little son when the other kids, cruel as they are, keep showin' him newspaper stories callin' me a killer or worse."

"They treat you real bad, Al," I said.

"Every time some kid falls off a tricycle, every time a black cat has gray kittens, the cops and the newspapers holler, 'Get Capone!' They've hung everything on me but the Chicago Fire."

Al didn't feel he was an outlaw, certainly not a bandit or bank robber. He saw himself as an entrepreneur, operating mostly within the law, but corrupting it only when he needed to—as well as being an influential figure in Chicago's power structure. There was talk of his running for mayor.

He also knew his life was in danger wherever he went. The incorruptible element of law enforcement wanted to nail him as much as his rival bootleggers. When we drove at night, he was always surrounded by a bevy of bodyguards in bullet-proof vests. In restaurants, we'd sit in the back of the room facing the door and near a curtained window in case he had to leap to safety.

Al half-heartedly worked out in the Metropole Hotel's gym, where I'd toss him medicine balls and hold the punching bags steady for him. To sweat off some weight, he'd go to the Jewish steam bath on Fourteenth Street, where clad only in large, white towels, we flagellated each other's backs. Then he'd put the weight back on by sending out to a deli for ridiculously huge mounds of brisket. There was nothing he liked better than golf, although he was a duffer. I caddied for him. Al stored his gat in his golf bag while on the green, and once, not waiting for me to hand him a putter, he fumbled around in the bag and accidentally hit the gun's trigger. He winged himself in the leg and I had to run him to hospital to have it patched up.

Then there was Dolly.

As our relationship grew and we saw each other more and more often, I found myself in a quandary. She was sure to find out I had lied when I told her I was studying for a degree at the University of Chicago, while I was ever less comfortable with my early visions of unending love.

But those thoughts vanished instantly when I went to the modest room she shared with her twin and saw her bloody body.

*They tell me you are wicked and I believe them, for I have seen your painted women under the gas lamps luring the farm boys.*

*And they tell me you are crooked and I answer: yes, it is true I have seen the gunman kill and go free to kill again.*

—Carl Sandburg

The coarse life of Chicago, despite its strength and cunning, was full of wanton death.

I entered Dolly's room because the front door had been left partially opened, something you didn't do in Chicago. At first, I wasn't sure which sister was the victim, they looked alike, but her twin Dalilah confirmed it was Dolly. Dalilah had come home just minutes before to discover the corpse in the bed. It appeared Dolly had been shot several times.

In shock, Dalilah was verging on hysterics.

"Who could have done such a thing, and why?" she said as she clung to me tearfully. "We were going to go to Hollywood together and become famous."

I had no answer. The easy explanation was that a simple burglary or a rape had escalated. Aside from waitressing around town and performing in the speakeasies, Dolly had been no gun moll. I knew of no enemies. The cops would have to sort it out. I was also in a state of shock. I hadn't known Dolly for more than a few weeks, but I'd carried, at least briefly, a torch for her. Although I admired her ambition and tenacity, I suspected it was somewhat disproportionate to her talent.

The cops questioned me, somewhat suspicious because of my job, ostensibly in a second-hand furniture store owned by one Alphonse Gabriel Capone. But I had a snug alibi, being on the links with Al at the approximate time of the murder. The detectives claimed to have no suspects and felt the murder was likely one of opportunity. There were no signs of a break-in and nothing appeared to have been stolen.

The papers got a fresh headline for a day—*Beautiful Emerging Star Found Brutally Slain*—and then the killing was stored along with the countless others that racked up in Chicago week after week.

But I didn't forget.

Dolly's grieving mother and father came to take her body back to Indiana for burial. Dalilah was so distraught she moved to a room in a nearby walkup. Al, as was his custom, sent an extravagant funeral spray of lavender and purple blooms to Dolly's parents. With me he was solicitous.

"Don't think the cops are gonna do much with this case, Choirboy," he told me at the Four Deuces, where I had first gotten to know Dolly. "But I'll have some of my boys look into it. She sang here in my joint y'know, so we all knew her. Damn shame, pretty girl like that. I also got a bunch of city detectives on my payroll and I'll make 'em work overtime. We got our own ways of snoopin' around. Fact is, we usually learn stuff faster than the fuzz."

A couple of weeks later he had a name.

"There's this mug up in Wabash Heights. You met him once. Been goin' around hinting that he knew lots about the Dolly murder case. There's some guys who blab too much when they get a little liquored up. Like to boast. Of course, it may mean nothin.'"

"Don't keep me in suspense, Al."

"Benito DeGrazia."

Brother of Guido, the guy I'd laid low at the Four Deuces.

I told Al about the incident at the club, but that Guido had no idea it was me who knocked his lights out, which was apparent when we held our parley in the Loop. And to my knowledge brother Benito never even knew Dolly.

"Tell ya what, Choirboy, I'll have Two-Fingers McCord politely invite Benito in and we'll just ask him. Keep it simple and direct. Just so's we don't stir things up, we'll leave your name out of it."

Which is how Benito wound up tied to a chair in the basement of the Four Deuces, while I was out doing some business for Al near the Union Stock Yards.

Later, Al filled me in.

"Benito was real cooperative," he said. "Of course, it took a few hours to get anything out of him, but, thanks to the persuasion of Two-Fingers, you can take Benito's name off the suspect list. He had nothin' to do with it. We asked him how he knew so much about Dolly and the murder, and he hemmed and hawed, but finally admitted that he'd been drinkin' too much and was simply shootin' his mouth off about what little he did know. You know, braggin.'"

I said, "Then that leaves us back where we started."

"Naw, we know who done it. Benito told us."

"Who?"

"His brother."

Guido, it seems, never gave up trying to find the mystery man who'd cold-cocked him. At last, his puny brain figured out who could give him a clue. Dolly. According to Benito, Dolly played dumb at first, and even after she was shoved around she still wouldn't open her trap. Frustrated and in a fury, not to mention having been cold-shouldered, Guido pumped five slugs into her.

I said, "We've got to let the cops know, Al. When Guido learns that Benito blabbed to us about it, he may make a run for it."

"Naw, Benito won't squawk. He ain't gonna tell nobody nothin' ever. I think his head got ahead of his hat. The tunnel down at the Deuces was put to good use."

I didn't need for Al to paint a more visible picture.

"I'm not sure torturing and killing Benito was the right way to go about it, Al."

"Choirboy, there's gobs of people in Chicago that got me pegged for one of them bloodthirsty mobsters you read about in the storybooks. The kind that tortures his victims, cuts off their ears, puts out their eyes with a red-hot poker, and smiles while he's doin' it. Now get me straight, kid. I ain't posin' as a model for the young. I got to do a lot of things I don't like to do. But I ain't as black as I'm painted. I'm human. I got a heart in me. And it seems to me it was worth it to find out who done in Dolly."

Investigative Reporter. Crusading Journalist. First Amendment Hero. There's a lot to be said for those mighty words in my chosen trade. But to protect my sources I'd bitten off more than I could chew.

"Al, you've advised me to get out of the business. Go legit. Maybe I oughta step down and head back East."

"And do what?"

"Something in fish. Crabs, maybe. Yeah, crabs. In Baltimore, you can't go wrong with crabs."

"Y'know, Choirboy, what we do here is hard, dangerous work. When a fellow busts his ass at any line of business, sometimes he just wants to go home and forget about work. He don't wanna be afraid to sit at a window or an open door. I ain't had no peace of mind for years."

"You've also complained to me about your health."

"Somethin' I picked up from one or more of the hookers I been around since I was a kid. It does funny things to my mind. Once in a while, I don't think straight. Everyone knows me as a nice guy, but occasionally I get into these uncontrollable rages. And every second I think I'm in danger of death. I don't want that happenin' to you, Choirboy. Crabs sounds good."

"About Guido…"

"Ain't your concern no more. When it comes to Guido and his Wabash Heights gang, let's say your pal McTeer is gonna be very pleased."

Before I left, Al gave me a diamond-studded belt buckle like the one he wore, replicas of which he handed out to a favored few as friendship tokens.

I managed a goodbye to Dalilah who was packing her bags for Hollywood. She said she was going to pick up where her twin had left off, and most people wouldn't even know the difference. The first person she was going to call on when she got there would be Menachem Stoneman of Rinestone Studios.

At Darrow's, I loaded my grip for the return East on the Capitol Limited. I asked if he had any parting thoughts.

He did. "While our soldiers were fighting in Europe the United States adopted the drastic, absurd Prohibition law, which is resented by half the population. The result is what any student of human nature or government easily foresaw. From the instant it went into effect our citizenry has waged virtual open warfare. Put *that* in your story."

"And it hasn't stopped anyone from drinking."

"Neither have we stopped buying and selling. That's led to a whole new industry, one headed by the likes of Al Capone. So long as their business is outside the law, the bootleggers and dealers are obliged to make laws of their own."

"There's also a lot of hypocrisy, Clarence. Those who actually buy the stuff rarely hesitate to condemn those who sell it."

"If you could gradually kill off everyone who ever drank, or wanted to, and leave the world to the Prohibitionists—my god, would any of us want to live in it?"

---

Darrow's words stayed with me on my return to Baltimore and the publication of my front-page exclusive: "Inside the Mob: An Investigative Reporter's Own Story. By Gart Booker Asquith III."

Mencken approved, although he consistently criticized my syntax. He had just published a new book, *Notes on Democracy*. At his usual table at Hotel Rennert, I pointed out a piece in the *Sun* about Chicago officialdom hosting a summit meeting of all the local gangs at the Sherman Hotel.

"They're trying to bring peace among the mobs, Henry. The article specifically cites the murders of two mobsters in Wabash Heights, Guido and Benito DeGrazia. Amazing. The bootleggers are so brazen and so public that the city of Chicago itself is trying to act as mediator. It shows how far our country has failed its people."

"Darrow is quite correct. As far as the Prohibitionists go, the urge to save humanity is always a false front for the urge to rule. The kind of man who expects the government to adopt and enforce his ideas is the sort whose schemes are the most absurd."

Henry railed against absurdity, ignorance, and superstition—yet I suspected that even he knew nothing would change.

I said, "Henry, do you know what's playing at the movies right now?"

"Film ranks low in my hierarchy of diversions."

"*The Gold Rush* with Charlie Chaplin, Lon Chaney in *The Phantom of the Opera*, *Ben-Hur* starring Ramon Navarro, and Buster Keaton in *Go West*. You know, I've never been to California."

"If I read between the lines correctly, Taggart, m'boy, you seem to be inclined to do so."

"Hollywood is where a serial killer is bumping off film actors. If the movies could talk, I imagine they'd tell us who the murderer is. Maybe I can find a way to talk for them. Dolly's sister Dalilah is already out there trying to become famous."

"I see it this way. Movies are still in the Wild West stage of culture, and have yet to produce a single authentic artist. That said, once we get used to the cinema, then truth will cease to be stranger than the fiction so many admire."

And that's -30- for this reporter.

> *You're my gangster, you're like Al Capone*
> *You're like Caesar stepping onto the throne*

> —Madonna

# THREE

# HOMICIDE IN HOLLYWOOD

*Hooray for Hollywood*
*That screwy ballyhooey Hollywood*
*Where any office boy or young mechanic*
*Can be a panic*
*With just a good-looking pan*
*And any barmaid*
*Can be a star maid*
*If she dances with or without a fan*

—Johnny Mercer

Skullduggery was afoot in Hollywood.

As an undercover reporter still in my salad days, I needed to get to the bottom of it, but Baltimore, despite its indelible history and its seedy, aquatic charm, was a far piece from the glamour of the movie capital. Local sage H.L. Mencken, my mentor, was skeptical of the film capital as a subject, although I'd been pushing it ever since I returned from Chicago. Photoplays had been around for more than a decade, Henry pointed out, and now, in the midst of the Roaring Twenties, the cinema had failed to prove itself as art.

As if to make his case, he told me, "I watched that Charlie Chaplin film—something about the Klondike, a mustachioed gold prospector, and a dancehall girl—but, despite the incessant laughter of the gallery, I crept out before the credits. Then and there, I concluded that of all of man's escape mechanisms, death is the most efficient."

"All beside the point," I argued as we guzzled bootlegged beer at Henry's choice table near the Rennert's semicircular bar, ever watchful for Prohibition agents and their stoolies. "The fact is that the movies are now America's primary form of amusement."

"Is that so, Taggart, m'boy? I've always considered human life, which is basically a comedy, as man's chief form of amusement."

"Henry, if you've read your own Baltimore *Sun*, you're aware that Hollywood film actors are being bumped off one by one. Three at least. All unsolved. Now, *that's* a story."

"Of interest out there, not here. I do read my own gazette, even its tedious radio listings, trashy movie ads, and the church service announcement on Saturdays. But they're snippets lifted from the wire. They serve as fillers placed deep within the paper's bowels to justify the ads. Juicy material for William Randolph Hearst's rags certainly, but the distinguished *Sunpapers*, morning and afternoon, have aspirations. And remember, we're in America, where murder is as tasty and available as apple pie."

"Hollywood counts for something, Henry: romance, adventure, escape."

He snorted. "It may be the cinematic capital but it's also the cynosure of popular culture, which I detest in all of its manifestations. Images that move give me vertigo. I once tried to read the actors' lips to understand what they were alleged to be saying on the screen, but it seems they were simply mouthing gibberish. After I read about the trial of one Fatty Arbuckle, I instantly put it out of my mind."

I didn't want to dwell on the sensational rape and murder case against the pudgy screen comedian. Although Fatty was cleared, its sordid aspects would have only stiffened Henry's skepticism toward my Hollywood project. Plus it had nothing to do with the cinematic felonies now underway.

A recent poll of women by a New York tabloid suggested that Mencken was tied with Rudolph Valentino, Douglas Fairbanks, and

Charlie Chaplin as among the most fascinating men in the world. Henry shrugged it off as balderdash.

He said, "I received a note from Valentino not long ago. The poor man wants my advice on how to deal with a hostile press. I find actors to be blatant and obnoxious posturers and windbags. Hollow and incompetent. As for comedians, their work bears the same relation to acting as a bishop is to religion—or a hangman, midwife, or divorce lawyer are to poetry."

Henry, as the *Sun's* most influential figure, had been my mainstay when I went undercover to expose the Klan and, later, as I infiltrated Al Capone's mob, both resulting in front-page scoops. Still, I was only two steps above that of copyboy, so before the front office would spring for my Pullman fare, I had to sell him on the idea.

"Henry, what if the Hollywood murders were all committed by the same killer?"

"I remain unimpressed. Let the deplorable Hearst exploit it. He's on record as admitting proudly that his newspapers are all about underwear and crime."

"Let's beat him at his own circulation game. He's cut into our readership now that he's merged those two second-rate local papers into the *News-American.*"

Henry and the *Sunpapers* were old school, so it was unlikely adopting even a sliver of Hearst's brand of yellow journalism would budge either. I had an ulterior motive in landing the Hollywood assignment. Dalilah Darling, twin of that aspiring actress murdered by a Chicago gangster, was in Hollywood trying to metamorphose into a star. In California, as I'd been enamored of both the victim and her sister, I could kill two birds, so to speak, and combine amour with murder. Or was that too much like Hearst's underwear and crime?

Henry said, "I've a low opinion of Hollywood, but not just because it's run by Jews."

Frequently, he was carelessly dismissive of racial and religious minorities, often casually using crude language that never appeared in his published writing. Perhaps he was aware that, as America's most influential critic and intellectual, such tactlessness would taint him.

But I didn't see how he could be anti-Semitic. He edited *The American Mercury* with George Jean Nathan, who was Jewish; was godfather to the son of his publisher, Alfred A. Knopf, also Jewish; and most of his fellow musicians in his amateur musical ensemble were Jews. He even defended Jewish shopkeepers shut down by the city on Sundays, condemning it as unfair to brand them as outlaws for refusing to keep two sabbaths in a row. He once told me that in literary matters Jews were far more intelligent and more honest than Christians. In fact, he said, he'd rather keep company with a Hebrew than a Methodist.

Finally, I understood. Henry held negroes in benign indifference because they were of no threat to him, but Jews were intellectually and artistically his equals; thus, his competitors. When it came to insults Henry was hyperbolic but nondiscriminatory: Russians barbaric, Scots vulgar, Poles ignoramuses, Dutch money grubbers, Norwegians yokels, Greeks unmannerly, Texans uncouth, Chinese and Japanese at the civilized bottom rung. However, he liked Germans for their practicality, common sense, and straightforwardness. Such generalizations were nutty. He'd opposed America's entry against the Hun in the Great War, for which the *Sun* rightly sidelined him during the duration of the conflict.

Raising his glass to his lips and swallowing, he savored the hops so cruelly slandered by the reprehensible temperance movement.

He said, "I happen to be acquainted with one Menachem Stoneman, who with his partner Uri Rinehart founded Rinestone Studios in Hollywood. I found Menachem to be an obnoxious blowhard when he was operating a seedy nickelodeon here on Light Street, although I'm delighted he figured out how to exploit the movie racket. Pity he has to be in Hollywood to do it."

My jaw dropped doltishly.

"Henry, *that's* the place. Rinestone Studios. The murdered film actors were all on Rinestone's payroll. Now you *have* to get me inside. Write Menachem Stoneman. Telegraph him. Phone him. Tell him about me. I'll do anything at his studio from lugging water, emptying urinals, to removing dead bodies. Just as long as I infiltrate it."

Henry was absorbed in contemplation for a few moments, but I could see he was coming around, obviously impressed by my contagious enthusiasm.

Henry said, "Menachem often behaves hysterically. Once, he got into a plotz, as he would say, over the price of lobster, which he never ate on religious grounds. That said, I got along decently with him, and my personal bootlegger kept him well supplied with sacramental wine, so he owes me. Maybe I could get you in as a screenwriter. Perhaps a long-distance call to Hollywood is in order." He eyed me narrowly. "But I'm uncertain your credentials as a fledgling reporter at the *Sun* are sufficient to land you a Hollywood job."

"Henry, if anyone can make it happen, you can."

It was going to jell. I could feel it down to my argyles.

---

A few days later I was at the corner of Baltimore and Charles streets running copy in the *Sun*'s newsroom when Henry beckoned me to his desk.

He asked me, "How much are we paying you here at the *Sun*?"

"I'm vastly overpaid at thirty-five smackeroos a week."

"How would you like to earn five hundred-fifty a week?"

"In my dreams."

"Taggart, m'boy, you are no longer Gart Booker Asquith III. Your name is now Wilson Collison, actor, vaudeville performer, and co-author of the farce *Getting Gertie's Garter*."

"Wait, wasn't that a hit play on Broadway?"

"It ran at the Republic Theater for fifteen weeks with one hundred-twenty performances. I was cajoled into seeing it by my *Mercury* co-editor Nathan, who claims to be qualified as a theatrical critic. But I survived for only fifteen minutes before I was able to crawl into the protective clutches of an emergency squad, which administered adrenaline in the form of gin. The witless plot, if it can be called that, involves a moronic husband who tries to keep his wife from finding out about an inscribed jeweled garter, which he gave as a gift to a former flame, thinking it was a bracelet. It's feebleminded, harebrained, ludicrous, and senseless. Not to mention asinine. In other words, perfect for Menachem's moving pictures. You don't think for a moment that one of these days it won't be purloined by Hollywood?"

"But how can I—"

"You, Taggart, m'boy, will be assuming the identity of Wilson Collison, unbeknownst to him, and are headed to Hollywood to become a screenwriter at Rinestone Studios. I've arranged it directly with Menachem, who is adding Broadway playwrights to his stable of writers to give his films more class—unlikely as that will be. He at least knew something of *Getting Gertie's Garter*, it having received passable reviews in the press, and he, as far as his brain went, was crudely impressed with your Broadway credentials as I depicted them. I exaggerated. Who was I to disabuse him?"

"And if he discovers I'm not the real Wilson Collison?"

"You'll be banished from Hollywood for life. But for now you'll be one of Menachem's many writers, well paid for doing little more than sketching elementary plots and spelling out simplistic captions for—what are they called?—the intertitles. It's not as though you'll be composing actual dialogue like Eugene O'Neill, the playwright, or a novelist such as James Branch Mandell, much less fashioning descriptive scenes that ring of poetry in the way of William Butler Yeats. Some would call cinematic putrescence barely writing at all."

"And did I hear you right? Five hundred and fifty a week?"

"Your hearing's unimpaired."

"Then I may never return to the *Sun*."

"It won't last, trust me. In addition, no matter who you are, Menachem will hate you."

"Hate's nothing but fear, Henry. Didn't you once say that?"

"Taggart, m'boy, against my better judgment, I may soon join you in Hollywood where I've been invited to appear in a moving picture.

Portraying myself, of course. It's the scheme of *The New Yorker* carica-
turist Ralph Barton. He is married to actress Carlotta Monterey, which
seems to give Barton the idea that he can also direct films. It would provide me the opportunity to confirm directly my suspicion that Los Angeles is a place devoid of any and all intellectual pretensions. A visit to the
grand temple of Aimee Semple McPherson to receive her blessing would
also be in order. I'll look you up once I'm out there."

―――――――

With no direct passenger service from the East Coast to LA, I took the
Capitol Limited to Chicago to connect with the Santa Fe Chief out of the
Dearborn Station. From Chicago, the odyssey would put me into LA's La
Grande Station in sixty-three hours.

I'd no time in Chicago to reunite with my ally Clarence Darrow, the
legal conquistador, but part of the layover was spent with a few of my
bootlegger amigos, who hosted a clam dinner for me at Al Capone's Four
Deuces on Wabash Avenue. The beer wars had been vicious, but, incredibly, my mobster pals, for the moment, were still kicking. They knew me
as Tommy the Choirboy, and I saw no reason to disillusion them.

Two-Fingers McCord said to me, "Too bad Capone couldn't join us.
He's down in Cuba scouting for new opportunities. He's also been house
hunting in Miami Beach. Al wants a quiet, loving Florida retirement place
where he can fish and bounce his grandkids on his knee."

Two-Fingers told me that just before Al embarked to the Sunshine
State, he hosted a gala for three unsuspecting mob defectors at an Indiana
roadhouse. The feasting and toasting ensued heartily for hours until Al
suddenly produced a Louisville Slugger and methodically bashed in the
noggins of the three double-crossers. To a round of applause, he told the
gathering, "I love youse guys but this is how we deal with traitors."

I said, "Gosh, that doesn't jive with the big-hearted Capone I know, the
convivial soul who invites his neighbors in for home-cooked spaghetti."

Two-fingers said, "A few cracked skulls don't mean that Al ain't a
nice guy."

Capone and I had wrapped up our business on a high note, but it was just as well for my health that he was out of town.

Two-Fingers said, "I thought you went back east to get into the fish business, Choirboy."

"Crabs, to be specific."

"Then why are you goin' to LA?"

"Actually Hollywood. I'm planning to break into the movies."

"Ain't that a corker. Say, if you need any muscle send me a wire. I ain't never been to Hollywood. Bet you could use a little protection out there. Guess there are plenty of babes too."

---

When I stepped off the Pullman in LA, I found myself appropriately impressed by the La Grande Station's peculiar red-brick Moorish architecture with its myriad towers and onion-shaped dome. Outside, on Santa Fe Avenue, palm trees swayed placidly in the breeze sweeping in from the Pacific. I was used to the odor emanating from Baltimore's Inner Harbor, that of dead fish and oil slicks. LA, I found, wasn't the drowsy California municipality I'd expected but a spry, thriving, metropolis whose bustling, sidewalk-jammed population was approaching a million—despite, deceptively, the surrounding alfalfa fields ornamented by intermittent oil derricks. Still, other than the terminal, I saw little so far that was quaint or memorable. A tacky sterility pervaded, and I suspected its swelling size wouldn't be an improvement. In fact, I wasn't sure why LA even existed or why anyone would want to live there—other than to make movies.

Rinestone Studios had sent a limo, which was waiting outside the station to ferry me to my temporary roost on Sunset Boulevard, the Thousand and One Nights Bungalows, where in the distance on brown, shrub-covered hills, a giant sign reading "Hollywoodland" stared down tackily to proclaim a future subdivision. The furnished bungalows all faced inward to a courtyard overflowing with bougainvillea, jasmine, trailing vines, olive trees, and fan palms, with a swimming pool at the far end.

It wasn't as ritzy as I had expected, but it beat my shabby room on West Biddle Street in Baltimore.

My driver, an unemployed actor named Andrew Vabre Devine, who had the most grating, raspy voice I'd ever heard, promised to pick me up the following morning to whisk me to the studio, where I was to meet the emir of entertainment, Menachem Stoneman. If the talkies ever became a reality, clearly the burly, high-pitched voiced chauffeur, who said his goal was Westerns, had no future in the movie business.

"Call me Andy," he said, handing me his card, which was de rigueur for even the lowliest of Hollywood's lowly. "Anytime you need a lift, let me know."

My first order of business was a call to Dalilah Darling's Hollywood 46 number. She'd known me as Tommy—whereas now I was the established playwright Wilson Collison. I couldn't come clean, so, as an undercover reporter, I'd have to finagle something convincing to protect my new identity.

Dalilah seemed delighted to hear my voice and suggested she pick me up that night for dinner at Musso and Frank Grill on Hollywood Boulevard, the favored hangout of movie types from actors to producers to directors to writers. Dalilah assured me it was a place where stars were born—a mecca of hope that also had grub.

"I watched Greta Garbo eating breakfast there last week," she said on the phone. "Miss Garbo is Louis B. Mayer's current favorite, the lucky vamp. She prefers her eggs poached."

I first thought that if I was to enjoy mobility in the vast lands of LA I'd either need to rent wheels or buy a junker, and with my Mencken-motivated movie money about to pour in I'd be able to afford it. But ultimately I was to rely on Andy Devine's hearse and Dalilah's get-around buggy.

---

She picked me up in an open Marmon roadster painted two-tone red. Pecking me on the cheek, Dalilah was just as ebullient as I remembered.

She wore the same bobbed hair, blond, that her late twin had and her sweet, cupid's-bow lips were identical. She seemed to have mostly overcome the trauma of her sister's murder.

"Nice car," I said as I sank into the leather of the passenger seat.

Shifting the machine into gear, she said, "Guess who I got it from. I'll give you a hint. He's known as 'The Handsomest Man in the World.' And sometimes as 'The King of the Photoplays.'"

"Fatty Arbuckle?"

"What?"

"Sorry, sometimes my jokes fall flat."

"Francis X. Bushman," she said. "Frankie's latest movie at MGM is called *Ben-Hur*. I haven't seen the picture but based on the title I think it has something to do with a man who is transformed into a woman. Anyway, Frankie just broke up with his wife Beverly Bayne, and he celebrated by buying a bigger Marmon, which is why I have this one. In spite of all the gossip, we're just friends. I mean, he's got five kids after all. When would he even have the time? He was once a sculptor's model and posed in the nude. Frankie's a Capricorn. He owns five Great Danes, and… and…"

Dalilah bumped her gums non-stop until she suddenly heard herself talking.

"I'm so silly, Tommy. Enough about dippy, old me. You must hate me for my blather."

"Weren't you going to follow up on King Vidor at MGM? Seems to me the director answered Dolly's letter back in Chicago telling her to look him up."

"Mr. Vidor blew me off. It happens all the time. I've put it out of my mind. Now tell me all about yourself. And what brings you to Hollywood?"

Before I could answer, she suddenly braked the Marmon after spying a miraculously convenient parking spot in front of Musso and Frank. Inside, the maître de, whom she seemed to know, whisked us to a table. Dalilah ordered Mary Pickfords for both of us.

"A Mary Pickford?" I said, wincing at the thought.

"Yum. A cocktail created for Douglas Fairbanks, her hubby, by a bartender in Havana. Do you know Cuba, Tommy? It's where all the smart people from the States are going. We'll have to get down there one of these days. For the fun stuff, like drinking and dancing and gambling and you know what. Mary Pickfords are made with rum, pineapple juice, a teaspoon of grenadine, and a maraschino cherry. These days, it's all I drink."

One sip proved the concoction to be as sweetly grotesque as it sounded, although I nodded in seeming approval. The bar at Musso and Frank was three deep in tipplers as though Prohibition never existed. It was amazing how a rotten law could be so blatantly disobeyed by good people, and, in the right locations, barely enforced. Little wonder Havana seemed so civilized to Americans.

Over our disgusting cocktails, Dalilah resumed her monologue as if it had never stopped.

"I just had a screen test at First National. They have a huge lot, Tommy. Sixty-two acres in Burbank. The director, John Francis Dillon, told me I was magnificent. I tried out for the role of Poppy La Rue in *The Half-Way Girl*. It's all about an actress who's stranded in Singapore and winds up working as a hostess in the red-light district. I know I'm going to get the part. I just *know* it. Mr. Dillon called me a natural."

She went on to tell me about the rooms she shared with another aspiring actress, Virginia Sweet, whose mother owned a vineyard in Sonoma County, and of the fantastic nightly Hollywood parties they went to and their glorious times at the beach at Santa Monica and the picnics in Griffith Park and the jaunts up to San Francisco, all while dropping the names of the rich and famous. Once, on the arm of Warner Baxter, she dined at a banquet hosted by William Randolph Hearst at his castle in San Simeon and was flown by Wiley Post in a borrowed Boeing Model 40 biplane back to the Calabasas Memorial Airport.

I sensed a degree of desperation on her part as she raved about her seeming accomplishments. It meandered through dinner and then dessert, both of which she insisted on ordering for the two of us because,

"That's what Charlie Chaplin always has here: baked escargot, grilled lamb kidneys, creamed spinach, lyonnaise potatoes, and brioche-bread pudding. So you just *have* to try it."

As much as I'd been stuck on Dalilah and her late sister, I was left with the sinking feeling that their looks might not compensate for their vacuity, although I was willing to withhold final judgment. I also suspected that, despite the glamorous life she depicted and the myriad dropping of names, Dalilah's were likely days of relentless frustration, rejection, and indigence. She shared digs with another girl. Someone gave her a car—whether it was really Francis X. Bushman, I was uncertain—but I doubted she'd been to Hearst's castle, and it was unlikely Wiley Post ever flew her in his plane. Hopeful actresses were superabundant in Lotusland, and perhaps Dalilah was searching for stability, in particular for a butter and egg man. Young women with similar aspirations were hat-check girls at night while waiting in line as extras during the day. At the same time, an ambitious looker like her could be useful to me—purely in the interests of investigative journalism, of course.

From across the table, Dalilah took my hand. "Tommy, I've been going on and on and on. You must think I'm awful. Did you keep yourself entertained on the train?"

"Mostly I read Dreiser."

"Who?"

"He's the—"

"And you still haven't told me why you're in Los Angeles."

In the interest of truth, I settled in to lie like hell.

"First, I have an admission. My name's not actually Tommy."

Her eyes widened in surprise, her mouth an O.

"Wait, Dalilah. I can explain."

"But you were a volunteer at Mr. Capone's soup kitchen while studying at the University of Chicago. All lies?"

"Not entirely. You see, I'm a playwright. My real name's Wilson Collison. I went to Chicago using a nom de plume—"

"A what?"

"An assumed name to research Al Capone for a three-act I was writing called *The Rackets*. Florenz Ziegfeld's interested in turning it into a musical with the score by Jerome Kern. Dalilah, it was the only way I could get inside Capone's mob."

"So you were never a student and not from wherever you said."

"I come from Glouster, Ohio, where my father was the mayor. I dropped out of sixth grade to be a printer, but found I had an aptitude for showbusiness so I became a vaudeville juggler and later joined a repertory company in Buffalo as an actor. But I also had a writer's knack, and my play *Up in Mabel's Room* became a Broadway hit. Then I wrote other stage comedies, the latest being *Getting Gertie's Garter*."

"*You* wrote that? Hazel Dawn starred in it. She also made thirteen movies right here in Hollywood. I *love* Hazel Dawn. I have her autograph on a napkin from the Brown Derby. She always ate the Cobb salad."

"Which is why I'm here. To be a screenwriter at Rinestone Pictures."

"Oh my God, that's the bee's knees. Do you know Menachem Stoneman? He's the biggest big shot in Hollywood."

"I'm inked-in on his calendar tomorrow."

Dalilah, now fully engaged, beamed in awe, my original baloney pushed aside. No longer was I some nobody she knew back in Chicago, but a honcho in the movie-manufacturing biz—or so I let her believe.

"What do I call you now? Wilson, Wil, Willy?"

"Willy is fine," I said. "But most important is that series of murders involving actors connected with Rinestone Studios. It could result in an interesting screenplay. Maybe, with all of your contacts, you could give me a hand. The same killer may be responsible. We might even be able to nail him before the cops do."

Thrilled, she clapped her hands with their perfectly manicured nails.

"I'd adore doing it," she said. "I actually had a date with one of the victims, although I didn't know him well and the poor man was such a bore. A police detective even talked to me. It was so exciting being part of an investigation. Although, you should know that they weren't killed at the studio, but here and there around town. And none of them were actual stars, not like Pola Normand, Rinestone's biggest. They're paying her millions of dollars. I'd kill to have her job." She put her hand over her mouth. "I didn't mean to say that so loud. People might think I meant it."

Gaffe aside, she now basked in the shadow of my presumed brilliance, and I wasn't about to let her down.

"You're so intelligent, Willy, speaking French and all. I see why you're a playwright. As for Mr. Stoneman... The poor man. His wife doesn't understand him."

"You know her?"

"Not exactly. You see, Menachem—Mr. Stoneman—saw me sipping a milkshake at Steinmetz's Pharmacy on Vine Street and invited me to his private office for an exclusive screen test. It went on for hours and hours over gin rickeys, and his secretary was told to hold all his calls. But so far nothing suitable has come up for me to test for. Or at least that's what he says. Willy, I also sing and dance, which I demonstrated for him. I had two weeks of ballet lessons back home in Indiana. Menachem promised to fly me to Havana on the Pan Am Clipper, but he's always out when I phone and never calls me back."

"Tell you what, Dalilah. When I finish writing my first screenplay at Rinestone, I'll make sure there's a part in it for you."

It was clear how she afforded her lifestyle of chichi parties, dinners, and a Marmon roadster: the generosity of others, which is why I, gladly, picked up the check at Musso and Frank. Dalilah was a sweet kid. Maybe we'd have more in common if she had known the name of Theodore Dreiser—unless it was all a Dumb Dora act.

---

In the morning, Andy Devine was waiting outside the Thousand and One Nights Bungalows to run me to Rinestone for my parley with the Caesar of Celluloid.

"Golly gee, Mr. Wilson," Devine said to me in his awful, grating voice, "I'd love to work in films even if it's only as an extra, but so far I'm just drivin' folks around town. The rest of the time I lifeguard at Venice Beach. Maybe you could put a good word in for me with Mr. Stoneman."

"Will do, Andy."

"I joined an amateur theater group, the Montecito Heights Players. Thought I'd get a little acting experience on the stage. I only have one line in this play we're rehearsing, a Western, so tell me how I sound: 'There'd be a lot more peace in this here territory if that Luke Plummer had so many holes in him he couldn't hold his liquor.' Whad'ya think?"

"Andy, you're a natural."

"I can climb on and off a nag and fire a shooter at the bad guys with the best of 'em, Mr. Wilson, so I'd be aces in a cowboy movie: a William S. Hart or a Broncho Billy or a Tom Mix. Any advice?"

"As they say, Andy, never squat with your spurs on."

Rinestone Studios on Melrose Avenue was a big Hollywood player, up there with First National, Paramount, MGM, United Artists, and Warner. Menachem Stoneman, known as a tyrannical penny pincher, knew that movies were so magical that even the dogs he cobbled in swift succession, as memorable as flossing, were gold. But Rinestone did pump dinero into the films of its biggest grosser, Pola Normand, who even had her own hairstylist, press agent, and punkah wallah.

The first thing I noticed after I arrived was that Menachem spoke in all caps. And that was even *before* I penetrated his office threshold.

"FOR FUCK'S SAKE, WHY THE FUCK ARE YOU WASTIN' MY FUCKIN' TIME?"

The office door was closed, but from outside I could hear his strident, New York-accented voice, and nobody had to tell me who it was.

"IF ADOLPHE MENJOU AIN'T HAPPY AT PARAMOUNT HE CAN GO TO FUCKIN' WARNER, BUT I CAN'T STAND HIS PHONY FRENCH FACE AND GREASY LITTLE MUSTACHE."

I said to the prim secretary sitting at her desk outside, "If that's Mr. Stoneman, he sounds pissed. Did he get up on the wrong side of the bed or did his wife and girlfriend commit a double suicide or something?"

The secretary arched her eyebrows reproachfully. "Why, no, Mr. Stoneman's fine, quite merry in fact. He just got the studio's quarterly earnings reports so he's walking on air."

"But…"

"Oh, he's always like that."

"SO CLARA BOW IS WITH ANOTHER STUDIO, I STILL FUCKIN' WANT HER OVER HERE."

"Is his partner that way too?"

"I've never even seen Mr. Rinehart. He's the studio's money person in New York. Mr. Stoneman's the quiet, delicate, artistic one."

"YOU'RE THE WORST FUCKIN' TALENT AGENT IN FUCKIN' HOLLYWOOD."

The door to the inner office burst open, and a baldish man in a gaudy, checkered jacket strode out, as Stoneman bellowed from behind, "Don't ever fuckin' come back. I never wanna see your ugly puss again." Then he added, "And don't forget about our golf date at the Hillcrest on Sunday."

The baldie said, "At our usual tee-time, Menachem. And remember, it's your turn to tip the caddies."

"Oh, and Charlie, tell Adolph Zukor, Jack Warner, and Irving Thalberg to all go fuck themselves."

"I already made a note."

As Charlie left, the secretary said to me, "Mr. Stoneman will see you now."

"That's easy for you to say."

Menachem was pretty much as Henry had described him, although his face was a bit more ferret-like than I expected, but, in his favor, his suit did not come off a rack.

"Who the fuck are you?" he demanded as I stood, obedient as a seeing-eye dog, in front of a desk about the size of the *Mauretania*. Menachem's hair was waxed to a watertight impermeability.

"Uh, Wilson Collison."

"Who?"

"The playwright?"

"Is that a fuckin' question or don't you know who the hell you are?"

"I'm working on that."

"What's your schtick?"

"Huh?"

"You don't understand no English? What the fuck did you write?"

"*Beyond the Horizon, Anna Christie,* and *The Emperor Jones.*"

"Never heard of 'em."

"Aren't you going to ask me to sit?"

"If I wanted you to fuckin' sit I would of told you. You gotta lot of chutzpah. Who the hell sent you?"

"Mencken."

"*Henry* Mencken? I hate that shlemiel with his cheap cigars. Opinions. Always got opinions about stuff. Who is he to have all them opinions? Walks into the nickelodeon I run in Baltimore once and stiffs me out of a nickel. One time, he sells me a Bible he says is a first edition signed by the author, but it turns out it's a Gideon he stole from a hotel room—and he signed it himself. Won't give me my five bucks back either. Fuckin' goniff. What's he to you, for christsake?"

"Because of Henry, you've hired me as a screenwriter for five hundred fifty a week, starting today."

"Why the fuck did I do that?"

"Because you want to give your films class. My best-known play is *Getting Gertie's Garter.*"

"Okay, you're hired."

"You saw my play?"

"Of course not."

"It would make a great talkie someday."

"There ain't gonna be no fuckin' talkies. And I don't give a shit whatever those assholes at Warner is doin'. Nobody wants it. You can't sync it right with the pictures. It's too expensive. Would slow down my production schedule. Half my actors have speech impediments or don't speak good English. You'd have to enclose the fuckin' camera in a big, glass box to hide the noise with no way to pan or zoom in. The theaters would have to spend thousands to hook up new equipment and speakers and shit. I may not be right, but I ain't never wrong."

"Then I guess a movie in color is also out."

"I'll believe in color when I see it in black and white. Can the crap, garter guy. I wanna hear about *now*. What are you workin' on?"

I had it all thought out.

"A script set at a movie factory in Hollywood, where film actors are getting bumped off in serial fashion by an unknown murderer, although I'm thinking about making the killer the noxious head of the studio."

He nodded in vainglorious approval as if he'd had the idea himself.

"I like it, I like it. I want it on my fuckin' desk by Friday. This Kraut I got in a temporary trade deal with Warner will direct. Name of Ernst Lubitsch. Speaks American like crap, but as long as he can say 'action' and 'cut,' I can live with it. Schlep over to James Branch Mandell at the Writer's Shack. He's the story editor, even though he can't write for shit. I may fire him and replace him with you, although you probably ain't worth shit either."

"I appreciate your confidence in me, Mr. Stoneman."

"If I had any friends they'd call me Menachem."

"Certainly, Mr. Stoneman."

"And don't forget. I got a timeclock down there so you gotta punch in or you're out."

"I'll be as regular as Milk of Magnesia."

---

First, Menachem wasn't kidding about the timeclock, an intimidating black box with an evil face mounted on a wall. Second, James Branch Mandell was not only a drunk but was Prohibition's biggest fan.

"I didn't start boozing until after they told me I couldn't," he said to me shortly after my arrival at the Writer's Shack, a squalid, single-story corrugated enclosure plumped down in the midst of a ramshackle sprawl of studio buildings and sets. Mandell had the fermented features of a man in perfect compatibility with his alcohol-fueled debility, although I wasn't clinician enough to know whether it was solely his choice.

Offering me a flask, he said, "Have a drink on me. Something else Prohibition taught me. Drunks hate to imbibe alone. Fortunately, the Shack is brimming with us."

I'd expected to hear a cacophony of Underwoods helmed by a frantic assortment of writers, sleeves rolled up, ties askew, clacking away at what would become celluloid masterpieces. Instead, I observed a seedy mishmash of unshaven louts, about a dozen, some with their feet on their desks counting z's, others engaged in animated sessions of gin-inspired gin rummy.

I saw instantly that I'd fit right in.

"Don't worry about the timeclock," Mandell told me. "If you don't show up someone will punch it for you. If none of us show up, we pay the porter extravagantly to punch the fucker for all of us. Some flunky from the front office collects the time cards and replaces them with blank ones. But they pay us no matter what it says on the cards or how little or how much we work."

The room was a malodorous mess: overflowing wastebaskets, wadded papers strewn on the concrete slab that served as the floor, empty bottles, pastrami remains rotting in corners, a woman's brassier draped over a ceiling light fixture. Seeing scores of paper airplanes dangling from the ceiling, I asked Mandell what they meant.

"It's the work of some Irish guy who came here claiming he's the poet W.B. Yeats. He didn't realize that verse has no place in silent films, so he's been reduced to writing intertitles that rhyme even though they have nothing to do with the plot. When he wrote, 'She ran off to join the circus but tripped and hurt her rectus,' Menachem had a hissy fit, so Yeats changed it to 'She ran off to join the circus but was canned for too much flatus.' That one passed. Anyway, Yeats folds the planes, then goes to the sidewalk and dips the paper noses in fresh dogshit. When he comes back he throws the planes at the ceiling, where they stick quite nicely. Personally, I see it as an artform."

I said, "I notice things are a bit loose around here."

"As your boss, I strictly enforce a single rule. One of us stands watch at the window at all times. We draw straws for daily watch duty."

"What are we watching for?"

"Menachem Stoneman. Sometimes he pays a surprise visit, although we're usually tipped off on account of we have a mole in his office. Menachem likes to make sure he's getting his money's worth out of us. He thinks busy is the same as prolific. Whenever he invades our den we look eager and engaged. But I don't think he's fooled. He's fired each of us several times over, but he forgets to tell payroll, so we still get our checks every Friday. Once, I told him I didn't want to be story editor anymore. I wanted to direct, and I'd quit if I didn't get the job. He told me I can't quit, only fired, and that I have a nine-year contract."

"Is that true?"

"I don't know. I never saw a contract."

"But you do actual writing here."

"Depends on what you call writing. Name the action, suggest a plot, capsulize novels, preferably those without a copyright, and any one of us will turn out a finished script in half an hour. It's not like we have to put actual words into the lips of the characters. Writing a movie is what a stick-figure drawing is to art. The script goes to a director, who usually chucks it and comes up with something else that he jots down on the palm of his hand, often influenced by the light or the camera angle or the boobs of the actress or how many extras he has or the size of his hangover. We spend more time on the title than the story. I figure all this will change if or when the movies switch to sound. Then the directors will depend on us to put sense into the mouths of the actors."

Now, of course, the screens were silent save for the fact that every theater in the country provided an orchestra, pianist, or mechanical piano to accompany the action—even if the music didn't quite match.

Mandell looked at his watch. "Say, how about a little lunchee? On me. Which is easy for me to say since lunch is a perk."

The studio commissary was non-alcoholic, so Mandell made sure we fueled up before he and I stumbled from the Shack into the maze of studio stages, prop facilities, dressing rooms, carpentry shed, machine shop, zoo, stable, and cheaply constructed sets with storefronts resembling an Old West town, Brooklyn street corner, New England village, even a Chinatown. The goal was to make a movie without the expense of going on the road—even if the story was set in Shanghai, which is why there was a thirty-five-foot plywood pagoda. Studio lots took up scads of real estate, dirt cheap in Southern California, but personifying just how artificial—make that phony—Hollywood was. However, for audiences, phony wasn't necessarily a bad deal if they got their quarters' worth.

Over Reubens at the commissary, where the writers commanded their own table, Mandell asked me, "What's your name again?"

I told him.

"The Broadway playwright?"

"Um, yes."

"That's funny. Seems I remember meeting a Wilson Collison back East once, I think at Keen's Steakhouse, but I don't quite remember the face."

"I have that quality," I said. "A face no one remembers."

"I'll drink to that."

And drink he did.

I, of course, had long known of James Branch Mandell, who preferred to be called Branch. His admired coming-of-age first novel, published by George H. Doran, was in the running for a Pulitzer. For a time, he was considered to be on par with H. Scott Fitzgerald, and Mandell's name seemed to be on everyone's lips. No fete in New York was complete without him. His third book dramatizing his torturous hitch as a doughboy in the merciless trenches of the Great War in France was a tour de force. Mencken, at the time co-editor of the *Smart Set*, gave Mandell a luminescent review and published several of his stories.

But something happened. As his celebrity ballooned, Mandell's literary output not only dropped, but the critics began to view it negatively, sometimes scathingly. Even Mencken turned on him, and when Henry crossed you off it was over. Some of Mandell's antics, which involved casual nudity, bloody noses, and chorus girls of dubious reps, made the papers. Particularly two notorious incidents, one in Oyster Bay and later on the Champs-Élysées when he and Fitzgerald got into slugfests and each time Zelda smashed a wine bottle over Mandell's head. His sales got so bad, Doran, his long-time publisher, ordered him to repay not just one advance but all of them. No surprise that he washed up on the Hollywood shore, emasculated, but raking in buckets of doubloons, more than he ever did as an author. Most of it went to bootleggers, bimbos, and a Bugatti Grand Prix Roadster.

Meanwhile, Fitzgerald's latest novel *The Great Gatsby* had just been published. Mencken wrote that despite *Gatsby*'s basic triviality, it had a fine texture and a careful, brilliant finish, while Gertrude Stein maintained that Fitzgerald would be read well after his contemporaries, such as Mandell, were forgotten.

"I sold my soul," Mandell told me boozily one night during an unending speakeasy crawl from Pasadena to Altadena. "Once, I was mentioned in the same breath as Nobel laureates. Now I write cheesy Western plots involving gunslingers, cattle rustlers, and the pretty schoolmarm, or worthless farces in which actors throw pies into each other's faces, which you might call a pie for a pie. I once wrote a brilliant script set in ancient Greece in which a son murders his father, the king, and sleeps with the king's widow, the son's mother. They called it derivative. Derivative, they said. I'm a hack, you're a hack, and soon all who step foot in the Writer's Shack will be entered into the Hacks' Hall of Fame. What happened? I ran out of things to say and the booze filled in the gaps."

I assured him he wasn't a hack, that he was in a temporary literary dry patch, and that he would stage a comeback—but we both knew I was lying. I once chanced upon a pristine first edition of Mandell's celebrated antiwar novel on the sidewalk ten-cent table at a second-hand book dealer on Vine Street. I was almost tempted to buy it.

I had little pull at Rinestone but gradually ingratiated myself with those who did—producers, directors, cameramen—which is how I was able to work Dalilah in as an occasional, paid-by-the-day extra. Even so, most mornings she still had to stand in line hoping to be called up for something, anything, while waiting in vain for Menachem to return her calls.

One day, our movie maharajah, his silver hair jelled into something solid, bushwhacked the Shack. He found us—having been early warned that we were about to be waylaid—pounding our respective typewriters like piledrivers through bedrock.

"That's what I like to fuckin' hear," Menachem brayed. "The harmony of typewriter keys. But that don't mean I'm gettin' my money's work out of you pishers. None of you schlubs is worth what I'm payin' you. All you do is kvetch and once in a while maybe move a few words around. Y'all oughta quit to save me from takin' the time to fire you. Hey, new guy, you. Yeah, the garter guy from New York…"

He was obviously talking to me.

"Get over here and tell me about that fuckin' project I gave you to work on."

"Project?"

I remembered chatting him up about my bogus movie murder scenario, but since Ernst Lubitsch had quit and I never turned in a sentence, I figured it had gone to the place where the angels strummed golden ukes.

Mandell came to my rescue. "Willy, he means the one about the history of the Crusades."

"Oh, *that* project. I finished the First and Second Crusades, and I'm now in the middle of the Third. I should have Four through Nine by next week."

"Next fuckin' *week?*"

"Maybe this week."

"That's more like it,"

"But it covers lots of ground, Mr. Stoneman. The years ten-ninety-five through twelve-ninety-one."

"Remember to keep it short. Lots of interest in the Crusades. Everyone's talkin' about 'em over at the Brown Derby. Even the dishwashers. That movie's gonna make Rinestone a fortune. I'm tryin' to hire Clara Bow to co-star in it with Pola Normand. So be sure to give 'em juicy parts."

"Yessir, anything you say, Mr. Stoneman."

"*Anything* I say? I don't want no yes men around here, garter guy. I want everyone to tell me the fuckin' truth even if it means costin' you your jobs. Now you schmucks get back to work and gimme some new clichés I never heard of."

After Menachem split in a cloud of volcanic sulfur, I snatched at Mandell's sleeve. "Why the hell didn't you tell me he wanted a script about the Crusades?"

"I didn't know it myself. But neither did he. Doltish ideas float in the air around here like excelsior. Besides, he's all juiced up about making some pirate crap called *Buccaneers of the Briny Deep*. What's the problem, garter guy? Go the library. The closest branch is in Hancock Park. They've got an encyclopedia. You'll be back in sixty minutes and can wrap up the Crusades script before cocktail hour. Oh, oh, duck." He pointed at the ceiling. "W.B. Yeats is shooting paper airplanes again."

Then Tyler Reed Desmond, the actor, was found dead of a gunshot wound in his bed in Room 264 at the Hollywood Hotel. He too had been a player at Rinestone, the fourth such victim. Which meant it was time for Dalilah and me to powwow. I called in James Branch Mandell as the cavalry. Sometimes, Mandell's looking through the bottom of his glass was all the perspective I needed.

---

Our command center was my living room at the Thousand and One Nights Bungalows. I outlined developing a true-crime epic, something just shy of a documentary with Hollywood at its core. With only a pang of conscience, I kept the fact that I was actually working undercover for the *Sun* to myself.

Our first order of business was chalking a blackboard detailing the victims and their circumstances; however, the productions had overlapping studio personnel, inevitable when a sausage factory churned out wurst by the score.

Vernon Fishman. July 1. Santa Monica. Gunshot. *The Two Musketeers*.

Harlo Wilcoxen. August 3. El Segundo. Gunshot. *When a Man Marries*.

Oswald Trumbo. September 5. Ventura. Gunshot. *Rifles on the Range*.

Tyler Reed Desmond. October 6. West Hollywood. Gunshot. *Noisy on the Northern Front*.

"Those murders must be connected in some way," I told my fellow conspirators, "and it's our job not only to prove it but to identify the baddy. Let's beat the fuzz since they don't seem close to finding the killer. It could turn into a bang-up screenplay. How about this for a title? *Homicide in Hollywood*."

Mandell, his nose overly infused with his ruddy complexion, said, "I already envision excited theater audiences from Fairbanks to Fort Lauderdale, Nome to Neptune Beach, and Anchorage to Apalachicola—if you admire my alliteration."

Sighing, her lips in her familiar cupid's pout, Dalilah said to him, "Are we going to have to put up with your sarcasm all night?"

"Oh my, and I always thought I did sarcasm so well. Or so my ex-wife tells me."

"You might at least take this seriously," she said. "People are dead."

He said, "I'm no detective, only a formerly celebrated novelist, but because all the victims had been cast in Rinestone movies, the killer is almost certainly someone on the studio's payroll. We should start by ruling out anyone at the studio who could *not* be the murderer."

"That's silly," she said. "Rinestone has hundreds of employees. Me for example. Three of the murders occurred *before* I was hired as an occasional extra. By your logic that rules me out as the killer."

"Not so fast, dolly," Mandell said. "You get around and know lots of people in and outside the studio."

"My name's Dalilah. Dolly was my sister."

"In your case, you might have had grudges with the victims even before being hired as an extra. We can't rule you out."

"I dated one of them, Harlo Wilcoxen. But I have an alibi for the night he was killed. I told the police all I knew. And so did my roommate, Virginia Sweet, who dated two of the victims, Tyler Reed Desmond and Vernon Fishman. The police cleared Ginny as well. She's an up-and-coming actress at First National, Hollywood's biggest studio. She had a small role in one of Mary Pickford's films. Ginny and I like to party, and so what if we get around a lot. That doesn't make us killers, Mr. Mandell."

"Call me Branch."

"I'd call you Mr. Bluenose if yours didn't look like a Pacific sunset. Hollywood may seem big, but it's actually a small community where everyone knows everyone else. It seems to me, *Mister* Mandell, you're an even likelier suspect because you and your co-writers fashioned the scripts for the movies they acted in."

I was newly impressed. Whatever happened to Dalilah's naïve little girl pose? Some schtick she used to attract sugar daddies? Mandell, much as I liked him, was acting like an ass, as usual.

He said, "Hey, little lady, with the crap we write, we'd be more likely to kill ourselves before dispatching the actors."

"Little lady. So condescending. Willy, why did you bring this man in? He's not on the team."

I said, "Guys, let's stop squabbling. Branch is here because he's been at Rinestone longer and knows everyone there. He can make connections and get us into places. Let's rule out ourselves as suspects. But I agree with Branch that the killer's someone inside. It's too much of a coincidence that four Rinestone actors just happened to be randomly murdered by a person or persons outside the studio. Why don't we look for any connections the victims may have had with each other?"

"I concur," Mandell said. "This calls for a little drinky poo now that we're in agreement. How about you, kid?" he said to Dalilah. "Scotch?"

"So now I'm a *kid?* I'm only drinking Mary Pickfords, but Willy keeps forgetting to buy the maraschinos."

"Wow, we've got a little wildcat here, Willy."

"C'mon, Branch. We all have roles in this caper. Let's focus. What about my original concept that the head of the studio did it."

Mandell said, "Menachem would more likely to *be* murdered than to be the murderer."

"But not if he'd impetuously signed some poor schnook to a long-term contract, changed his mind, but legally couldn't get out of it. He might bring in a hitman from Chicago."

Dalilah said, "I have to own up to something. As I told Willy, I spent four hours closed up in Menachem's office, but I don't remember much except for the gin rickeys he pumped into me like plasma transfusions. And he never even gave me a job. It was Willy who got me in as an extra."

Mandell said, "*Four* hours? The more we know you the more we learn. Guess at Menachem's age certain things take longer."

"I don't care for your innuendo, *Mister* Mandell. Unless, in your state of mind, you're simply confused."

"If I look confused it's only because I'm being cogitative."

"Well, la-di-da. Don't be so hard on yourself."

"I'm not. Loads of people are willing to do it for me."

She grumbled, "I never got that role over at First National either. I was sure I was going to get it. The director told me I was a natural."

Mandell snapped his fingers. "How about an entire change in direction? A whole new plot. Let's bump off the profane, dictatorial studio prick instead of the four actors, then have the thespians come under suspicion. So it's not a true story. Just a movie. We're accustomed to making up stuff—like paper planes with dog-shit noses."

I said, "Branch, we agreed this is supposed to be true crime movie, so let's stick to the facts."

"Which are?" he said.

"To start, from the newspapers we've learned that two of the victims were married, two were not. They ranged in age from twenty-eight to forty. Only Desmond earned enough to act full-time, the others supplemented their income doing odd jobs or day labor. Outside of appearing in Rinestone films, they seem to have had little in common—although each died of bullet wounds from a thirty-eight, if the gendarmes are right. There were no known witnesses and no suspects as far as we can tell."

Dalilah said, "About the murdered actors. I don't think any of us actually saw the final movies they were in. Maybe there's something in their films that could give us a clue: the way they behaved or their expressions or mannerisms or something."

Hey, the girl did have an original thought. My first impressions of her were out of whack.

I said to the skeptical Mandell, "What about it, Branch? Can you arrange a private screening of their last movies for us?"

"Is the pope Catholic?"

Dalilah said, "Was that ever in question?"

Telling Branch to go for it, I suggested to Dalilah that she talk up the murders at the Hollywood parties she went to.

"Even if it's just gossip. You know everyone. It could pay off."

"My roommate gets back tonight from Sonoma. Ginny and I will hit the party circuit big-time. There's safety in twos."

After Dalilah squealed off in her roadster, Mandell said, "That tootsie's good on the eye, Willy, but she's a lightweight."

"Clean your eyeglasses, Branch. Obviously, she's more than what you think you see."

---

Purveyor of endless inebriating nights, Mandell enjoyed a plethora of blind tigers—by some estimates thirty-thousand of them throughout the City of Angels. Since the start of Prohibition's noble experiment the number of liquor purveyors, all unsanctioned, had doubled.

As we settled into the screening room, he said, "I could be throwing 'em back with more convivial companions at King Eddy's." His favorite speakeasy was in the King Edward Hotel on East 5th Street, which used a piano storefront as cover. "I hope I'm not wasting valuable drinking time."

Although Mandell had bitched that it was a useless exercise, he seemed resigned as he joined Dalilah and me after studio hours with only the sentry in his box at the gate. One of Mandell's pals, a projectionist named Sal, threaded each of the last four movies, all three or four reelers, in which the victims appeared.

We suffered through the films, one after another. They weren't bad so much as rotten. *The Two Musketeers* had swashbuckling swordfighter Vernon Fishman in seventeenth-century France easily dispatching a multitude of villains and escaping with the beautiful young duchess he'd rescued. It was called *Two Musketeers* because Menachem didn't want to pay for a third actor with top billing. Harlo Wilcoxen in *When a Man Marries* is an alcoholic Bostonian banker who hits rock bottom but recovers his faith, redeems himself and wins back the hand of the woman he'd lost. In *Noisy on the Northern Front*, Tyler Reed Desmond single-handedly rescues his buddies encircled by the depraved Hun and returns a hero to small-town Ohio, falling into the arms of the sweetheart he'd left behind. Oswald Trumbo in *Rifles on the Range* bests rustlers, gunslingers, and a corrupt sheriff, and woos the gorgeous schoolmarm who nurses him back to health after a bullet wound. It wasn't clear why whooping, wild Indians suddenly materialized as they weren't part of the plot.

The films were predictable and clichéd, the acting either hammy or wooden, costumes hemmed with safety pins, shoddy sets of painted plywood, and inept cinematography—as one would expect from a commodity rushed out in the studio's inexorable production schedule. And every film had some half-baked love angle. Fresh, mass-produced fodder like this filled screens from sea to sea to lure eager patrons, nickels and dimes clutched in their sweaty palms, back the following week.

"Told you," Mandell said, passing his flask around, which, under the circumstances, both Dalilah and I availed ourselves of. "As Menachem would say, you gotta see this shit to see why you shouldn't see it."

I said, "I admit, the films and the actors had zero in common. And how about that dueling scene in which Fishman clumsily drops his sword and the other actor helpfully picks it up and hands it back to him? You'd have thought they would have reshot it."

"On our production schedule? Retakes are strongly discouraged. Directors live in fear of going over budget and, in the Writers Shack, there's a phrase known as 'Incurring the Wrath of Menachem.' Someone scratched those words like a mantra into the wall over the door."

I said, "Or that take where Trumbo is chased on horseback by a horde of outlaws, and when he reaches back without looking and fires his pistol once, six bad guys fall off their horses simultaneously. It could be a clown act."

"At Rinestone, we take our comedy seriously."

"Why are Indians always depicted on film as ruthless savages, stripped of any nobility?"

"Subtlety is not a strong point in the celluloid world. American Indians are not a major demographic and the movies have not been kind to them."

"That pivotal battle scene in *Noisy on the Northern Front* was filmed at night so you couldn't tell what was going on except for bursts of fireworks."

"Because in daylight everyone would see how cheaply it was staged. Besides, it would take too many extras, even on a battlefield fashioned on a cramped back lot."

Dalilah sniffed. "I don't know why you two are working for a film studio if you feel such contempt for the movies. I love them. Even with their flaws. As do people like me all over the world. They're stories, magic, and for a little while we're able to fly from our humdrum, sometimes depressing lives."

"With your looks, you're hardly humdrum, sweetheart," Mandell said.

"Don't sweetheart me, *Mister* Mandell. What I'm trying to say is that the movies let us escape into different worlds, to see people other than ourselves, heroic or exotic, or to find ground with a flawed person who by the end redeems him or herself."

Wow, I thought. It sounded as though Dalilah had studied film at UCLA—where a more popular major was football cheerleading.

I said, "In other words, Dalilah, you believe a bad movie is still a good movie."

"That's not exactly what I said. Willy, I just think you two are being too hard on those films. Not everyone reads *The American Mercury*. Most are perfectly happy with *Photoplay*. To them, Adela Rogers St. Johns is a more influential writer than H.L. Mencken. Besides, while you were seeing all the flaws, I was looking for something that could connect them all—and I found it."

Mandell said, "The hell you say. I saw the same movies you did. They were all of different genres and time periods. Nothing in them was alike, from costumes to sets to the execrable acting."

"But there was. In each film there was at least one scene in a restaurant, kitchen, dining room, or saloon. They all showed a table. And on the table was a bottle of wine. And no matter where or when the film was supposed to have taken place, the bottle of wine was always the same."

I said, "So what? Wine's ubiquitous. At least until Prohibition. But even now—"

"You don't understand," she said. "The wine bottles all carried the identical label. Why would that same wine be in films representing all those different times and places?"

"That's easy," Mandell said. "The prop people are lazy. They put out the identical bottle each time simply because they had it. Besides, how distinctive could the wine label be?"

"Quite distinctive. It shows a pelican in flight. That's the wine's name, El Pelican. How many labels are there like that? I happen to know it's a wine bottled here in California. I recognized it because it shows up at so many of the parties I go to."

Mandell said, "Nah, doesn't hold water. Or in this case wine."

"But we were looking for something that would link each film, and the wine does."

I said, "Dalilah, you may be on to something. A California-labeled wine bottle that appears in films set in eighteenth-century France, on the battlefields of Europe, in proper Boston, and a cowboy saloon in Arizona. Makes no sense. Branch, who was the property person involved in those movies?"

"Edith Elvira Elland. Middle-aged and a real sourpuss. Rumors have it she got the job because she was Menachem's mistress before she divorced her second husband and became a lesbian. You're not implying that she's our murderer?"

"We've agreed that the killer is likely someone at the studio. Let's talk to her."

Before that could happen, Hearst's Los Angeles *Examiner* found a witness the cops had overlooked in the killing of Tyler Reed Desmond. The frenzied front page quoted a neighbor as saying that shortly after gunshots were heard, a man in a trench coat and hat was seen leaving Desmond's West Hollywood bungalow.

"Guess that rules out a woman as the killer," I said. "That excludes Edith Elvira Elland."

"Don't be so sure," Mandell said. "Witnesses are notoriously unreliable about what they've seen. Besides, what about your idea that some hitman did the actual deed? I kind of like that theory."

"Dunno, Branch. Maybe we're coming up with too many complicated plotlines for our movie. Rinestone Studios likes stuff simple."

---

Edith Elvira Elland was harried when Dalilah and I found her on the set of *Buccaneers of the Briny Deep*. She was busily tracking the props used by the actors performing on a full-sized, plywood replica of a pirate ship's deck, while an unconvincing miniature of the ship was being filmed separately in closeup on an artificial pond. To make it move as it floated on the water, the crew was blowing it around with a huge electric fan. It looked like a kid's duckie in a bathtub.

I saw that Elland was keeping a checklist on a clipboard of all her props, which included swords, flintlocks, caplocks, a skull and crossbones, even a pegleg. When she carelessly put the list down, I surreptitiously picked it up—but not for long. She saw me studying it and snatched it from my hand.

"That's not for you to handle, young man. Who are you and who's that young woman you're with?"

Disdainfully, she eyed Dalilah, who was wearing a cloche hat and a short skirt that only teased her knees.

"Wilson Collison, ma'am, a new screenwriter from New York. Dalilah Darling here is an extra. James Branch Mandell, the story editor, sent us."

"Since neither of you are working on this film, why would Mr. Mandell do that?"

"As I said, I'm one of the writers—"

"But not on *this* project."

"Because I'm a freshman here, and I'm trying to learn all I can so I can properly type the prop names in my next script."

"Totally unnecessary," she harrumphed. "Sets and props aren't your department. I take care of that."

I saw that Elland, while wound as tight as a ball of rubber bands, was fully in control when it came to her beloved props. But she was also a one-hundred percent battleax. Would she ever give loaded guns to the actors in a staged shootout? Not unless she intended to.

"And what about *her?*" Elland said, indicating Dalilah.

"She's new too and also trying to learn the business. She has a particular interest in props and sets and wardrobes and stuff."

"Neither of you should be on this stage unless you have business here."

"A quick question, Mrs. Elland. Pirates drink lots of grog, right?"

"What does that have to do—"

"How is it served in the film? From casks into, what, mugs?"

"Of course casks. And mugs. For the pirate crew."

"How about wine?"

"Wine also, but only for the captain and his lieutenants."

"Bottles of wine?"

"Yes. Wait, why are you asking me all this?"

"Bottles of El Pelican?"

She turned white, visibly shaken.

I said, "But El Pelican wine wasn't around in pirate days, was it, Mrs. Elland? Why have you been putting El Pelican bottles in some of your recent movies? That's not a very realistic prop for the times and places, is it? And always turned in such a way that the camera sees the label."

"That's none of your concern."

"Just trying to—"

"You must leave the set or I'm reporting you to Mr. Stoneman. He wants nothing to slow down production, which is what you're doing."

"Don't get sore, Mrs. Elland. I think you've told us plenty for now."

Dalilah and I blew the set.

"Jesus, Willy, you weren't subtle at all. You should have let me handle it. I might have actually gotten something out of her."

"Could be we're tooting the wrong ringer, but I think she's hiding something."

"Maybe those El Pelican wine bottles were or are being used as some sort of signal."

"If she intends to use El Pelican as a prop in this new pirate film, that might mean another actor is about to wind up in a wooden kimono."

"Willy, we should check the cast listing for *Buccaneers of the Briny Deep*. Immediately."

I was starting to admire this young woman, who had the look and style of a flapper but was thinking more like Charlie Chan.

Thanks to Mandell, we finagled the film's production notes, script, and the list of cast members and crew. *Buccaneers of the Briny Deep* starred Rinestone's two best-paid players: Pola Normand as Glendora, a pretty passenger on board a merchant ship captured by pirates led by the evil Captain Coffin, and Ramon Martinez as Starbuck, the handsome first mate who changes his plunderous ways and goes straight after falling for her. Glendora and Starbuck lead a mutiny resulting in the vile pirate chief walking the plank, and, in true devotion, the two cinematic darlings go on to ply the high seas

*Extreme Long Shot (XLS). Fade.*

That Martinez bore no resemblance to anyone with the white Anglo moniker of Starbuck and in real life crudely spoke only Spanish with a weighty Mexican accent was irrelevant as far as Rinestone was concerned. It was an asinine action spectacle with crewmen, knives clenched between their teeth, energetically monkeying up and down the rigging, canons exploding, muscular hand-to-hand combat, and endless cutlass waving. One scene had Coffin and Starbuck celebrating the spoils while swilling down a bottle of red, but nothing in the script suggested El Pelican.

"What do we do?" asked Dalilah. "Tell all the actors that if they see a bottle of El Pelican on the set, someone's about to be murdered—or has been?"

"Perhaps we frightened Elland off, although she doesn't seem the type to be easily spooked."

"Willy, I have another confession. I'm not only familiar with El Pelican wine, I know the woman who bottles it."

---

Virginia Sweet's mother, Charmayne, won her vineyard in Sonoma County's Chalk Hill as part of a divorce, although she lived mostly in Bel Air, leaving the fruitage to a manager. Prohibition didn't prevent the cultivation of grapes, and while wine production was curtailed, most of California's vineyards still produced vino on the QT.

Dalilah and I sat side by side sharing a boxed lunch on the wooden bleachers of the Hollywood Bowl. It overlooked a canvas shell arched above a stage guarded by two giant urns rescued from the Fairbanks film *Robin Hood.* The concert venue had been plopped down on a hillside naturally shaped like an amphitheater. Normally subdued and empty during the day, it was a strategic, anonymous place to hold private conversations like ours.

Dalilah told me that Virginia was constantly on the outs with her mother, which was why Virginia and Dalilah shared rooms at the Villa Suprema on Wilshire Boulevard.

Dalilah said, "Charmayne's overbearing and tries to keep Ginny on a tether. She seems to think Ginny will run off and marry the first guy she thinks she's in love with. Charmayne doesn't want her daughter to do anything that would interfere with her screen career, and she's afraid an early marriage would do just that. A few months ago, Ginny had an abortion in Mexico, although she refused to say who impregnated her, not even to me. Her mother drove her to Tijuana to get it."

"Does Charmayne see her daughter as a cash cow?"

"God, no. She took her ex-husband's last dime and sent him packing back to Philadelphia. Charmayne's mansion is in conspicuous bad taste. She has a butler, maid, cook, and gardener. But Ginny would rather share a cramped bedroom with me than live with her."

"Ginny had access to the wine from her mother's vineyard, and you've said that she dated at least two of the murder victims."

"Maybe all of them. She doesn't tell me everything she does or who she sees. Ginny works at First National, so she's never even had an opportunity to smuggle El Pelican bottles into Rinestone's prop department. If she had, Elland would know about it. Besides, what motive would Ginny have to kill anybody?"

"What if her romantic relationships were exposed? Blackmail maybe. She had an abortion, illegal everywhere in the States. First National could fire her, wreck her career. Not even Rinestone would want her. You know what the climate's like in California right now, especially after the Fatty Arbuckle debacle. Hollywood's under siege for—you name it—sex orgies, homosexuality, drug parties, drunkenness, prostitution, obscenity. No doubt the Bible thumpers could add a few more to the list."

"And this Will Hays is going to do something about it?"

"He intends to show that the film capital can tidy up its act. If Ginny were implicated for her conduct she could kiss her movie career goodbye."

Hays, the former Postmaster General, was the industry's new over-lord, hired to clean up Hollywood and fashion some sort of movie code—preferably something toothless.

"Willy, I'd know if she had a secret career as a murderess. She doesn't even care that much about the movie business. Ginny would like to settle down with a stockbroker or an accountant—even a grease monkey if he's well endowed—and share a little white cottage surrounded by poppy fields, rose bushes, and jacaranda trees, and maybe a view of the hills."

Then, Dalilah gave me an offer I couldn't decline, although it sounded more like a decree.

"Willy, you need to meet Ginny. She and I've been invited to a party at the Cocoanut Grove in the Ambassador Hotel, and you're my date. And, what the heck, I'm inviting Branch, awful as he is, to be her escort."

With a thousand guest rooms and bungalows sprawling over twenty-seven acres of terraced gardens, the Ambassador, built along the newly-paved road to Long Beach, was the most gaudy, splendiferous, and ostentatious hostelry in America—and its Cocoanut Grove nightclub was the fabled Hollywood playroom of everyone who was anyone, or, like me, pretended to be.

"Wear your tux," Dalilah instructed.

---

So our quartet could arrive in style, and because Dalilah's Marmon road-ster was a cramped two-seater, Andy Devine chauffeured us. The rabble, not knowing better, might have thought we were actual muck-a-mucks rolling up in their Daimlers, Rolls Phantoms, and Duesenbergs.

As the Ambassador's epaulet-clad doorman assisted us from our showy oil burner, Andy said, "Golly gee, Mr. Wilson, with all those big-shots inside maybe you could put in a few more good words for me."

"Any bigshot in particular?"

"Yeah, all of 'em."

I didn't have the heart to tell the poor chump he was never, ever going to make it in the movies.

Mullen & Bluett on Wilshire had come to my rescue with a penguin-suit rental that nearly fit my medium build, so when I waltzed into the Moroccan-styled Cocoanut Grove with Dalilah on my arm it wasn't completely obvious that I didn't belong—and not because of my only slightly darker complexion. As I'd once donned the hood and robe of the KKK, not to mention the duds of a Chicago gangster, I knew how to dress for a role. And without a bit of shame.

If any Prohibition agents had infiltrated the soiree, where booze flowed like an irrigation conduit, they were either in disguise, on the take, or too drunk to notice. The boisterous bash was hosted by the head of United Artists, Joseph Schenck, and his film-star wife Norma Talmadge to celebrate Valentino's new sequel *Son of the Sheik* and the heartthrob's imminent departure on a nationwide publicity tour to culminate in New York City.

The lush, papier-mâché coconut trees, fake coconuts, and plastic palm fronds had been pillaged from the Oxnard Beach set of Valentino's original *Sheik*, while padded, mechanical monkeys, their electric eyes blinking, swung from the branches. Was that a real-life monkey among them? Indeed, John Barrymore's pet primate Clementine. Magically transformed into an endless depth of sky, the sapphire ceiling sparkled with stars, buoyant clouds, and a full moon that glimmered over a cascading waterfall. The entertainment, proffered by the Cocoanut Grove Orchestra, was broadcast live on Radio Station KFI.

Before we were seated, we spotted William Randolph Hearst, arm in arm with his paramour, Marion Davies of Cosmopolitan Pictures. Breaking loose, Dalilah beelined it to the newspaper magnate and, like a kissing cousin, popped him a smacker on the cheek. My god, she and Hearst *were* like that, and, spare me, I'd doubted her. Later, she told me that "William and Marion" had been flown down from San Simeon by their mutual friend Wiley Post.

Virginia Love and Branch Mandell shared our table. Ginny bore a gilt-edged resemblance to Dalilah, both dressed in frilly gowns, Dalilah's black, Ginny's red, each garment elaborately beaded and fringed, with tasseled boas, and on their heads cumbrous feathered hats. Little wonder their appointment books were chockablock with invitations. Branch was predictably cranky, out of his element, preferring the fugitive atmosphere of a speakeasy, although he appreciated the club's fluidic open bar and its tasteful centerpiece, an ice sculpture of the Manneken Pis. I wasn't sure what he made of Ginny as his date, but, based on his prickly relationship with Dalilah, I suspected the worst. And Ginny probably felt the same.

I gazed around the bursting nightclub, finding it a lark to identify the celebrities whooping it up to overbrimming flutes of champagne: Valentino and his wife, Natacha Rambova, of course; Buster and Natalie Keaton; Harold and Mildred Lloyd; Pickford and Fairbanks; Lillian Gish and her close friend, producer Charles Duel; Charlie and Lita Gray Chaplin; Gloria Swanson and her husband Herbert Somborn, owner of the Brown Derby; Clara Bow and her cameraman-boyfriend Arthur Jacobson; Maurice Chevalier, over from France. And for the hell of it Aimee Semple McPherson, who was known around town as a party girl for Jesus, safely returned from an alleged kidnapping that had made headlines.

The not-so-famous were also there, such as Jack Donovan Foley, the young genius who was developing sound effects for the talkies over at Universal. But the money-minded masterminds behind the camera dominated the premier tables: Jesse Lasky; B.P. Schulberg; Irving Thalberg, boyish but looking frail; Adolph Zokor; Marcus Loew; the Warner Brothers, three of the four; Louis B. Mayer; William Fox; Samuel Goldfish, now Goldwyn; and, naturally, Menachem Stoneman, whose abrasive voice cut like a scalpel across the smoky clamor. I was praying the combustible potentate wouldn't notice me, forcing me to pay homage at his table while he referred to me as the garter guy from New York.

If an earthquake justifiably demolished the Cocoanut Grove that night, the entire Hollywood movie industry would end in a single wallop, which, if Mencken had his way, would not be a non-positive.

Then the all-powerful Hearst columnist, Louella O. Parsons, sniffed out her first scoop of the evening, confirming gossip initially spread by a busboy: Scott and Zelda Fitzgerald had crashed the party. On hands and knees they'd crawled to the entrance of the club barking like mongrels begging for scraps. Some sap cut the velvet rope and on all fours they wriggled across the floor honing in on the bar by instinct. They were the only souls in the club lacking formal attire, which fazed them not.

When the self-martyred Mandell, conquered by Fitzgerald in the literary wars, learned of the duo's unheralded presence he nearly had apoplexy and girded his loins for battle.

He said, "For christ's sake, I last saw those two on the Champs-Élysées when Zelda broke a bottle of Château Cheval Blanc over my head—for the second time. She's batshit crazy and Scott thinks he's Gene Tunney when he's drunk. Believes he's a tough guy because Hemingway gave him a couple of boxing lessons and a quick tutorial on bullfighting. Where *is* that bastard?" Mandell rose in a fighting stance. "I'm gonna kick the—"

I grabbed his arm, pulled him back to reality.

"Branch, don't do anything stupid. Everyone in Hollywood's here. You get into a brawl with Fitzgerald—in this place, right now—you're through in this town. Then what?"

Mandell cooled down to something slightly less than the temperature of an oven-roasted goose. He, above all, knew he had zero literary options and no place else to survive.

"Oh, what the hell. Where's the fucking liquid-bearer? I need to place a standing libation order."

However, it wasn't a waiter who materialized at our table, but Scott himself with Zelda clinging to his arm.

"I say, old boy," Fitzgerald said, Princeton-like, to Mandell, "fancy meeting you here of all places. Mind if we pull up a pew? How about we let bygones be bygone?"

I thought there'd be fireworks and another melee, but, somehow, Mandell managed to contain his inner fury. As I observed the Fitzgeralds sitting there, both seemed diminutive, particularly Scott. Somehow, I'd imagined that he, the Jazz Age's most celebrated voice, would have commanded more bulk.

"What are you two doing in California?" Mandell demanded of Fitzgerald. "Doesn't seem like your kind of place."

"Would you believe that a mere month ago Zelda and I were in Paris with Ernest and Gertie and Alice, but we rushed back to the States because of a nibble from First National to write a screenplay, *Lipstick*. It's based on a clever little idea of mine in which a young woman wears magic lipstick that makes every man in town want to kiss her."

"Sounds like a piece of shit."

"And you would know shit, old boy."

"What you mean to say in your idiotic script, Scott, is that it's not a kiss you're writing about, but a fuck."

"Little doubt, but I understand that Hollywood's drafted a new code, rather like the Ten Commandments, only without the etched granite. So, yes, fuck is out, kiss is in. Zelda and I are staying in a bungalow right here on the Ambassador's grounds, and when we over-heard the music and laughter from this wondrous party next door, we couldn't resist."

Zelda interjected, "And how's your head, Branch?"

"Couldn't be better, Zel, and, as I think about it, I believe you knocked some sense into me. Twice."

"Probably more sense than my stupid husband, whose been running around panting after this cheap little starlet who had a bit part in *Stella Dallas*."

"Nonsense, Zelda, my dear," Fitzgerald said. "I've only been trying to develop her literary taste by recommending clever books such as *This Side of Paradise, The Beautiful and the Damned,* and *The Great Gatsby*. Branch, old boy, I would have suggested to her your marvelous war novel—what's its name?—but it's out of print, unlikely ever to return."

Zelda said, "Scott's full of shit, as usual. The girl's seventeen. Imagine him indulging in a cutesy, artsy relationship with a child—just prior to fucking her."

"The hell, Zelda," Fitzgerald said. "And simply because you were irate didn't mean you had to burn all your clothes in the hotel bathtub. Didn't you realize how expensive it would be to replace them? Our movie money's about to run out."

"Why did you drag me out here, you bastard?" To all of us, she said, "I detest this town, which closes up by ten unless you're invited to some half-baked party where nobody talks about anything but movies, movies, movies. There's nothing to do but to look at the view and to eat, and I hate looking at views—especially where there's nothing to see. And I despise their food. Have you ever heard of some ghastly thing called a tamale? If I ever escape this dump I'm never again going to watch a moving picture or even get close to an actor—unless I admire the heft of his *cojones.*"

As the couple bickered, Mandell, smiling, settled back, becoming more and more loose, realizing he no longer had to wage war against the Fitzgeralds. The faltering lovebirds were perfectly capable of conducting combat between themselves.

Mandell was ebullient after the thirsty Fitzgeralds, bored with our company, finally abandoned our table to refuel at the bar. He became so cheerful that he put his arm around Ginny and gave her a spirited smooch on the lips.

He told us, "Scott thinks I'm a bum for taking refuge in Tinseltown, but he came to the same place for the same reason: making a quick buck while hyping some script that's too imbecilic to ever reach the screen. But he'll be back. Like me, he's going to sell out because one day no one will read him anymore. And Zelda? When she goes, it'll likely be in a plume of smoke."

Ginny pulled away from Branch's arm, but not because of his friendly gesture, which she seemed to have fancied.

"Oh my god," she said, "do you see who's sitting at that table near the stage? My damned *mother.* She's here to spy on me. And look who she's with. That properties lady from Rinestone, Edith Elvira Elland."

We saw, indeed gawked. Although we couldn't make out their actual words, the two women were yelling at each other, on the verge of a catfight.

"I love it," Ginny said. "I knew it wouldn't last, those two."

"Wouldn't last?" I said.

"You didn't know, Willy? My mother and Elland are lovers."

Suddenly, a tearful Elland stood, knocking over her chair, and shoved through the nightclub revelers leaving Charmayne with her lips as straight as the backbone of a herring.

After her very public contretemps with Elland, Charmayne, a handsome woman in her forties, threaded her way to our table to introduce herself, but Ginny shriveled into a tight, defensive ball, refusing to acknowledge her mother, much less acquaint us.

Following a short, taut interlude, Charmayne muttered through her teeth, "I see I'm not welcome at this table. A mother needs to look after her daughter. Something you disgusting people won't do."

The atmosphere at our table was tense as Charmayne pirouetted like a one-legged ballet dancer, and we remained icily silent until she stalked off, disappearing into the party crowd.

"She's still watching me," Ginny said. "I can feel it."

Film impresario Joseph Schenck, who cut his teeth running Palisades Amusement Park in New Jersey, mounted the stage to introduce Valentino, congratulating the actor on his brilliant, new film sequel and pending publicity tour, and presenting him with a gift of a life-sized stuffed camel. Valentino, in accented English, voiced his appreciation and, to a round of applause, provided a demonstration of nostril flaring, his trademark in his romantic film scenes.

My own slightly deviated septum precluded nostril flaring, which no doubt had impacted my love life.

After the industry's unflagging movie czar, Will Hays, mouthed a few pious words on how sensationally Hollywood was policing itself, Schenck introduced the floorshow, which opened with a chirpy vocal rendition of *…at night when you're asleep / into your tent I'll creep …*and culminated in the descent of a colossal block of ice, inside of which posed au naturel an aspiring actress who displayed an abundance of pubic glory. After the ice was chipped away, she emerged to warm applause in full flesh, smiling but shivering, her toes blue. It was unlikely, however, that the poor girl, good sport that she was, would ever land more than an occasional role as an extra, if that.

Shortly before dawn in my bungalow bed following the gala, Dalilah whispered to me, "Flare your nostrils, Willy, and I'm all yours."

I tried. I really tried.

But there were four murders to attend to, and at the top of our must-do list was another consultation with Edith Elvira Elland.

But she had disappeared.

---

Rinestone's newest feature film *Buccaneers of the Briny Deep* debuted with shameless fanfare at Sid Grauman's Mandarin Theater on Hollywood Boulevard, replete with spotlights searching the California skies for ticket prospects, and a line of limos depositing red-carpeted first-nighters who strutted into the ridiculously ornate theater while basking in flashgun bursts and the cheers of adoring fans pressed against the velvet ropes. Built to resemble a red pagoda enveloped by Tang Dynasty-style fire-breathing dragons, bulging Buddhas, and guardian lions, the neon-lit movie palace with its copper roof was an affront to respectable architecture, although it did boast of a booming Wurlitzer organ and on major film premiers a sixty-five piece orchestra. It was Hollywood at its flamboyant worst—or best depending on the perspective.

The last of the luminaries to enter, of course, were the film's stars, Ramon Martinez and Pola Normand, holding hands and blowing kisses to their swooning, rose-petal-throwing worshipers. Rinestone didn't discourage the wild gossip columns and fan magazines speculating that Ramon and Pola were sweethearts in true life and about to announce their engagement. It was great press or as Menachem candidly once told us in the Writers Shack, "Hoopla sells shit." In real life, however, the two stars despised each other, with Pola calling Ramon an illiterate little greaser who forgot to take a bath, while he contemptuously referred to her as "la puta."

In its forecourt, the Mandarin Theater had begun a bizarre practice of impressing the faces of popular film figures into wet cement-like death masks—until it actually happened and it was decided to use profiles only.

Rinestone should have added a disclaimer to every reel of *Buccaneers of the Briny Deep*: "No actors were shot and killed during the filming of this photoplay." If El Pelican symbolized the murder of an actor in a given flick it never happened in this one, although we still needed another audience with Elland, our only real suspect. She had, however, become elusive after the *Pirates* filming was completed, allegedly going on retreat in Agua Caliente, Mexico. Rumor had it that she'd been drinking heavily.

But, shortly after the curtain fell at the movie premier, eagle-eyed Dalilah spotted Elland amid the crowds pouring roach-like from the Mandarin Theater. We stalked her as she entered a Studebaker parked several blocks away and trailed her in our limo, Andy Devine at the wheel, to a villa at the Garden of Allah Hotel. After she entered the abode, the lights inside snapped on, leading us to conclude that we had found her hideaway and that she was living alone.

All we had to do now was to make her talk, but based on our first run-in with her, that wouldn't be easy. It briefly occurred to me to wire my gangster pal in Chicago, Two-Fingers McCord, and bring him to Hollywood. Two-Fingers's ability at persuasion led to the killer of Dalilah's sister, so if anyone could make Elland squeal, it was him. But I ruled it out as, well, overkill.

We waited until the next morning to return to the Garden of Allah, but there was no answer at Elland's door, which proved to be easily jimmied. Inside, she was nowhere to be seen, so we took advantage of her absence to rummage through her closets and drawers, even under her mattress. It was illegal. We were trespassers. But what the hell? What must one do simply to solve a few murders? Elland seemed to be a solitary, unsentimental being. The only things we found of interest, apart from a depleted bottle of El Pelican and a single, empty wine glass, were photographs of Charmayne Love and Sister Aimee torn in half, as well as a flier from the Foursquare Church in Echo Park promoting salvation as represented by the quartet of man, lion, ox, and eagle.

---

As he'd threatened, Henry Mencken came to town.

It was a whirlwind trip, Henry barely having time for me. After visiting obliging newspaper editors in Dixie, he arrived in LA from New Orleans on the Sunset Limited through what he called the ghastly wilds and dreadful deserts of the Southwest.

We drained illegal fermented fluids downtown in a booth at Cole's P.E. Buffet in the Pacific Electric Railway's terminal building on East 6th Street.

"Taggart, m'boy, these cross-country passenger train excursions are exhausting with no facilities for a decent drink. I'm more content in the comfortable speakeasies of the major cities. Not unlike establishments such as the one we're in, only cleaner."

He'd been greeted by a cohort of Valentino's, actress Aileen Pringle who escorted him on a round of obligations that included dining with Louis B. Mayer, tea with Mary Pickford, and handball with Menachem Stoneman.

But the highlight was his performance in a thirty minute, self-indulgent film directed by *New Yorker* cartoonist Ralph Barton: *Camille: The Fate of a Coquette*, which included an elaborate cast of walk-ons, including Paul Robeson, Charlie Chaplin, Sinclair Lewis, and Theodore Dreiser, with Anita Loos as Camille. Primarily, the film was a muddle of drink-guzzling partygoers in open defiance of Prohibition.

It never made it to the box office.

"While the cinematographer cranked the camera," Henry told me, "I had nothing more to do but to sit and savor libations directly from the bottle, which I would have been inclined to entertain in any event."

As a celebrity himself, he found most of his visit a blur of interviews, parties, lunches, and dinners with a multitude of Hollywood stars and biggies. He'd just published still another in his essay sequence, *Prejudices: Fifth Series*, which had received considerable attention. Like the Fitzgeralds, he was staying in a bungalow on the Ambassador's grounds.

"Los Angeles is all I expected," he told me. "It's a genuine horror, and if I described it literally in the *Sun* I'd be laughed down as the earth's damndest liar. Here they erect garish Spanish palaces and stuff them with Grand Rapids furniture. I can state with absolute accuracy that this land of quacks and frauds is the one true and original arsehole in all of creation, nine times worse than I figured."

"Isn't there *anything* you like?" I asked.

"Outside of its lemon groves and eucalyptus trees? Only its gaudy sexual society and its beautiful, intelligent women. But enough about me, Taggart, m'boy. How have you been now that you're a successful, highly-paid screenwriter?"

I was quick to explain that I hadn't written anything, save for a few hastily composed outlines under duress, and that I was still focused on my undercover investigation into that series of murders, the victims all actors at Rinestone Studios—which, I reminded him, was why I had come in the first place.

"So who did it, the butler?" he gleefully joshed, foreshadowing the contrived whodunnits of Mary Roberts Rinehart. United Artists had recently released a film version of Rinehart's Broadway play, *The Bat.*

"I'm close, Henry. And I think the answer lies somewhere at the Foursquare Gospel temple of Aimee Semple McPherson. I've reason to believe a key suspect named Edith Elvira Elland may be there."

"Excellent. I'm shortly to entrain for San Francisco to visit the poet George Sterling, protégé of the late Ambrose Bierce, but calling on Sister Aimee's Angelus Temple ranks high on my itinerary. Evangelical bullrings are of a particular interest of mine, having been to many in Baltimore's back alleys, and the Holy Rollers always put on a bully show. There are services this coming Sunday are there not?"

The infamous Aimee was under investigation by the DA for perjury, criminal conspiracy, and obstruction of justice. She had gone missing during an outing at the beach in Santa Monica, and was declared dead, a suspected drowning. A month later she turned up in a Mexican border town claiming she'd escaped from a desert shack after being chloroformed and kidnapped for ransom by mysterious captors. Because there had been a dozen unrelated ransom demands, the press, led by Hearst, thought it more likely she had run off with her randy radio engineer, Ken Ormiston.

It wasn't hard to zone in on Aimee's Angelus Temple with its massive domed roof and a watchtower for round-the-clock prayers. It blighted the landscape like a giant, concrete pustule—but, with my co-conspirators, I was in good company when I landed there.

---

Andy Devine collected us in his gas-guzzler, although Ginny, the newest member of our cast, was in and Mandell was out—at least for this go around after he learned of Mencken's visitation. Branch remained outraged that Henry had disparaged his later work, which caused him to lose favor in the book-buying world. This translated into Hollywood or death. He chose Hollywood. Mandell didn't forgive easily, be it a literary slight or a wine bottle or two over the skull.

During the limo ride to the temple, Henry, the old roué, became quite chummy with Dalilah, who buttered him up unashamedly.

She said, "I just love your *American Mercury*," she purred. "Never miss an issue. And I so admire the novels of Theodore Dreiser. Your discovery, I believe?"

Henry all but blushed.

"No, no, Theodore was quite established before my ringing endorsements. As you know, he's been denounced by his enemies, and the law, protecting our fragile sensibilities, has been called upon to occasionally put down his books. But he is *the* American novel. I've been informed by the best legal minds at Johns Hopkins that our First Amendment only applies to political speech, not to that involving free expression otherwise. Thus, governmental censors, abetted by the God-fearing, currently prevail. Therefore, we must have God's approval before reading a book. Despite it all, Theodore's most recent *An American Tragedy* is striking, don't you think?"

"Of course, Mr. Mencken. I absolutely *adored* it."

"Call me Henry."

Dalilah seemed to be quite taken by the bard, while I sat stone-faced.

Andy deposited us at Sister Aimee's Roman Coliseum-like basilica on Glendale Avenue, where seven thousand worshipers could revel in the stained-glass windows, baptismal tank watered by a real stream, and sections dedicated to faith healing and yammering in tongues. Two twin steel towers mounted on the roof like clothesline poles beamed out Aimee's KFSG, which gave her radio voice to all the faithful unable to cram inside her tabernacle.

"My word," Henry said, as he gazed at the edifice, "the hideous architecture is of the early Norddeutscher-Lloyd Rauchzimmer school with modifications suggested by the Standard Oil Company of New Jersey. It appears to have been cheaply made, so I doubt that it cost much, but then nothing in Los Angeles appears to have cost much. The town is inconceivably shoddy. Oh woe, take me back home to Charles Street."

But I saw that as soon as we entered the chateau, Henry was in a milieu that fueled his natural antipathy toward ignorance, nescience, and occultism.

"I'm going to enjoy this," he said, chuckling. Then he whispered into my ear, "You have one bright, intelligent young woman in Dalilah, Taggart m'boy. Don't lose her."

We managed to find four seats in one of the higher elevations, although not exactly scraping the ceiling—it was a dome, after all—so that we enjoyed a panoramic view of the vast gallery. Runways loped down the center and along the walls leading to a proscenium arch, under which was parked a grand piano on one side, an organ on the other, and below the stage a full brass band in Salvation Army-style uniforms. At any moment I expected them to rise up and play "Ta-ra-ra Boom-de-ay."

Henry said, "This arena is packed with the most enlightened minds of the thirteenth century, Taggart, m'boy. To their credit, they no longer believe the earth is flat, but remain convinced that prayer cures when medicine fails."

The pageantry began with an acrobatic quartet contorting themselves into a human crucifix while singing "Dry Bones," followed by adorable six-year-old twins augmented with ukulele performing "Jesus Wants Me for a Sunbeam." From the hall's rear, a brother thrusting a miter into the air led a phalanx of pilgrims escorting Sister Aimee to center stage marching to "Onward, Christian Soldiers." The brethren were dressed alike in white robes, similar to the Klan's but lacking hoods. Aggregations of varying numbers and sexes mounted the dais to yodel hymns, and then Sister Aimee, wearing a gangling white robe under a plum-hued cape, her abundant chestnut-brown hair piled aloft, herself led the choir in ditties of beseeching and praise.

Henry said to me in a low tone. "Sister Aimee seems to be a woman quite in charge. Hard to believe she would ever have allowed herself to be kidnapped. She brings to mind the madam of a certain fancy house on a busy Saturday night."

"You've been to it?"

"Only on Mondays, the slowest night. Hallelujah."

Finally, an ever-in-motion Sister Aimee, with a flunky following her with a mic to broadcast her every syllable, launched into her act, which involved speaking in tongues, sharing words of praise and salvation, and promising eternal life—but *only* to the faithful who mailed donations in any amount to Foursquare Gospel, Echo Park, California, checks and money orders gladly accepted.

Meantime, Dalilah and I scanned the crowd for evidence of Edith Elvira Elland, but there were so many performers festooned in white, like laundered sheets on a line, it was hard to tell, even assuming she was one of them.

"Worry not, Willy. I brought my opera glasses."

Uproarious, hand-clapping gospel canticles nearly shook down the house for the grand finale, and finally, the sated, post-orgasmic crowds began to thin.

Henry nodded in satisfaction, saying, "As orgies went, Taggart m'boy, this was spectacular. That heinous effort by the law to jail Sister Aimee seems disingenuous to me. The poor woman has two sets of enemies: the clergy who resent her raids on their customers and the local Babbitts who think she's making Los Angeles look ridiculous—although the town doesn't need her for that. Unless I err, I actually believe our Heavenly Father is on her side."

"You don't believe in the Heavenly Father."

"If the notion gives one a little hope in a hopeless world, so be it. That said, Christian theology, like every other, is not only openly opposed to the scientific spirit, it's also opposed to all or any attempt at rational thinking. It's the habitual and incorrigible defender of bad governments, bad laws, bad social theories, bad institutions, and maybe even bad teeth. Skin a chimpanzee and it would take an autopsy to prove that he or she is not a theologian."

Suddenly, Dalilah shouted, "There she is!" She pointed toward an elusive figure in white disappearing into a doorway off the stage. "I told you I'd find her. Let's go."

The four of us sprang from our seats to pursue Edith Elvira Elland to a robing area off the currently empty speaking-in-tongues section. We found her, sobbing, sitting alone on a folding chair.

"Mrs. Elland," Dalilah said, "perhaps you remember Wilson Collison and me from the studio. This is Mr. Mencken. And you know Ginny."

"What do you want?" she sniveled between sobs.

"It's about El Pelican, the wine."

"That *again?* Can't you see that I'm in distress? I wouldn't even be here if had I someone to talk to?"

Grasping our opportunity, we sat, then eagerly scooched our chairs up to surround her, although Dalilah did the talking.

"But you *do*, Mrs. Elland. Us. We're all, uh, Rinestone Studio friends of yours. Trust us. You can tell us anything."

Elland's snot oozed and Henry gallantly handed her the hankie that was usually pleated in his breast pocket.

"I'm at the end of my harness," she said.

"We're here to help."

Damn, Dalilah was good. Sometimes the best secrets are those spilled to near strangers, such as in a bar. From Elland, they came gushing out. The services of Two-Fingers McCord were absolutely not required.

We learned that Aimee hadn't been kidnapped, nor had she run off with Ormiston, the radio schmuck. She and Elland had absconded to a desert oasis hideaway. The two were secret lovers, but their torrid affair collapsed upon prolonged intimacy, and Aimee was the one who bluntly, unexpectedly, broke it off.

Today, the tearful, beseeching Elland had come to the Angelus Temple fervently hoping to repair the breakup. But Aimee rebuffed her. It was cruel.

Elland said, "I banded with Aimee when I was on the rebound from my rupture with Charmayne Love. It seems I'm unable to eternalize any sort of a relationship. They've all fallen to pieces like little shards of glass. My husband deserted me. Foolishly, I thought Menachem cared for me, but no. To him, I'm mere bric-a-brac, and he lets me keep my job at Rinestone purely out of pity, and he isn't known for having sympathy for anyone but himself. And Charmayne? I hardly have the words to speak about her. So now here I am."

Pathetically, the poor woman had revealed her deepest despair—and I knew what was in our minds as we exploited her vulnerability: how were we to ask, and receive a candid response, about the El Pelican wine bottles and the four Hollywood murders?

Dalilah said, "Mrs. Elland, perhaps we might ask…"

"What?"

"It's about those…"

"Those?"

"As I'd tried to say before, the…"

Finally, Henry broke in, "My dear lady, I've been told by these fine people all about those observable El Pelican bottles in the photoplay of each actor who was so violently dispatched. You supplied those bottles. Are you the killer?"

Henry had a way of cutting to the nitty-gritty.

Elland broke into still more tears, but, amid the sobs, her story took shape.

"I despised what Charmayne was doing, as I told her again and again, but she refused to listen. It's what led to our breakup. Every time she revealed her plans to murder one of those men, I protested. But I was in love with her, you see, so I couldn't go to the police."

We heard a noticeable gasp from Ginny. She had no idea.

"I didn't know how to stop her or what to do. But on each occasion that Charmayne marked an actor for death, I made certain a bottle of her El Pelican appeared in his film. It was a symbol of my anguish, one I thought she alone would grasp, and perhaps take to heart. I'd no idea anyone else—you—would even notice it."

Dalilah said, "But *why*, Mrs. Elland? What did those men ever do to Charmayne?"

"They threatened to steal away her daughter. Virginia here is a silly, flighty girl who falls in love too easily and so cheaply."

Ginny, almost as if she were an inanimate object, sat in stunned silence as she heard Elland malign her character.

"Charmayne had grand plans for Virginia, wanted her to become big. I mean truly spectacular. An international star. More so than Pola Normand or Mary Pickford or Greta Garbo or Clara Bow. The poor girl doesn't have it in her, of course, and she kept falling in love with the wrong sorts of men, those of limited ability and doubtful futures, and terrible actors to boot."

Ginny covered her face with her hands, too distraught to say a word.

"To guard her daughter's career and to make sure that the men Virginia was bedding were out of the picture, Charmayne tracked them down one by one and shot them to death."

We let this sink in for a moment until Dalilah said, "But a witness saw a *man* leaving the home of Tyler Reed Desmond, the fourth victim."

"Charmayne *always* dressed like a man when she went out to kill. I mean, really, who would expect a woman to be an assassin?"

To Ginny, I voiced an obtuse observation, which I instantly regretted for its blatant insensitivity.

"It must be devastating to hear this about your mother," I said. "But on the positive side, you'll no longer be tormented by her—and the Hollywood film industry can at last be declared safe."

Elland's eyes popped in astonishment, saying, "Are you people naïve? Do you really think Charmayne limited herself to just film actors, any more than Virginia did? How about that Mexican gardener who was found shot to death on Olivera Street; an insurance man in Echo Park; the police detective who worked out of the Wilshire Station on West Pico Street? Virginia here slept with them all and Charmayne killed them all. Shall I go on?"

The weight of her words dropped like a ton of bricklayers, and the thought of how narrowly confined to Hollywood our suspicions had been suddenly seemed shallow, oblivious, and embarrassing.

Finally, I said, "How many victims?"

"I lost count."

Dalilah said, "Mrs. Elland, Are you prepared to tell your story to the police?"

"What choice do I have? I've nothing left."

I said, "You have us—as long as I get an exclusive with you before the cops are called. I've got a story to write."

"Shut up, Willy," Dalilah said.

---

Thus, the case of the Hollywood homicides was cracked by, well, I'd like to say yours truly, but it was Dalilah who actually put the who into the dunit. Nevertheless, I labored on a penetrating inside account for the *Sun*, which would lead to a Pulitzer, I hoped, under my true byline. But I wasn't going to admit yet to my Hollywood chums that I wasn't actually Wilson Collison until after my story appeared in the *Sun*.

The scandal scored oversized LA headlines, Hearst leading the pack, with front-page photos of a defiant Charmayne Love being led in handcuffs by the bulls to the clink, her daughter weeping histrionically, along with sleazy autopsy headshots of all four Hollywood film victims.

There were also references to Charmayne's eight other non-Hollywood killings. Then the *Examiner* landed another biggie. To hide the murder weapon she had ordered her butler to dispose of her .38 in the La Brea Tar Pits.

Mandell said to me, "Hey, garter guy, you must be proud. The scoop's all yours, and now you have the makings of a great screenplay."

"Nix on that, Branch. You take the screenplay. I couldn't have navigated Hollywood and the studio system without you, but I'm through with it now. There's no one in the movie capital better equipped to write the script than you, which you need to avoid the Wrath of Menachem. I understand Warner is about to release a film in which Jolson actually sings, so when the talkies take over you'll have the words for them. And what's this about you and Ginny Love?"

"We're now an item one may tie with a bow. Ginny's been through perdition what with her abhorrent progenitor and all, so I'm taking her to Palm Springs this weekend. Not only is she going to give up acting, she's also giving up actors. By the way, I've joined the Tarzana Chapter of Inebriants Incognito, and I've been dry for four days straight."

Henry was also finished with LA, about to push on to the only slightly saner but eminently more literary San Francisco.

"Taggart, m'boy, I'm poised to bid adieu to the City of God's Messengers, where homeopaths, chiropractors, snake oilers, and other quacks formerly marked the landscape, but which now swarms with swamis, spiritualists, Christian Scientists, crystal gazers, and their allied necromancers. Gullible pickings it is for real estate speculators, oil-stock brokers, and sellers of the Eiffel Tower."

"Plus you had the rare opportunity to see Aimee Semple McPherson in the flesh."

"Indeed. As the local pastors weren't up to the town's juicy opportunities, in traipses Sister Aimee armed with the oldest tricks out of Billy Sunday, Gipsy Smith, and the other time-honored hell robbers. To them, she adds capers from her own circus days. In some infinitesimal way, I shall miss it here."

Alas, Henry never saw George Sterling in San Francisco. The poet was a suicide delivered by cyanide, a vial of which, labeled "peace," he had carried for years waiting for the right moment.

As for Andy Devine, he landed a role in a series of two-reel comedies from Universal called *The Collegians*.

He proudly told me, "It's not a Western, but golly gee, Mr. Wilson, it's a start."

Shortly following Andy's words came the flash that Valentino, on his publicity tour in New York, had died suddenly of peritonitis from a perforated ulcer.

Dalilah Darling and I never had more than a casual affair, although for moments, in my effort to nostril flare, it almost seemed like it. But I was willing to try again.

She said, "So, Willy, you're returning to Broadway to work on your stage plays."

"Which is another complicated issue I need to talk to you about, although it'll take some explaining. But, more to the point, I'm going to Havana."

"*El Cocodrilo?*"

"*Si.*"

"Ah, you also speak Spanish."

"Dalilah, you told me once that Cuba's where all the smart people in the States go now that the drys have crimped their style. Open gambling, booze, live sex shows, gangsters. A corrupt and sordid Caribbean paradise, and a tiny sliver of fascism controlled by our beloved America. A story's there and I aim to tell it from the inside."

"So you'll be in Havana while I stay in Hollywood at Rinestone Studios struggling to land even silly walk-on parts and drinking myself to oblivion at insipid parties, not to mention clawing off married lechers."

"You once suggested that you preferred *Photoplay* over *The American Mercury*, Dalilah."

"Did I really?"

"What's the truth?"

"What do you think? By the way, Willy, *Sister Carrie* is my favorite novel, and I actually loathe drinking Mary Pickfords. But it's hard to find good-quality scotch these days."

With those words, Dalilah made it clear, she was not only a terrific actress but she was smart as hell.

I said, "Menachem claimed he'd squire you to Havana. He lied. He's a four-flusher. But when I get to the Caribbean, I'll send you a ticket and, perhaps, you'll join me. I have other cases to crack and more stories to work on. Dalilah, after your work on the El Pelican wine murders... I could use you."

"I'm beginning to think you're more of a reporter than a playwright."

"Which is what we need to talk about. Meantime, Havana, *por favor?*"

"*Maravilloso, estupendo.* I've been learning Spanish from Ramon Martinez."

And that's -30- for this reporter.

> *This is the song at the end of the movie*
> *When the house lights go on*
> *The people go home*
> *The plot's been resolved*
> *It's all over*
>
> —Joan Baez

# ——FOUR——

# ~~HELL~~ HECK IN HAVANA

*Not so far from here*
*There's a very lively atmosphere*
*Everybody's going there this year*
*And there's a reason;*
*The season opened last July*
*Ever since the USA went dry*
*Everybody's going there and I'm going too!*

—Irving Berlin

The swells from the States were overrunning this Caribbean mecca, marking it as their own. But with any luck, I'd be back in the safety of B-more before my undercover piece hit the *Sun*'s presses. Safe from the bruisers and bootleggers, the hatchet men of the malevolent American sugar and fruit consortium, and the Machado death squad known as La Porra.

It made sense for me to stay at the Sevilla on Calle Trocadero in La Habana Vieja. The hotel was just off the Paseo del Prado and a little above El Capitolio, which was still under construction. I could easily stroll down to Museo Nacional de Bellas Artes to absorb the local culture. With Prohibition still inhibiting the States, El Vevado, the downtown district, was where the action was. Cuba's biggest hostelries and casinos

128

were there: the Plaza, Saratoga, Inglaterra, Ambos Mundos, Santa Isa-bel, Raquel. Ground was being cleared for an extravagant new hotel to be called the Nacional de Cuba up by the broad esplanade known as El Malecón, which would look down on everything else.

The tourists were immune from Cuba's dangerous intrigues.

But not investigative reporters such as myself.

Cuba had been on my mind for some time. With the US officially dry and repressed by sanctions on everything from gambling to books to art to sex to women's reproductive rights to shopping on the sabbath, the Caribbean island almost seemed like a liberated American state. As well as the Western Hemisphere's Monte Carlo.

Except for Machado's La Porra.

---

Prior to my Hollywood mission, Henry had extolled the pleasures of Cuba. As usual, we were in the Rennert Hotel indulging at Henry's favored table. After covering the Great War in Europe, he'd been return-ing to the States from Spain via Cuba on the *Alfonso XII* when the *Sun* cabled him to remain on the island and report on an insurrection.

"I adored Havana, the food, and its people, Taggart, m'boy. And it was an ideal place in which to cover a revolution."

Although it didn't amount to much.

Gomez, the ex-presidente, staged a military coup against the current *jefe*, Menocal, who'd suspended the constitution. Henry barely had time to develop a decent hangover in the local cantinas before Gomez was pinched and the insurrection petered out. It was a tame affair, according to Henry, who noted that the island's balmy climate seemed to nourish political malfeasance.

He said, "A pity there's no revolution in Cuba at the moment for you, Taggart, m'boy. But wait a day."

However, Cuba was more than revolution. It was also an island of corrupt politicians, secret cops, greedy American tycoons exploit-ing the economy, mobsters attracted to the open gambling, and the never-ending supply of booze itching to be bootlegged to the dehy-drated US.

Henry characterized America harshly. "It's the habitat of puritanism, the haunting fear that someone, somewhere, may be happy." Whether in print or while quaffing a beer, he railed against the lunacy of Prohibition and the sermonizers who'd imposed it. "There's now more drunkenness in our failed Republic, not less. There's more crime, not less. Respect for the law hasn't increased, it's diminished. Cuba may be problematic, but at least you can buy a drink without the Apostles of the Lord threatening to put you in jail."

I'd have plenty of cash to throw around when I went to Havana thanks to a well-heeled patron. Henry identified him only after my relentless badgering and the promise of springing for another round of potables.

"It must remain our secret." He lowered his voice to a whisper. "It's Pierre S. DuPont, the industrialist and one of the world's richest men. Pierre and his brother, Irénée, are ardent foes of the Volsteadians. They've formed the Association Against the Prohibition Amendment. It even has an official song called 'Light Wine and Beer,' which I've promised to per-form on the piano at my Saturday night music ensemble."

---

After wrapping up my Hollywood adventure, I hopped the Sunset Lim-ited from LA to New Orleans, the New Orleans-Florida Express to Jack-sonville, then the Orange Blossom Special to Miami. There I boarded the Eastern Steamship Line's *S.S. Evangeline*, sometimes called the booze cruise, to Cuba. The magazines and newspapers were awash in ads describing Havana as the *Paris of the Caribbean* and touting its wondrous night life as filled with *gambling, water sports, and old-world charm* with the *American dollar welcome*, and *English spoken everywhere*.

For the purpose of my covert enterprise, I planned to portray myself as the scion of a distinguished, well-to-do line of New England socialites: Niles Tinsley Aldrich IV, family lucre bulging in my pockets and salivat-ing to invest in something, anything, in Havana—on the up and up or not. In real life, I continued to inhabit my squalid room on West Biddle Street in B-more and drove a two-seat Dixie Flier, currently mounted on blocks in an alley.

I was flush with hush-hush DuPont wherewithal, leading me to dub the cash "DuPonts," as well as my movie money from Menachem Stoneman's Rinestone Studios. I'd offered to buy Dalilah Darling tickets for the Pullman from the Coast plus the ferry to Havana, but she insisted she'd arrange her own transit and meet me there. She was going primarily for the thrill. Her independence was what I liked about her. As an actress, she sometimes put on a beguiling but phony little girl pose that seemed to attract sugar daddies—but when it came to her onions she knew a Vidalia from a Bermuda.

My exclusive on the cinema capital's magniloquence, movie madness, and multiple murder, "Homicide in Hollywood," had finally appeared under my byline: Gart Booker Asquith III. It put me in fine stead with the *Sun*, and I couldn't have done it without Dalilah. But I had enough nom de plumes to confuse Albert Einstein, which had to be sorted out for her once she arrived. But undercover newshounds were occasionally rewarded with the big sleep, and I wasn't quite ready to join their feathered choir.

---

As the *Evangeline* rounded the inlet on the island's north coast guarded by El Morro and La Cabaña, the two ancient forts on the opposite shore, I saw that Havana Harbor was bustling with watercraft of all sorts and sizes from scows to steamers. Standing at the rail, I struck up a conversation with an amicable Cuban who was returning after visiting relatives in Miami. He told me he worked at the Hotel Sevilla.

"Which is where I'll be staying," I said.

He broke into a toothy smile. "Then no doubt our paths will cross. I am the *cantinero*—the bartender—at the rooftop garden. Ask for Javier. I will see that you get extra, special attention. In fact, I will be on duty tonight."

"How about all those boats in the harbor, Javier?" I asked. "I've never seen so much seacraft in one place."

"Rumrunners. Our harbor is teeming with them. They make a fortune shipping booze up to El Norte, and, with the American coastline so big and the US Coast Guard so small, they only sometimes get caught. Although the Americans have planted spies in Havana in the hopes of identifying the smugglers."

"How do you know so much about it?"

"My cousin Hector owns one of those boats. Besides, bartenders like me know everything worth knowing in Havana."

I intended to crew on a rumrunner to the US shore after I found an obliging captain—perhaps Javier's cousin—and, assuming I wasn't thrown to the fishies, return to Havana in one piece.

Javier said, "Would you care for the service of a limousine while you are in Cuba? My cousin Ernesto is in the business."

"Sign me up, Javier."

"Then have a panatela on me. I get them wholesale. Another of my cousins is in the cigar trade."

We docked at the Sierra Maestra terminal across from the Plaza de San Francisco in La Habana Vieja, where I bid adios to Javier. Customs was a joke. Cuban officialdom was delighted to have us and waved the eager, thronging passengers through, showering us with rose petals. The *Sun* had a stringer in Havana, but I figured I'd stay clear of him so that my undercover status wouldn't be jeopardized.

Javier's cousin Ernesto skillfully chauffeured me to my hotel through the winding, cobbled streets and colonial plazas of the city's oldest section with its venerable cloistered churches, narrow alleyways bedecked with laundry flapping out to dry, and balconied casas with old men in suspenders playing dominoes on the sidewalk. And, incongruously, a ragged hurdy-gurdy man with a fez-wearing monkey on a leash begging with a tin cup. Cuba may have become a trap for American tourists in desperate need of quenching their thirsts, but real people lived there as well.

The tiled Moorish facade of the Hotel Sevilla was ornamented with double arches, columns, and mosaics. Its American parent, the Biltmore chain, had added a ten-story wing, where I opted for a seventh-floor suite. I wanted to arrive in style as part of my pose, and the limo provided the perfect touch. I was effusively greeted by the lobby crew like the fabulously wealthy American jackass I'd made myself out to be. In addition, I'd had embossed business cards printed with a bogus Boston address and my alias *Niles Tinsley Aldrich IV* below which were the words *Entrepreneur, Investor, Philanthropist*. I ostentatiously passed out the cards to everyone from desk clerk to maître d'hôtel to dishwasher to shoeshine boy. You never knew.

Dalilah was to wire me at the Sevilla in care of said Niles Tinsley Aldrich IV, and her telegram was waiting for me at the front desk. I would meet her the following day at Rancho Boyeros Airport, nine miles southeast of the city. I wondered how she arranged it. Pan American Airways was still hashing out details of its new flying clipper service to Cuba, but for now only operated a Key West to Havana mail route.

I was welcomed to my plush Sevilla suite with a bottle of champagne on ice and an enormous basket of flowers and sweets, a nice upgrade from my Biddle Street hovel. After a dip in the outdoor pool, a therapeutic massage from a giantess who sang to me a beautiful song she called "Son de la Loma," and a rejuvenating nap, I beelined it to the Roof Garden to partake of intoxicants—just as the Caribbean sun submerged in brilliant streaks of reds and purples.

At the bar, I encountered a delighted Javier, who embraced me like a long-lost cousin, of which, as it turned out, he had many. His enthusiasm was energized by my slipping him a friendly roll of DuPonts, modest by American standards—but US currency, more powerful than the Cuban peso, went a long way in Havana.

He said, "My customers from El Norte love my mojitos and daiquiris, but for you, I mix my specialty, a careful blend of ron añejo, vermouth blanc, Curaçao, grenadine, and a secret ingredient. It is called the cóctel colosal mortal. It will put you to ease, make you cheery, and calm your nerves. Cuba is a nation that runs on rum, and you will love the island so much you will never want to leave."

It took a mere two sips for me to find that Javier was unerring about both his cóctel colosal mortal and the island. As dusk assembled the stars and the Caribbean breeze caressed my flesh, faraway America seemed like a grim, forbidding fortress, filled with rage and guns and Jim Crow and desperate lives and awful food and the criminalizing of cocktails.

It was through Javier that I met a cordial expatriate American, Henry Kime, and his companion, Mary O'Kane, Venezuelan and ex-wife of an American engineer. Adoring Havana so much, the two were there to stay. Kime was vague on what he did, other than to say he enjoyed a bit of family money and owned a house in Miramar that came with a Chinese chef. His biggest vices, he told me, were driving a canary-yellow convertible Packard Tourister at top speed and smoking imported Turkish cigarettes. O'Kane worked with Kime in some fashion, but it wasn't clear in what way.

Following a few rounds of cóctel colosal mortals, and after Kime and O'Kane bid adieu, Javier said, "The night still holds promise, Señor Niles, so may I recommend the roulette wheel at our newest casino, Take the Gold, where my uncle Nestor is a pit boss? Or perhaps the ladies might interest you, in which case I suggest the Smiling Mustache, where you should ask for my cousin Imelda. She is head procuress there, and she will make sure you meet the most shapely *jineteras* in all of Havana."

"A show perhaps?" I said.

"Ah, the Tropic Thunder has the most stupendo music and dancers in the entire West Indies. One of my older brothers Estevan is the stage manager and he will sit you at the choicest table. Or maybe another kind of show, all live on stage: girls and or boys in any combination, even a celebrated collie who performs admirably. It is where my sister Tranquila is the overseer, and she will sit you close enough to touch."

"I think I'll save that for my to-do list."

"The fights, maybe. We got bare-knuckle, kick boxing, luta livre, jai-alai, and if you like animals, dog fights, rat fights, cockfights. No more bullfighting though. It is too cruel—to the toreador. If you desire to hit the pipe, we got opium dens in our Chinatown, Barrio Chino de La Habana. A third cousin of mine is half-Chinese. Goes by the name of Chin."

"It seems you have a large family, Javier. Hope there's no bed shortage."

"It is big, Señor Niles, which is why I can get you whatever you want, wherever you want, and when you want it."

"I'd like to meet your cousin Hector."

"You would like a cruise in his boat around Havana Harbor?"

"Quite a bit farther. I'll also be looking into some nice investment opportunities. The liquor export business, perhaps, for pharmaceutical and philanthropic purposes, of course. I need to meet the necessary people."

"Señor Niles, fortunes are to be made in Havana—if the right person has the right amount of funds to put up. President Machado is holding a reception at his palace this very week. He encourages all sorts of investment opportunities throughout Cuba. One of my cousins, Amador, is a secretary to the president. I will see that you receive an invitation."

"Along with a guest?"

"Certainly."

"Have I given you my business card?"

"You have, Señor Niles, and your card will take you far."

"Have a few more. I've got plenty."

Javier always referred to me by my first name, a form of comity all of his family members would apply toward me and Dalilah—which I liked.

---

I had engaged Javier's cousin, Ernesto, to remain on call for me, and the next afternoon we headed out in his limo to Rancho Boyeros Airport. There was little traffic on the dusty road. The terrain was mostly flat with leafy, undulating tobacco and black bean crops growing in the copper-colored soil. Occasional farmhouses with roofs of thatched palms and shaded by banana and coconut trees were a sharp contrast to the teeming streets of Havana.

Ernesto was a graceful singer and entertained me in a lovely tenor as he drove.

> El arroyo que murmura y que la luna retrata,
> Cuando sus rayos de plata, atraviesan la espesura.
> El sinsonte de voz pura, que alegra el monte y el llano.

"Which in English, Señor Niles, is about a murmuring stream and the silver rays of the moon that reveal a thicket in which a mockingbird sings in a pure voice, cheering the mountains and the plains as well as a palm that sways in the wind."

"I didn't fully grasp all the Spanish, Ernesto, but the sentiments are beautiful."

He pointed out the sights as he drove, notably Oriental Park Racetrack where a little over a decade earlier, Jess Willard, a Kansas cowboy, knocked out the invincible black Galveston Giant Jack Johnson to claim the world heavyweight championship. The kayo came in the twenty-sixth round of the scheduled forty-five-round bout to the satisfaction of the white bigots wanting to dispel the myth of an invincible black boxer.

Because most visitors to Cuba debarked by ship, Rancho Boyeros Airport was not a hive of activity as I waited on the tarmacadam for Dalilah's arrival. When a high-wing monoplane taxied in on the airport's single runway, I figured it had to be her.

She alighted in the company of a lanky man with a patch over his left eye: Wiley Post. I recalled my skepticism when she claimed that Wiley had flown her to LA from San Simeon. As usual, Dalilah dressed the part. No flapper pose this time, she was garbed cunningly in a pilot's outfit, which included a leather helmet, goggles, knickers, and boots.

I said to Wiley, "Must have been a long flight from California to Cuba. How did you stay awake?"

"We did a bit of barnstormin' on the way," he replied in his Texas-Oklahoma drawl. "Picked up a little extra cash. Almost like my flyin' circus days with Burrell Tibbs and his Texas Topnotch Fliers."

"Is there a lot of engine noise in the cockpit?"

"Say again? Can't hear too good."

"I said a limo is waiting to drive us into the city."

"Can't stay, pardner. Gotta fuel up *Winnie Mae* here and head back to Key West for a few repairs. I'm modifyin' this old Lockheed Vega, gittin' it ready for a flight around the world. If Lucky Lindy can fly solo from New York to Paris in thirty-three hours with just a single tuna sandwich—and get hisself a big ticker-tape parade—I figure I'll be able to aviate the world's first solo flight with a thermos of tomato juice, a few packs of gum, and a carton of zwieback."

We watched Wiley soar from the landing strip into the air, tilting *Winnie Mae*'s wings to say so long before turning into a speck in the cloudless, Caribbean blue. Dalilah told me he lost his eye in a drilling rig accident when he was working in the Texas oil fields.

"He bought an old Canadian-built Canuck with the insurance money. Only went as far as the sixth grade, but he has a certificate from the Sweeney Automobile and Aviation School in Kansas City."

I said, "Not sure I want to fly in one myself. Those crates sometimes come down hard."

"Not if Wiley's the pilot."

It would not be the last I saw of Wiley Post.

As we rode into Havana, Dalilah asked the inevitable: "So who's this Niles Tinsley Aldrich IV, care of the Hotel Sevilla, I've been sending wires to?"

"Me. Actually, not me. Not the real me anyway."

I went through the convoluted process of explaining my role as a newshawk who used various pseudonyms, not the least of which were Wilson Collison and Tommy the Choirboy, to go undercover to look for more than back-page fodder, finally disclosing that Gart Booker Asquith III was my actual moniker.

"Although Henry thinks Gart is crude and calls me Taggart. But for our time in Cuba, best to get into the habit of calling me Niles."

Instead of being sore by my deceptions, Dalilah was amused, accustomed to an occasional artifice of her own. I also revealed that my mother was of mixed race, allowing me to claim I was part negro, thus accounting for my slightly tawny complexion, which most people assumed was simply from the sun. It was how I'd been able to infiltrate the KKK, I explained.

"You'll have your own room in our suite at the Sevilla," I said.

"Am I to play the role of your faithful wife?"

"Mistress, I think. Faithful or not. All dolled up and out for the hunt. It'll make me seem more convincing as a fat-cat American on the town and looking for deals."

She said, "If I get you through this exploit will I get a byline too?"

"Um, I'll have to think about that."

"I'm getting thirsty. Did you bring your flask?"

"We're not in America, Dalilah. No need for flasks here. I understand the priests at Catedral de San Cristobal, where Christopher Columbus's remains were once interred, keep an open bar. They call it holy water—although my source was drunk at the time. We'll stop on the way; however, champagne on ice awaits in our suite."

"Did I see your nostrils flare like Rudolph Valentino's, Niles?"

———

Ernesto claimed us for the short haul to the Palacio Presidencial at Calle Refugio No. 1, even though it was within walking distance from the Sevilla. On Calle Colon, we passed what was left of a building, now a gaping hole of rubble, still smoldering, guarded by police.

"What happened here?" I asked Ernesto. "Looks like some sort of explosion."

"The work of the Abecedario, known as the ABC, revolutionaries who are trying to do away with Machado and his henchmen. Until yesterday, there had been a flower shop here. One of Machado's accomplices, a captain named Herrera, was lured to the shop thinking it was an arsenal for the ABC. Instead, he triggered a boobytrapped bomb, and now there is not enough left of Herrera for his mother to bury.

"And that is not all, Señor Niles. The ABC is taking responsibility for gunning down Clemente Vazquez Bello, one of Machado's closest allies, as he was leaving the Yacht Club, still in his boating shoes. But you do not have to worry. The ABC is not after visitors such as yourself and Señorita Dalilah."

"Why are they called the ABC?"

"It is a society so secret even its own members do not know the names of the others. They identify themselves only by designations like A-1, B-3, C-6. That way, if La Porra tortures them, they can only reveal letters and numbers, not names."

"You seem to know a lot about them."

"When you drive people from place to place, as I do, you overhear many things. Me and my cousins are very well informed."

Dalilah said, "And what's this La Porra?"

"It is President Machado's secret police, which has powers even the regular authorities and the military do not have. Very, very dangerous. They will kill anyone, important or not, who publicly opposes Machado. Which is why there are few street demonstrations anymore, although the students at the university are quite agitated. Sometimes people just disappear never to be heard from again. But everyone knows La Porra is responsible."

I said, "I get the impression you're not enthusiastic about Machado."

"He is a criminal. Before he joined the war against Spain and became a brigadier general, he was a cattle thief. Then he ran a sugar mill and later an electric company. Mysteriously, all the records exposing his criminality were destroyed in a fire. After he became president, he decided Cuba's term limits need not apply to him. So he rewrote the constitution to give himself six more years in office. Again, do not concern yourself, Señor Niles. I am sure he will be very, very *simpático* to you."

Machado's palace was a domed edifice with lavish European touches. Although jaded by the wonders of Hollywood and Aimee Semple McPherson's temple of grandeur, I was duly impressed by this Caribbean marvel. Dalilah and I were dressed to make a splash, I in an elegant three-piece, doubled-vested worsted. She, wearing a bejeweled head band, was stunning in a short paisley dress with sequined bat sleeves and a plunging V-neck.

After being escorted inside by a file of saber-bearing military officers, bolstered by a contingent of heavily-armed coppers, we were greeted by Amador, another of Javier's cousins, an impeccably-garbed man with a neat mustache.

"Señor Niles, I presume, and your lovely guest, Señorita Dalilah," he said, bowing formally. "As the president's social secretary, let me say we are delighted to have so prominent an American visitor. My cousins have told me all about you. Allow me to escort you to the Salon de Espejos where President Machado is most anxious to make your acquaintance."

As we followed Amador and his retinue, Dalilah hissed at me, "Try not to talk too much like a hick, Niles, or they may find out you are one."

I whispered back, "It's my shtick. I want 'em to think I'm easily conned."

"That shouldn't be difficult."

Dalilah adopted her dumb-blonde act.

The Salon de Espejos had been built to make an impression, although I was uncertain why it was necessary in a relatively poor island nation that was often one hurricane away from disaster. The room's arched windows, mirrored surfaces, glowing chandeliers, and marbled panels were dizzying. The complexity of it made it hard for me to focus on Machado, not to mention the fact that, as a dictator, he was unassuming. His ordinary face and high forehead were accented by round tortoise-shell eyeglasses, and I noticed he had only three fingers on his left hand, the result, as I later learned, of a misapplied cleaver while working at a butcher shop in his youth. He was effusive as Dalilah and I were introduced.

"We adore our American visitors," he said, trying to polish me like an apple. "And I assure you, we Cubanos will make certain your stay here is pleasant and productive. We especially admire distinguished and, shall I say, *substantial* personages from Boston."

Batting her eyelashes, Dalilah said, "Gosh, y'all sure do have an impressive house, Mr. President. How many rooms you got?"

"There are thirty-eight. Here on the ground floor, in addition to our Salon de Espejos, we have the Golden Hall, the chapel, and the meeting room of the Council of Ministers. The main telephone exchange is here and the city's power plant. And in the rear is a stable for the police horses and a barracks for my, shall we say, safety inspectors."

"I adore your floors."

"You are quite perceptive, Señorita Darling. Most people would not notice such things. The floors and staircases are made with the famous Carrara marble of Italy. Tiffany and Company in New York created all of the interiors. And the room in which we are standing was designed to resemble the Hall of Mirrors in the Palace of Versailles, France."

"And it's *sooo* big!"

Machado all but blushed. "With its great dome, from which can be seen lovely views of the Harbor, my palace is the tallest structure in Havana."

She said, "I guess your personal quarters are upstairs. I mean, with your bed 'n' all?"

"Indeed. I would enjoy showing it to you personally." He cleared his throat. "Perhaps later."

I said, "We don't have anything this grand back home. Of course, our public library is nothing to sneeze at, but still… Being from Boston, Mr. President, I appreciate Havana's old-world flavor."

"We Latins are proud of our heritage. Did you know that the first book to be published in the Americas was not in what would become the British colonies but in Mexico City in fifteen-thirty-nine?"

"Golly," Dalilah said, "do you mean an actual, real book like with words?"

Machado chuckled. "Yes. A printing house in Seville, Spain, sent an Italian named Giovanni Paoli to Mexico City to open a branch. The first book he published was entitled *Breve y más compendiosa doctrina Christiana en lengua Mexicana y Castellana*, which translates in English as *A Brief and more compendious Christian doctrine in the Mexican and Spanish language*."

"I'd just love readin' it sometime."

"Alas, no copies are known to exist."

I said, "Mr. President, you may have heard how open I am to business opportunities here in Cuba."

"My aide Amador has informed me of your interest in investing in the Pearl of the Antilles, Señor Aldrich, which we welcome enthusiastically."

"Perhaps sugar, although I heard that your sugar exports have been off."

"No, no, no. It is true, that sugar prices did fall, but they have now fully recovered. It is a marvelous investment. I should know. Before I engaged in politics, I operated a sugar enterprise known as the Central Carmita. The business climate here is superb. New hotels and casinos are opening right and left. I have just built the longest road in all of Cuba, the Carretera Central, which runs the entire length of the nation from La Fe to Baracoa. I also ordered the construction of a new national capitol building, designed to resemble your capitol in Washington. And it was I who commissioned the bronze sculptures of lions along the Paseo del Prado."

"But, of course, getting here from the States will always be a bit thorny. You are an island, after all."

"But not that remote, Señor Aldrich, as you may know. Pan American Airlines is about to begin a new passenger service from Key West to Havana, and in my honor, it is naming the plane the *General Machado*. Not only do we have regular ferry service from the major ports in Florida and New Orleans, but the West India Fruit and Steamship Line is operating a railroad ferry from Miami to Havana, which means visitors never have to leave their passenger compartments to arrive from across the sea in comfort."

"You've certainly convinced me, Mr. President. And when I come across the right opportunity, a generous finder's fee is involved—if you catch my drift."

"Indeed. I shall have Amador make all the arrangements on your behalf. You will meet the island's most esteemed business executives. And I guarantee that your government in Washington very much approves of my administration."

"But there is one troubling item. I understand a terrorist group called ABC is going around setting off bombs and shooting people on the street."

"Do not bother yourself about it, Señor Aldrich. It is a tiny, pesky group of troublemakers who are of no threat to our American guests. They are simply gnats that are being slapped away. I assure you we have ways of dealing with them and those who support them."

It was then I fully noticed any number of burly men garbed in tight-fitting suits who seemed to be stationed in strategic locations throughout the Salon de Espejos. Clearly, they weren't tourists.

"La Porra?" I asked Machado as I nodded toward the brunos.

"Safety inspectors," he replied. "For everyone's protection."

The presidential reception was crowded, but I saw two familiar faces: Henry Kime and Mary O'Kane, whom I'd met at the rooftop bar at the Sevilla. We struck up a conversation and Kime suggested we leave for drinks at Los Jardines de la Tropical, a beer garden along the nearby Almendares River. The grounds were scattered with waterfalls, fountains, gazebos made of poured concrete, and a large dance pavilion. Our drinks were strong, the music infectious, and Kime and O'Kane knew everyone in sight.

Kime, who claimed to have a little vaudeville experience, seemed to hold his firewater well, even when he climbed on the table to sing William Shakespeare:

*And be you blithe and bonny,*

*Converting all your sounds of woe*

*Into hey nonny, nonny.*

*Hey Nonny Nonny*

*Hey Nonny Nonny*

*Hey Nonny Nonny*

*Hey Nonny Nonny*

*Hey Hey Hey*

Dalilah and I were making progress.

She asked me after we returned to our suite, "Are you keeping notes?"

"In my spiral notebook, which I hide under my mattress."

"Don't lose it, Niles. If anyone finds it…"

---

The glow from the slot machines was what you first noticed when you waltzed into Take the Gold Casino on Calle Empedrado, Havana's newest, swellest, swankiest gambling destination. Its floors, walls, and draperies were of deep shades of crimson with velvet ropes suspending gargantuan crystal chandeliers from the gilded, frescoed ceilings. The slots clanked, clinked, and clattered, but the players at the one-armed bandits were silent and grimly intent, anticipating a jackpot that rarely came.

A sea of hopeful humanity jammed the gambling tables in the cavernous main room. It was all roulette, baccarat, craps, blackjack, tuxedos, evening gowns, martinis, champagne, and Gauloises distributed by leggy cigarette girls in high-topped boots. The communion of jazz, live, floated in from the lounge. I recognized Zez Confrey's "Kitten on the Keys."

The mob, down from New York, ran this joint. They intended it to be a class act, bad taste or not.

I was spiffy as all get-out in a tux with a white vest, starched collar, black bow tie, and pocket square, my hair slicked back. Dalilah provided a flash of color in a canary-hued, backless straight cut with a mondo bow at the waist. A jeweled headband gave her the look of an Egyptian princess. For emphasis, she waved like a baton her unlit gasper in an opera-length cigarette holder.

Javier's Uncle Nestor turned out to be more than a mere pit boss at the Take the Gold Casino. He was the boss of all pit bosses and was well compensated. Habaneros employed by the American casinos were paid in US dollars, not the weaker Cuban peso.

"Señor Niles, your reputation precedes you," Nester said. "I am told that President Machado speaks highly of you, and I assure you that here at the Take the Gold Casino your every desire will be met. And Señorita Dalilah, you grace our humble casino with your beauty."

Dalilah beamed. "This here place is the bee's knees."

I said, "Nestor, as you know I'm seeking investment opportunities, so I'd like to have an audience with the in-crowd."

"It has already been arranged. I will escort you to a very private room for serious baccarat players only. You may conduct business there uninterrupted with, as you say, the in-crowd. Perhaps, Señorita Dalilah, you would enjoy a special game of American roulette while Señor Niles is occupied."

The mob was strictly a man's bastion.

She said, "I'll just leave you big, busy men to all your boring old business talk, probably stinking up the place with your nasty cigar smoke. Niles, deary, meet me at the roulette table after you're done. And how's about givin' me a little extra sugar to play with? I'll miss you."

I passed her a roll of DuPonts. She blew me a kiss.

"Ciao."

The private room was empty of dealers smoothly shuffling cards and placing chips at the oval baccarat pulpit. It was being used as a conference table, around which sat half a dozen bozos puffing on panatelas. I knew hoods when I saw them, having, in the line of duty, infiltrated the Capone mob, and these palookas with their bent noses, glad rags, and pinkie rings were no exception. Save for one. He was short, alpine forehead, beaklike nose, eyeglasses thick as tea cups, and looking almost like the dazed academics I'd see walking across the campus at Johns Hopkins.

Nester said, "Señor Niles, let me introduce you to Señor Chaim Blum of New York, who will make the other introductions. Adios, señores. Vaya Con Dios."

With that, Nester took a powder, leaving me to make nice with this racketeering array.

Blum, the man in the specs, said, "Mr. Aldrich, my associates and I are all principals in Take the Gold and other casinos, hotels, and entertainment venues here in Havana. But we're always seeking new investors to join us—as silent partners, of course. Silent?"

I said, "I'm all about discretion."

He went around the table introducing me to the gathering, their last names I mentally recorded for my notebook: Ajello, Bianchi, De Luca, Segreto, O'Malley.

Blum said, "A few of the others couldn't be with us just now, notably Lansky and Luciano who are tied up in New York, but they're here in spirit. Please, take a seat, Mr. Aldrich. Let me pour you a glass of imported Amarone della Valpolicella from nineteen-twenty, which was a superb year."

I quipped, "A a superb year for the wine, but not for America's wine drinkers. The Eighteenth Amendment and all."

One of the mugs, De Luca, said "I hear you're from Bean Town, but how's about Chi-town?"

"Chicago? Uh, never been there. So much violence I understand."

"Well, I been there and you look a little like some wiseacre I saw that was connected to Al Capone. It was in a speakeasy called the Four Deuces on South Wabash."

I chuckled nervously.

"That wouldn't be me. Obviously. I've never met the gentleman or been to the—what?—Four Deuces. But I've certainly heard of him. We do receive the newspapers in Boston, notably the *Globe*, which has the city's finest society pages."

De Luca said, "Capone's gonna be arrivin' here in Cuba at the end of the week. He'll be shackin' at the Hotel Sevilla. Word's got it, him and his mugs is gonna take over the entire sixth floor in that new wing."

"Capone? Sevilla?"

"You look a little agitated, but we ain't gonna let no Chicago punks do us no dirt or muscle us out of our territory. New York's got this here place locked up, and we don't need no outside competition from Capone."

My stomach sank. Capone and I would be staying in the same hotel in the same wing with my floor directly above his. What if he recognized me as the Tommy the Choir Boy who dished out vittles in his soup kitchen and tossed medicine balls to him for exercise? Not to mention my nabbing Fats Waller to entertain at Al's birthday party in Cicero. I'd be found out, my cover here blown. And he'd certainly recognize Dalilah, whose twin sister was offed by a rival mobster who was deep-sixed by Al's guys. Plus Capone, who always looked for his name in the papers, might associate the guy he knew as Tommy the Choirboy with my *Sun* scoop about the syndicate. It would dash my Cuba investigation—and maybe even give me the big adios. The walls were closing in.

But I played it with my usual aplomb, saying, "From what I've read, Mr. Capone appears to have a somewhat tarnished reputation."

De Luca said, "That what you call it? Tarnished? The prick's got a bad rap, but he's still a bum. Anyhow, it don't matter. He ain't movin' into Cuba. We don't want no gang war. Bad for the bottom line. Down here we're considered legit."

"But how would you keep Mr. Capone out?"

"We got amigos in high places. That's why we don't need a bunch of triggermen down here—except once in a while to fit cement shoes on a double-crosser. Machado's on our payroll and he's got tons of muscle behind him. To make him happy we gave him an honorary gold key to our casino. Also, the government of our own US of A has plenty of pull here and it don't wanna see nothin' stirred up. 'Cept maybe about the rumrunners to America—although that ain't happenin' yet. Hey, Chaim, I ain't speakin' out of turn am I?"

"Not at all," Blum replied. "As a potential investor, Mr. Aldrich needs to know the facts, and nothing here said today will leave this room. Perhaps, gentlemen, now that our distinguished visitor has been edified, we should get down to business. Mr. Aldrich, what have you to say to *us?*"

Without hesitation I said, "It's all about ducats, shekels, folding stuff, mazuma, and long green. It's why I crossed the Straits of Florida to get here. However, Mr. Blum, so I know who I'm talking to, what exactly is your role in your organization?"

"I pulled strings to get us established here. Some of my associates from up north excel in Tommy guns and getaway cars, but I prefer calculators and tabulating numbers. The Habaneros sometimes refer to me as

Pequeño Genio, even though my formal education stopped by the eighth grade. My colleagues at this table are the heads of various enterprises in New York, where Prohibition proved to be quite profitable."

De Luca said, "With America on the skids, Cuba's got unlimited possibilities. We was all competitors in the past, but we're now united as a single operation, all sharin' in the spoils. A lot of us mugs even bought homes here in Cuba, mostly in Mariano, which ain't far from La Playa Beach. It demonstrates our commitment."

Blum said. "Now let me ask *you* a question, Mr. Aldrich. Your interests are…?"

"Alcoholic spirits. I'd like to get involved in the export-import business. America remains fertile ground for the right goods. Also, it seems the time for investment in Havana real estate is opportune. I'm hoping I can still get in on that new Nacional de Cuba hotel."

"If I may be so bold, just how much are you planning to invest?"

"I think I'll start small just to see where it leads. Say one, perhaps two."

"Two…?"

"Million, of course. Three, maybe. Depends on how it goes."

The hoods eyeballed one another, impressed as hell.

Blum said, "We shall meet further to sort out the details, Mr. Aldrich. And let me emphasize that all we discuss here is privileged, with everything that implies. In the meantime, may I pour you another glass of Amarone della Valpolicella, as well as offer you a cigar? Not just any cigar, but a Hoyo de Monterrey, which is what you smoke if you want to feel like a Cuban."

De Luca said to me, "You sure you never been to Chicago?"

---

My mind was a morass of confusion as I worked my way through the wagering throngs to where Dalilah was playing roulette, the ball clicking as it bounced hypnotically along the circling wheel's rim. She was in the company of our new friends, Kime and O'Kane. The pout on Dalilah's face seemed to look as if she'd lost every DuPont I'd given her to play with.

I said, "That's why it's called a game of chance, doll, and why the best chance is always the house's."

Her sour expression dissolved into a grin.

"It was duck soup, Niles. I didn't quite break the bank. But how does five grand sound?"

"Five grand as in w-i-n-n-e-r?"

"Let's just say the paella's on me. That's a lot of kale."

"A year's salary."

It was a cheerful bit of news that accompanied the four of us into the lounge where the jazz was holy and where Dalilah splurged on the drinks. But after she and I returned to our suite the euphoria wore off as I told her about Capone's imminent arrival.

"We'll have to bail from the Sevilla," I said. "We can't risk being spotted by Capone and his cronies. Our cover will be blown—and for me, maybe for all time."

"But we've made our base here. We have all these contacts, particularly with Javier and his family and with Henry Kime and Mary O'Kane. It's where we get our mail and telegrams."

"What's the alternative?"

"Disguises. In Chicago. everyone knew me as a blond. What if I suddenly turned into a brunette? You have dark hair. What if it changed blond? And how about your wearing a little paste-on mustache that you can take on or off? You'd appear almost Cuban. We'll look so far out of context Capone and his crew won't recognize us."

The gal had brains, looks, and style. But she wanted to share my byline, and I wasn't sure I'd go that far.

Ultimately, we decided to hole up in our suite and exist on room service. But Capone had to cut his visit short, so our exile didn't last long. We got the juicy details from Javier over cóctel colosal mortals at the Roof Garden.

Al and his entourage, arriving in a private plane from Miami to Rancho Boyeros, decided to check out a pool hall near Oriental Park Racetrack. He thought he might use it as a front for his bootlegging operations. But it didn't take long for him to learn the potential was lousy. The New York syndicate was simply too well established. In the final analysis, Al was both a businessman and a realist. Traveling with Al was my old crony Two-Fingers McCord, who'd helped me snatch Fats Waller and who nailed the killer of Dalilah's sister Dolly. It would have been nice to share a few with Two-Fingers, but it was not to be.

After checking into Room 615 at the Sevilla, Al went to the Gran Teatro de La Habana to watch the tenor Francesco Dominici perform as Rodolfo in Puccini's *La bohème* followed by a crawl through the Tropical Gardens and a blur of other cabarets. At six the following morning, he was coarsely awakened by Machado's secret cops, who claimed the American Embassy wanted him third-degreed about rumors Al was planning a bombing spree to celebrate May Day—or wherever day Capone intended. He prudently departed Cuba by air that afternoon.

In a way, I was sort of sorry I didn't run into Al. I almost liked him. He wasn't all *that* bad—for a mobster. He may have put some of his competition into cold storage, but he never robbed Wells Fargo. As far as I knew.

---

Most of all, Cuba was music.

And dance.

In Havana, the Tropic Thunder on Calle Progreso was el supremo. The music began with a native ensemble consisting of multiple congas, chekerés, claves, and cowbells. Who would have thought such instruments of rhythmic percussion could produce an African-Cuban beat so infectious you never wanted it to end? It quickened your heart and rattled your bones long after the percussionists had packed away their instruments.

As Javier promised, his older brother Estevan, the nightclub's stage manager, had made sure we occupied table numero uno, best in the house, center front, close but not too close. A posse of waiters fetched outlandish cocktails decorated with fancy swizzle sticks and tiny umbrellas plus a never-ending aggregation of piquant hors d'oeuvres.

Dalilah and I, as usual, were in the company of the well-informed Kime and O'Kane along with several American tycoons who controlled anything producing a buck in Cuba: sugar, fruit, tobacco, mining, timber, rail, telephone, and power. US investors owned such a whopping slice of Cuba's agriculture and industry, it might have been Louisiana or Florida. The island was up for grabs.

Hobnobbing with these big kahunas was a shrewd move, or so I thought at the time, and I intended to make the most of it.

So far, the subterfuge Dalilah and I had perpetrated had taken us to the right places, and just the mere promise of our money—without actually spending it—drew suitors like a moth to flame or a fly to shit. Disengaging from our deceit might be a problem down the road, but for now, we were taking full advantage of it.

We were dressed for a casual night on the town, I in herringbone tweed with a club tie, even though I'd never belonged to a club, and she in a velveteen party dress accented with emerald and gold sequins.

Next to me at our table was a portly bigwig named Bathurst Wormwood, who'd been stuffing my ear with the illustrious history of his ancestors dating to the Norman Conquest and claptrap about his family crest and coat of arms. Wormwood was a pill, yet was potentially useful. He was not only president of the Consolidated Sucrose Corporation of America, which controlled the lion's share of Cuba's sugar production but was head of the spurious Cuba Development Association, an off-the-record cartel of entrepreneurially-oriented moguls whose decisions could make or break the island's economy.

The CDA made sure its officers, directors, and stockholders always scored first. It was hard to decide which had the most clout in Cuba: the mob, Uncle Sam, a president who elected himself, or the cartel. But one thing was certain: it wasn't the Cuban people.

However, such trifles were easily ignored at the Tropic Thunder, where the music was clamorous, the dancers spirited, and the audience—forgetting the Spanish flu epidemic from only ten years ear-lier—was packed into tables so closely aligned that the massive room seemed to be a single breathing entity.

The floor show opened with such subtly and beauty that I was unpre-pared for a pending spectacle that would put Florenz Ziegfeld to shame. It began with a plaintive ballad called "Siboney" sung by salon singer Rita Montaner, better known as Rita de Cuba, who was once married to bandleader Xavier Cugat:

> *Siboney, yo te quiero*
>
> *Yo me muero por tu amor;*
>
> *Siboney en tu boca*
>
> *La miel puso su dulzor*

Henry Kime whispered a translation for me, "It's either about a girl or maybe a place—I haven't decided—and how the singer would die for Siboney's love."

The beautiful name Siboney haunted me as the pace on the stage quickened and the song merged into a sensual tango performed by a bevy of elegant couples dressed in orange and yellow, the women in svelte, nar-row skirts that furled at the hemline, the men wearing vests and tight-fitting slacks that tapered to the calf.

Then the lights dimmed, the music faded, and… crash!

We heard an explosion of cymbals and watched pastel billows of mist enveloping the stage. Suddenly, the lights flashed on and off at their bright-est, roving in geometric circles as three dozen stiletto-heeled women in spectacular gowns emerged through the vapors, high-stepping in exuberant but precise choreographed formations. They were all smiles and teeth and boobs and legs and feathers and headdresses, some with faux wings on their backs, while acrobats on trapezes swung and swirled above their heads.

Thunder and lightning permeated the room like an intense summer storm with the orchestra reaching a full crescendo as the dancers kicked and somersaulted in perfect timing illuminated by multiple spotlights irradiating in searchlight patterns. Then instant blackness and stunned silence followed by wild applause.

Yipes, the show was incredibly tacky yet as colossal as the pending Second Coming of Christ—or perhaps the Folies Bergère in which Josephine Baker danced in a skirt consisting only of a string of bananas. The Havana crowds ate up the razzle-dazzle, and nothing on the mainland came close to it.

I pledged to name my first-born Siboney.

After the lights went up, we smoked and sipped our drinks as Bathurst Wormwood said, "I say, Aldrich, I see you're wearing a club tie. Choate, is it not?"

"Huh?"

"Or perhaps Phillips Exeter?"

"Well…"

"I went to Deerfield Academy myself, where they still remember me as Batty, before going on to Dartmouth. Hmmm. On second thought your tie appears to be that of one those clubs at Roxbury Latin. Have I got that right?"

"You're amazing. Roxbury Latin it is."

"And you went on to…?"

"Ah, Brown?"

"Decent enough school, I suppose. If you care for Rhode Island. Ever run into a chap named Boddington while you were there? Played rugby."

"Boddington? Indeed. Will never forget him."

"Wonder what he's up to these days?"

"Playing polo and living off his fortune no doubt."

"Thought he'd lost a leg. His horse fell on him."

"By jove, Mr. Wormwood, I must have been thinking of some other Boddington."

"Call me Batty."

"And I'm Niles."

Damn, I thought, how did I fall into that hole? And why the hell did I wear a club tie? Not that I knew what a club tie was, having dropped out of a second-rate theology school to work on a newspaper. The only club I'd ever been in was a handbell choir. And Brown…? My ass.

Wormwood, assuming he was talking to a kindred soul, wouldn't let up on me, but as a journalist and failed theological student, lying came easily to me.

He asked, "May I ask what branch of the Aldrich family you spring from?"

"The Dorchester branch, Batty. My lineage goes directly back to Sir Absalom Aldrich, who designed All Saints Church, Oxford, was canon of Christ Church, and author of two tracts in defense of Anglican principles. The first of the Aldriches in America settled in Massachusetts in sixteen-thirty-nine, although a distant aunt was hanged as a witch in Salem. Justifiably. She *was* a witch."

"Hear, hear," he said.

"But enough about me. I'm more interested in the Cuba Development Association, which I understand is doing marvelous work on the island. I'd like to know how I might support it."

"Shall we retire with our cocktails to a more sedate corner so that I may speak confidentially?"

After we repaired to a remote table near the bar, Wormwood said to me, "We are duty-bound to keep the local laborers under our thumbs and the hungry politicians well fed. The Bolshevists are attempting to incite the workforce after we imported lower-wage labor from Jamaica and Haiti to replace Cubans in the sugar mills, the fields, and the port. The Reds formed what they call CNOC, the Confederación Nacional Obrera de Cuba, to organize workers, unionists, and reformists of all stripes. Niles, all these loathsome communists want is more, more, more."

"Greedy bastards, Batty."

"As a result, we've had violent strikes by port and railway workers and even at my sugar works. Fortunately, Machado has come down hard on the unions, raiding their offices and jailing or deporting their leaders. One of them, a rabble-rouser named Alfredo López of the typographic workers, mysteriously disappeared, and there has been no sign of his remains."

"Good riddance."

"Then there was Enrique Varona, a railroad worker and union activist, who was gunned down by an unknown assassin."

"To your credit, I'm starting to suspect that the Cuba Development Association has played a positive role in all of this."

"Officially, the CDA exists as a humanitarian organization committed to stamping out poverty, educating youth, and promoting moral, Christian values. In other words, it aims to do away with any activity that threatens profits and disrupts production and output. We've imported certain specialists from the mainland to work secretly under our guidance, which is terribly expensive, and must, of course, be paid for off the books. Therefore, Niles, this is one area that could benefit from your support, monetarily or otherwise."

"I respect your candor in revealing these things, Batty."

"And I, speaking for the Cuba Development Association, appreciate your willingness to promote our cause, the details of which, of course, must remain confidential." He clapped me on my back. "We speak the same language—and we're from the same tribe, are we not?"

No, we were not, nor I would have wanted to be a part of the man's tribe any more than I needed a family crest and a coat of arms. The only crest in my world was the *Sun*'s masthead, which read *Light for All*. I suspected the henchmen Wormwood's cartel imported from the US also worked hand in bloody glove with Machado's La Porra.

"By the way," he said. "That Boddington chap we talked about? Now, as I think about it, his name was actually Baddington."

My interchange with Wormwood led me to believe I was witnessing two Cubas: the first in which decent people were simply struggling to get by; the second was of an island exploited for power and gain. I'd been reading a small book of poetry in translation composed by the martyred poet José Martí, who may have thought much the same when he wrote:

*I have two countries: Cuba and the night.*
*Or are they one? No sooner does the sun*
*withdraw its majesty than, dressed in long*
*veils with a carnation in her hand,*
*Cuba appears to me a silent widow.*

Overwhelmed by the regurgitating floor show at the Tropic Thunder, Dalilah and I in the company of Kime and O'Kane, ditched the oligopolists, and drove in Kime's yellow Packard to a small setting on San Ignacio near the docks: the Libido, where Javier's sister Tranquila was the overseer. As a theater in the round, the views of the performers were excellent from all angles. The room was relatively crowded, and the audience appeared to be mostly mainland tourists.

But the players were of mixed races and sexes who performed unashamedly in the buff, assuming a variety of poses while utilizing an eclectic array of toys and instruments, even a bathtub. The groupings of the entertainers were astonishingly varied and included couples, triples, and even larger aggregations arraying themselves in combinations and positions I had thought were humanly impossible. The performance of two midgets was particularly arresting. The lighting was excellent and the hall had fine acoustics.

Such displays in the repressed, puritanical States were unthinkable: the corrupt product of sinners and back alleys and dark basements with vice raids and jail terms an ever-pending threat. Nor were our books or magazines permitted to titillate. But when it came to titillation I was all for it. In literature in America, profanity did not exist—as if real people never spoke a dirty word. When actress Mae West got ten days in the bastille for corrupting the morals of youth after a few double entendres in her stage play *Sex* you had to wonder more about the mores of those who jailed her. Pockets within America's vast dominion believed that blasphemy was a crime against God as was the teaching of science. Life, for the rest of us, simply went on as best it could.

Still, to my mind, the Libido's bodily pageantry became repetitious and boring. After the performers reached their climaxes, retiring to the wings, and the porters emerged to mop the stage, we adjourned to the rooftop bar at the Sevilla for a round of Javier's cóctel colosal mortals. There, we compared critical notes on what we'd just seen.

Dalilah said, "The collie didn't do much for me but I thought the donkey performed admirably."

O'Kane said, "I feel it could have benefited from a little musical accompaniment by that old hurdy-gurdy man in Habana Vieja."

Kime said, "I thought the drinks were weak. I believe they shortchanged us on the booze."

We were all impressed by the size and stamina of a seven-foot-tall contortionist from Tanganyika sporting a bone through his nose, but we agreed that a substantial number of the women were simply too passive.

"Just going through the motions," Dalilah asserted with authority. "And some of the men took too long to get there."

Finally, the talk turned to Cuba and its tarnished sweetness. I pressed Kime, who never seemed to go to an office, on what he actually did in Havana as he'd been so reticent about it, and Mary too, since she worked with him.

Boozily, Kime said, "Don't suppose it'll hurt to tell you since the four of us have gotten on so famously, and it's unlikely you'll spill the old coffee beans."

He paused as a sly smile came to his lips.

"Mary and I are spies."

"Huh?"

"For America."

---

To say it was awkward to now socialize on friendly terms with Henry Kime was an understatement. I now wanted the goods on him for my story, and yet I didn't have the heart to blow his cover. I almost felt complicit even while, in my current guise, acting under the banner of a free press. To make it worse, I was about to crew on the *Indies Pearl*, the rum-runner owned by Javier's cousin, Hector. This while Kime's driving force was trying to crush those same rumrunners.

While Dalilah and Mary O'Kane were off shopping—or whatever gorgeous flappers on the loose did in Havana—Kime and I strolled along the sultry, tree-lined Paseo del Prado, which stretched up to El Malecón where the waves crashed over the seawall bringing the smell of salt and fish. After taking in the mansions of the decadent rich lining the boulevard and gawking at Machado's hideous bronze lions, we sat on one of the marble benches.

I said to him, "So you're spying in the name of the good old Red, White, and Blue. Engaged in depriving desperate, thirsty folks on the mainland of their meager rations of booze."

"Someone has to do it, Niles. God knows the incompetents in our State Department and the consular office here can't or won't."

"But *you* imbibe, Mary too. I've seen you, slightly tanked, mount a table and belt out 'Hey Nonny Nonny.'"

"Yep, like all but the most tightly wound, we also like to dip our bills. However, Prohibition's the law in the US, and laws, even bad ones, must be enforced or else all we'll have is lawlessness. I don't care for Prohibition any more than you do."

"So it's actual cloak and dagger stuff you guys do."

"A lot of it is paperwork: checking Customs declarations, clearance papers, cargo manifests, that sort of thing. But some of it is dangerous, which is why I carry a concealed pistol even though it violates Cuban law. The local constables, if they found out, would clap me in jail. I've had to pull my weight on any number of occasions to avoid the hoosegow without giving myself away. Also, I had to fashion my badge, since the powers that be in DC refuse to give me one."

"A toy sheriff's badge, which suggests that you're working on your own."

"Technically, a private contractor. You might say I'm a dry agent in charge of my own little bureau. I estimate there are three hundred vessels of all kinds now in Havana Harbor engaging in smuggling."

"Resulting in mucho moolah, I suppose."

"The best bootleg prices are name-brand imports from Scotland and France: White Horse, John Haig, Glenlivet, Martell. The lowest are for gin, which Americans can brew in their bathtubs, even though it may taste like piss."

"But booze is legal in Cuba, Kime, and so is its export. Not much you can do with your homemade badge."

"On the contrary. When a known rumrunner departs Havana Harbor we assume it's heading for the States with a cargo of contraband—even though it may carry a phony bill of laden claiming its destination is elsewhere. Mary and I chat up politicians, gamblers, port workers. We learn who's smuggling, where the goods are stored, on which boats the swag's loaded, when the runners sail from the harbor and return. Then we alert the US Coast Guard, which dispatches its cutters to engage the traffickers, arrest the crews, confiscate the ships, and destroy the cargo. A few shots over the bow usually stops the runners, and now the Coast Guard has bigger, faster boats that can overtake them."

"It's an awful large ocean out there for the Coast Guard to cover," I said.

"But a bit smaller now that the US has extended the three-mile limit to twelve."

"The Coast Guard was founded to provide safety and security on the nation's waters. How does it like acting like a police force?"

"They hate it. It fell to them by default, and they're undermanned and underequipped. Niles, did you know that smuggling liquor from Cuba to America adds up to half a million cases of alcohol a month? And because of me, we're making a dent in the trade. But do you think I get any thanks from our politicians in Cuba or Washington? Hell no. I'm doing it all on my own. I'm supposed to get a salary and expenses and enough money to hire a few extra agents, but I haven't been paid in months. Our government doesn't have its heart in liquor enforcement. So it does only what it has to do to keep the drys in the States happy."

"What's your pal Machado and his cronies doing, if anything?"

"Lip service. His government collects export duties on all ship traffic, which is especially lucrative on the best Cuban aguardiente and rum. The bastard knows he can't go too far in bucking the US, so if he plays ball the Americans leave him alone. Our country has no beef with dictators as long as they're *our* dictators. Anyway, why should Machado want to address a problem that's not Cuba's—nor that of most of the civilized world?"

"Cuba should tell America to go jump into the lake—or in this case the Caribbean."

"Won't happen. Ever since we first occupied the island, the US has held an outrageously unfair treaty over Cuba's head. It's named for a Senator Platt, which not only grants us a big military base in Guantanamo in perpetuity, it allows Washington to militarily intervene in Cuban affairs anytime it wants. Cubanos are rightly afraid that on some flimsy pretext, the Yankees may again occupy their land. It was bad enough when the Spaniards dumped on Cuba, but now the Yankees do it too."

"While you and Mary were trolling Havana's hot spots with us, Dalilah and I thought we were all just out for a good time."

"Everyone has a good time in Havana—except the Cubans. But for me, club crawling isn't *all* work. How about that seven-foot Tanganyikan with an appendage almost as long as his height?"

I stifled a laugh. "Yeah, his appurtenance was nearly as extravagant as the floor show at Tropic Thunder. Dalilah was especially impressed."

He'd been too candid with me, aching to share his story with someone he trusted, yet remaining dedicated to his mission: dismantling the rum-runners. I wondered if he'd pegged the schooner I'd be sailing on.

To celebrate my last night before shipping out, Dalilah and I went on the town, sans Kime and O'Kane, nearly breaking even at the casinos and blitzkrieging our way through the juice joints. We got back so late that I, heavy-lidded, skipped updating my notebook to include my conversation with Kime and turned on the snores.

It would be an oversight that saved his life.

———

Hector, the captain, thought my crewing on his schooner was the mere whim of some crazy, filthy-rich American eager for a bit of excitement and adventure. He tried to talk me out of it but changed his mind after I flashed a wad of DuPonts.

"It is dangerous, Señor Niles," he said, stogie chomped at the side of his mouth.

All he lacked was a peg leg and an eyepatch to make him look like Wallace Beery in *Treasure Island*—but the pollution from his cigar was so bad I was sure it couldn't have been rolled by Cubans.

"Anything can happen at sea," he growled. "You never know when a squall will come up. Or some competitor in the rum corridor tries to take your ship and cargo and throw you to the sharks. Or sink it to the bottom. Or the American Coast Guard seizes your ship and tosses the crew into a squalid jail somewhere in swamp-infested Florida."

"It's just what I'm looking for, Hector."

"It is merely a lark for you, is it not?"

"When I woke up this morning I couldn't decide whether I wanted to change the world or to go back to sleep. So I reckoned I'd just hop into your canoe."

"*Loco turista.* What do you know about being a hand on a sailing vessel?"

"Zero. Nor as a swab on any other kind of boat. But I figure that, unless I tap the keg too much, I can heft enough cases of rum to earn my salt."

"You could slow us down, get in our way, and become a problem. And I do not intend to be responsible for anything that happens to you. In fact, I might have to throw you overboard myself."

"All men are equal before fish, Hector, aside from the humpback anglerfish, but that's another story."

"I pay my crew good. Sixty American dollars a month. But I am paying you *nada*. It is you who pays me. Up front."

"Looks like we have a bargain, Hector. Shake."

"On board the *Indies Pearl*, you will refer to me as Captain."

"I've been brushing up on my nautical terms, *El Capitano*. So far, I've learned ahoy, anchor, and abandon ship."

"You may not think it so funny, Señor Niles, if we are hit by a gale and you are not only threatened with the loss of your cargo but also your *estúpido* life."

Newly minted as a deckhand, I reported to Tallapiedra Wharf at an inky, ungodly hour to labor with Hector's four-man crew, none of whom spoke English. The ninety-foot *Indies Pearl* started life as a fishing boat but running rum was more lucrative and certainly less mundane. Loading the ark proved to be back breaking, at least for one so quiescent as myself. Even though Hector pitched in, we were still lugging cases from the pier to the *Indies Pearl*'s lower deck as a glorious Caribbean sunrise flowered in the east—either the glory of God's grace or the simple refraction of the sun's rays as the earth revolved. I reckoned we moved a fifteen-hundred cases of imported top-label scotch, bourbon, rum, and cognac, plus two hundred kegs of malt. The ship was so weighted with cargo it sat low in the water.

Officially, as the clearance papers showed, we were off to Trujillo, Honduras, and Tampico, Mexico, with a cargo of three-hundred cases. Hector had fudged the customs numbers to avoid higher duties.

Just beyond the harbor, he checked his compass and altered course from west to north, straightaway to the southern US coast. He estimated the entire voyage, including contact and delivery, would take three days, barring unforeseen issues.

It was an old schooner, built long before the turn of the century, and it wasn't well cared for. The ship was badly in need of paint and some of the deck's planking had rotted. I hoped the hull was in better shape. It had been outfitted with an engine, which Hector ran to navigate from the harbor, through the channel, and into open water. He told me the second-hand motor—which he proudly described in boring detail as a 120-horsepower Fairbanks-Morse single-screw semidiesel—was reliable. Some of the time. The engine sputtered and spat, roaring like an enraged tiger, yet it somehow clung to life.

The first thing I noticed once at sea was the schooner's odor, which I would long remember, the sum of all that had come since the boat's first hour of christening. The briny stench of dead fish, of course, but also of decayed wood, mold, rotting canvas, diesel, linseed, pitch, turpentine, rubber, seawater, even of human waste and sweat. To a wine connoisseur, the myriad delicate nuances in a fine red or white might be detected, but there was nothing subtle in the effluvium of the *Indies Pearl*.

The water was choppy and I felt the rock and sway as the two-masted took on its sails. I tried to pitch in, but the skipper told me to keep my *norteamericano* hands off the *maldito* rigging and bone up on my *estúpido* nautical terms somewhere out of his sight. Hector liked my DuPonts but didn't care much for me. A seadog I was not.

Unlike the *Evangeline*, on which I arrived in Cuba, the *Indies Pearl* wasn't built for comfort, only speed and endurance with every available space, even a portion of the topdeck, loaded with cargo. Its only semblance of a head was a metal bucket, which Hector ordered dipped into the sea after the crew filled it. Mostly they relieved themselves over the rail. To sleep or rest meant reclining on the hard deck or trying to find small comfort by lying on the cases of hooch in the cabin below.

Hector hated palavering with me but grudgingly explained that the *Indies Pearl* planned to coordinate with the mainland's black-market mob, which would arrive in speedboats to claim the cargo. It was now harder to link up since the US had extended its territorial waters—not to mention more danger from the Coasties. The risks were greater, but so much dough was involved, it was worth the gamble.

Most of the time the voyage was boring—how much gazing at water from horizon to horizon is that interesting?—and I found myself using scrap paper to play tic-tac-toe with myself and losing. I noticed the crew, including *El Capitano*, freely ingesting more than a few nips from the cargo. One of the mates served as a kind of cook, heating over a camp stove on deck *arroz moro*—garlic, rice, and black beans—and dishing it out with metal spoons and plates.

Chomping on his usual stinking cheroot, Hector, at the wheel on the poop deck, motioned me over.

"Look to our stern, Señor Niles, and tell me what you see. No, I said *stern*, not bow. *Idiota*."

I did, but all my boneheaded, landlubbering eye saw was the usual expanse of sea. He tossed me a pair of binoculars.

"Look closer."

I saw what appeared to be a sail or sails.

He said, "We have been followed since we left port. I know that ship, the *El Diablo*. It is a three-masted with a bigger crew than the *Indies Pearl* and faster."

"Hijackers?" I said.

"*Ciertamente*."

Hector ordered one of the crew to take the wheel while he led me to a padlocked storage room below deck.

"Do you know how to use a gun, Señor Niles?"

"I saw William S. Hart shoot one in a Western once."

"You should learn. This is our arsenal."

I had packed a persuader in Chicago, but it was mostly for show.

He unlocked the door and displayed an array of munitions from gats to scatterguns to Chicago typewriters.

"I told you this is *peligroso*—dangerous—work, and every member of my crew is prepared to use these weapons in case of hijackers or if the American bootleggers refuse to pay cash up front. Once we've safely delivered our cargo to the whiskey peddlers, it is no longer our concern, and we return to Havana with mucho American dollars while not stinking of fish."

"What's that oddly shaped contrivance?" I asked. "Looks sort of like a stovepipe."

"It is a tube-fired rocket launcher developed by some Yankee named Goddard during your Great War with the Boche. The war ended before it saw action, and only a few were made. Some renegade dealer sold it to me as war surplus along with lots of rockets. It is called a bazooka because it resembles an *estúpido* musical instrument that is, by the grace of God, forbidden in Cuba. I have been practicing with it in the mangroves observed only by flamingos, and now is the opportunity to use it for real. And while there is still time, maybe you should practice with a revolver."

Hector saw me as some effete, moneyed Yankee, unprepared for a real *hombre*'s work, so I spent the afternoon fiddling with a British-made Webley semi-automatic, firing randomly at seagulls. But every seagull I shot at escaped my bullet, making it clear I'd never be a marksman. In disgust, Hector returned the revolver to the locked arsenal, explaining that he didn't fully trust even his own crew, much less than me.

He said, "Since the *El Diablo* has more sail than we got, it can catch us. But it does not have a motor like us, so we can escape if we use both sail and diesel. It thinks our engine is busted, as it often is, but you see it is working. However, I am inclined to let the pirates catch us."

"Why don't we take advantage of our speed and just vamoose?"

"To teach them a lesson. Would that be adventure enough for you, Señor Niles? You are paying for it, are you not? Do you not want to have some fun?"

"Not if it means landing in Davy Jones's locker, whoever Davy Jones is."

"If we go down, the *Indies Pearl* has a life raft. Unfortunately, there would not be enough room in it for you. If this old, rotten ship sinks, I have nothing to lose. My marine insurance is up to date and will more than cover the loss."

There was just so much an investigative reporter should expect while on assignment, and going down with the ship wasn't one. Alas, I couldn't just hop onto a Pullman and flee unless its wheels ran on water—although for True Believers, unlike me, anything under God was possible.

Hector killed the Fairbanks-Morse and ordered the crew to partially trim the schooner's sails to slow its speed, allowing the *El Diablo* to get ever close.

Until it was within hailing distance.

He then broke out the munitions and the crew trained their weapons on the interloper.

From the opposite deck, a man using a megaphone shouted to Hector, "Ship ahoy, heave to leeward and prepare your peccant, putrid scow for boarding."

Hector, also with a megaphone, answered in kind, "Damn your soul. By St. Boogar and all the saints at the backside of purgatory, I shall have thou hide if ye try to board."

I was hesitant to interrupt at a hairy moment like this but, baffled, I said, "*El Capitano*, what's with all the salty, old English lingo?"

"English is the language of the sea, is it not? Carlos and I have been speaking it since we played pirate as kids."

"Carlos? You *know* each other?"

"Of course. He is my cousin. We grew up in the village of Cojimar, where we played together in the old Spanish fort. Our fathers were fishermen. We *despreciamos*—despise—each other."

From the *El Diablo*, Carlos shouted, "Do not try to jaw me down, you sod-witted fustilarian. By thunderation, there shall be the devil to pay if ye do not comply."

Hector responded, "Ye best clear thou deck as I am about to trim thy sails, you moldy spotted toad."

"Bejabbers, you cream-faced loon, I shall deliver a broadside that will send your bucket to the bottom."

"You whoreson cullion, you were born to give our family shame. You shall not lay a hand on my cargo."

"Which you shall immediately transfer to the *El Diablo*, you lily-livered loitersack, after which I might allow you to sail on."

"Verily, we are at loggerheads, you defiler of all that is holy."

I was enjoying this colorful repartee until Hector ordered me to help him hoist the bazooka to his shoulder and arm it. It was heavy but he was more than *hombre* enough to heft it and, by his assertion, well practiced.

He said, "This will not be a warning shot, Señor Niles. I have had it with Carlos, who has insulted me and embarrassed our entire family."

Without another word he pulled the trigger.

The tube-fired rocket unleashed itself with a roar that struck the *El Diablo* middeck, resulting in a fiery explosion and blaze that instantly pitched the schooner to its side. If Carlos's crew intended to open fire on us, it was too late and forgotten as the men dived into the water to escape the inferno.

"Throw them lines," Hector ordered his crew.

In the end, the survivors, all eight of them including Carlos, were pulled from the sea and stood dripping on our deck as we watched the enkindled *El Diablo* slide to the bottom accompanied by a great slurping sound as it was swallowed.

Carlos snarled to Hector, "*Un burro ignorante.*"

Hector replied, "*Follador de cerdos,*" which by my faulty Spanish translated into "pig fucker."

"What will our Aunt Hermosa say when she learns you sank my ship using some sort of crazy canon?" Carlos said.

"She will say I am a brave and thoughtful nephew, a warrior, and a credit to our family."

"*Cabron.*"

"*Hijo de puta.*"

Hector ordered me to break into the cargo and pour rum for everyone, including our prisoners.

It was well after dark when we reached the territorial limit, arriving at the coordinates Hector had supplied to the American bootleggers, who, following a series of signals using lanterns, arrived in several speedboats.

When they climbed aboard, one of the hoods said, "You're fuckin' late."

Hector said, "We had to fight off pirates."

"We gotta work fast. We spotted two Coast Guard cutters in the area."

"But first you pay."

*El Capitano's* well-armed crew enforced his words. Hector put me and all our hands, as well as Carlos and the other captives, to work. By dawn, we'd offloaded the cargo. The bootleggers sped off, presumably to isolated inlets and shores along the coast where the booze would be conveyed to convoys of trucks and shipped to the parched cities of the States. Truly, a service to an America in need.

At dawn, we had barely begun our return to Cuba when we were intercepted by two US Coast Guard cutters, which fired a shot over our bow. The young captain of one of the vessels boarded the *Indies Pearl* demanding to see our papers. He carried only a sidearm, and, while outnumbered, appeared unintimidated by our tough-looking crew.

Hector said, "We are in international waters, lieutenant. You have no authority here."

"The canons my cutters have trained on your ship say we do."

"Why did you stop us?"

"We had reliable information from Havana that you'd be in this approximate location at about this time. I need to inspect your cargo hold."

I knew immediately the Coast Guard lieutenant was acting on information supplied by Kime and O'Kane.

Hector handed him the customs papers and bill of laden, then led him to the lower deck, now empty of cargo.

"What's in that padlocked storage area?" the lieutenant asked.

"Sporting equipment."

"Open it."

When he did, I observed the amazed expression on the lieutenant's face when he saw the munitions, including the bazooka and rockets.

"As I told you, lieutenant, sporting equipment."

He said, "Your papers show you had a shipment of liquor to Trujillo, Honduras, and Tampico, Mexico."

"Delivered."

"How do I know the papers aren't forged?"

"They have the seals of the customs agents."

"Which may also be forged."

"That would certainly be a surprise to me."

"Then what are you doing way up here? You're hundreds of miles off course."

"We got caught in a big gale and lost our compass."

"Also, I see you have an extraordinarily large crew for a schooner of this size."

"As Good Samaritans, we rescued a number of deckhands from a ship in distress."

"Personally, captain, I believe your *Indies Pearl* is a rumrunner, and one of these days we're going to catch you red-handed and confiscate your ship."

"You remind me of one of my nephews, lieutenant. I would like to offer you a drink. Unfortunately, I have no alcohol on board."

"And no compass. How will you find your way back to Havana?"

"Dead reckoning."

---

As soon as we docked at the Tallapiedra Wharf, where Hector was to load a fresh cargo, I called from a phone booth to tell Dalilah I was safely back and would join her shortly at the Sevilla.

"Niles, whatever you do, do *not* come back to the hotel. They found your notebook under the mattress and are looking for you."

"Who is *they?*"

"Everyone."

"Are *you* safe?"

"They think I'm just some helpless, deceived tootsie you're sleeping with."

"What's the plan?" I asked, feeling about as useful as a clock without hands.

"We need to leave town. Stay out of sight as best you can. La Porra has all the key places staked out. The gangsters are also looking for you. And so are certain associates of the Cuba Development Association."

"Had no idea I was so popular."

"I'll pick you up as soon as I make sure I'm not being followed."

"Ernesto's limo?"

"Absolutely not. They don't let Ernesto out of their sight. Leave the wharf and go directly to the Plaza de San Francisco de Asís across from the ship terminal, where it's usually crowded. Wait by the white-marble fountain, the Fuente de los Leones. I'll meet you there. And don't look conspicuous."

"Easier said."

What a sap I'd been. There were plenty of places I might have hidden the notebook. But under my mattress? For cryin' out loud, I screwed up.

My clothes were stained and stinky after three days under a hot sun at sea so I blended in well enough among the port workers—until I got to the plaza, which was filled with stylishly-dressed tourists toting maps and cameras.

With my hand out, I crouched in the shadow of the fountain like a beggar—who looks at beggars?— until Dalilah appeared holding a white straw hat

"Put this on," she said.

"Straws aren't my preferred attire."

"It'll help you look like you just stepped off the liner lusting for a drink, the nearest roll of the dice, and a good lay."

She daringly wore white, wide-legged chiffon trousers, a cloche hat, and dark glasses.

"Take my arm and try to look like a tourist," she said as we walked toward the street. "I have a car waiting. It was a bitch slipping from the hotel unseen, but Javier got me out through the kitchen."

The car was the familiar canary-yellow Packard Tourister convertible, its top up, with Kime in the driver's seat and next to him O'Kane. His car couldn't have been more conspicuous. Kime gunned it somewhat recklessly as he navigated through Habana Vieja, startling the peanut vendors, flower girls, and chorizo sellers.

He said to Dalilah and me, crouching in the rear, "Stay down until we get to the city's outskirts. I love this car and don't want to see it riddled with bullets."

To Dalilah, I asked, "Where are we going? And how do we get the hell off this isle?"

"From the airport in Camagüey, three hundred miles southeast. Nothing's safe for you in and around Havana, from the harbor to the rail stations to Rancho Boyeros Airport. I brought sandwiches, water, and rum for our trip."

Kime said, "I know the route and where the filling stations are, so I'll get you to Camagüey. I can fix a flat, but if we have a breakdown you're on your own."

I said to him, "You're probably the only human in Cuba not completely pissed at me."

"If you'd mentioned me in your damned notebook I'd be gunning for you too. I carry, you know, and I'm not talking about a flask."

"You certainly had us fooled, Niles," O'Kane said. "We thought you and Dalilah were just some rich, carefree tourists from the US. Instead, we find out you're muckrakers."

I said, "I prefer the term, factfinders."

Kime said, "You could have blown my cover and Mary's. When Dalilah told us you were in trouble, I thought it was something to do with the mob, gambling debts maybe. Then I learned why you're *really* here. Do you plan to write about Mary and me when—or if—you get off of this island? Because if you do—"

"Kime, I guarantee you'll be described only as my Numero Uno Unnamed Source, and Mary as Numero Dos. Your secret's safe." To Dalilah I asked, "How did the bad guys get on to us in the first place?"

"We flashed a lot of money around but spent very little, which apparently raised some eyebrows. Then I learned that Bathurst Wormwood of the Cuba Development Association was particularly suspicious. He had second thoughts after his conversation with you at Tropic Thunder. Didn't think you had the right accent for a Boston Aldrich, nor did you seem to know anything about club ties, and your Aldrich history was nonsense. Plus there was something about a Boddington or Baddington. Also, no one with any class would pass out the cheesy sort of business cards you did. Wormwood apparently got the ball rolling. He let Machado's henchmen know, who in turn informed Chaim Blum and his gangsters. And then the rumrunners were alerted, meaning we'll never escape the island in a fishing boat."

"How did they get my notebook?"

"After I returned to our suite after shopping in El Vevado, I saw the place was torn up. Drawers open, closets emptied, suitcases ransacked, all our belongings strewn around. And there were five or six thugs waiting for me, demanding to know more about what was in your notebook, which they'd found and read. But mostly they wanted to know where *you* were. They boasted they were La Porra, and I rather had the impression they were slightly ill-tempered."

"They hurt you?"

"Shoved me around a little. I got the bejesus scared out of me. They found it amusing."

I said, "What did you tell them about my whereabouts? Not as a deck hand on Hector's rumrunner, I hope. Hector might be compromised."

"I said you'd gone to the provinces of Villa Clara, Las Tunas, and Cienfuegos to look at investment opportunities, and I had no idea when you'd be back. I put on the best little girl act I've ever done. I would have done Rinestone Studios proud. They bought my story, thought I was some naïve floozy only good for a lay. One of them even tried to make a date with me. He was rather good-looking. A little scary, but I have a thing for dangerous men. Why the hell did you put that damned notebook under your mattress? Didn't it occur to you that anyone searching for incriminating evidence would look there?"

"Flagellate me all you want, Dalilah. Just don't tell Mencken. He has a low enough opinion of humanity as it is, and I don't want to give him more ammunition."

She sighed, rubbing my shoulder. I'd like to think she did it fondly— but wasn't going to bet the farm on it, if I had had a farm.

"It's part of the adventure, Niles, which is why I'm here in the first place. Too make matters even worse, La Porra stole our money, every last chalupa, including all my roulette winnings."

"That's a drag."

"We're cleaned out, forced to rely on the kindness of strangers."

Kime said from the driver's seat, "Don't look at me. I'll get you as far as Camagüey, but I'm still waiting for Uncle Sammy to pay what he owns me."

We drove in silence, looking askance every time another car appeared. Kime navigated the back roads wherever possible. Occasionally we'd see a flash of blue as the roadway veered near the sea. Cuba's arteries weren't all that great, some of them barely paved, and with Kime heavy on the pedal, it made for a bumpy ride.

He asked me, "What's losing your notebook going to do to your story—if you live to write it?"

"I'll reconstruct it from memory. There's lots stored in my mind, so it won't be all that hard. Plus I have Dalilah here."

"Does that mean I'll be getting my byline?" she said.

"Um, that's still under review."

Near to Santa Lucia Beach, Camagüey, the capital of Camagüey Province, had once been burned by the pirate Henry Morgan. Kime drove us directly to the landing field, a primitive affair consisting of a ramshackle, terra-cotta roofed building and a hanger. No one seemed to be around, and I saw no planes taking off or landing.

I asked Kime, "Are there regular flights out of here to the States?"

"You've got to be joking."

"Then how—"

Dalilah said, "I arranged for Wiley Post to fly us to Miami. Sent him a wire from the hotel. Which means the bad guys might find out about it. Wiley was still in Key West making repairs on the auxiliary exhaust ports in his plane's cylinders."

Kime said, "Sorry we can't stick around, kids. It's a long drive back to Havana, and if I'm to keep cracking down on those rumrunners I've got a shit-load of work to do. And, yes, Niles, I knew your captain-friend Hector was smuggling hooch and I notified the Coast Guard. Say, we don't get the Baltimore *Sun* down here. Maybe you could send me a copy once your story comes out."

"By airmail," I promised.

We exchanged goodbyes, Kime's final words being, "Hey Nonny Nonny."

After he and O'Kane took off, Dalilah and I camped for the night in a corner of the empty hangar, a dirt floor with the smell of oil and hydraulic fluid. The sandwiches she'd brought were stale and about to go bad, but the flask of glorious Cuban rum, delicious enough to drive a teetotaler mad, made up for the grub.

"I have to tell you about something else," she said. "ABC, the Abecedario, those revolutionaries trying to bring down Machado? You remember they only identify themselves by number. It turns out Ernesto is B-7. Javier is A-4, Amador C-2, and so on. Their entire family are members. Ernesto confided in me. I have that knack. It's another reason we couldn't escape in his limo. He's being watched twenty-four hours a day—and most of his relatives are too."

"You were made for this work, doll."

"Byline?" she nudged.

Despite the abrupt end to my legwork in Cuba, I was lucky to have escaped with my life. I had Dalilah to thank for that. I slipped my arm familiarly around her shoulders. As she snuggled close, she murmured seductively, "So what do I call you now that you're no longer Niles Tinsley Aldrich IV?"

"Gart will do. Although you know that Mencken prefers Taggart."

"In that case, Taggart, you're awful gamy after three days on some filthy schooner baking in the Florida Straits."

"I thought my good looks would make up for the odor."

"Are you flaring your nostrils again?"

Sometime after daylight, as we took off in Wiley's *Winnie Mae*, I peered down through a cockpit window at the diminishing airstrip and saw several cars on the runway along with a number of men pointing what appeared to be handguns up at us. I saw flashes but heard nothing over the engine roar of the Lockheed Vega. We were being fired upon. I deliberately forced it out of my mind as Wiley Post safely piloted us over the azure depths of the Straits of Florida.

---

From Miami, Dalilah hit the rails for Hollywood, still determined to break into film. Wiley flew on to Roosevelt Field, Long Island, to prepare for his round-the-world flight. I returned to B-more and my West Biddle Street warren, where I slept for two days straight to free myself from the stress of Havana.

In the short time I was there, I'd gotten to love Cuba, although I never had time to visit the Smiling Mustache, where Javier's cousin Imelda was the head procuress, or to smoke dream sticks at the opium den run by a third cousin named Chin. I would miss Javier, Ernesto, Amador, Nestor, Estevan, Tranquila, Hector, Carlos, and all the other members of Javier's immeasurable family who made my expedition so indelible. And I hoped they all survived Machado and his death squad.

At the *Sun*, I spent two days at the Underwood pecking out my story, which later Henry Mencken toasted with several rounds of forbidden libations at his preferred table at the Rennert.

I had given Dalilah her byline, reading, *with help from…*

"What's next for my favorite globe-trotting reporter, Taggart m'boy?" Henry said. He'd recently published his latest jeremiad, *Prejudices: Sixth Series.*

"Washington politics maybe. There's always some sort of scandal in DC. However, I'm thinking more about something cultural: riding over Niagara Falls in a barrel; flagpole sitting; joining one of those bunion derbies known as dance marathons."

Henry grunted, as he did when he felt disgust. "The capacity of one human being to bore another is vastly greater than that of any other animal, and I fear you're boring me almost as much as the dinner party, the epic poem, and the science of metaphysics."

"Henry, there's a two-square-mile area of upper Manhattan called Harlem where an extraordinary literary and cultural movement is taking place. Sheltered from the worst of Jim Crow, it's the scene of what's being called a renaissance. I think the *Sun*'s readers are entitled to get the inside dope and I'm just the guy to do it."

"Taggart, m'boy, while I admit to expressing mixed feelings about certain minorities, I've championed in my *American Mercury*, the work of W.E.B. Du Bois, Countee Cullen, James Weldon Johnson, and Langston Hughes."

"Good, Henry. It's a start."

"It's been a long time since I was in the field, but I find that most of today's newspapermen are simply journalistic castrati who seldom abandon the safety of the newsroom. They never feel the wind of the world in their faces or see anything with their own eyes. Aside from the *Sun*, most newspapers are purely devices for inciting the ignorant to be more ignorant and the crazy crazier. But there is hope for you, Taggart, m'boy. If Harlem's renaissance doesn't work out, there's always some Cuba waiting somewhere."

Henry stoked his Uncle Willie Perfector.

And that's -30- for this reporter.

> *Cuba, where all is happy*
> *Cuba, where all is gay!*
> *Why don't you plan a wonderful trip*
> *To Havana? hop on a ship*
> *And I'll see you in C-U-B-A*
>
> —Irving Berlin

# ——FIVE——

# JITTERBUGGIN' WITH THE RENAISSANCE

*On the day when the Savoy*
*leaps clean over to Seventh Avenue*
*and starts jitterbugging*
*with the Renaissance,*
*on that day—*
*Do, Jesus!*
*Manhattan Island will whirl*

> —Langston Hughes

It was that ugly happening at the Cotton Club on Lenox Avenue that got Carlo so damned mad, and for some folks in Harlem it changed things a lot. Carlo didn't take insults lightly, particularly if they were directed at his pals—even more if his chums were dark-skinned, and that meant most of them. Then Casper Holstein, the negro rackets czar who ran the black mecca's biggest numbers operation, got involved and that pissed off Cotton Club proprietor Owney The Killer Madden, who was still walking around with five bullets embedded in him. So things got dicey. Also, I fell in love with Zora Neale Hurston.

Although I'm getting ahead of myself.

---

As for Harlem, no one knew it better than Carl Van Vechten—Carlo to his friends—who had made the mistake of being born white to a rich banking family in Cedar Rapids, Iowa. He was a cohort of my mentor Henry Louis Mencken who knew everyone worth knowing, and often published them in the pages of his *American Mercury*, a rag for intellectuals. Van Vechten was, indeed, worth knowing, and the two dined together whenever Henry entrained from Baltimore to the Big Apple on magazine business. His sojourns always being shorter than longer, he refused to abandon the beloved place of his nativity for any length of time. Both men shared the same publisher, the house founded by Alfred and Blanche Knopf, and Henry was godfather to the Knopf progeny.

Like Carlo's Cedar Rapids, for me, Baltimore, where I began, was also a far piece from Harlem. As a miscarried theology student turned idolatrous newshound, I was intrigued by the new Harlem Renaissance, about which the literary, tuneful, and artistic connoisseurs were so rhapsodic. It was as if blacks had never sung, danced, authored, or painted before. Now, with my applauded front-page Cuba exposé behind me, I intended to witness the soul of this artistic movement, which would make for a timely byline in the *Sun*.

That I was part negro but light-skinned enough to pass for white had nothing to do with the assignment. Mostly.

At his consecrated table in the Hotel Rennert at the corner of Saratoga and Liberty, where he openly defied Prohibition despite the ever-present threat of agent provocateurs, the Bard of Baltimore invoked the name of Carl Van Vechten.

"First of all, there would be no Harlem Renaissance without Carlo, our era's most recognized eccentric. Agreed, negro writers, artists, and musicians of every stripe would still exist, but not all together at that one place and time. Just as the Renaissance is many things, so is Carlo, who, as a Caucasian, thinks that dullness is an unpardonable sin and that most whites are dull. Life to him is a grand performance. He believes that if even the repetition of breathing becomes mundane, then life fails as art."

"Breathing is evidence of life, Henry, something physiological. The esthetics of art is something else."

"You're starting to think like me, Taggart, m'boy. Look at it this way. Man is the only animal who devotes himself to making others unhappy. This is evidenced by the creative energies of the drys, the holy, and those who consider women purely as birthing mechanisms. By default, that's art. Carlo lives in the shadow of himself, and until now his best-known books were about his beloved cats, although if one believes a writer's reputation survives on the subject of pet cats then he's a damned fool."

Henry was a man of unyielding convictions, and while he had little to say on the subject of felines, he celebrated heroes who tossed dead cats into sanctuaries; the object being to prove to stupefied worshipers that their gods were fraudulent and that lightning would not strike them dead. The liberation of the human mind was never advanced by dunderheads, he said, and although I, somehow, passed muster with him, I suspected he never graded me more than a B-minus.

I said, "Didn't I read something about a controversy over Van Vechten's most recent book?"

"Indeed, although it's not the content that's causing a stir but its incendiary title, which, Taggart, m'boy, I'm almost reluctant to repeat in recognition of your delicate, bleeding-heart sensitivities. Carlo, as a non-black, wrote a candid, positive portrayal of negro life as it is in today's Harlem, which might have gone little noticed. But he titled it, despite the objections of the Knopfs, *Nigger Heaven*, which to many of his friends, white and black, was unthinkable. To Carlo's achievement, it became a best seller and has gone into multiple printings—with the added benefit of being banned in church-corrupted Boston, as are most of our best books. Knopf was so convinced book collectors would flock to this novel it offered it in a signed, limited edition of two hundred and five copies; ten on Borzoi rag paper signed by the author and lettered from A to J; one hundred ninety-five copies on Borzoi rag paper, numbered and signed."

I said, "Wait, Henry. Isn't that the novel in which *you* are a character?"

"As Russett Durwood, who as editor of a journal called *The American Mars*, a riff on *The American Mercury*, fires wily bon mots at American life and culture. It's not unflattering to me, I'm pleased to relate, although the novel's protagonist, a negro author named Bryon Kasson, seems to believe that Durwood is a player in some cosmic plot to destroy him. Carlo mailed me a first edition in which he inscribed the words, 'with reverence and reverences.'"

"Was that when you first got acquainted?"

"No, a decade earlier when Carlo sent me a thank-you for my decent review of his book of music criticism in *The Smart Set*, which I was coediting with George Jean Nathan. I noticed an aphorism on Carlo's letterhead reading, *A little too much is just enough for me.* However, I fear he immerses himself in fads so it wouldn't surprise me if his obsession over the Harlem Renaissance will lag at some point. He's been talking about taking up photography."

"Then I'd better leave for New York immediately before it's too late."

"And I shall phone Carlo to discuss your impending arrival. When you get there you might look up a young black poet named Countee Cullen. I published a poem of his in the *Mercury*, which attracted some attention. I recall a stanza that goes, *The cries of all dark people near or far / Were billowed over me a mighty urge / Of suffering in which my puny grief must merge…* He's now one of the most discussed negro authors in the country."

"I have a lot to learn about the Harlem Renaissance," I said.

"And you should also know that physically Carlo's not an attractive man, although he once said of himself that charm kills ugliness, and he is, indeed, quite charming. Dorothy Parker, however, once saw him coming toward her in the Algonquin Hotel lobby and fled in fright to the gent's room, where she, unfamiliar with the lavatory's geographics, stepped into a urinal."

"I'll watch where I walk."

"Carlo's arteries have been hardened by the ill effects of alcohol. He cranks himself up like a Victor Talking Machine and repeats the same refrain without letup. I once heard him reprise the identical canticle three-hundred and fifteen times in the same sitting. Luckily, there's an easy way to stop him. Simply slip him a double dose of Glauber's salt, which you may obtain at any rural feedstore."

---

I stepped off the Capitol Limited and walked up the stairs into the grand atrium of New York's Pennsylvania Station, a Beaux-Arts edifice so magnificent I knew instantly that it would defy the ages—like Egypt's pyramids, the Parthenon, and the Great Wall of China. Seeing the soaring dome of glass and steel, I gawked slack-jawed like a first-time tourist—a demeanor Henry would characterize as being that of a yokel. Subtle motes of dust floated in the sun's rays flooding down through the lofty skylights. But I caught myself, closed my mouth, and attempted to appear like the hard-boiled, cynical journalist I was fashioning myself to be—although no one in the bustling, crowded terminal seemed to notice me. While I was almost insulted by their slight, I was aware that for a reporter anonymity was often useful.

Unfamiliar with New York's labyrinthine transit system—I knew only that the IRT ran underground up to Harlem—I engaged a Checker to the Van Vechten apartment at 150 West 55th Street. According to Henry, Carlo had insisted that I bed on his living room couch until I found more permanent, albeit cheap, accommodations. Pierre DuPont, Henry's Prohibition-foe accomplice, wasn't financing this venture as he'd done when I penetrated Cuba, and the *Sun*, despite Henry's influence, was getting chintzy about my expenses.

Van Vechten was waiting in the doorway of his apartment as I stepped from the elevator. I could hear the tinkle of a piano and a babble of voices behind him.

He said, "You've timed your arrival perfectly, Mr. Gart Booker Asquith III."

"Ah, Henry has informed on me."

"Marinoff and I are having a few people in for drinks and a little entertainment, after which we'll be heading to the Cotton Club to hear Fletcher Henderson. I understand he's added a brilliant cornet player to his band: Louis Armstrong, who used to be with King Oliver."

Van Vechten was tall, somewhat paunchy, with sandy hair. But his protuberant front teeth, which looked as though they were trying to break free from the bastille of his mouth, were his most remarkable facial component. I was at first distracted by those jutting teeth, but as time went on I, subsumed by his natural, infectious charisma, was to grow so accustomed to them that they became barely noticeable.

I observed a woman holding a bulging purse standing next to his door, and as Van Vechten ushered me in, I stood aside to allow her to enter before me.

"No, dear boy," Van Vechten said. "She's not going in. The lady's waiting for her husband who is inside. He's been unfaithful to her and she's waiting with a pistol in her purse so that she can shoot him."

As he escorted me into the apartment, I said, "Thanks for letting me flop on your couch, Mr. Van Vechten."

"Any friend of Henry Mencken's… And call me Carlo."

I knew little about culture, other than that too much good taste was in bad taste, but even I saw the Van Vechtens' spacious rooms were a study in aesthetics: paintings, sculptures, rare books, antiques. The gathering was in Carlo's drawing room, which, under a magnificent chandelier of what I learned was Venetian glass, were Persian carpets in patterns of purple, raspberry, and turquoise. The room was crowded with some two dozen men and women, most of whom were black, poised, and well-dressed. A slender white man sat at a piano, surrounded by several people who appeared to be captivated by his music.

Carlo said to me, "I'll introduce you to as many of my guests as I can. Meanwhile, as you can see, my bar is fully stocked. I just got in a fresh shipment from my favorite bootlegger who runs a speakeasy in the West Forties, although I'm not allowed to mention his name. But I can say that he also supplies intoxicants to Jimmy Walker, our beloved mayor. That's

George Gershwin at the piano, by the way. Oh, and over there is my loving spouse, Fania Marinoff. My divorced first wife was so furious after Fania and I wed that she demanded the back alimony I owed, so when I couldn't pay I spent four months in the hoosegow. As a former actress and dancer born in Russia, Fania prefers to use her maiden name, which is why I rarely refer to her other than Marinoff."

She was diminutive and dark-haired, and Henry's alkaline description of her was uncannily accurate: she, paired with Carlo, looked like a tugboat pulling an ocean liner.

Among those I hobnobbed with that evening were poets Langston Hughes, Claude McKay, and Countee Cullen, the young man Henry wanted me to call upon; singers Ethel Waters and Paul Robeson; *World-Telegram* columnist Heywood Broun; Alfred and Blanche Knopf; Salvator Dali, said to be some sort of surrealist; hoofer Bill Bojangles Robinson; the Harlem philanthropist Casper Holstein, who boasted that he had no talents except for getting rich by running numbers; and Zora Neale Hurston, a promising young writer garbed like a Chippewa Indian, replete with fancy beadwork and a headband with a feather, her outfit the gift of a lady who was so captivated by so-called primitive cultures she was called Godmother.

As far as journalistic research was concerned, I was sitting on a gold mine. I had lots to enter into my reporter's notebook and vowed it would stay safe, unlike the one confiscated by Machado's La Porra in Cuba.

Suddenly, the partygoers were distracted by what appeared to be gunshots in the hall.

"Relax, everybody," Van Vechten said. "Either the lady outside shot her husband or she missed. Story over."

Ethel Waters, who had starred in the musical *Plantation Review*, fell into a good-natured dustup with Van Vechten.

She said, "Hell no, I've not read your book, Carlo. It has such a nasty title. I almost didn't come here tonight on account of it. You should be spanked."

"You may not approve of the N-word in the title, Ethel, but the second word, Heaven, represents Harlem. Metaphorically, it's where Africans sit in the theatrical gallery that is New York from which they stare down at the white faces in the orchestra's good seats. Occasionally, the whites turn their hard, cruel faces toward the balcony to laugh or to sneer, but they never beckon. It never occurs to them that the black people above them can rain objects down on them, that the wretches in the balcony could swoop from their so-called Heaven and rightfully take their place in the seats below."

"My, you're passionate about this," Waters said. "Perhaps I should get past the title."

"I see myself as a witness. Despite what W.E.B. Du Bois claims about my novel—he calls it cheap melodrama—it's about negroes as they actually exist in the new city of Harlem: the rich and poor, fast and slow, intellectual and ignorant. My book means well."

"Mr. Du Bois is a champion of basic rights for black folks and a great man. So he's correct about a lot. Still, maybe some of us have the wrong idea about your book. You're not like most whites, Carlo, the good ones. But they annoy me, always complaining about their mental pains and psychic aches, and lots of guilt. You, however, have life and enthusiasm, and being rich hasn't got you down—yet. But I have another complaint. Are you up to hearing it?"

"Ethel, complaints to me are like beer gushing from a keg."

"It's your damned food. Rich white folks' victuals. That fancy stuff over there on the table? Caviar you call it. Looks to me like buckshot. Or maybe I should say buckshit. And what's that borsch you're always serving? It's just beet soup and it's cold, which is enough to kill your gizzard."

"I've no choice," Carlo said. "My wife's Russian."

"I prefer baked ham, string beans, grits, and lemon meringue pie. I'm having you and Fania over for dinner next week."

"Marinoff and I will be there—if she's still speaking to me, which is usually the case."

"Don't bring borsch."

Carlo gathered the guests round the piano.

"Ladies and gentlemen, it's time for the entertainment portion of our soiree. George here needs no introduction, other than to say he's rehearsed any number of his songs at this very piano."

Gershwin said, "I'm going to play a little piece I'm working on called 'Harlem River Chanty.'"

The tune, as his fingers flew over the keyboard, had a familiar ragtime cadence, highly syncopated. Ragtime was a staple of Tin Pan Alley—although its origins were undoubtedly African—but George gave it the Gershwin touch. The critics were already describing as a masterpiece his *Rhapsody in Blue*, which Paul Whiteman's orchestra had introduced at Aeolian Hall just four years earlier.

After a round of cheers, Gershwin said, "My brother Ira's been working on lyrics for it, but he's having problems trying to find the right word to rhyme with chanty. All he has so far is panty."

Then the youthful poet Langston Hughes recited his latest verse:

*Good evening, daddy!*
*I know you've heard*
*The boogie-woogie rumble*
*Of a dream deferred*
*Tilling the treble*
*And twining the bass*
*Into midnight ruffles*
*Of catgut lace.*

Polite applause.

Ethel Waters, accompanied by Gershwin, sang in her clear, perfect voice.

*Am I blue?*
*You'll be too*
*If your schemes like your dreams*
*Done fell through*

The guests were entranced, as was I.

Countee Cullen, inspired by the English Romantic poets, recited:

> *I cannot hold my peace, John Keats,*
> *I am as helpless in the toil*
> *Of spring as any lamb that bleats*
> *To feel the solid earth recoil*

And Claude McKay:

> *Desire naked, linked with passion,*
> *Goes strutting by in brazen fashion*

Paul Robeson, who earned his law degree from Columbia while playing in the National Football League, sang a cappella in his unearthly, sonorous voice:

> *I gets weary, and sick of tryin'*
> *I'm tired of livin', but I'm scared of dyin'*
> *But ol' man river, he just keeps rolin' along*

Zora Neale Hurston recited something from a book of folklore she had been putting together, but as it was about hoodoo and in dialect, it went over my head. I had no idea at the time that I would soon share a bed with her, although Henry had once warned me to never sleep with your sources. Unless, of course, it led to a damned good story.

Finally, they pulled back the carpet, and, accompanied by Gershwin at the piano, the dapper Bill Bojangles Robinson, his derby cocked at a jaunty angle, performed a tap dance so lightly it was as if he was bouncing on air, and to hell with the neighbors on the floor below. Ethel sang along as he tapped.

> *The beauties of creation*
> *Will never lose their harm*
> *While I roam the old plantation*
> *With my true love on my arm*

I was roiled. I'd just experienced the cream of the Harlem Renaissance. And it was Van Vechten who had brought them all together.

Carlo announced to his guests, "Grab your flasks. We're headed up to Lenox Avenue to hear Fletcher Henderson's band at the Cotton Club. We'll commandeer two taxis, three if necessary. And to those of you unable to join us, I wish you eighteen housebroken vestal virgins as well as purple parrots and evergreen boots."

I was game of course. It would be my first foray into Harlem. I learned that when downtown whites went there to party it was called *van vechtening around*. Carlo wouldn't have had it any other way.

But damned if the night didn't go all to hell.

---

It was once known as Club Deluxe, but when Owney Madden was sprung from Sing Sing, he took over the lease from heavyweight champ Jack Johnson—kayoed by Jess Willard at Oriental Park Racetrack in Havana—and changed the name to the Cotton Club. Owney figured to make it his prime outlet for bootlegged beer, and in order to draw customers from the white precincts he starred the top negro performers in America.

The Cotton may not have been as flashy as the clubs I'd seen in Havana—with their open gambling, sex, and extravagant floorshows—but Owney made sure there were scads of potted palms around to give off a jungle vibe. And his so-called high-yellow dancers and chorus gals wore only the necessities, top and barely bottom. The place wasn't cheap. With a two-dollar minimum, and, as a high-class joint, patrons were required to keep their flasks in their pockets or purses, not store them on the floor, and never on the table. Owney's distillery in the basement of the building next door made sure his booze, which he sold at premium prices, never ran out.

To keep it copacetic, a squad of unobtrusive, tuxedo-clad bouncers kept order. Duke Ellington's was the house band, but Owney also brought in guest performers like Fletcher Henderson and Cab Calloway. The music was broadcast on Saturday nights over RCA's WEAF, the station that carried the Silver-Tongue Tenor, the Happiness Boys, and the Ipana Troubadours. Publicity you couldn't buy.

We barreled out of our Checkers at the frantic corner of 644 Lenox at 142nd where the Cotton Club was a panorama of flashing lights, neon signs, and bellowing billboards heralding the symphonious spectacle awaiting within. The street was lined with taxis and limos from downtown.

Led by Carlo, our group of partygoers, half-blottoed, lurched to the club's front door where we were stopped by a poised, tuxedo-clad man, nary a hair out of place.

"Sorry," he said. "There ain't no more room inside."

Carlo said, "That's absurd. The Cotton Club has seven-hundred seats. There are only a dozen in our party. Certainly, you can accommodate us. We just came from downtown."

"So does everybody else."

"Then why are *we* being kept out?"

"You look intelligent, sir, so lemme be up front with you. You got a mixed-race group here."

"So? This is Harlem, and the Cotton Club stars the best black entertainers in the world."

"We got a strict policy, one that we're firmly enforcin'. This joint's for Caucasians only. I'll let you and the other whites in your party in, but not the rest."

"Carlo said, "Fletcher Henderson's on stage tonight. It's an all-black band."

"All the performers here is black. So is the chorus girls. Ditto the waiters and kitchen staff. But we got a whites-only clientele."

"I demand to talk to your superior. And what's *your* name?"

"Name's George Raft."

Who may have been New York's most urbane doorman.

Casper Holstein pushed his way to the front saying, "I recognize you, Mr. Raft. You're a hoofer. I've seen you in vaudeville."

"And someday you're gonna see me act in the photoplays. But right now I'm between shows and workin' for Mr. Madden. I'm also his wheel man."

"Do you know who *I* am?"

"Yeah, you run the numbers rackets here in Harlem, the Bolito King. But that don't cut no ice here because you're also black. So you ain't gettin' in either—unless you change your pigment."

Carlo said, "This is outrageous. Where is Mr. Madden?"

"The boss is pretty busy. He's gotta big joint to run."

Holstein said, "You want to start a gang war over an insult, Mr. Raft? We're in Harlem, so you're not the only one to have a lot of muscle behind you."

Raft ran his fingers with their manicured nails over his slicked-back hair.

"Tell ya what," he said. "Why don't you all wait here while I go talk to Mr. Madden." He turned to another torpedo, saying, "Sal, how about keepin' an eye on the door."

Carlo was fuming.

He said to us, "There are other big clubs in Harlem we can go to. How about Small's Paradise?"

Holstein said, "Same as the Cotton. Ditto Connie's Inn and the Nest Club. Negroes work in those places, but can't buy a drink. I figured we'd have a problem."

"How could I have been so uninformed?"

"But there are a few friendly clubs, Carlo: the Savoy, Lenox, Renaissance Ballroom, Striver's Row, Bamboo, Leroy's. Just because it's Harlem doesn't mean you won't find Jim Crow."

Finally, a flashy-suited Owney Madden appeared shadowed by George Raft. Owney made his dough uptown but his double-breasteds and finger rings were definitely downtown.

He acknowledged Holstein, saying, "What brings you to my club, Casper? You seem to be a bit pissed."

"Mr. Van Vechten and his friends want to go in and hear that new cornet player Louis Armstrong everyone's talking about. But your guy here won't let us through the door."

"Casper, Casper, Casper. We're pals, right? You got the lion's share of the numbers rackets here in Harlem, and I've never interfered. But about the Cotton Club. I know I've been loose about it in the past—you've been here before at a good table—but I gotta enforce my policy of no blacks as customers if I'm gonna keep patrons coming here from downtown. They're the ones with the dough, and I want ermine and pearls."

"They come to Harlem just to gawk at us black people, Owney. It's called slumming. They look at us like we're apes in some zoo."

"They come for the entertainment and to get laid, drink booze, and buy dope. But they don't wanna share tables with no negroes. However, this here's a big town. You people got your own places."

Carlo broke in. "See here, Mr. Madden, it's time negroes are treated like humans, especially in Harlem. That this is happening in the black capital of the world is appalling."

"I know all about you, Mr. Van Vechten, and about the good work you been doin' for the black race, gettin' their books published and their art in galleries and museums and their plays in the theaters. And I know that life ain't that easy for black folks in this town or anywhere else."

"Just how would *you* know, being white?"

"Hey, don't tell me I always had it soft. Born so poor and Irish that my widowed mother put me into an orphanage back in England. She brung me to Hell's Kitchen when I was six. Barely survived growin' up. It wasn't until after I joined the Gophers Gang that I learned how to protect myself, especially from the Hudson Dusters, our rivals. They don't call me Killer Madden without no reason."

"As a white man you can go anywhere you please," Carlo said. "Black people in our country don't have a choice."

"You think I can go anywhere? The Dusters cornered me once at the Arbor Dance Hall and pumped eleven slugs into my body. Five of them bullets is still in me. Then the state dumped on me for gunnin' down Little

Patsy Doyle and sent me up the river for eight long ones. You believe a prison cell is goin' anywhere I wanted?"

"Maybe you're a criminal, maybe not, but whatever you are it's not the same as being born black."

Owney pulled out a smoke and motioned to Raft to give him a light.

"I'm a respected member of this here community, Mr. Van Vechten. I done my time. And I run a decent joint. So here's what I'm gonna do. I'm cuttin' a five-thousand-dollar check to the National Association for the Advancement of Colored People and handin' it over to you."

A worthy compromise, I thought, and more than generous.

"Five-thousand dollars isn't enough," Carlo said. "It'll never be enough."

Owney flung his barely-smoked fag to the sidewalk.

"Then I got only three words to say to you: Fuck you. And *none* of youse people is gettin' into my club. I don't care what color you are, not even if your skin is as white as an Irish nun's ass."

Eyes tearing in anger, Casper Holstein said, "It's over between us, Madden. We had a truce and a good thing going. But you can't talk Mr. Van Vechten like that. He's Harlem's best friend."

"You been gettin' awful uppity with me lately, Holstein. I been puttin' up with you in the interest of good relations, but now I'm thinkin' about branchin' out into the numbers myself. There's lots of opportunity up here, so you'll be hearin' from me." He motioned to Raft. "George, make sure these here people don't ever darken my doorway."

---

Our party, dispirited, broke up. Casper suggested we head to the Savoy Ballroom, where all comers were welcome. But the festive mood had dissipated. Carlo, Marinoff, and I, cabbed it back to West 55th Street alone. He was despondent.

"I failed tonight, Gart. I should have handled Owney Madden some other way."

"You did your best, I think."

"Sometimes I get nasty and abusive when I drink, as Marinoff here will attest. But usually, I pass out before I become worse. I just wake up with a hangover and remorse."

"Owney's a mobster. There was nothing more you could have done. Most people seem to take to you."

"I don't expect knee-bends from anyone, still… Also, I might have held a five-thousand-dollar check in my hand for the NAACP. I came away with nothing."

"There is that."

"And now there may be a gang war."

"Gang wars are always about money. And I heard that directly from Al Capone."

"They're also about saving face."

Carlo and Marinoff made me comfortable on their sofa, but before he retired to his bedroom he said to me, "Apple blossoms and mignonette, Gart."

---

Sometime before dawn as we slept, a bomb blast severely damaged the Cotton Club and caved in most of its windows. A black porter mopping the lobby lost both legs. Nobody knew who did it.

But an aggrieved Owney Madden had a pretty good idea.

A week after the blast forced the Cotton Club to shut down for repairs, Casper Holstein was snatched. Five armed men in two cars crammed him into the rear of a Packard Club sedan. Casper's chauffeur took after them but lost the kidnappers after the getaway car squealed north on Seventh Avenue. A kidnapping in Harlem, like your usual murder and mayhem, rarely made the papers, but this one reached the front page of the *Times* with the headline, RICH NEGRO SEIZED FOR $50,000 RANSOM.

The article, however, came out well *after* the abduction because everyone in Harlem including the fuzz kept a lid on it.

---

Downtown, they called it Jungle Alley. Uptown, it was known as Swing Street. Officially it was West 133rd between Lenox and Seventh. It was lined with so many speakeasies, cabarets, and jazz joints occupying brownstone after brownstone after brownstone that nights were a cacophony of soul interwoven with a contagious beat that quit only at sunrise: Pod and Jerry's, Basement Brownie's, Covan's, Mexico's, Edith's Clam House, Monette's Supper Club, Log Cabin, Barbecue Club, the Nest, Bank's Club, Hansberry's Clam House, not to mention Pig-Foot Mary's, who sold what she was named for on a sidewalk corner.

At first blush, Harlem didn't appear dissimilar to any big city, even reminiscent of portions of Baltimore. But Harlem was also a state of mind. I saw that during the day it was dull and ordinary, with men headed to their labors, others standing in clumps smoking reefer, women pushing baby carriages, and the occasional drunk in the doorway. It was transformed at night, flooded with white tourists out to celebrate. But Harlem's nights had been ripped from the people who lived there, and its sparkling, superficial surface merely coated over despair and bitterness.

Still, there was music everywhere. Somehow, the jungle rhythms of Africa had been tamed into American-style jazz and dance, often tempered by some lonely voice in a window singing the blues or a haunting trumpet echoing from a rooftop.

While white visitors flocked to the gangster-run clubs, the real people of Harlem celebrated, if they celebrated at all, at rent parties, where a buck would get you through the door, and for another quarter or fifty cents, all the bootleg you could drink, with chitterlings thrown in—and music so close and personal you could almost taste the sweat on the faces of the musicians.

I had my first and last chitterling at a rent party, where Carlo told me, "The problem with Prohibition, Gart, is that it makes everyone drink."

The Volstead Act never stopped anyone from draining a bottle. While the misbegotten law was inconvenient, Harlem's thousands of speakeasies made things less cumbersome. They looked like barber shops, newsstands, coffee houses, poolhalls, smoke shops, and cafes, which they were, but inside you could quench your thirst in any way you wanted, as long as you were aware of the sometimes dubious quality of the booze. The cops rarely busted them unless they got to be too obvious, a nuisance, or made some sort of ruckus. For Harlem's black bootleggers Prohibition was a bonanza.

By dawn, the Harlem streets, which I'd first assumed would crackle with daybreak anticipation and optimism, were again workaday, as ordinary humans went about their unremarkable routines.

---

Jungle Alley was where I, still unaware of Casper Holstein's kidnapping, was palling around with Countee Cullen. After learning of my Mencken connection, and that I was writing an article about the Harlem Renaissance for the *Sun*, he agreeably took me in tow.

Soft-spoken, dignified, and poised, Countee always wore a well-pressed suit and tie. He might have fared well as an Oxford don. I was a little intimidated. He was, after all, a Phi Beta Kappa from N.Y.U. with a master's from Harvard, and had published three admired books of verse. Excelling at mathematics, languages, and English lit, he worked summers as a waiter in Atlantic City.

He told me, "Mr. Mencken made me visible when he published my poem 'The Shroud of Color' in *The American Mercury*, so I got off to a quick start."

I said. "Henry never publishes anything he doesn't like."

"He was unaware at first that I was black. Mr. Mencken told me that I wrote like Shelley or Keats. I was almost afraid to disabuse him about my race for fear I'd be treated like a dog performing tricks, which is often the case."

"He's also published Langston Hughes."

"Poetically, my major competition. But we don't write the same way or about the same things. I'm not even sure Langston's jazz verse belongs in the austere literary expression known as poetry. His riffs are interlopers in the company of poetry that is truly beautiful."

Countee and I ducked into a basement joint called Tillie's Chicken Shack, which had several wobbly tables presided over by Tillie Fripp, a former roadhouse cook who looked like a figure from an antebellum plantation. Tillie's biscuits were on the house. At night, her customers, sated by Jungle Alley's jazz, lined up to get in, and no how much of a big shot you thought you were, even if you were Killer Madden or the Bolito King, you waited your turn.

I was amused watching so distinguished a gentleman as Countee Cullen tear into fried chicken and sweet potatoes with gulps of bootleg beer in between.

He told me the ordinary black citizens stared blankly when they heard the phrase "Harlem Renaissance," coined by black socialist Hubert Henry Harrison in his radical paper *The Voice*. The movement had developed through the impetus of rich, white intellectuals such as Van Vechten and Charlotte Osgood Mason, but hadn't quite reached the ordinary mind.

Countee said, "For them, it never pays the rent or boosts their wages, and most have never even read a line of poetry or a novel or even admired a painting."

"Much as Carlo is working to educate the uneducated," I said.

"The white influence on negro artists is okay with me. As there are no black book publishers, it's satisfying that a white one would bring out my work,"

He was cagey about his early life—although Carlo had told me Countee had been born in Kentucky and was raised by a grandmother in New York. After her death, he was taken in by Frederick Cullen, pastor of Salem Methodist Episcopal Church, Harlem's largest congregation. Countee adopted Cullen's last name.

Our talk turned to Van Vechten's controversial novel.

"His title's a sore spot with me," Countee said, "and I told him it was a mistake. I actually distrust Carlo's motives. He may be exploiting black artists for financial gain. Has he somehow, perhaps unknowingly, betrayed the negro race? And that's also his own fear. He told me so, and about his recurrent nightmare that he himself is a negro who is being pursued by white-sheeted evil."

Two big-league events were in Countee's near future. He'd been awarded a Guggenheim Fellowship to study in Paris and he was about to wed Nina Yolande Du Bois, daughter of W.E.B. Du Bois. He was looking forward to the Guggenheim, the wedding not so much.

He said, "Whether in Paris or here, I don't want to be considered a negro poet, but simply a poet. I've also been mischaracterized as a racial poet. If that's the case, it's a bitter and unfortunate irony because I see no distinction between white and black poetry. Art transcends race. Black artists have more to gain by writing in the tradition of English and American poetry than any nebulous ancestral yearnings toward an African inheritance, which is why I wrote, rather cynically, *Spicy grove, cinnamon tree / What is Africa to me?*"

"But how many black artists think of poetry in the scholarly way you do?"

"We must stop erecting barricades between the races, Gart. Black authors should never write antagonistically. It only strengthens the bitterness of our enemies. Even though I do address racism in my poetry, I don't want to be known as the Black Keats."

"Isn't it possible that the African-roots poetry of Langston Hughes might actually encourage whites to better understand black artists?"

"Why? Because I can't hear the eternal tom-toms beating in the negro soul? I've been accused of racial self-hatred, thus proving I've been vanquished by whiteness. I deny it, Gart. You don't need the influence of the jungle to address racial conflict. I'm now working on a poem about a man who was murdered by a lynch mob over his innocent relationship with a white woman—and, like Christ, is resurrected."

I was tempted to tell Countee about my own mixed-race mother but backed down. As a reporter, I was supposed to be an observer, not a participant—a dictum I was about to disregard.

He said, "I hear you've been sleeping on Carlo's sofa. I have a bed in a rooming house on West One-Hundred Thirty-Sixth Street. It's called Niggerati Manor because the landlady Iolanthe Sydney believes in Harlem's creative energy and gives rooms rent-free to black artists. Zora Neale Thurston, Langston Hughes, the theatrical director Harold Jackman, and Wallace Thurman, who edits the black literary journal *Fire!*, all stay there from time to time. I use it as a quiet room in which to write or for the occasional tryst. As I normally sleep at my father's parsonage, you're welcome to stay at Iolanthe's. She'll make an exception for you."

I jumped at the chance, and after our chow at Tillie's, we ambled up Lenox Avenue to West 136th. Niggerati Manor was a narrow, four-story building, more tenement than brownstone. Inside, the walls were painted with panoramic red and yellow phalluses, which Countee insisted was part of the building's quirky appeal, along with its hooked rugs and wicker furniture.

"Who's not charmed by a phallus, no matter the color?" he said. "It's one of God's greatest inventions. Queers of all sexes can be comfortable here."

Countee's room was threadbare, with a narrow bed, one chair, and a desk with an old Underwood. A single framed picture was on the wall, an artist's conception of Jesus. Raised in a church parsonage, Countee was acutely religious.

We sat side-by-side on his bed.

"Do you find my space here adequate?" he asked.

"It reminds me of my room on Biddle Street in Baltimore, only better."

"May I recite to you one of my poems?"

*Locked arm in arm they cross the way*
*The black boy and the white,*
*The golden splendor of the day*
*The sable pride of night.*

Not unexpectedly, Countee placed his hand on my thigh.

Without flinching, I said, "I think not."

Slowly, he removed it.

And so I moved into Niggerati Manor.

---

If Casper Holstein was pissed he didn't show it, and he wasn't the worst for wear after his kidnapping.

I went to see him at his Turf Club on West 136th Street, a five-story brownstone lavishly decorated inside with racing regalia: pairs of shiny jockey boots, brightly polished horses' bits, and colorful prints of thoroughbreds on the walls.

My connection with Carl Van Vechten gave me a ticket to Harlem that most white reporters would never have.

Casper explained that he was at his Turf Club at about midnight when he phoned a lady friend who lived in a building he owned on West 146th Street, telling her his chauffeur would deliver him there in his brand new Lincoln within twenty minutes. He never got to her door. The driver and a few neighbors saw gunmen, who may have been lurking in a hallway, drag him to one of two cars waiting outside and speed off, eluding Casper's chauffeur.

Shortly after the abduction, one of the kidnappers phoned the Turf Club to demand a seventeen-thousand-dollar ransom and not to go to the police. Soon after, Casper himself called the club to warn that if the dicks were notified all they'd find would be his dead body. The Turf enlisted three-hundred people, all agreeing to remain silent, to search for Casper by combing the tenements and basements and asking questions, which, with so many involved, inevitably got back to the bulls. Casper was venerated in Harlem. Hundreds were on his payroll: runners, collectors, even his bodyguards who were absent the night he was shanghaied. Casper had sent them home because the hour was so late.

The kidnappers were incredibly inept. One of them walked into a bank and tried to cash a three-thousand-two-hundred dollar check made out to Holstein that had somehow fallen into the kidnappers' hands. Rebuffed by the bank, the dimwit again phoned the Turf Club to up the ransom to fifty-thousand dollars, claiming the check was proof that he had Casper. They could see the check for themselves if they went to a certain address in The Bronx—which the constabulary promptly proceeded to do, making the first of five arrests.

Now, at the Turf Club with me, following his release, Casper was jovial and cheerful, even suave, his tailored suit impeccably creased. He held out a huge stack of telegrams for me to read.

"They all congratulate me on my release," he told me. "I have a lot of friends."

I asked him how it all played out.

"Some mug put a gun to my head and said, 'Stick 'em up.' Then I was hustled into a car with the engine running. They made me wear smoked glasses so I couldn't see where they were taking me. But they treated me pretty good. Four of them were white and one was a black gentleman I happened to know as a friend."

"You *knew* one of the kidnappers?"

"He apologized for getting involved. We all make mistakes. They took me to a house somewhere, and I was given a plate of chicken and lots of vegetables. When I said I was on a milk-only diet, they brought me a glass of milk. One of the whites was especially kind, the sort of gent I'd like to know better if he hadn't been a kidnapper. They moved me around a lot, took me to another house, although very apologetically. I had a diamond ring worth two-thousand dollars, which they took, as well as seventy-two dollars in cash.

"Eventually, they told me they were sorry, it had all been an error, so they drove me to Amsterdam Avenue and let me out. They returned my ring but kept the seventy-two dollars, although they gave me three-dollars for cab fare back to the Turf Club. One of the kidnappers, the nice one, told me if I was ever broke he'd stake me to the races."

"Five suspects are now behind bars."

"Yeah, the police took me downtown to finger them in a lineup. But I couldn't because of those smoked glasses they made me wear."

"But you knew one of them, a friend."

"You know how it is." Wink, wink.

"It seems like a very odd kidnapping, Mr. Holstein. The cops said the men they arrested were petty hoodlums and probably working for someone. Any idea who orchestrated it?"

"Of course. But in Harlem, we prefer to deal with things ourselves without involving the law."

"What about Owney Madden? You had quite a run-in with him at the Cotton Club, which was later bombed. Didn't he say he was going to run you out of the numbers racket?"

"No one who plays the numbers in Harlem is going to deal with some Irish mobster. Between me and my friendly competitor, Madame Stephanie St. Clair, the two of us have the local numbers business sewed up."

I learned that numbers betting was factored on any winning three-digit combination, such as in parimutuel horse racing. Casper based his on the Spanish game of Bolito, which is why he was called the Bolito King. He operated more or less in the open.

"The cops have better things to do than to bust anyone for taking two and three-dollar bets," he said. "Besides, I'm very generous to local law enforcement."

The racket had made him rich, by all accounts pulling in as much as twelve-thousand dollars a day. Casper had been a porter, a doorman, and a messenger boy on Wall Street, where he learned about statistics and how to manipulate numbers. Now, as Harlem's leading philanthropist, he was financing dorms at black colleges, creating a Baptist school in Liberia, and supplementing the incomes of any number of Harlem Renaissance artists. The day before his kidnapping, he'd sent a large consignment of lumber to black hurricane victims in the Virgin Islands, where he was born.

As for his kidnappers, the goons were all released since Casper couldn't—or—wouldn't identify them.

But congenial as he appeared, it would take Casper a long time to forget the indignity of being kidnapped, no matter how polite his abductors were. Plus he was still out seventy-two dollars, excluding the three bucks they gave him for cab fare.

And one other thing. Like Owney Madden, Casper also employed guys with guns.

---

In what was a deliberate accident on my part, I bumped into Zora Neale Hurston, who was lugging a typewriter down the stairs at Niggerati Manor where her room was a floor above mine. She was staying there temporarily until she moved into a flat on the Upper West Side. Zora remembered me from the Van Vechten party as an eyeglasses-wearing, reticent, pasty-fleshed out-of-towner who was sleeping on Carlo's sofa. And I remembered her, not only because of her delicate features, flashing eyes, and colorful Chippewa Indian dress, but because she was Zora Neale Hurston. There was only one of those.

"What are you doing here?" she demanded as if I was either lost or out of place, which perhaps I was.

I told her I was staying in Countee's room while I researched an article on the Harlem Renaissance.

"So Carlo's sofa wasn't good enough for you?" she said.

"Harlem's closer to my work."

"What makes you think some white person can get closer to anything in Harlem other than drinking or getting laid?"

"And you believe I'm white because…?"

Zora rolled her eyes, obviously considering me a wiseacre.

"I've got to go now," she said. "This typewriter's damned heavy and I can't stand on these stairs wasting time talking to you."

"Where are you going with that thing?"

"Not that it's any of your business, but to the pawnshop. I'm broke, and my benefactor says she's spent enough on me this month and has cut me off until the next payday. Not that I'm complaining. Godmother's the most gallant woman on earth, the spring and summer of my existence. But I've got to make a choice. Either keep the damned typewriter or go hungry this week."

"For a writer, that's a pretty hard decision," I said. "Not sure what I'd do. Probably starve."

Yeah, as if I'd actually do that.

She snorted, tossed her hair, and, barely managing the heavy type-writer, stomped down the rest of the stairs and out the front door. I stood in paralysis, more cowed by her than not.

Carlo had told me of Godmother Charlotte van der Veer Osgood Mason, widow of a wealthy doctor, who was an ardent primitivist so obsessed with African-American culture that she'd taken under her wing any number of black artists. With some of her pets, Mason signed contracts, which, in return for modest allowances, meant they effectively ceded to her the rights to their work.

I also learned that Zora had recently returned from an expedition to the Deep South to research negro folklore and that Mason had not only financed the trip but bought her a car, a Nash coupe that Zora called Sassy Suzie. It was a daunting adventure in the Jim Crow South: a mouthy, young black woman with a camera dangling from her neck traveling alone—although with a .45, which she had no qualms about flashing if the circumstances warranted. And there were plenty of those: fat racist sheriffs, the Klan, the innocent violation of sunset laws, and more often than not on the roadways no place with a roof for colored folks to relieve themselves.

That night, I spent the evening cavorting with Countee Cullen in Jungle Alley, and by the time I got back to Niggerati Manor, I was feeling medicinally as though I could do cartwheels. My room, however, was barren and lonely, and I despised the framed picture of Jesus Christ staring down at me. Fuck you too, Jesus. At times like this, feeling sorry for myself, great thoughts would pop into my brain—as one did that night. I collected Countee's Underwood, walked up one flight, and knocked at Zora's door.

She was pissed when she answered, saying, "Do you know what time it is? I was almost asleep. What the hell do you want?"

"You told me you were pawning your typewriter, so I brought you a new one. It's Countee's. He's not using it. He's never here anymore, too busy trying to decide between a future with Harold Jackman or Yolande Du Bois."

"This typewriter's for me?"

"The piece of paper in the roller has your name typed on it."

"Get the hell in here, you fool. I happen to have a bottle of gin I've been saving for a special occasion and this is it. What's your name again?"

---

Zora and I talked till dawn, the first of our many conversations about books and writers and the black experience. Far better educated than I, she'd studied at Howard, Hunter, Barnard, and Columbia. Once, she traveled with a Gilbert and Sullivan theater troupe—although as a maid, not a performer. She had been married once, perhaps twice, a veteran of any number of liaisons, although she was coy about her relationships.

Most lately, she had been putting her field notes on black folklore together as a book, but Mason, her mentor, had placed a hold on it. Zora was also co-authoring a play with Langston Hughes called *Mule Bone*. She admitted she was at first romantically attracted to Langston, but concluded that he was asexual.

"I love Langston, but he's as weak as water," she said. "Also, when we work as co-authors he tries to claim full credit, which is something I'll need to discuss with Godmother. She also mentors him."

I told her about my crush on Ruby Glam, the adorable black singer I'd wooed at Aunt Ethel's Rib and Okra place in Royal Prong, North Carolina, where I had infiltrated the local Ku Klux Klan, a band of racists so inept they'd forgotten to bring matches to a cross burning. To escape the state's fornication statutes, Ruby and I almost ran off together, but the miscegenation laws were too much for us to overcome. Zora seemed doubtful about my Klan experience, even though I could have shown her my clippings from the *Sun*. Still, I didn't reveal to her that my mother was of mixed race.

Zora described her research into negro folklore.

"Many are tales I remember from growing up in Alabama: Brer Rabbit, Ole Massa, how God weighed up the dirt to make mountains, the hoodoo magic, the deadly damnation powders you feed to your enemies, and about the Congo Square conjure woman who generates dance rhythm by beating the shinbone of a donkey on a skull."

When she told me she too was a conjure woman, which made her a pagan, I kept a straight face, or thought I did.

"Inside, you're laughing at me," Zora said, "but I know things that white folks will never understand."

"Such as?"

"Ghosts always feel hot and smell faintish. Some ghosts grow fat if they eat too much. They love to dine on honey. A spirit newly released from the body is likely to be destructive, which is why black folks always throw a cloth over the face of a clock in the death chamber and cover the looking glass. Unless they do that, the clock will never run again and the mirror won't ever cast a reflection. A fresh egg in the hand of a murder victim will stop the murderer from escaping far from the scene. And if a murder victim is buried in a sitting position, the murderer will be fast brought to justice. When it rains at a funeral, God's so displeased he washes human footprints off the face of the earth."

"Have you told the police about these revelations?"

"You scoff, Gart, but hoodoo burns with all the intensity of a suppressed religion. Belief in black magic is older than Christianity, and who is to say which of the two superstitions is superior to the other."

Of that, I could not dispute.

Zora and I had many such discussions over time until late one night as I was tossing in my sleep, I was awakened by a soft tapping at my door. It was Zora.

"Do you have space in your sheets for a black woman, Gart?"

I did, and that night, after our sensuous coupling, I revealed to her that, white as I appeared, I was of mixed blood. It didn't faze her. Zora was like a brick wall that would loosen up bricks only a few at a time, if at all. She insisted I accompany her on her ritual pilgrimage to Charlotte Mason who, although white, was such a legendary figure in the Harlem Renaissance she had put leashes on any number of black writers and artists.

"I adore Godmother, but I need to straighten her out about a few things," Zora said.

I hoped.

---

*He wore his coffin for a hat, calamity his cape.* Countee Cullen's own words in his first book of verse, which might have been the epitaph for his wedding to Nina Yolande Du Bois. The planned pageantry at Salem Methodist Episcopal Church, Seventh Avenue and 129th Street, was trumpeted in black circles as the wedding of the decade, if not the century. To Countee, it was a death sentence.

Twelve-hundred engraved invitations were sent out to the apogee of black society. I didn't receive one but Countee gave me special dispensation to attend. He said, "It'll make nice fodder for that story you're writing, Gart."

We'd taken to meeting regularly at Tillie's Chicken Shack, where the reserved Cullen was forthright with me as he described the catastrophe he knew was about to happen.

"Yolande's mind is good but she's barely read a word of my poetry," he said. "She has utterly no interest. I'm not sure why I proposed in the first place. Maybe to keep up appearances. Gart, she doesn't love me."

"Then why—"

"We've got to go through with the wedding. Our families expect it, and things have gone too far for us to back down now. They've already pumped thousands of dollars into this thing. But Yolande's infatuated with a saxophone player she met at Fisk, Jimmy Lunceford, who heads a band called The Chickasaw Syncopators. They've just made a record for Columbia predictably titled 'The Chickasaw Stomp.' She's still carrying on with him. Her father doesn't approve, of course. He insists that she marry someone more academic and with excellent family connections, such as myself. If she doesn't, he's threatened to disown her. He's hired a guard to follow her whenever she goes out, although more times than not she manages to give him the slip."

Yolande's father W.E.B. Du Bois was the most famous African in America, and in the negro realm his word was all but law. His only rival was the black intellectual Alain Locke. Du Bois had founded the NAACP and edited the monthly magazine *The Crisis*. If there was anything resembling a spokesperson for the black race in America, Du Bois was it.

Countee said, "While he's supportive of the Harlem Renaissance, he says he doesn't give a damn about art for art's sake, that art is best utilized for propaganda in equalizing the races. He unhinges me, Gart, and he insists I refer to him as *Doctor* Du Bois. He's a freethinker, not part of any religion, yet he's entered into an unholy alliance with my minister stepfather who's just as enthusiastic as Dr. Du Bois about the wedding. My stepfather and mother have no children of their own, so I'm the closest they have to one. For the finale of our wedding ceremony, Dr. Du Bois wanted to release into the air two-thousand white doves, but we managed to talk him out of it. However, he's held firm on the damned balloons."

I said, "You mentioned that Yolande doesn't love you and that she's involved with Jimmie Lunceford. But how do you feel about *her?*"

"If the truth be told, I'm in love. No, not with her but with Harold Jackman, my wedding's best man, whose been my closest companion since we were students at De Witt Clinton High School. Don't look at me like that, Gart. You know I have feelings toward men, and I still find you attractive even though it didn't work out between us. In our society, it's impossible for me to publicly express my true impulses, which is why marriage to a woman is of strategic importance. Being known as queer in addition to being black would ruin me. So now you understand why Yolande and I have to complete this charade."

Indeed, it appeared to be a disaster in the making. I could offer no words of encouragement. And I don't think even a Henry Mencken could figure this one out.

The Du Bois-Cullen nuptials was a Harlem guest-list gazetteer that included Jean Toomer, Alain Locke, Jessie Redmon Fauset, James Weldon Johnson, Wallace Thurman, Nella Larsen, Anna Bontemps, and too many more to mention. Yolande boasted of sixteen bride's maids in green and white gowns, a matron of honor, and a flower girl. Countee had a boy ring bearer and nine groomsmen, including Langston Hughes, who vowed never to enter society again if he had to rent another swallow-tailed tux. Van Vechten was to serve as an honorary groomsman, but got to the ceremony so late it was too crowded to get in. I managed to squeeze through the door, but had to crouch under the pipe organ, constantly being bumped by the organist's knees.

Guests began arriving at the tabernacle in the early afternoon, well before the start of the ceremony. New York City police, alleged experts in crowd control, blew it this time. Two sergeants and thirteen patrolmen were dispatched to keep order, but they were outnumbered. Because of overcrowding at the nearby 125th Street station, trains were ordered to skip that stop. Even before the organist from the Union Theological Seminary played the "Wedding March" from *Lohengrin*, six-thousand people, mostly uninvited, had crammed into the church's nave, balcony, vestibule, sanctuary, choir loft, and overflowed into the surrounding streets.

In the chaos, nine people were injured and twenty-five arrested, some for theft. Someone ran off with a jewel-encrusted chalice that was used to hold the precious blood of Christ, although it was empty at the time, as well as a life-sized plaster cast of the Virgin Mary, which had realistic glass eyes that seemed to follow you around the room. It turned up later as a centerpiece in the bar at Small's Paradise.

Throughout Harlem, flasks were raised in speakeasies stylish and seedy to celebrate the glamorous couple. Black weddings were rarely reported in the white press, and never in the society pages, but this one made the *World, Mirror, Daily Racing Form, New Yorker Volkszeitung,* and *The Jewish Daily Forward.*

After the wedding, Countee and Yolande went their separate ways. Yolande continued to be bad with Jimmie Lunceford, now known as "The New King of Syncopation" and who became a headliner at the Cotton Club, while Countee Cullen ran off to Paris with Harold Jackman.

I was expecting fireworks to light up the skies when Conjure Queen Zora and I arrived at Godmother's penthouse at 399 Park Avenue. In fact, knowing of Mason's autocratic reign, I was counting on it.

She was a small yet imperious woman with snow-white hair who received us from her great-great grandfather's chair, which she occupied like a throne. I was introduced as a writer interested in the Harlem Renaissance, but the stone-faced Mason didn't seem to be impressed, and, because Henry Mencken was often reviled by his many enemies, I didn't want to risk invoking his name. She was decidedly uninterested in me, and never once addressed me directly. Perhaps if I had looked black, it might have been different. Zora and I sat on low stools looking up at her as if we were her subjects.

"Godmother, you sit with eternity," Zora gushed, "and I'm so grateful for your faith in me."

"Did you bring them?" Mason snapped.

"I did, Godmother. All sorted by date."

They were Zora's receipts for various expenditures, which Mason would either accept for reimbursement or reject, depending on her mood. The two women had entered into a contract in which Zora, as an employee, was paid two-hundred dollars a month. In exchange, Mason acted as her agent in collecting all manner of black material obtained by Zora, including music, folklore, poetry, hoodoo, conjure, and any expressions of negro art or related material. This included Zora's own writing, which she was not permitted to "use, publish, or present" without Mason's permission.

Mason thumbed through the receipts.

"What's this item for eighty-five cents?"

"Uh, sanitary napkins, Godmother."

"I approved a similar item just last month and it was less."

"I ran out, Godmother. I had an unusually heavy flow."

"And what's this three-dollar item from the apothecary?"

"Colon medicine, Godmother. You know how my insides are always acting up."

"My dear, did you not make an appointment with my own doctor, which I told you I would take care of?"

"No, Godmother, I didn't want to run up my costs. You're already too generous. But, and I hesitate to say this, what I really need is a new pair of shoes."

"We agreed you were only going to have one pair of shoes at a time."

"But my big toe is almost poking through the shoe on my right foot."

"Zora, my dear, I pay you generously every month and make little demands on you. I expect you to keep your costs down, and that includes your shoes. And remember I bought you a camera and an automobile."

"Which I park in New Jersey, Godmother, where it costs less. I know how unselfish you are, and that's why this sun-burnt child adores you so much. But there's something else, Godmother. As you know, I came back from the South with many pages of material on negro folklore. I've put them together as a book, which I call *Mules and Man*. I think it's ready to be published."

"No."

"But I've shown it to a number of people, including Carlo, and they all say it should be in print."

"I said no. I don't mind if you place items here and there with my approval, but you are not ready to publish a book. Your writing is showing improvement, and I believe you have the potential for brilliance, but any substantial work you attempt to publish at this time would only damage your career, and I'm not prepared to allow that to happen. I have too much invested in you."

"But isn't being published part of the writing process, Godmother?"

"Do you wish to terminate our contract?"

"Oh, of course not."

"Then say no more. You will continue to convey to me all you write and I'll let you know if I feel it is ready to be published."

I wanted to yell, but kept my trap shut. Why the hell did Zora drag me here to witness her humiliation by that woman?

Zora reached out, putting her slender, brown fingers over Mason's arthritic hand.

"Godmother, when you speak to me I suddenly recognize all of my terrible weaknesses and failures, my utter stupidity and lack of vision."

"Do not depreciate yourself, my dear. I have confidence in you."

"Still, I'm amazed that you continue your love and certainty. Please, please always see me with your inner vision, and I hope I'll forever be your Conjure Queen."

"Enough of such chatter, my dear. It was good of you to call on me and to introduce me to your young gentleman friend. But now you must go. I've scheduled high tea with some very important people who have just debarked in New York from England. Royalty, in fact."

On the way down the elevator, Zora said to me, "Don't say a word, Gart. Not a fucking word."

---

I went places, talked to people. And learned a lot, such as that things had been heating up for Owney Madden. He was leaving the Cotton Club in the early morning hours in his black Peerless Model Six-90 sedan, George Raft at the wheel. As they headed south on Lenox Avenue, two cars pulled alongside and opened fire with submachine guns before speeding off. Nobody was hurt, although George's hair was mussed. But the Peerless was shot to hell and Owney was pissed. Really pissed. That car cost a bundle. To make matters worse, nobody saw nothin'. And even if they had, they still saw nothin'.

Owney, who once called himself, The Best Shot in New York, had been trying to go legit—mostly. He bought into other clubs around town, including the Stork, El Fey, and the Silver Slipper. Not only that, he had a delectable new girlfriend: Mae West, the blonde bombshell who was the leading lady in a Broadway play she composed herself, *Diamond Lil*—and who had spent ten days in the slammer for her raunchy show *Sex*. Plus Owney had gotten into the boxing game, buying pieces of Jack Dempsey and Max Baer.

But despite his good intentions, he felt misunderstood and under siege, with the cops constantly harassing him, busting him for every little infraction, such as jaywalking, littering, and spitting on the sidewalk.

"I'm gettin' too old for this," he bitched to his pal George, who later told me all about it. "I already got five slugs in me and I don't need no more. I'm thinkin' about dumpin' the Cotton Club, sellin' my share to my partner Big Frenchy De Mange, and lettin' him carry the weight. It looks like Vincent Mad Dog Coll has been tryin' to muscle in, and who wants a war with Mad Dog? That mug's crazy. I might retire to some peaceful little town out in the sticks somewhere. Ever hear of a place called Hot Springs, Arkansas? Bet I could be happy in a burg like that, maybe buy a little spa or something—even if they don't speak our language down there."

Nobody knew who Owney's would-be assassins were, although the gunmen seemed to have shot high and wide and not in between. A lot of folks speculated that it was just a calling card left by Mad Dog Coll. I was putting my money on Bolito King Holstein, although I never found the solution.

None of this meant, however, that the Cotton Club would change its white customers-only policy anytime soon.

---

The money was too good to turn down. Zora decided to abandon Harlem after receiving a fourteen-hundred-dollar fellowship from the Association for the Study of Negro Life and History. With the blessing of Godmother, she was to head solo to Florida in her puny Nash to revisit the South's turpentine camps, sugar cane factories, cotton fields, phosphate mines, sawmills, and bawdy houses, and to absorb as many oral histories as she could. She expected to be gone for two years. Two years. Perhaps renting some little house somewhere down there.

I was unhappy with her decision. Either she was being selfish or I was. Maybe both of us. We'd finished one pint of so-so bathtub gin and, as the first one hadn't made us blind—so far—we were poised to crack another. I had turned Countee's annoying, phony face of Jesus against the wall. Who wanted the Lamb of God ogling a naked man and woman guzzling sheepdip in a narrow bed with busted springs?

"I think I'm in love with you," I told her as we lay on my damp sheets on the eve of her departure. We were both sweaty from our lovemaking. There was no response, only a pregnant pause. "I thought you felt the same, Zora. At least wait until I wrap up the research for my Harlem story before you go. I'm almost through."

"So when you finish, then you'll leave Harlem? If I wait, what after that? Would you go to the Deep South with me or back to Baltimore? I do have feelings for you, Gart, and for a man who's more white than black, you're decent enough in bed. But, unlike you, I don't use the term 'love' loosely. I have too much work to do and want no distractions. Also, I'm not going to disappoint Godmother. We just renewed our contract for another two years."

"Godmother, Godmother. When are you going to strike out on your own, Zora? You don't need her. The woman's holding you back. It could be years before she lets you publish a book. She sits on a goddamned throne while you bust your ass. What does she do but collect your work and throw you pittances in return?"

"Shut your mouth, Gart. She's the dearest little mother of the primitive world, God's flower and my flower. Life's a road with one end in heaven, the other in hell, and Godmother has dragged more than one of us to paradise from the fate of everlasting blindness."

"Why did you take me with you to see her in the first place? It was an embarrassment."

"Because I wanted to give you a piece of myself, a part that most people will never see, my vulnerable self. It was a gift. Something you'll probably never grasp. Besides, you have your own Godfather, this H.L. Mencken you're always talking about. Everyone in America knows of Mr. Mencken, even those who don't read him. Who is he but a distasteful cynic who pronounces on things he may not even understand? He might have published a few black authors in his *American Mercury*, but I hear he often speaks unkindly of us and dismisses out of hand those he calls hebes, hillbillies, lintheads, beaners, and greasers. When are you going to strike out on *your* own?"

"Touché, Zora. But in Henry's defense, if there's racism or anti-Semitism in him, it's so casual and unintentional that he's oblivious of it."

"And that makes it right?"

"He judges everyone the same way, measures them against his own intellectual standards."

"Then why does he put up with *you?*"

In a flash of anger, I sat up in bed.

"That's cruel, Zora. And unfair."

"I'll tell you why he does, Gart. Because you're just as cynical as your mentor. You just don't know it yet. Mr. Mencken is still grooming you. Besides, how much do you *really* know about black people anyway?"

"I told you. My mother—"

"What's the negro's most visible characteristic?"

"Uh…"

"I'll explain. It's drama. That's why we're so imitative. Know what I mean by drama, Gart? I'm talking about mimicry. Our use of gestures in place of words. Bet you never even noticed. And, despite our casual exteriors, we're filled with restrained ferocity, which often comes out in our music and dancing. Also, we have angularity, by which I mean that every artistic impulse of the negro is sharply defined: dancing, storytelling, sculpture, singing. What did I tell you when we met on those stairs when I was toting that typewriter to the pawnshop? That no white person can ever get closer to anything in Harlem other than drinking or getting laid.

"Carl Van Vechten has only touched the surface, and, in spite of his Harlem novel, he knows much less about black people than he thinks he does, Gart. He wasn't even aware that the Cotton Club refuses to admit black customers. How obtuse? So you once carried on with some black girl in North Carolina. Who cares? You're still about as white as it gets, no matter what you claim about your mixed-race mother."

"You're too hard on me, Zora. I came to Harlem with a sincere purpose. To write about the Renaissance as I saw it and to share my understanding of it."

"Good for you, Gart. You have your labors cut out for you, As for me, I have much to do in addition to my research. I'm going to put together a volume of negro work songs for piano and guitar. All primitive music started with the drum, and singing is an attenuation of the drum beat. The closer to the primitive, the more prominent the drum. Langston and I are still working on that play we're co-writing, and I'm thinking about developing an opera with Paul Robeson. And I've just finished a study of Cudjo Lewis, the last survivor of the final slave ship to reach America, a manuscript called *Barracoon*. I'm going to drop it off with Godmother on my way out of town."

"But she'll leave it in limbo too while you're running off below the Mason-Dixon Line to God knows where. It's all a form of escape for you."

"I'm not going South to run away from anything, much less my blackness. I intend to embrace it, to celebrate it. It's hardly an escape. But you wouldn't understand these things."

"You're wrong, Zora. I may not like all I hear, such as your refusing to commit to me or your leaving, but I do understand. I know much more about the black experience now—or at least I see it better—because of you. You've given me so many insights that when I publish my story in the *Sun*, it will show an awareness of the Harlem Renaissance that it wouldn't otherwise have."

"Dear, dear, Gart. I shall miss you. Say, where's that other flask of gin? If we hurry we can finish it off before dawn."

Outside, through the open window, came the voice of a girl singing, possibly from some rusty fire escape, and it was all too painful for me to hear.

> *Gee, but it's hard to love someone*
> *When that someone don't love you.*

*I'm so disgusted, heartbroken too*
*I've got those downhearted blues.*

———————

You could hear the stucco-faced Savoy Ballroom at 596 Lenox at 140th long before you saw it. Its block-long mahogany-floored ballroom easily accommodated five thousand people, and the Savoy was never content with just one band, but two, alternating through Harlem's nocturnal frenzy. Langston Hughes captured the mood when he wrote,

*I could take the Harlem night*
*and wrap around you,*
*Take the neon lights and make a crown,*
*Take the Lenox Avenue busses,*
*Taxis, subways,*
*And for your love song tone their rumble down.*

It was my last day in Harlem before returning to Baltimore and Henry, and Carlo insisted that I learn the Lindy Hop at the Savoy before capping things at what turned out to be a sordid speakeasy called Sambo's. To be candid, the entire night was mostly a blur of color, light, sound, and bodies—but there was much to be said for that. We entered the Savoy through a chandeliered lobby and walked up the mirrored stairs to the orange and blue accented ballroom where the bands of King Oliver and Chick Webb were facing off on two raised bandstands, one at either end, so the music was nonstop.

The heart and soul of the Savoy may have been African, but it was owned by a white Jew named Moe Gale. Which wasn't unusual. Jews owned most of the small shops in Harlem; Greeks and Italians the restaurants, gangsters the big cabarets, and WASPs the banks. The blacks were left with the churches.

Carlo had gotten us one of the best spots in the home of happy feet, a round-topped table at what was known as the Cat's Corner, which was reserved for the hall's most talented dancers. It was also closest to the stage where, as we took our table, King Oliver's nine-piece Dixie Syncopators, with Oliver on trumpet, were blasting his hit "Dippermouth Blues."

The waiters brought us glasses of root beer and ginger ale, which we liberally spiked from our flasks, so by the time King Oliver introduced a special guest star I was without a care. But I sobered up quickly when I saw the guest was Fats Waller. Our table was near enough to the stage that I was afraid he might recognize me as the apprentice hood who had kidnapped him to perform at Al Capone's birthday party in Cicero, Illinois.

"Carlo, trade seats with me."

"What for?"

"I need to have my back to the stage. You don't want to know, Carlo, trust me."

Fats was his usual, expansive self, who polished off his set with "Honeysuckle Rose" and left the stage to thunderous applause. King Oliver picked up the beat with his famous "Doctor Jazz," and it was then that I felt someone tapping my arm.

Fats. I knew had to be Fats. All three-hundred pounds of him. He'd spotted me. I was a gonner. And this time, I wasn't packing. But, no, it was a towering Amazon of a woman with skin as dark as the night and bright red fingernails like claws.

"Dance, hon?" she said.

My response wasn't particularly astute, although I said it with conviction.

"Huh?"

"We're gonna do the Lindy Hop, hon."

"The Lindy what?"

Carlo said, "Get up, Gart, it's a dance and she's a Lindy Hopper. I had it all arranged. You're going to do the Lindy with her. They invented the Lindy here at the Savoy, so that's another part of your story."

"I, I don't know how to do it. They didn't teach dancing in theology school."

She said, "No problem, hon. My name's Jasmin. I'll teach you."

She grabbed me by the arm and pulled me to the dance floor, crowded with mixed couples. Few places, even in New York, permitted dancing by couples of the opposite race, but at the Savoy, dancing had no color line. The only thing anybody looked at on the dance floor were the flying feet.

Jasmin squared off side by side with me, our arms around each other's waists. She was a head taller than me.

"It's an eight-count pattern, hon, that starts with the right foot, known as the rock step, then triple step, walk, walk, triple step. Repeat. Got it?"

"Well…"

Before long, as King Oliver rocked, I was doing something with my feet, but I wasn't sure it could be called the Lindy or much of anything else. I was self-conscious, acutely mindful of my ineptitude. My eyeglasses started to steam. But I took some comfort in that no one but Jasmin seemed to be aware of me, and I was resigned to the fact that I couldn't hide my embarrassing performance from her. Even in high heels, Jasmine's steps seemed perfect. The couples on the packed floor danced with such well-practiced exuberance, I didn't see how they avoided colliding with one another, but they didn't. I thought again of Langston Hughes's words.

> Dance with you till day—
> Dance with you, my sweet brown Harlem girl.

Jasmin walked me back to our table, where Carlo applauded.

"You forgettin' somethin', hon?" she said to me.

"What?"

Carlo said, "She wants her tip, Gart."

Jasmin told me, "Maybe you oughta stick to the conga line, hon. It's only one-two-three-kick."

Nicely tipped, she ambled off on those clicking high heels, satisfied, while I collapsed in my chair draining my spiked root beer at the same time.

"Do you think Charles Lindbergh ever does the Lindy?" I asked Carlo.

"Lindbergh's on record as saying it's just as easy to stand as to sit, so my guess is he has."

Chick Webb's band took over, then again King Oliver. I got drunk as much on the music as the hooch.

Somehow, at some godforsaken hour, we found our way to a reeking tenement, where a man sat in a window holding a long chain attached to the front door.

"Where the hell are we?" I asked Carlo.

"Sambo's."

"What street are we on?"

"It's known as Vaseline Alley."

The man in the window said to Carlo "What's the password?"

"Goldfarb sent us," he replied.

"Who's Goldfarb?" I whispered to Carlo.

"No one. It's the password."

The man in the window pulled the chain, which opened the door. We entered and walked down a flight of stairs to a packed basement jammed with men dancing with one another. I soon learned they were steeplejacks, longshoremen, bricklayers, chimneysweeps, truck drivers, a smattering from Wall Street, Columbia professors, and three or four stage actors. I saw a low platform with a three-piece band and a singer, heavily made up in a garish blonde wig and long skirt. It was clear the singer was a man, although he sang "Red Lips, Kiss my Blues Away" in a clear contralto.

"Carlo," I slurred, "I don't see any women here."

"If you did, it would be quite an imposition, wouldn't it? Although if it's any comfort there's lots of crossdressing. Ah, I see my friend Clinch Jackson."

Carlo took me to him, a muscular black man, and the two kissed on the lips.

Carlo said, "Clinch is a welterweight with twelve wins, four losses, and one draw. Such a darling boy. Oh, and here comes my dear friend Rudy. Be nice to him, Gart. Rudy's a sandhog who had to be dug out of a collapsed subway tunnel last month, and he's still a little shaky."

Rudy and Carlo embraced.

Carlo said, "Oh look, two of my favorite gonsils are here: Claude McKay and Alain Locke. Let's go over and say hello."

I lost track of things after that, but when I awoke with a hellish headache, I was alone in my room at Niggerati Manor. I felt so lousy that I turned the picture of Jesus so it faced the room again. Well, dammit, it couldn't hurt. There was a scribbled note on the bedside table. It was from Carlo that read, "Do good, dear boy. I'm giving up the writing game. I've already informed the Knopfs. I've just bought a new camera and will be taking up portrait photography in a big way. Come sit for me. Royal purple dachshunds with silver legs to you. Carlo."

---

When my story on the Harlem Renaissance appeared in the *Sun*, it was widely praised for its insights into one of the most important cultural movements in modern America. Publicly, I took full credit for the article, but it couldn't have been written without the remarkable people in Harlem I'd come to know and love. Carlo sent me a wire of congratulations, calling me "The New Mencken."

I had concluded in my piece that I saw no way for America to completely redeem itself for its brutal treatment of the black race and the failure of the federal government to declare lynching as illegal. I felt the same way about the injustices perpetrated against men who loved other men, which forced them to crowd into sleazy, secret speakeasies like Sambo's, ever in fear of being dehumanized by the police. Even Henry had once concluded that every decent man in America was ashamed of the government he lived under.

But I saw to my shock that the editors, in their wisdom, had deep-sixed my fervent conclusions from the story.

---

Dalilah, my Hollywood flame who'd rescued me from Cuba, had just finished the starring role in a hit Rinestone Studios talkie called *Shelter from the Storm.* She was now in demand and said to be dating her leading man Ramon Martinez. James Branch Mandell, the burned-out screenwriter I knew in Hollywood, had sobered up and had published a new novel that was nominated for a Pulitzer. Even Henry, Mandell's nemesis, was impressed.

While I was happy at my friends' success, I was still stuck in Baltimore, uncertain of my future. But I had been thinking a lot about it.

"What's next, Taggart, m'boy?" Henry asked me over one lager or three at his regular table at the Rennert.

I said, "The Roaring Twenties are about to merge with the nineteen-thirties and whatever that'll bring, the end of an era. I think it's time for me to go down to Washington and dig into what's going on. Everyone knows about hanky-panky down there. Teapot Dome still lives. All I have to do is prove it. With your political contacts, Henry, you could get me a job with a congressman, maybe as a speechwriter."

"Consider it accomplished. I know just the lawmaker. He's an ass, but that should be of no surprise. If a politician found he had cannibals among his constituents, he'd feed them missionaries for lunch."

I had no idea then how badly the twenties were going end, and that even the repeal of Prohibition wouldn't make it any better. But I was on the story.

And that's -30- for this reporter.

> *The gracious city swept across the line;*
> *Oblivious of the color of my skin,*
> *Forgetting that I was an alien guest,*
> *She bent to me, my hostile heart to win,*
> *Caught me in passion to her pillowy breast;*
> *The great, proud city, seized with a strange love,*
> *Bowed down for one flame hour my pride to prove.*
>
> —Claude McKay

## — SIX —

# THE CRASH

*Why, hello there, mister iceman. Where have I seen your face?*
*Please don't try to tease me, mister, just because I lost the race;*
*I was once a great big banker, worth a million for a time,*
*But I lost the whole kaboodle in the fall of twenty-nine.*

—W. Lee O'Daniel

Damn that Shipwreck Kelly, always perching on flagpoles and stuff, and cutting into news that mattered. Shipwreck broke his previous record for flagpole sitting at Baltimore's Carlin's Park that early fall of nineteen twenty-nine: twenty-three days of resting his butt on a padded seat sixty feet in the air. He would eventually surpass his record, which was just the kind of nonsense folks wanted to read about. Mencken would call it blatherskite. I dragged my heels but the *Sun*'s city desk made me snap to and cover the story. However, in the long run I got the last laugh. Shipwreck helped me to crack a scandal that involved corruption, perfidy—and murder. And damned if Henry didn't get engaged to be married.

———

The nation's economy was hot, sizzling, and ablaze. So, with Henry's encouragement, I invested into stocks what little I'd managed to cull from my meager salary at the *Sunpapers*. Money didn't grow under a mattress, so just about everyone with even a small bundle was speculating on the market. He directed me to his Charles Street broker, Hyman Katz, who performed the viola in the Saturday Night Club, a small group of amateur musicians with whom Henry played piano.

"Worry not, Taggart, m'boy," he said. "Hyman is one of the better ones—if you catch my drift."

I knew Henry wasn't talking about Hyman's qualifications as a stockbroker.

"Furthermore, he can't play the viola worth a damn," Henry added, as the two of us transgressed against the Eighteenth Amendment at the Hotel Rennert bar, which by all appearances sold only Hires Root Beer, Royal Crown Cola, and bratwurst.

Henry's Saturday Night Club, a major adjunct to his life, focused on the German music that he adored—*always* German. It was, to him, the only music.

"I raise my stein upon high to salute Bach, Beethoven, and Brahms," he said, "although it's hard for me to imagine any of them being proficient at billiards."

After consigning to Hyman all I had to invest—my life savings—I relaxed in the knowledge that my capital was working for me. Hoover had assumed the nation's highest office from Coolidge, successor to the late, scandal-ridden Harding who at least looked presidential. Henry maintained that Hoover was a transparent fraud, and while Coolidge had lacked a single idea in his skull he at least managed not to be a nuisance.

Henry said, "With Coolidge as President it was almost as good as not having a President at all," but he predicted the days of so-called Coolidge Prosperity were unlikely to last.

With that in mind, he offhandedly recommended I not dump my nest egg into one basket. Nonsense. I may have been somewhat callow, but, presumably, I had a long life ahead, so I was undeterred by the risks.

Now convinced that my dough was in good hands, I was poised to take on a new reportorial assignment: looking into shady dealings in the nation's capital. Henry had received a mysterious cryptic message suggesting that something was amiss about a proposed military hospital at Fort Belnoir in Fairfax, Virginia. A bill to approve it was before a congressional committee chaired by Representative Seymour A. Skutch (R-Md), a man Henry lampooned without mercy, although in a way that the moronic Skutch thought was praise. There were few, if any, politicians Henry extolled. And he believed that the real test of truth was ridicule, as he provided day after day.

He told me, "A politician is professionally dishonorable. He makes so many compromises and submits to so many humiliations that he's indistinguishable from a streetwalker. Skutch in particular has the bombastic air of a cock on a dunghill."

The unsigned message, delivered in a sealed envelope anonymously to the city desk, consisted of three symbols: a sketch of a cow with a dollar sign in its mouth, a pair of wings perched on what looked like a snake, and what may have been an antique cannon mounted on wheels. Attached to the note was a partial clipping of a *Sun* article on the proposed hospital at Fort Belnoir.

"What am I to make of this, Taggart, m'boy?"

"The cannon obviously refers to something military. Fort Belnoir no doubt. I don't know about the rest—but with a little practice the artist might turn out some decent work someday."

To complicate the mystery, a week after Henry was given the note with the mysterious symbols, the body of Skutch's speechwriter, Frank Morhouse, was found under a desk in the House Chamber, which sparked little attention. There were no visible signs of foul play, and Skutch's office insisted his passing was the result of a bad heart. But what was Morhouse doing so late at night under a desk in that empty chamber? Poor Morhouse's untimely death was a bit of luck for us. We jumped at it.

As the death left an opening on Skutch's congressional staff, Henry suggested in a call to the congressman that I fill the vacancy. Flattered by Henry's attention, Skutch responded by hiring me sight unseen at a pay scale much better than my salary at the *Sunpapers*, although not as good as my weeks in Hollywood.

I said to Henry, "This could open the door into a new world of politics for me: guiding democracy from the inside."

"Like a circus being run from inside a monkey cage, you mean."

For this assignment, my nom de plume was Kevin S. Clarke, a virtual boy wonder with a gift for writing stunning prose in Henry's Johns Hopkins adjunct class on Journalism, Goethe, Nietzsche, and Comparative Religion. I'd never gone to Hopkins and Henry taught no such class, but few on Capitol Hill, especially Skutch, would doubt Henry's word. Politicians on both sides of the aisle lived in fear he might single them out in his *Sun* column, subjecting them to mockery, which made him both powerful and despised.

He said, "I enjoy politicians abundantly more than professors. They sweat in greater proportions and they're vastly more amusing."

"Henry, this anonymous note. Do you suppose the death of Skutch's speechwriter could be connected somehow? If so, I might find myself dead too—before Hyman Katz earns me my first million on Wall Street."

"If journalism's about the truth, remember that truth isn't enough. Danger be damned. You must expose and denounce the false. Washington will always hatch more Warren G. Hardings, Taggart, m'boy, so stay alert. Newspaper work's only dull when you're writing obituaries—unless it's your own. And you'd better take that note with those cryptic symbols with you. It may come in handy."

I'd just left the *Sun* office and was at the corner of Baltimore and Charles about to mount my ancient two-seat Dixie Flyer for the short haul to DC when the copyboy who had my old job corralled me. He towed me, mentally flailing and howling, back inside to the city desk.

The editor, Simon Legree—not his real name because he may outlive me—said, "Asquith, I know you and Mencken have been cooking up something, but we're shorthanded. Need you to pay a call on this flagpole sitter called Shipwreck Kelly before you go. Know where Carlin's Park is, out on Reisterstown Road?"

"Yeah, my favorite attraction is the tea-cup ride."

"Get your ass up there and gimme twelve-hundred words. I'm also sending our best photographer, A. Aubrey Bodine. Don't get in his way."

When it came to daily journalism, or the presumption of it, there were some things not even Henry could change. The flagpole story I was assigned to may have been a meadow muffin, as they said in West Virginia, but Bodine's photos would give it a little class.

---

Carlin's Park, known as Baltimore's Million-Dollar Playground, had mushroomed since it opened in nineteen-eighteen. In addition to its original roller coaster and other amusements, it now had a thousand-foot swimming pool patterned after the baths of ancient Rome, a roller rink, boxing ring, dance hall, and a vaudeville theater. The pleasure ground followed the quaint custom of our day: black people could work and perform there but otherwise were not admitted. That would certainly infuriate Carl Van Vechten in the unlikely event he'd ever bother to show his face at Carlin's Park. Carlo had converted a room of his Manhattan apartment into a studio and darkroom, and was now taking stunning photographic portraits of the era's major figures. He vowed to snap at least one shot of Henry doing something in contemplation, such as studying his cigar or snapping his suspenders.

I spotted Shipwreck from the parking lot, which was easy because a human being attached to the tip of a pole was a sight one was unable to ignore.

When I reached the scene of the stunt, which was roped off to keep the onlookers from crowding too close, I hollered up, "Mr. Kelly, it's Gart Booker Asquith III, *Baltimore Sun*. I'd like to do an interview with you."

He bellowed back, "You're too far away, Scoop. Come on up."

"Huh?"

"Put your keister in that sling and we'll hoist you up to eye level. Bring along a cup of fresh Joe and cigarettes and the latest newspaper when you come up."

Not on your life, I thought. I wasn't the most physically adventuresome guy in the world, although I did successfully arm wrestle an Irish gangster on the Capitol Limited to Chicago and once cold-cocked a hood when he wasn't looking. But I realized that if I didn't land the interview, I'd never be able to blow town to work on my congressional piece. Simon Legree owned my derriere. So I climbed into the sling and the park's flunkies turned a crank to slowly lift me up to where Shipwreck was sitting on a cushion attached to the pole. He had one leg strapped to the staff. I wasn't sure how secure he'd be if he, say, fell asleep and slipped off his perch.

Shipwreck had no fear of heights, but I was spooked and clung to the sling's straps so tightly my fingers throbbed. He thanked me profusely for the coffee, which he sipped while puffing a Camel. He was in his late thirties with thinning red hair, and despite his chunky build seemed to be roosting comfortably.

I followed Henry's basic first rule of journalism: never, ever pose a yes or no question unless you only want a yes or no answer.

"How many days have you been up here?" I asked.

"I reckon it's been close to three weeks."

"How do you relieve yourself?"

"The usual way. But I can tell you I mostly have a liquid diet."

"How do you sleep?"

"Sitting up, Scoop. I'm used to it. As you can see, there are a couple of holes in the pole that I can stick my thumbs down into. If I start to lean in my sleep I'll feel the pain in my thumbs and that wakes me up. But I can go as long as four days without sleep, so it don't worry me much."

"You've adopted a strange career, Mr. Kelly."

"Call me Shipwreck, a nickname I got after I escaped from drowning when the *Titanic* went down. But never call me Aloysius."

"Wait. You were on the *Titanic?*"

"Clung to the iceberg after the ship hit it for two days before I was rescued by a Panamanian trawler. I've also survived three other shipwrecks. Plus I lived through a train derailment, two airplane crashes, and four automobile smashups. I've been a stunt man, a movie double, prizefighter, steeplejack, window cleaner, and a high diver. I'm the luckiest idiot on the planet."

"How'd you get into this racket?"

"In Philly. A pal dared me to climb a flagpole outside of Wannamaker's, and it attracted such a crowd, the department store gave me money to keep on doing it. The rest is history. I'm actually paid for what I do. Sometimes as much as a hundred clams a day."

"You've started a fad, Shipwreck. Flagpole sitters are now out there everywhere trying to top your record."

"And I'll beat 'em all, Scoop. I'll be looking for other projects after I wrap up things here. Have my eye on Atlantic City's Steel Pier. They got a pole that's two hundred twenty-five feet in the air. Say, I don't like to be rude, but I'm gonna have to break off this interview on account of it's time for me grab my looking glass and shave. A man on public view like me has gotta look dapper. Also, I wanna catch up on the latest in the sports section. I see the A's are gonna start junkballer Howard Ehmke in the first game of this year's Series. But, listen, Scoop, if you wanna stay in touch, here's my card. Just call my wife Vivian. She knows where to find me."

Which is exactly what I would do.

———————

I'd been looking forward to making a grand entrance in our nation's great hometown: walking up the three hundred sixty-five majestic steps of the U.S. Capitol Building for the first time and absorbing the magnificence. But, no, on the phone I was directed by Skutch's chief of staff, a man named Ben Gunn, to the House Office Building, just south of the Capitol. The white-marbled, colonnaded building on Independence Avenue appeared impressive enough. I learned that Theodore Roosevelt had laid its cornerstone in nineteen-six, an occasion in which he coined the term 'muckrakers.' But it paled in comparison with the Capitol itself. Recently, there had been calls to rename the House habitat for Joseph Gurney Cannon, once the powerful Speaker of the House.

Inside, a guard directed me to Skutch's second-floor office, where I was met by Gunn who showed me to an empty desk, one of several where the congressional staffers sat. All appeared to be busy at whatever they were supposed to be doing, and I took instant note of a fetching dark-haired woman working a typewriter's keys.

Gunn told me my desk had been that of poor Frank Morhouse before his untimely death at the age of thirty-two.

"Then I have a few years left," I quipped, knowing immediately it wasn't funny. I quickly changed the subject by saying I'd always thought the congressional offices were in the actual Capitol.

Gunn said, "That's where the congressional leadership is, but the rank-and-file has been here for more than twenty years. But you can actually walk from here to the Capitol through a tunnel. The Senate's offices have a subway, although they're on the north side."

"Is there anything the congressman wants me to write immediately?"

"Morhouse had been working on a speech the congressman is to deliver this weekend at the Crab and Seafood Fest in Mount Vernon Place in Baltimore. Since Morhouse never finished it, that's your first assignment. It's a rush job. You'll find his notes on that and other speeches in the works in his desk drawer. By the way, I expect you to clear everything you write with me before it goes to the congressman."

"Everything?"

"Everything. Representative Skutch is a busy man."

"When will I meet him?"

"He rarely gets in before noon except when an important vote is scheduled."

"Any tips on what I'm to say in this Crab and Seafood Fest speech?"

"The usual platitudes about crustaceans and the American Way. You come recommended by your Mr. Mencken so you figure it out."

Damn, it looked like I was going to have to do some actual work. I also had a feeling Ben Gunn didn't particularly care for Henry, and likely for good reason. Skutch was a conservative windbag about whom Henry, in his *Evening Sun* column, had engaged in some wicked lampoonery. The gullible Skutch, notorious for his hissy fits, fell for it, but everyone was afraid to tell him otherwise. Henry wrote:

While it is difficult to praise the buffoons, boors, brutes, and barbarians who infest the diminished Halls of Congress, it is easy to single out Maryland's own congressional representative, one Seymour A. Skutch. I have known Congressman Skutch for many years since the bankruptcies of his several businesses, notably a billiards parlor on Light Street and a haberdashery on East Lombard, setbacks that have in no way diminished his enthusiasm to incur further financial ruin. The most dangerous man to any government is the one who is able to think things out without regard to prevailing superstitions and taboos. Inevitably such a man comes to the conclusion that the government he lives under is dishonest, insane, and intolerable. I give Congressman Skutch high marks for never reaching such conclusions due to his indominable faith in the status quo. A good politician is just as unthinkable as an honest burglar, and it has never once been suggested that Congressman Skutch was ever a burglar. In general, a congressional member is one who can sit on a fence and yet keep both ears to the ground—and the ground, no matter how dank, is precisely where Congressman Skutch has tirelessly positioned his head. It requires true physical stamina to reach so low and remain there. Further, whenever you hear a politician speak of his love for his country, it is a sign that he expects to be paid for it. I can state emphatically that Congressman Skutch adores his nation—as he attests so vociferously each and every Fourth of July. I for one hope that his reign will be long and for him so personally profitable that he will continue in office. This column survives only by writing about inconsequent, sophistical, casuistical, Pecksniffian, and pharisaic political figures such as the indefatigable Congressman Seymour A. Skutch. Excelsior!

Skutch loved it! He proudly framed the Mencken column and mounted it prominently on the wall of his congressional office. Skutch was so grateful, he entered the column into the Congressional Record and was willing to say yes to any request Henry might make. Aside from a few possible exceptions, such as demanding that Skutch divorce his wife or give up his girlfriend—although Skutch could likely be induced into jettisoning the wife. "And take my mother-in-law too."

---

The first thing I did was to forage through Morhouse's desk, not only looking for his Crab Fest notes but any material that might shed light on possible hanky-panky at Fort Belnoir, not that I was optimistic. Morhouse had been a doodler if not an artist and his favorite topic appeared to be the U.S. Capitol Building. He'd made any number of relatively decent sketches of the building and its great dome, inside and out. But drawings were drawings, especially those of a familiar landmark. What I needed was the sort of info that would lead to something revealing, assuming Morhouse knew anything. I found his Crab Fest notes and any number of doodles and sketches and random jottings that looked to be the sort of drivel Skutch would mouth before a crowd. But nothing that appeared to be useful.

The young woman I noticed when I first walked in introduced herself. Cerys McLean, staff assistant in charge of community liaison, whatever that was. She sat on the edge of the chair by my desk.

"They didn't waste any time in filling Frank's job, did they?" Cerys spoke in hushed tones so as not to be heard by others in the office. "He was buried only a few days ago at Oak Hill Cemetery in Georgetown. I was there. It was sad."

I said, "Apparently the congressman is making several speeches soon, including one this weekend. So they wanted me to go to work sooner than later. Did you know Frank Morhouse well?"

"We were… friends."

"What sort of person was he?"

"Frank loved mountain and rock climbing. Was indifferent to heights. Although he was athletic, he suffered from low blood pressure for which he was taking medicine. But I saw him on the day of his death and he seemed perfectly fine. Because his body was found in the House chamber, the coroner was called in, and pronounced it a heart attack."

"An odd place to die," I said

She said, "You don't always get to choose where you're going to go—or when."

"Was he happy here?"

"Writing political speeches wasn't Frank's first choice. He never cared for all the backroom stuff, and he didn't seem comfortable working for a politician. Frank loved puzzles and games, and he wanted to draw a comic strip for the newspapers. He especially liked the Sunday comics in the Hearst papers. But he never got the chance." Tears welled in her eyes. "Excuse me, I can't speak on the matter anymore."

"I'm sorry if I upset you, Miss McLean."

"It's not you. I told you that Frank and I were friends. Actually it was a bit more than that."

She put a handkerchief to her eyes and abruptly left the office just as Congressman Skutch strode in. He pumped my hand and invited me to his inner sanctum. I was quick to notice that Skutch's facial expression could turn from a goofy grin to a scowl in seconds. But most often he left his mouth open in what looked like a sense of bewilderment. And when he spoke it often seemed as though he had memorized words cobbled together from KKK tracts.

Skutch said, "Henry Mencken spoke highly of you."

"He's spoken of you as well," I replied.

"I want my Crab Fest speech this weekend to be a humdinger."

"Any salient points you'd like me to emphasize, sir?"

"The threat to this democracy of ours by anarchists, communists, freethinkers, atheists, homos, liberal Democrats, and those who would end Prohibition and allow our sacred nation to wallow in sin and disgrace.

Also, we got to promote racial separation as a fact of life, as well as the freedom to practice our noble Christian religion in all the public schools and the halls of government. For example, by law, the Ten Commandments oughta be posted in bold letters in the lobby of each government building in our great land: city, state, and federal. And a cross placed atop every public building. Ours is a Christian nation with all that that implies. And say something nice about crabs too."

It was instant confirmation that the Mencken column Skutch had so proudly framed had gone well over his head. I was prepared to carry on in the Mencken tradition.

"I should have no problem, sir," I said, "and I'll get a rough draft to you before the end of the day."

"Gunn takes care of all the little details. Give it to him. But I got a lot of other speech ideas I need you to write about. They just keep poppin' into my brain. One of 'em is a plan to utilize the government printing office to publish inexpensive editions of the Bible to be issued to every public school in America as textbooks."

"An ambitious project, sir."

"I'm also going to offer an English language-only bill. If it passes, all newly arrived foreigners must speak English within two years or be deported. Also, they all got to be hosed down at the border on account of the diseases they bring in."

"Excellent, sir, but what about Fort Belnoir?"

"Huh?"

"That proposed new military hospital in Virginia. It's before your own Special Committee on Hospitals and Veterans Concerns. The papers seem to think that a private developer, Black Industries, has the inside track to win the contract."

"Complicated, damned complicated. See Gunn about that. I got to devote my time to the important stuff. Like deliverin' that Crab and Seafood speech you're gonna write me. It better be good."

I realized that this job was going to be even more fun than I had thought. For Representative Seymour A. Skutch, ignorance had been no obstacle to his political career, and it was my duty to help further it.

------

*Oh a crab is a pal*
*Who would travel a mile*
*Simply to get a smile*
*And make dinner worthwhile*

—Anonymous

Congressman Skutch never expected to be hit by noisy demonstrators from not one but two crab-rights groups at the annual Crab and Seafood Fest in Baltimore's Mount Vernon Place. It happened under the shadow of the towering, one hundred-seventy-eight-foot tall monument honoring George Washington, which at the top boasted an illuminated sculpture of the general resigning his commission as commander-in-chief. The tower, dating to eighteen-fifteen and the first dedicated to Washington, was so tall, that neighbors in the fancy homes surrounding the square were first afraid it would collapse on them.

Skutch was to be a prime speaker at this gala event held annually at the height of crab season. As his speechwriter, I had to attend with him in case he needed last-minute rewrites to his script, which I'd knocked out with all the banality, vapidity, and cliché I could muster. He loved it, thought it would be as everlasting as the Gettysburg Address. Ben Gunn came too but stayed in the background as he usually did.

The Crab Fest was Baltimore's biggest event, far exceeding the fanfare and hoopla of the Preakness Stakes at Pimlico a little to the north. Colorful tents and stalls ringed Mount Vernon Place in the city's historic heart, with vendors selling every variation of crab: steamed to baked to soups to crabcakes on sticks. Henry maintained that crabs could be concocted in fifty different ways and that all were transcendental. For the uninitiated or skeptical, there were also oysters, shrimp, and lobster, while merchants hawked seafood-themed wares, artists displayed their creations, and kids thrilled on rides as a panoply of music came from strolling performers. A couple dressed as crabs danced the Lindy Hop sideways.

Personally, I despised the process of eating a steamed crab, grotesque as it was, in which there was so little flesh it took an eternity to figure out how to empty it and pick out the little slivers of meat. It also required using a mallet to crack open the tiny legs. What's more, the crab's guts were filled with green stuff known as tomalley, which effectively was shit, but which connoisseurs euphemistically called mustard or crab butter. Who were they fooling, especially those who spread tomalley on saltines to eat? The process of dissecting a crab needed to be accomplished by hand, which left debris under the fingernails and the eater's hands stinking of dead crustaceans for days. It was so messy, the crabs had to be consumed on top of newspapers, the *Sun* being the favorite. Did one of the sea's ugliest inhabitants really warrant an annual ritual? To me, their best use was putting day-old crab remains inside the hubcaps of your boss's car.

Both cheers and boos rose as Skutch mounted the stage where he was to follow bromides by the governor, mayor, senators, and other dignitaries. I kept my head low, hoping none of my *Sun* colleagues would spot me. As Kevin S. Clarke and working undercover, I didn't want to explain why I was associating with the likes of Seymour A. Skutch.

The jeers came from two camps: the Society for Understanding Crustaceans (SUC) and the American Crustacean Liberty Union (ACLU). Apparently, some internal conflict led the pro-crab group to split into two factions, each trying to drown out the other.

Using a megaphone, one of the protestors yelled, "Crabs aren't inanimate objects. They're living, feeling individuals."

A competitor, also with a megaphone, bellowed, "Crabs feel pain. They need their claws just like you need your hands."

And so it went.

"We demand the ethical treatment of crabs."

"Justice for crabs."

"Crabs suffer too."

"How would you like to have your legs broken with mallets?"

"Crabs feel fear just like humans."

"Crabs value their lives and those of their children."

"Crabs have unique personalities."

"Would you want to be steamed, boiled, or baked?"

"Crabs are Godfearing beings."

It didn't take Baltimore's Finest long to clear the square of the demonstrators although several heads were cracked in the process.

Given the unexpected protest, I rose to the occasion and adroitly adjusted Skutch's remarks to fit the situation, slipping him my revisions. I first feared he wouldn't be able to read my squiggles or stick to the script, but I had to give him begrudging credit. Armed with a megaphone, he utilized every word down to each comma and period. He stumbled only once on a typo. Skutch even had to stop from time to time to ingest the applause.

"My fellow Americans, what you saw here today was a disgrace, dozens of communistically-inspired radicals out to abolish our cherished American Way, and what can be more American than eating piles of steamed crab on a stack of old newspapers? That demonstration was a perfect example of America's rot from within, which, unless we are vigilant, can lead to irrevocable decay stretching from the amber waves of grain to the majestic purple mountains above the fruited plain and from sea to shining sea. And, no, crabs are *not* Godfearing. They've never read the Bible. Crabs never even went to Sunday school. Not one crab has ever been baptized. If God didn't want us to eat steamed crabs he wouldn't have invented steam.

"Let this be a lesson, my fellow Americans. Remember that we must never lose sight of the enemy within, the foreigners, the liberals, the co-called academic elites, those who would snatch away our guns and our crabs, and above all the atheists, the Jews, the Muslims, and the so-called freethinkers who jeopardize our true Christian beliefs, an insult to the one and only God. My brethren, symbolically go with me down to the Harbor so that, in the precious oil that slicks the waters, we may wash away our sins and gird our loins for battle against this menace. Until then, pray for the good health of former President Coolidge and for the success of our sublime new President Hoover, who will lead us to continued greatness as ordained by the magnificent men of Wall Street and, above all, by our valiant Christian God. Amen."

Personally, I thought my line about washing away our sins in the Harbor's precious oil slicks was inspired.

The applause and cheers were long and hearty, and at that moment I knew I was unlikely to top the cynicism that Zora Neale Hurston in Harlem had perceptively seen in me when I couldn't see it in myself. I tended to identify with T.S. Eliot's poem that read, "I should have been a pair of ragged claws / Scuttling across the floors of silent seas." That way, as a bottom feeder myself, being steamed and consumed would have been my only fear.

Skutch, who clapped me on the back, said, "Kevin, a masterful speech. Far better than anything that damned Frank Morhouse ever wrote, may he rest in peace."

As Skutch, Gunn, and I started on our separate ways, I noticed the congressman talking to a young man I didn't recognize. I thought little of it until I saw the two enter the gallery at the base of the Washington Monument and shut the door behind them. After what seemed to be an interminable amount of time Skutch emerged alone, straightening his tie and adjusting his suitcoat.

---

I started to get to know Cerys McLean better, and sometimes we took lunch together. She'd show me the sights, walking me through the tunnel that led from the House Building to the Capitol itself. The tunnel, which had entrances to a cafeteria, cobbler, barbershop, and beauty parlor, was lined with artwork, the product of an annual congressional competition for teenagers.

I couldn't help but feel a jaundiced sense of pride as I stood for the first time inside the Capitol's rotunda gazing up at the great, soaring dome. It was a much different, more profound, experience than viewing it from outside at a distance. The Capitol was still under construction when the British burned it in the War of 1812, and its restoration and expansion continued even as the rebellious South's army menaced DC from the far side of the Potomac. Part of the construction was completed, to our shame, by slaves. Nevertheless, I saw it as sacred ground, and it was hard to imagine that an edifice such as ours would ever again be defiled.

Cerys had grown up in the District where her father, until a stroke, had worked on the Capitol's maintenance crew as an electrician. She'd had to drop out of Hood College after two years to help her party-faithful family, but it led to her congressional job. Being raised in DC by a father employed at the Capitol, she got to know the building from bottom to top.

She pointed out that the dome was actually two cast-iron domes, outer and inner, with a not-so-secret stair in between that she, led as a child by her father, had frequently climbed. He often repaired the lighting fixtures and wiring at the farthest reaches of the dome. The metal stair led to a room called the Tholos at the dome's highest point, above which rested the Statue of Freedom.

"Shall we climb it, Kevin?" she asked. "There are three hundred sixty-five steps, just like the Capitol steps."

"Uh, I'm not so good with heights," I replied, thinking of my ordeal in interviewing Shipwreck Kelly at the top of a flagstaff. "Why would anybody go all the way up there anyway?"

"It's a wonderful place to hide. It's where I went after I learned of Frank's death. No one would look for me there. You can be alone in that place, which is not open to the public, no matter how many hundreds, perhaps thousands, of people below pass through the Capitol every day. And from it, you can see for miles. At night the Tholos is illuminated from within. My father did all the electrical work."

For now, I was satisfied by simply gazing up from the Rotunda with its statues and busts of American Presidents and murals of great events in American history, and where celebrated patriots would lie in state. One hundred-eighty feet above, a great fresco by Constantino Brumidi called "The Apotheosis of Washington" served as the dome's canopy.

Cerys said, "Below us is the Crypt, which was intended to be George and Martha's final resting place, but the Washingtons were content to remain at Mount Vernon. Right now the Crypt's empty, so visitors park their bicycles down there."

It sounded like it might be a good place to make a pass, but I wasn't going to rush it. Cerys was still mourning Frank Morhouse. However, one evening she accepted my invitation to go to the movies, where we watched the new RKO talkie, *Rio Rita*, a musical with Bebe Daniels, John Boles, and the comics Wheeler & Woolsey. The film's finale, which was in Technicolor, floored us. Afterward, we went to the Old Ebbitt Grill on F Street NW, the District's oldest restaurant, where I again brought up the subject of Frank. At the moment, he was all I had to go on.

"I, I can't discuss it," she said.

"Too painful?"

"Not now, Kevin. But there are things. Dangerous things."

"Involving the congressman?"

"I didn't say that. I never said that. This is Washington. Favors are exchanged. Deals are made. Money changes hands. But you're probably already aware of that."

She was hiding something. I knew it. And I almost sensed a feeling of fear within her.

I had rented a room on K Street so I wouldn't have to commute up Highway 1 through all those little hamlets to B-more every night. I didn't have much to do with myself in the evenings but listen to the radio: my favorites being Rudy Valle's "Fleischman Hour" and "The Hour of Charm" with Phil Spitalny's All-Girl Orchestra.

Often I stayed late at the congressional offices to snoop when nobody was around. Even though Skutch kept his desk locked, I was able to jimmy it. In a drawer, I found a bottle of moonshine, a substantial collection of French postcards, a variety pack of prophylactics, and what appeared to be a number of love letters apparently from someone named Shelly who was not only not his wife but who was also a lousy speller. In addition, I saw a woman's wig, blond. What would a man be doing with something that? But I found nothing that appeared to be directly linked to the Fort Belnoir bill.

---

In September, as the events at the Capitol unfolded for me, the stock market started faltering, but my broker assured me that any hiccups were just hiccups. The economy was splendid, Herman Katz insisted, noting that Henry Ford was bragging that a new car came off of his assembly line every ten seconds and that one-third of all American households now owned radios.

What could go wrong?

Still, I was getting rattled, even though the market edged back up during the first three weeks of October, then sputtered again. However, on the seventeenth, it rose to such a high level that Hyman boasted he was confident stock prices had reached a permanent plateau and from there would go nowhere but up.

I started to feel more relaxed.

Then on October 24, a huge selloff began—although before the end of the trading day, the tide was turned by investors taking advantage of the losses by buying up huge blocks of securities. Hyman told me the loss averaged out to just ten points. No reason to panic.

"Bad, yeah," Hyman said. "They're calling it Black Thursday. But listen, Gart, the market's always bounced back. So don't do nothin' stupid and sell off. You'll be hit with too big a loss. Just hang in there. Take it from both me and Herbert Hoover. He just gave a speech saying that the nation's financial health is sound and prosperous."

"Hoover should know," I said. "I suppose."

Henry was of little help. He'd already jettisoned most of his stocks, putting half of his investments in the bank, and the other half in his cookie jar. But I decided to wait it out. And Hyman appeared to be right.

After that fateful Thursday, the market held firm and again seemed relatively stable.

---

As Cerys and I became more chummy, she loosened up about Frank and some of her apprehensions. We were alone in the congressional office after hours when she told me that Morhouse was never acrophobic, but, despite his athleticism, sometimes suffered from dizziness, fainting, and blurred vision. Doctors coined a word for it: hypotension, meaning low blood pressure.

She said, "Something in fertilizer is used in small doses to treat hypotension: potassium chloride, which is an important mineral. The body needs it for normal functions. On his bad days when Frank lost his breath and felt weak, he relied on potassium chloride powder, which he mixed with water, to get back to normal."

With Cerys opening up to me, I also became more candid, although not telling her I was an imposter posing as a speechwriter to dig for a story. But I showed her the note with the cryptic symbols that Henry had received suggesting mischief involving the Fort Belnoir military hospital.

"Where did you get this, Kevin?" she asked.

"Uh, it was just something I spotted in the office trash, along with a newspaper clipping about the congressman's hospital hearings. I liked the artwork."

"I'm positive Frank drew it. Maybe he wanted to say something without calling attention to himself. But it's odd it somehow wound up in the trash and you found it."

"Guess I'm just naturally curious. Maybe after he died someone cleared out his desk. But what do the symbols mean? A cow chewing on a dollar sign, a pair of wings perched on top of a snake, and an old-fashioned cannon mounted on wheels."

She said, "I was a volunteer at Providence Hospital for two summers, so I can tell you about the wings and the snake. It's actually two snakes coiled around a staff. They call it a caduceus, the symbol of medicine. The US military adopted it."

"And a cow with money in its mouth?"

"Easy. A cash cow."

"Jeeze, Cerys, you're quick. Never thought of that. And clearly, the drawing of the cannon refers to Fort Belvoir. That's pretty certain."

"It's not certain at all. I believe it means something entirely different. What is a cannon anyway?"

"A cannon is… well, a weapon."

"Go on."

"A long-range piece of artillery."

"And what else?"

"Large caliber?"

"Try again."

"A gun. Wait. Gun. Gunn, with two n's? As in Ben Gunn, Skutch's chief of staff?"

Suddenly, thanks to Cerys, it all became clear.

I said, "Military hospital, cash cow, Gunn. End of story. How did you dope all that out?"

"I play the crosswords in *The Washington Star*. Kevin, the clipping mentions Black Industries, which is owned by an important Republican donor, Lamar Black. He wants the contract to develop the hospital, and he meets often with Mr. Skutch socially. And they both have an interest in freshwater fishing."

"Bet they're trying to hook a lot more than fish. I'm supposed to write a speech about the hospital bill. Skutch is planning to deliver it to the American Society for Colon, Rectal, and Ocular Surgery."

"Kevin, I've come to trust you. A lot. So I'm going to confide in you. It's no secret that big money is involved in the hospital contract. Lamar Black's company is among the bidders. Like you, Frank had more than the usual access to our congressional office. It's how he found out that the process hasn't been on the up and up."

"Payoffs, bribes. I'll bet Gunn is Skutch's bagman"

"We don't know for sure. But I do know Frank compiled a lot of compromising material: letters, receipts, even an incriminating check that had gone astray. I never told you before. He planned to turn the evidence over to J. Edgar Hoover."

"Why didn't he?"

"He was waiting for the right time. But he really didn't trust Hoover, one of the reasons being that Hoover and Skutch were known to be friends, often having intimate dinners and going to the racetrack together. Hoover might not be sympathetic to anything negative about a fellow believer in the American Way. Frank told me that until he had the opportunity to release the documents so they would stick, they'd stay hidden somewhere at the Capitol where no one would find them."

"And you know where."

"No, he wouldn't tell me. For my protection, he said. But by the time he decided to give the files to Hoover, it was too late. He had that sudden heart attack and died."

"We're screwed."

"Um, not necessarily. Kevin, I said to you that Frank liked puzzles—which you can tell by the note with the symbols. He told me the secret documents were in a sleeve, they're waterproofed, and that Jefferson Davis wouldn't mind."

"Jefferson Davis? The traitor who joined the Confederacy as its first, last, and only president?"

"He was once a congressman, senator from Mississippi, and Secretary of War under President Pierce."

"Cerys, after the Rebs were whipped, Davis tried to escape by disguising himself in women's clothes."

"He may have been cowardly, but in the South, he's still a hero. Kevin, Congress lets each state contribute two statues of noted people to Statuary Hall. Mississippi's planning to install a bronze of Davis, although not for another year."

"Then that's no help," I said. "And Frank's other clues could mean anything. Let's look at some of the drawings he left in his desk."

We found about two dozen sketches he'd made of various items, including a charming pencil profile of Cerys. I wanted it but she snatched it out of my hand.

"I'm keeping that one," she said.

The others were sketches mostly of various aspects of the Capitol Building, some just shy of being schematics, in particular the Dome. A few had enigmatic markings and arrows that were likely known only to Frank. But one drawing was notable in that it depicted the outer parts of the Dome's summit. It showed that temple-like structure called the Tholos, upon which rested the Statue of Freedom rising from a pedestal engraved with the motto *E Pluribus Unum*.

I said, "The Tholos is the place at the top of the Dome where you would go to hide. Did Frank ever go there?"

"Many times. With me. It's where we... we occasionally were romantic, although that's none of your business. But it was so glorious, Kevin. Watching the sun go down from there. The moonlit nights. The idea of the Capitol and its architecture entranced Frank, and the only building in the District taller is the Washington Monument."

"What's it look like up there?"

"It's circular and has twelve columns with windows in between to protect against the wind and the pigeons. You can see from every direction. All of Washington and far across the Potomac are a panorama. Frank loved it."

"Then he must have hidden the documents in the Tholos."

"No. It's bare, empty except for the view, no recesses or anyplace where something could be secreted."

"Damn, in that case, we're back where we started. That and Jefferson Davis."

"Wait," she said. "The Statue of Freedom at the tip of the dome is based on a design of a woman with long, flowing hair, wearing a helmet with a crest of feathers. She's wearing a full, willowy robe, like a toga, and her hand's on a sheathed sword."

"So?"

"It was the design of the sculptor Thomas Crawford, which had to be approved before it was cast in bronze."

"Where are you going with this, Cerys?"

"The Secretary of War was the one who approved the design, and ultimately the statue. And the Secretary of War at the time was..."

"...Jefferson Davis."

"And in Frank's sketch, Kevin, look where an arrow is pointing."

"To an abundant sleeve of the lady in bronze."

"In which are likely the very documents we want, and since it's outside they must be in a waterproof container."

I said, "How the hell did Frank get up there?"

"He loved climbing. He must have gone out between the columns in the Tholos, up the pedestal, and finally to the statue itself. It sounds reckless, but he loved a challenge, especially if it was high."

"Then all we have to do is to..."

"...climb up there and get it."

"Which is about impossible for most mortals without having a crew install scaffolding. And that would alert the Capitol's groundskeepers, maintenance people, Capitol Police, and the Bureau of Investigation."

"Not to not to mention the bad guys," I said. Then my febrile mind, although not as quick as hers, moved astonishingly fast. "Cerys, I know someone who isn't like most mortals. They call him Shipwreck Kelly. He's the one man I can think of who has the brass to climb it."

"Do you think you can get him?"

"We're, uh, old pals. He gave me his number in Carlin's Park. Shipwreck sat on a pole there for twenty-nine days, his record so far. I know you and Frank climbed the steps to the Tholos many times, but it's off-limits to the public, and even congressional members have to get special permission to access it. How did you manage? It must be kept locked."

"You forget, Kevin, that my father was on the Capitol's maintenance crew. When he retired after his stroke, he kept a memento: a full set of keys to every room in the building. There's no door in the entire Capitol that we can't unlock."

I called Shipwreck's number. His wife Vivian put me in touch with him in Cleveland, where an electrical storm had forced him to descend from the top of the transmitter tower of radio station WHK.

"It was either my coming down or being fried like a chicken," he told me on long distance. "I'm almost as burned up about having to quit the tower as being incinerated by lightning."

I told him I had a short job for him, one day's work, but perhaps his most spectacular feat ever. Mounting the Statue of Freedom at the peak of the Capitol Dome. It would pay two-hundred dollars courtesy of the Baltimore *Sun*.

"Hell, Scoop, I'd do it for nothing as long as I get the publicity."

"Only after the fact, Shipwreck, not before."

"In that case, it'll cost you two-fifty plus travel and expenses. What exactly do I have to do?"

"Just scoot up the statue and retrieve something I want that's hidden within a recess of her sleeve. Or I think it is. But, Shipwreck, no one here knows I'm with the *Sun*. I don't want to blow my cover, so keep mum."

"I'm with you, Scoop."

---

Shipwreck couldn't get to DC right away. He'd committed himself to a goldfish-swallowing contest in Buffalo. Ingesting goldfish hadn't caught on like flagpole sitting, but Shipwreck hoped that if he added his name to the stunt, it would become a big enough fad that it would lead to a lot of short-time jobs in between flagpoles. Shipwreck Kelly imposters stealing his name were springing up all over the country, so, often, no one knew who was the actual Shipwreck. He told the *Cleveland Plain Dealer*, "By God, there's only one Shipwreck Kelly. And that's me as far as I can tell, although I have to ask my wife occasionally."

While I waited impatiently for Shipwreck's arrival, damned if Henry didn't get engaged to be married. Who would have thought? It didn't seem to be in character, and he certainly didn't cut a dashing figure.

Sara Haardt was elegant with a soft Southern drawl, far more attractive than Henry deserved, although there was something frail, almost tubercular, about her. As it turned out, my observations were not incorrect.

Henry met Sara at Goucher where he had gone to lecture on writing and she was on the faculty. She'd already published some of her short stories, was laboring on a novel, and was planning to take a gig as a Hollywood screenwriter. They made an incongruous couple: he of average height and pudgy, she tall and willowy; he, in his words, who ate like a Cro-Magnon, she like an Armenian refugee. She was eighteen years his junior and theirs was a seven-year courtship. As one of the most eligible bachelors of the twenties, Henry was sometimes referred to as the German Valentino without the sex appeal and nostril flaring.

"The longest sentence you can utter with two words is I do," he once quipped. Finally, frustrated by his failure to commit, Sara decided that Henry was a closed chapter in her book—but somehow he managed to convince her to reopen the page.

I said, "Henry, I remember your saying that marriage is purely a financial matter pertaining to the cost of the wife's hats, but more importantly to the husband's cigars."

"I stand by the assertion. No married man is genuinely happy if he has to drink worse whiskey than when he was single. Sara's favorite drink is a revolting concoction of gin, Coca-Cola, and lime juice."

"Why at this late stage in your life did you decide to tie the knot?"

"Imagine this scenario, Taggart, m'boy. After a frustrating day and deep into a late afternoon, I stretch out on a divan before a fire, having enjoyed a cocktail or two. As I drift off, I see sitting at the edge of the settee, a handsome woman, young but not too young, with a soft, low-pitched voice. She talks of books, music, art, clothes, men, other women. No politics, no business, no theology. Nothing challenging or vexatious. I see the fine sheen of her hair, the glint of her white teeth, the arch of her eyebrow, the graceful curve of her arm. I again slumber, but only for an instant. When I again hear the murmur of her voice I awaken. Then once more I gradually enter that slippery hall of dreams. What could be more beautiful?"

"That's lovely, Henry. You should put it in a book."

"Such as the one I published in nineteen-eighteen called *In Defense of Women* in which those lines appeared? Taggart, m'boy, I decided it was time to make my blissful dreams come true. Sara may be from the South but at least she has German blood in her."

---

It was a Saturday when Cerys and I met Shipwreck at Union Station on Massachusetts Avenue. The notion that civic vandals might repurpose it for any other venture such as a hotel or department store was unimaginable. It was a majestic American landmark that, like Pennsylvania Station in New York, was destined to endure for the ages.

To avoid attracting attention, we whisked Shipwreck directly to the House Office Building, where we walked the tunnel to the Capitol, then to the Rotunda where the obscure stairway behind an unmarked door led up to the Tholos.

As we climbed the steps, Shipwreck said, "What the hell does Tholos mean anyway? I used to know a Greek guy named Harry Tholos who ran a greasy spoon in Hoboken."

Cerys said, "It's an architectural term meaning a circular structure."

Gad, the girl was smart.

I, at least, was breathless when we got to the top. Outside the Tholos, the wind was howling in recurring gusts.

"Hope you won't be blown away out there," I told Shipwreck,

"Hell, I sat for three days on a flagpole in Savannah during a hurricane once. Didn't faze me a bit."

"How are you getting up to the statue?"

"I'm goin' out that window."

"I just noticed it's sealed glass. Doesn't open."

"Which is why I brought a glass cutter, Scoop. I done my research. Don't want to break no glass. Disrespectful. Besides, I like things neat. I shave every other day on account of I believe in good groomin'. Say, here's what looks like a new pane of glass. Bet it's where that other fella cut through the window to get out, then replaced the glass."

Shipwreck neatly removed the pane, then leaned out to get a better view of the perspective above.

He said, "I estimate the pedestal's eighteen-feet high and the statue on it about twenty. That's nearly forty feet, which should put the statue's head at about two hundred eighty-eighty feet above the plaza. Where's this sleeve you say contains something? Won't ask you what. It's your business."

"Most likely it's a box or pouch wedged in the statue's right sleeve with the hand holding a sheathed sword. But I suppose it could be any-where. There are plenty of folds. All bronzed."

Shipwreck said, "The pedestal's made of cast iron and the sides are sheer, nothin' to hold on to. So I'm gonna rappel up it, which means me climbin' with a double-coiled rope that I'll secure to the statue. Whoever got up there before to hide that thing probably done it. If he did, so can I—and maybe even do him one better."

"How are you going to get the rope around the statue?"

"A lasso, Scoop. Just like cowboys in the Old West. Ever watch Hoot Gibson in the flicks? Or Tom Mix? Trouble is, I can't throw it from down here. Gotta climb from the Tholos to the pedestal's base. Which'll shorten the distance I need to throw the rope around the statue's head. Looks like there's just enough ledge around the pedestal to stand on tippy toes."

"What are you going to hold onto?"

"Nothin'. Simple matter of balance. Once I lasso the statue's head it'll be a cinch. I'll rappel up, grab whatever it is you want, and rappel back down to the Tholos. Just gotta make sure the window I'm goin' back into is the one without the glass."

Suddenly, the impossibility of it hit me. The idea that compromis-ing documents were concealed inside a statue at the top of the Capitol Dome was farfetched enough—let alone risking a man's life for them. If

Shipwreck fell, I was the one who got him into it. And I wasn't sure if it was even covered by the *Sun*'s insurance.

"Stop," I said.

"Huh?"

"I've changed my mind, Shipwreck. I can't let you do it. You'll still get paid."

"Too late, Scoop."

"You'll die."

"If you wanted to call it off you shoulda told me before I got off the train from Cleveland. So if you stop me, my fee goes up to a grand, and I'm also blowin' the whistle on you. Hey, I know what I'm doin'. Over the summer I sat on a ten-foot pole attached to a biplane flyin' over Manhattan. All I had was a strap around my legs in case of turbulence."

"That's crazy."

"This is duck soup. You want a whole construction team to spend a week installing scaffolding so you can go up there? I doubt it."

The next thing I knew, Shipwreck, equipped with rubber-soled shoes, a long coiled rope, and knapsack around his shoulder, swung up and out the window of the Tholos and disappeared. It was almost as if he had jumped into space.

"Oh my God, Cerys, I'm responsible for this. It's going to kill him. I can't look. You do it. Tell me. The suspense is killing me. What's he doing? I gotta know. What's happening? No, don't tell me. Yes, tell me."

"Relax, Kevin. Do you think Shipwreck would be doing this if he wasn't sure of himself?" She leaned out and looked up. "He's now standing, barely, on the ledge around the pedestal and swinging the rope and... He missed! He was aiming for the statue's head, but the rope just dropped into the air and is flapping around. It's the wind up there. Too much wind. A big gust could blow him off. Wait, he's coiling it again. He's swinging the rope. Letting go, and... Oh, no!"

"What? What?"

"He missed again."

"Call him back inside, Cerys—if he can even get down here. We'll simply tell J. Edgar Hoover about our suspicions. Let him handle it."

"They'll never believe us, Kevin. We have no proof. We need those documents. Wait. Shipwreck's trying again. There goes the rope. It's almost... almost... Hey, he did it this time! Despite the gusts. The rope's firmly around the head. Now he's rappelling up the side of the pedestal. He's almost reached the statue's feet. He made it! Now he's fumbling around the folds and crevices in the bronze looking for... Wait, I think he's found something."

She paused.

"What's going on?" I said. "What's he doing now? Is he coming down?"

"No, Kevin, he's... He's climbing to the top of the statue. And now he's..."

"What? *What?*"

"He's sitting on her head."

I joined Cerys at the window, looking up. There he was. Perched comfortably on the bronze-feathered head of the Statue of Freedom and smiling into the wind.

We shouted, almost in unison. "Down! Come down, Shipwreck. Get back in here."

Damned if Shipwreck didn't look as contented as an owl tenanting a limb of an oak. Eventually, it was bound to attract attention. Somebody down below, probably a tourist from Akron or Erie or Cicero, was going to notice him. And then... It would make things hard. Maybe impossible. But I wouldn't feel comfortable until those documents were safely in our hands

Shipwreck squatted on his roost for another fifteen minutes. For the bragging rights.

Finally, out of patience, I shouted up at him, "Shipwreck, if you come down now there's another hundred in it."

I'd put it on my expense account, and if the *Sun* refused to reimburse me I'd pay him out of my lucrative Wall Street investments.

"Make it two," he hollered back. "In the name of the Statue of Freedom."

Shipwreck almost made it sound patriotic—and the lady of the statue didn't seem a bit perturbed with a man sitting on her head. I realized that freedom in a democracy also meant being free from those such as religious zealots who would impose their notions, which is why the Statue of Freedom carried a sword.

He climbed down by the time crowds had gathered on the plaza below to gawk at the spectacle of some bonkers bozo ensconced on the head of a bronzed monument atop the Dome of the Capitol Building of the United States of America. Back inside the Tholos, Shipwreck tossed me a fair-sized plastic case that looked like it had once been a sample container for ladies' makeup.

"There you go, Scoop," he said. "Must be somethin' really good in there."

"Something that will bring down a corrupt politician."

I opened the box and there they were.

I was so happy I bussed Cerys on the lips, and for good measure Shipwreck Kelly got a smacker too. We exited the bottom of the stairs to the Rotunda, just before the Capitol Police swarmed up the stairs.

Cerys and I thought we were going to nail Congressman Seymour A. Skutch (R-Md), but it didn't happen that way.

---

Perfidy and Politics: brothers under the skin. Henry conveyed that proposition in his scathing columns, maintaining that every election was a sort of advance auction sale of stolen goods. And Congressman Skutch seemed to be the perfect stereotype of a conniving, baby-kissing handshaker, bloated with crude, right-wing bellicosity, his brain's fuel gage running on empty. His speeches, which I polished up smartly for him, reflected the mental aptitude of an adolescent chimpanzee, who at the least was capable of using a rock to crack open a walnut.

The trouble was that Congressman Skutch was an innocent man. And another thing we didn't know: Frank Morhouse's heart attack turned out to be murder.

He had collected in excruciating detail documentary evidence of how Ben Gunn had interacted with Lamar Black to ensure that the developer won the multimillion-dollar contract to construct that military hospital in Virginia. It included a daily log in which Frank detailed Gunn's clandestine meetings with two of Black's henchmen in and around Washington. Frank regularly followed Gunn to obtain photographic evidence as well. Tens of thousands of dollars were made in payoffs directly to Gunn, mostly in cash but some disguised as loans, as evidenced by the bank statements Frank had purloined.

The unsuspecting but greedy Black, founder of Black Industries, was under the impression his financial inducements were going through Gunn to Skutch, who knew nothing about it. Oblivious, Skutch's latest birdbrained scheme was an incentive to require that all public school textbooks be registered with the seal of approval by the National Bible Association.

Effectively, Gunn ran Skutch's committee and every element of the legislation, not to mention controlling the entire congressional office where everything had to go through him. He was positioned to stack the deck in favor of Black Industries. The hapless, pontificating Skutch had no idea of what was going on.

Ben Gunn, however, wasn't all that bright himself. I remembered that his was also the name of the crazed pirate in Robert Louis Stevenson's *Treasure Island*. With his new-found wealth, Gunn had bought an elegant rowhome in Georgetown, a winter bungalow in Sarasota, a Falcon Knight Roadster, and a Curtiss Jenny. He claimed that he'd come into scads of family money and everyone bought the story but Frank.

But things became dicey after Frank got careless and was discovered one night while tailing Gunn to the Tidal Basin for a rendezvous with Black's agents—as Frank's log later pointed out. Morhouse was roughed up by the two thugs who made the mistake of letting him go with a warning. Then Gunn tried to placate Frank with a bribe, but Frank knew, as he noted in his log, that no amount of money was enough, and that his life was in jeopardy. This prompted him to hide his evidence in a secure location, one that proved to be so sequestered it took Shipwreck Kelly to obtain it.

Our trove of evidence put me into a quandary. Cerys wanted to take it to the Bureau of Investigation on K Street and give it in person to J. Edgar Hoover. Whereas I had hoped to break the story first in the *Sun* to add to my successful run of scoops.

In the end, we did both. Hoover got the dope. I got exclusive first-story rights.

In pre-dawn raids, agents arrested Lamar Black, his two goons, and Ben Gunn. Hoover personally put Black into handcuffs so he could demonstrate his courage and pose before the cameras. Hoover even displayed a revolver that one of his agents had lent him for display purposes only. To make sure Hoover didn't accidentally shoot someone in the foot, the agent removed the bullets.

It was the biggest scandal since Teapot Dome.

Skutch decried the payoff scheme as duplicity, asserting that he was deceived by a congressional staff member he'd treated like his own son. Skutch not only denied any involvement, he even passed a Emotograph test administered by a young man named Leonarde Keeler, who predicted that his new lie detector would become commonly used in the future. How was it, Skutch fumed, that Ben Gunn had turned to Satan rather than the Holy Father?

Delivering the last speech I wrote for him, Skutch bellowed, "Outside the hallowed walls of Congress are the jackals who practice magic arts, the sexually immoral, the murderers, the idolaters, and everyone who loves and practices falsehood. I condemn those sinners to the fiery bowels of Hell."

I thought it was a spanking good speech, although perhaps not as strong as my Crab and Seafood address, and I hoped nobody noticed that I swiped it mostly out of the "Book of Revelations."

To win a reduced term, one of Black's heavies turned state's evidence and squealed on the others, making a dramatic admission on the witness stand: Frank Morhouse, the jury was told, was murdered in the wee hours inside the House Chamber at the Capitol, where Frank had run in a futile effort to escape his pursuers.

While the thugs held Frank down under a desk, Gunn injected him several times with potassium chloride. In small amounts, potassium chloride treats hypotension, but if administered in high doses will cause sudden cardiac arrest. The victim will die within ten to twenty minutes. A coroner isn't likely to recognize the potassium in the victim's blood-stream—since it's naturally present —and will inevitably conclude that the cause of death was heart failure. Gunn made the injections in obscure bodily locations: armpits, groin, and anus so no puncture wounds were obvious. Within five minutes Frank was unconscious and in fifteen minutes he was dead on arrival.

The perfect murder weapon and clean—though taking longer than a bullet.

While Skutch got off, there was one hanging question: the matter of the blond woman's wig I'd found when I rifled his desk, along with the love letters from a Shelly. Again, Cerys came through with the answer, which she had learned from Frank.

She told me, "You know that Mr. Skutch and J. Edgar Hoover are friends, but what you don't know is that they like to hold intimate parties in which they dress up in women's clothes. Mr. Skutch plays the blonde while Mr. Hoover is either a brunette or a redhead, depending on the day of the week."

"What about Kutch's love letters from some woman named Shelly?"

"Oh, Shelly's not a woman. It's a nickname for Sheldon."

The indictments and subsequent trial were great news for me, the dashing, bespectacled reporter who broke the inside story in the Baltimore *Sun*, which wouldn't have happened without Cerys. Pulitzer material for sure. My next problem was revealing to her I wasn't the so-called speech-writer who called himself Kevin S. Clarke, but Gart Booker Asquith III, crack undercover reporter, an identity dilemma I'd faced before.

Cerys said, "You lied to me, Kevin. Or Gart. Or whatever your name is."

"Henry calls me Taggart. He thinks it's more magisterial than Gart."

"You're missing the point."

"I had to change my identity, Cerys. I couldn't tell you I was a reporter. Not until after I landed the story."

"I suppose you're satisfied now."

"Not if you hold it against me."

I knew my answer was self-serving and selfish. I did tend to fall for some of the women I encountered on a story, in particular those who helped me the most. It was a failing. Henry had warned me about becoming romantically involved with a source.

"I'm unlucky in love, Gart," Cerys said. "Frank had principles and died for them. I'm not sure you have any. It's certain to me that you're more inclined to put your story first."

"I'm not *that* bad. My mentor Henry Mencken has his soft edges, and so do I. He recently got engaged, so he's open to marriage. Why shouldn't I be the same?"

"Are you proposing to me?"

"Well…"

"Keep asking yourself about the answer to that question. Because whatever it is I won't buy it. I have my own ideas as to where I'm going, and it doesn't involve you. My father has recovered sufficiently from his stroke, so I'm planning to take my vows as a nun."

No, no. no. I wanted to yell.

It was the wrong thing for her to do. Nuns and priests had adopted positions completely counter to human nature and I was certain it would become a struggle rather than a satisfaction for her. Those weren't even jobs in the normal sense. It was batty. Nobody in his or her right mind would take employment in journalism or accounting or law or any other profession if they had to declare celibacy.

Cerys said, "I'm taking the vows because I want to help people."

"Then become a teacher," I said. "Or a nurse or a doctor or a firefighter or a coalminer. They help people. The mission of nuns and priests isn't to help people, which may happen incidentally, but to spread their faith."

But who was I to advise anyone? My track record wasn't all that good, and my own cynicism was often self-serving.

As for Henry's Sara, she was not well. She suffered from kidney disease and was unable to bear children due to the loss of an ovary. When a bladder infection forced her to undergo surgery, the doctors found tuberculosis in her remaining kidney and gave her three years to live.

A distraught Henry told me that if she survived the surgery, he'd give her the happiest remaining years of her life. It was a promise he would keep.

He said, "There's no treatise on woman by man that's not a stupendous compendium of posturings and imbecilities. Even more ingloriously, I'm also likely to have failed. And if so, Taggart, m'boy, I'm full of sincere and indescribable regret."

Henry wasn't used to apologies.

---

After that Black Tuesday, the market managed to right itself, and at first seemed to be behaving. But it was a feint that only slightly delayed the knockout punch on Thursday, October 29, 1929, when Wall Street bit the dust like an aging outlaw in front of a saloon.

Frantically, I tried to reach Hyman on the phone. I either got a busy signal or no answer and by the time he picked up he sounded weary. Or drunk.

"Sorry, Gart," he said. "It's all gone."

"All of it?"

"Every dime."

By the standards of the rich, my investment wasn't much: four-hundred bucks. But it was all I had.

"What are we going to do, Hyman?" I asked.

"We? I can only speak for myself. You know the new Baltimore Trust Company Building on Light Street?"

"Yeah, the city's tallest. Thirty-four stories."

"As soon as I hang up, I'm walking there, taking the elevator to the top floor, and jumping out of the first open window I see. I hope I don't have to stand in line."

Hyman made good on his promise. Henry's Saturday Night Club was out one viola player, and the great economic boom of the twenties was over.

Puffing on his five-cent cigar, Henry told me, "During his Presidency, Cal showed no sign that he knew of any dark clouds ahead. The man talked only sunshine, when he talked at all. Now, as Herbert Hoover is being fried, boiled, roasted, and fricasseed, old Cal is safe in Vermont and catching up on his zzz's."

I said, "If Coolidge had run for re-election and won, how do you think he would have handled the crash?"

"By pulling down the blinds, stretching his legs on his desk, and snoozing away the afternoons. Some idiot emperor played the lute while Rome burned. Coolidge would have sawed wood."

"The nation's in financial ruin, Henry, but no one has told us why."

"It's like a cold. You don't know exactly how you caught it. There may be one reason or many. But in the end, you still have a cold."

"You don't seem to be worried about it."

"The easiest job I've ever had is making money. It's almost as easy as losing it. I'm pulling in thirty thousand per year, so what do I have to worry about?"

"And I'm out four Franklins."

"Look at it this way. The only thing you had to lose in the crash was money."

"I've also lost out on romance. I wooed Ruby, Dolly, Dalilah, Zora, and Cerys and struck out with all of them. Now, all I have is you."

"Love's like war, Taggart, m'boy. Easy to begin but hard to stop. It's the triumph of imagination over intelligence. Besides, to be in love is merely to be in a state of perceptual anesthesia—and I'm speaking of myself."

"Henry, give me your keenest advice."

"That's like asking me whether stairs go up or down. The best thing I can say to you about either money or love is not to drink the water downstream from your horse."

---

And so the Roaring Twenties came to an ignominious end, and, as a young man, I'd been fully caught up in it. It would be good to conclude my narrative on a reflective note. But the stirring words "Land of the Free / Home of the Brave" were mere platitudes unrelated to the nation's historical reality of violence, prejudice, and fear. Such a conclusion, however, would win me no favors. So rather than continue with inanities about bootleggers, Al Capone, bathtub gin, speakeasies, the Klan, mah-jongg, the Lindy, flagpole sitting, rumble seats, the talkies, and flappers, I'll simply let the era speak for itself.

Now, five years after the KKK staged its massive march in the nation's capital, which led me to gatecrash the Invisible Empire, I've decided to quit the news biz to write detective novels. In my first, the heroine will be Emily Dickinson, Crime Fighter.

And that's -30- for this reporter.

> *Every morning, every evening*
> *Ain't we got fun?*
> *Not much money, oh, but honey*
> *Ain't we got fun?*
>
> — Gus Kahn,
> Raymond B. Egan, Richard A. Whiting

# ACKNOWLEDGMENTS

Author's note. This is a work of fiction. While I've relied extensively on Mencken's own words from his enormous body of work, I'd like to acknowledge Mencken biographies by Marion Elizabeth Rodgers and Fred Hobson, as well as Robert S. McElvane's *America: The Great Depression, 1929-1941*, New York, 1984. Also: *The Harlem Renaissance: Hub of African-American Culture, 1920-1930*, by Steve Watson, New York, 1995. *Carl Van Vechten and the Harlem Renaissance: A Portrait in Black and White* by Emily Bernard, New Haven, 2012. *Zora Neale Hurston: A Life in Letters* by Carla Kaplan, New York, 2002. Additionally helpful were *A Thousand Thirsty Beaches: Smuggling Alcohol to the South During Prohibition*, by Lisa Lindquist Dorr, Chapel Hill, 2018; and *Capone: The Man and The Era* by Laurence Bergreen, New York, 1996. As always, my appreciation to my faithful writers' group, the venerable Bucks County Writers Workshop, which has given me more help and encouragement over a quarter century than I deserve.

# ABOUT DON SWAIM

Kansan by birth, Ohioan by education, Manhattanite by inclination, and Pennsylvanian by preference, Don Swaim is the author of several books of fiction and non-fiction, including the definitive fictional biography *The Assassination of Ambrose Bierce: A Love Story*. A veteran broadcast journalist, the audio files from his long-running CBS Radio feature "Book Beat" are now archived by the Ohio University libraries' special collections. He's the founder of the venerable Bucks County Writers Workshop and co-founder of the literary journal *Neshaminy*.

He manages to share a semi-rural Pennsylvania house with 9,000 books.

www.ingramcontent.com/pod-product-compliance
Lightning Source LLC
Chambersburg PA
CBHW021007260626
47169CB00006B/1984